A Second Spring

A Second Spring

Connie Monk

PIATKUS

PIATKUS

First published in Great Britain in 2007 by Piatkus Books

A CIP catalogue record for this book
is available from the British Library

*A catalogue record for this book is available from the British
Library*

ISBN 978-0-7499-0850-8

Typeset in Times by Action Publishing Technology Ltd,
Gloucester
Printed and bound in Great Britain by William Clowes Ltd, Beccles, Suffolk

Piatkus Books
An imprint of
Little, Brown Book Group
100 Victoria Embankment
London EC4Y 0DY

An Hachette Livre UK Company

www.piatkus.co.uk

A Second Spring

Chapter One

November 1944

In a rare burst of self-indulgence Rhoda washed her hair then luxuriated in a warm bath of more than the five inches of water recommended by the Government. Next she applied a face mask and lay down on the bed for twenty minutes while she felt her skin being drawn tighter and tighter as what she hoped would be a miracle restorer of youth set rock hard. Time up, she rinsed it off in cold water and peered hopefully in the mirror, trying to imagine it had done all it said on the packet, although she was honest enough to know the only real difference was the colour in her cheeks – probably put there by the cold water. Miracle or not, it was the best she could do and, with her mind on the new dress hanging in her wardrobe, she pulled on her underwear. After more than five years of war – and with Natalie's need for attractive clothes so much more vital than that of the rest of the family – impulse buying had long since ceased to be part of her life. But last Wednesday in town she had tried on the cherry red dress and been unable to walk away.

Taking it from the wardrobe she held the hanger at arm's length and just for a moment the excitement receded, leaving her with a sense of loss. What was the point in dressing herself up, trying to turn back the clock? Who would so much as notice what she was wearing? Alec? She didn't want to hear the question. Etty? Yes, Etty would notice. Natalie? No, bless her, she'd be far too excited to be home and with so much to tell them. The expensive dress that had taken the last of her coupons seemed to mock her.

Don't be stupid, she told herself. You bought it because you liked it, not because you wanted admiration. So, chin up, she put it on, turning this way and that, well pleased with her reflection. She'd just finished 'doing her face' when she heard the front door slam and a second later Alec's shout from the bottom of the stairs.

'Buck up, Rhoda, I thought you'd have your coat on and be waiting.'

'We've got bags of time.' She ran down the stairs, her coat on her arm. Would he notice? Would he say she looked nice?

'Come on, I've left the engine running.' He was already turning off the hall light ready to open the front door.

She crossed the familiar hall in the dark. Then her imagination carried her to the moment when Natalie would recognize them on the platform and she smiled. At the thought of Natalie, who could help it? 'I expected Etty would be with you. I thought we might have gone to the Green Monkey to eat for a treat.'

'She's coming home on her bike. There was a job she wanted to finish. Anyway Natalie will want to get home – she must have had enough of restaurants.'

Lucky Natalie, Rhoda thought, but over the years she had learnt when it was pointless to argue.

Their two daughters could hardly have been more different. Etty, the elder, worked in the family business and Rhoda smiled as she conjured up a picture of her. Then there was Natalie, two years younger and pretty as a picture. Life had always been kind to Natalie, but then so it should for she met each day with a smile and with hope. Now, at twenty, she was already making a name for herself travelling the country entertaining the troops – although if 'making a name' was an exaggeration, none of them would admit it. She would be home for five days, her first visit for more than a month, so it was no wonder that Rhoda had felt excited as she'd got ready.

At Waterloo Natalie climbed aboard the train, her mind leaping ahead as she imagined all she had to tell her parents and Etty when she got home. Already the corridor was in near-darkness and the blinds of each compartment were pulled down as soon as the shaded blue lights had come on. All that was normal, part of the life everyone had become conditioned to. Sliding a door open far enough to check if there was a spare seat, she saw there were already four people sitting on either side of the compartment, so she started to close it before trying further along the corridor.

'We can make room, we'll squeeze you in, won't we, chaps?' The invitation came from a jolly looking sailor.

'Not half we won't,' came a laughing rejoinder from his mate. 'You come next to me, miss, I'll squeeze you in right enough.'

The compartment was hazy with cigarette smoke, the occupants representing all three armed forces barely visible in the dim blue light.

'Thanks. If you really don't mind making room. I expect it's just as full if I try further along.'

The sight of her was a delight to all eight occupants: the sailors just docked and home on shore leave, those from a home station in the Air Force on a 72-hour pass and the soldier who said nothing but moved as closely as he could to the end of the seat to make space for one extra. At the start of their journey they had all been strangers but, all of them servicemen, there was a bond between them. By the time she joined them the barriers were already down – here was an atmosphere of camaraderie and goodwill.

'Ciggy?' Someone held his packed of Gold Flake ciga- rettes towards her.

'Are you sure you're all right for them?' Natalie replied.

'I managed to get some earlier, so we'll use mine next time.' She was enjoying herself. There could have been no better company – it carried her straight back to the previous evening and the clapping and cheering that ended her entertainment at an army base in Yorkshire. As if all that weren't enough to keep her spirits high, there was the other thought: another half hour and she would be getting off the train at Brackleford. Then – home! She had been travelling the country for more than a month and could imagine the excitement there would be, but she made an effort to join in with the laughing chatter of her new friends. When they asked her how far she'd been travelling, she told them not only where she'd been this time, but also over the last few weeks as she'd moved around, sometimes entertaining at factories during the workers' midday break, sometimes singing at service bases. If they'd thought she was something special when she'd opened the compartment door, her story raised her pedestal to even greater heights.

As good as her word, she passed her packet of Craven A around and the smoky fug in the compartment got thicker, the hoots of laughter louder. They were young and for a few days they were free men – like a gift from the gods they had the company of a gorgeously pretty companion. There were plenty of attractive girls about, friendly ones too, but, even more than the aura that came from her being a professional entertainer, there was something about Natalie that made them want to treat her well.

As a child she had been blonde, but now at twenty her hair was what she considered nondescript and her doting father called 'honey top'; it was worn in a popular pageboy bob. Her eyes were dark blue and made unforgettable by their fringe of long dark lashes, her mouth looked as though it wanted to be kissed – the same thought probably occurred to all her companions – and her teeth were even and very white. And there wasn't one amongst her companions who hadn't noticed her slim figure, the lovely curve of her bust, and her slender legs and trim feet in their high-

4

heeled shoes. It was a pity for them that her journey wasn't longer for it seemed no time before the train was slowing down as it approached Brackleford.

As she stood up, so too did the soldier who until then had remained silent.

'Let me get out first, then you can pass me your case,' he said and was rewarded by the smile that won her admirers at every turn. 'Is anyone meeting you?'

'My father's sure to be here,' she answered, peering along the dark platform.

It was the moment Alec had been waiting for. He honestly made an effort not to put her above everyone else, but in his heart there was no denying that between Natalie and himself was a bond that needed no words. Rhoda was forgotten as he hurried forward. Then Natalie's arms were around him.

'I'm home. It's so exciting, Dad,' she whispered, nuzzling against his neck. Then, she saw her mother and if the hug she gave her was less exuberant, her affection was just as genuine.

Amidst the excitement the soldier was temporarily forgotten.

'You travelled together?' Rhoda was the first to realise he was standing holding the case. 'Nat, aren't you going to introduce us?'

'I would if I could, but I can't,' Natalie said, laughing. 'We only met as we got off the train. Thanks for humping my luggage. Is no one meeting you?'

'No one knows I'm coming. I'm going to my grandmother's – she likes surprises.'

With that he raised his kitbag onto his shoulder and with something between a wave and a salute prepared to leave them. That he and Natalie were no more than passing acquaintances didn't surprise Alec – even in the near-darkness of the station platform it was clear he lacked refinement.

5

'Where are you heading?' Alec asked. 'On some routes the buses will have stopped at seven. Can I give you a lift?'

'I'm not going far – only to Russell Street.'

'We pass right by – I'll drop you there.'

So, with Rhoda and the nameless soldier in the back of the Morris Oxford, and Natalie by her father's side in the front – an arrangement dating back to the days when he'd driven to fetch his daughters home from school at the end of each term – they set off through the almost deserted streets of town. Instead of putting his passenger down at the corner, Alec turned into Russell Street.

'Tell me when we get there,' he said, driving slowly past the blacked-out houses.

'Almost there. Here we are, she's just beyond this tree. Thanks for the lift.' Then, to Natalie, 'Good luck with your singing. Perhaps I'll get a chance to hear you one of these days.'

'Put in a good word for me if anyone's listening. Natalie Harding – remember the name.'

'Sure thing.'

But as he got out of the car, someone hurried out of the front gate of a house on the opposite side of the road.

'I was just putting the key in the lock when I thought I recognised your voice. It's young Stewart, isn't it? Drat this blackout, can't see a thing.' The portly lady who bustled across the road was out of breath from the exertion. 'You never told her you were coming.'

'Gran likes surprises,' the soldier called Stewart answered cheerfully.

'Oh dear, but she'll be upset when she hears she's missed you. She went off only this morning to stay with her sister in Llandudno. Oh dear, and you've come specially. Can you get in? But what a homecoming – no one there for you.'

For a moment the soldier seemed uncertain.

'I used to have a key – well, of course I did. But I've lost it.' Then, his confidence returned, he put the well-

6

intentioned neighbour at her ease by assuring her that he would put up at Morland Hotel. 'And I bet she won't have locked the shed. In the morning I'll wander over and chop some logs for her.'

'She'll be pleased about that. She always boasts that you saw up the logs and chop the wood when you get a bit of leave. How long have you got? Oh dear, what a pity.'

'Seven days. But when I've chopped her wood, I'll get a train up to Wales. Aunt Flo will have a bed for me.'

All this time Alec had waited, the engine still running. He supposed the least he could do would be to take the fellow back as far as the Morland, but Rhoda had a better plan.

'Hop back in the car,' she called. 'We've a bed made up in the spare room. Come back with us for the night. In the morning, you can drive in with Alec.'

If Stewart Carling had known them better he would have realised that Rhoda's spontaneous invitation was in character, but on that cold, wet night he felt humbled by the warmth of their hospitality.

At Harding's Agricultural Engineers, the boarding planks firmly attached to the back of the lorry, Etty carefully steered the tractor into line.

'OK, here we go,' she called and started up the wooden incline. Despite British Summer Time being extended for the whole year, the evening of that first Friday in November was already sufficiently dark that she had to watch the side of the planks carefully as she drove. Even as a child she'd been fascinated watching implements being loaded ready for their return journey, restored to 'good health'. Wide-eyed and fearful, Natalie used to watch too, imagining a tractor veering off course and being thrown to the ground. 'Please don't stand so close, Etty,' she would call. '*Please.*' But Etty would have been conjuring up pictures of herself grown up and driving the perilous ascent. For her there had been nowhere more exciting than

7

those workshops at the cattle market in Brackleford, even though in those days she'd been too young to realise the struggle her father had to keep the business afloat. Now, though, everything was different. Etty had grown up, she was twenty-two and had served her apprenticeship just as she would have had she been born Alec Harding's son instead of his elder daughter. If she stopped to think about it – which she seldom did – she was aware of how different the atmosphere was in the workshops now from when she'd started her training at just sixteen. After five years of war, the previously neglected farming industry had at last become an appreciated and essential part of the economy of the country – in turn the agricultural engineers who serviced the farmers' old equipment and sold them their new machinery had thrived. Even in a reserved occupation it wasn't easy to find skilled men but, even so, Etty was the only female in the workshop.

'You off home now, Miss Etty?' Giles, the lorry driver, asked more out of friendliness than because he had any doubts. Of course she was off home, it was nearly seven o'clock and she'd been there since eight that morning. None of them worked longer hours than Etty, governor's daughter or not.

'Yep, that's me done. I'll just scrub some of the grime off my hands then I'm on my way. You too, Giles?'

'Reckon so. I'll get my time sheet and give it you before you go – the boss'll be wanting them in the morning.'

So, her strong and capable hands scrubbed, the time sheet deposited with the others in the drawer of her father's desk and the office door locked, Etty collected her bicycle from where she'd left it against the back wall of the workshop, called a cheery 'Goodnight' and pedalled off, leaving Giles to lock the double doors to the workshop. Although all the men worked at least seventy hours a week during the busy period, by that time of year it was only if there was an urgent job to be finished that anyone stayed beyond about six or half past. More often than not Etty went home

8

in the car with her father, but on this particular day she had made up her mind that she'd not pack up until the tractor was running well and had been loaded for an early start in the morning. There was nothing unusual in that – Etty hated leaving a job unfinished if an extra hour would see it done.

From Brackleford Cattle Market to Dewsberry Green where the Hardings lived was about four miles and Etty was almost halfway when she remembered the two rabbits Dougie Wright from Hamley Farm had brought just after her father had left for home. They'd been shot that morning and she knew her mother would be glad of them for the weekend, so she turned round and, head down against the wintry wind, started back along the dark road. The black-out had become an accepted part of life and, even if there had been no such thing, the lights of the town would have been far behind her. That night the darkness enveloped her, rain felt as though it froze as it hit her face. By now Giles would have gone, the place would be deserted and the workshop doors locked. But that didn't bother her; she had her own set of keys and in the workshop she could walk blindfold, knowing exactly where she had hung the rabbits on the far wall. Instead of opening up the double doors into the workshop, she leant her bike against the wall in Wilmott Street and went into the workshop that way.

In the pitch darkness the first thing she noticed was the thin strip of light shining from beneath the door of the office. Had she gone off without noticing she'd left a light on? She frowned, cross with herself and glad that she'd come back.

'Whatever are you doing here?' There was nothing unfriendly in her question to the young man at her father's desk, simply surprise. That was her first reaction. Andrew Clutterbuck was seated in the swivel chair with the desk drawer open. In his hand he had a time sheet. It was only the mechanics who kept time sheets – they and Etty herself, who insisted on being treated no differently from anyone else just because she was the boss's daughter. Andrew certainly didn't. 'You don't mean to say Dad asked you to come back in to do the wages?' she said in surprise, then added with a teasing note in her voice, 'I bet you don't even know how to work out our income tax.'

He answered in the same vein.

'You're right. The mysteries of income tax are beyond me, I'm happy to say.' Then, stacking the sheets and pushing them back into the drawer, he turned to her with a smile. 'No, of course your father didn't suggest any such thing. Pete Lewis was over at Maybury Farm – he'd not handed his time sheet in so I brought it and let myself in with it. I've written in today's time. Eight hours, he said. But I've put down ten. I know that's not an exaggeration.'

Perching herself on the side of the desk, she held out her hand for the time sheet.

'He always underestimates his hours, you know. He's slow, that's why he does it. Slow and frightened Dad'll give him the boot. That's what happened when he was with Marchand's. But Dad's not daft; he makes his own assessment. And I'm sure he adds the odd hour or so when Pete doesn't count travelling time.'

Watching her as she sat on the edge of the desk, Andrew let his mind wander. Especially this evening, dripping wet as she was, there was nothing of the glamour girl about Etty Harding with her tall, strong frame, her round face and rosy cheeks, her nondescript brown curly hair cropped like a boy because it was easier, he suspected. He let his thoughts carry him where they would as in his imagination he saw beyond the workman's overalls ... long, strong legs, firm thighs, a joy in living and, surely if only it could be tapped, a joy in loving. Etty did nothing half-heartedly.

Now, her face breaking into a smile, Etty said, 'Andrew, move your butt, Dad'll want to know we left the office locked. I've only come back to collect a couple of bunnies

10

Dougie Wright brought in. They'll be a godsend too. Nat's coming home this evening and it's not easy to come by a fatted calf. I'd ridden halfway home when I remembered them.'

Andrew returned the time sheet to the drawer with the others then stood up ready to leave. He had been with Harding's Engineers for nearly six months, a job that suited him admirably. His war service had been in the merchant fleet until about a year ago when his ship had been sunk in the North Sea. When he'd been picked up, suffering from hypothermia, he'd been taken to a military hospital. Pneumonia had followed, leaving him with a collapsed lung and his demobilisation.

Two years before the outbreak of war, he had come home from boarding school at eighteen having matriculated but with no clear idea of what he wanted to do, and had been in no rush to find out. His background was very different from Etty's: his wealthy stockbroker father ran a large estate in Hampshire – or more accurately a farm manager ran it for him. Andrew had always been more interested in agriculture than any of the professions his father seemed set on for him and until the outbreak of war, when he'd joined the Merchant Navy, he had spent his spare time on the estate. Once out of hospital, he'd no longer been satisfied with living at home and pottering around doing the manager's bidding, and he knew that, even if that had been what he wanted, very likely he would have found himself directed into something not of his own choosing. It was then that he had approached Alec Harding in a quest for work.

Despite Alec's initial doubts, there was something about Andrew that had made it impossible not to listen to his suggestion. A good-looking young man with his expensive well-cut tweeds and his highly polished and boned brogues, he looked like someone straight from the pages of a country fashion magazine – but how would he be received by the average hard-working, mud-on-his-boots tenant farmer?

11

'I know my limitations,' the young man had said. 'I'm not a mechanic. I'm not even a hundred per cent fit or I wouldn't be where I am. But I know from what Henry Dean, my father's manager, tells me that you visit the farms yourself and don't have a man whose job it is to keep a constant eye on the farmers' needs.'

'I've always made my own round of visits. It builds a good working relationship,' said Alec.

'Yes, of course it does. And, of course, with your experience you make a better job of it than I could – but if I'm on the road too, well, think of the ground we'd cover. Look, sir, I don't want a huge wage – if you'll just give me a try I'll willingly work for less than peanuts for a start,' Andrew said, enthusiastically.

'That's not my way,' Alec had answered. And so a wage had been agreed, not a vast sum but one they both saw as fair for a man with plenty of enthusiasm, a knowledge of farming, but no marketing experience.

Looking back on that unconventional interview, Alec had seen it as a turning point. Despite Andrew's appearance, his friendly manner was such that even the meanest working farmer soon came to welcome him. And he had enough intuition to recognise those who had the money to be tempted into more modern equipment, and those who relied on Harding's to keep their archaic horse-drawn ploughs serviced, and to supply their hayforks, milking stools and barbed-wire fencing. There wasn't a day when he returned to the cattle market without an order or two in his book, or one when he hadn't enjoyed every visit he'd made.

'My mind's like a metal detector,' Andrew once said with a good-humoured laugh to Miss Wheeler – Muriel Wheeler, who had looked after the office for some twenty years but still retained an old-fashioned aloofness that demanded the respect of that 'Miss'. 'It knows where there's the chink of brass. It's amazingly easy to give a hint of temptation for some new gadget or other. Those new

12

potato riddles, thank God they're home produced with quick delivery and don't have to come across the Atlantic. I've got orders for four today.' Work and enjoyment were all one to Andrew. Handsome and well groomed though he was, it wasn't his appearance that left a lasting impression so much as his honesty and his ability to find pleasure where others might see nothing but routine. The world was his friend.

Now, the drawer locked, he put his set of keys in his pocket and stood up to follow Etty out just as they heard the rain lash the window in a sudden gust of wind.

'Leave your bike and let me run you home,' he said, adding with a grin as she hesitated, 'Petrol? Is that what's bothering you? I'll "adjust the books" when it comes to logging my journeys.'

'A suggestion like that ought to make me refuse,' she answered in the same vein, 'but I'm not going to let it.'

'I should think not. What's more to the country's advantage – to cook the logbook on my mileage or let you catch pneumonia and not be able to keep the wheels of agriculture turning? All set?'

'Yep, I'll pick up my bunnies and then that's our lot. Just one proviso though, Andrew: if you take me home you must come in and meet Nat. They should be home by the time we get there. You'll like her. She's not a bit like me.'

He raised his eyebrows, his eyes alive with silent laughter. 'Is that supposed to be a recommendation?'

'What? Oh, I didn't mean it like that. I just meant that we're different. And of course you'll like her; no one could help it.` Nat and I are poles apart, but we get along famously.'

'A singer, isn't she? The girl in the picture on your father's desk.'

Etty nodded, pride in her younger sister apparent. 'Not the opera singer variety – she sings all the popular stuff. It goes down a treat with the servicemen. She's a natural – and prettier than any of those who are well known already.

13

Anyway, she's doing really well … has a busy time entertaining the forces and munitions workers. She goes all over the place – that's why it's such an event to have her coming home for a few days. You'd better find your way to the main door before I turn out the office light and lock up.'

'I've got a torch in my pocket. Do you want it?'

'As if I need a torch! I could go anywhere here with my eyes shut. When I was a kid that used to be one of my tests. And that was before we knew about things like blackouts. OK to turn off the light?'

With the rabbits collected and the doors locked, they set off. As he drove, Andrew let his mind dwell on Etty. He'd never met anyone quite like her. If she'd been male, he knew they would have been good friends. But she wasn't. She was a young woman with a warm and generous spirit, with physical strength and tenacity, with good humour – but with absolutely no regard for her personal appearance. If she changed out of those workman's overalls that had become her uniform, if she'd only take herself off to a good hairdresser instead of washing her hair herself and having it cut every month or so, and if she spent some of her clothes coupons on a frock – nothing too girlie, he conceded – then she needn't look half bad. But imagine suggesting it to her, imagine her hoot of laughter! By contrast he thought of Celia, his childhood friend, his teenage sweetheart and now his fiancée, gentle, utterly feminine in appearance. Sweet, ethereal Celia, even when they'd played together as children he had wanted to protect her. She was about a year his senior and now an officer in the WRNS, yet still he felt the same about her. In truth he seldom saw her these days. She was stationed in Plymouth and when she had leave she liked to spend most of it with her widowed mother. Perhaps that wasn't natural – he was sure his father thought it very odd, but then his father had never made a secret of the fact he thought theirs to be an odd relationship.

*

14

When Alec turned into the driveway and pulled up in front of Timberley, the Hardings' home facing Dewsberry Green, he found another car already parked.

'That's Andrew's car. What would he be doing here?' he said.

'Probably he gave Ett a lift. Company, that's nice!' Natalie was clearly smiling – Stewart could tell she was by her voice. 'It's turning into a party to celebrate me being back in the fold. Have we got lots of food, Mum?' She neither expected nor received an answer – they took it for granted that Rhoda never failed them.

It was an evening such as Stewart had never known at his home in Staffordshire or with his grandmother in Brackleford. Life had been a struggle for his parents but one they accepted as a blessing. Man wasn't put on this earth to look for pleasure or to indulge in what they saw as wicked frivolity. His father was in charge of their local Casual Ward, a nightly bed for the homeless provided for a few pence, accommodation for him and his family being part of the wage; his mother worked in a bakehouse situated a mile or so away, a mile she insisted on walking come rain or shine. There were never any arguments in the house, or an atmosphere of warmth either. Life was a serious business, its path unerringly straight and extremely narrow. Man's duty was to work – anything bordering on pleasure was viewed with suspicion. The result was a home dedicated to joyless labour where it was taken for granted that every nineteen shillings and sixpence had to do the work of a pound. It was a far cry from Timberley.

The Hardings were able to see their visitor for the first time once he was inside the house – until then he had been little more than a voice in the dark. Natalie must have seen him in the dim blue light of the railway carriage but, if she had, he had made no impression on her, thought Rhoda. His dark hair was cropped very short and there was nothing

15

outstanding in his features, although his appearance was pleasant enough. His hands looked strong, his teeth were very white but were marred by the fact that they weren't quite straight. Rhoda sensed that he was 'on his best behaviour', and yet he still managed to lack any natural grace. It was impossible not to be aware of the contrast between their two guests.

Andrew needed no persuading to stay, so there were six of them for supper. Etty brought in the steaming tureen of home-made vegetable soup and Rhoda followed with a breadbasket of home-made rolls. Even Harding hospitality couldn't rise to butter, but no one expected any. Soup was followed by fish pie and jacket potatoes, and that by apple crumble and custard. Shortages were a habitual part of life so, although it was a humble meal, no one was conscious of the fact. It spoke volumes to the two visitors.

That was Andrew's first encounter with Natalie. He'd known from the picture on Alec's desk that she was beautiful but he discovered something more: he suspected that she was the centre of Alec Harding's universe, his gaze hardly leaving her and his eyes carrying a message that was plain to read.

Stewart, too, noticed Alec's adoring expression and it didn't surprise him for he too found it hard not to stare at her. As she chattered, which she did almost non-stop, he was fascinated by her changing expression, her sudden burst of laughter, the way she held her head, the way she chinked her wine glass – filled with home-made elderflower wine – against her father's.

On Alec's other side sat Etty, a girl so different. Indeed she was so different that Stewart didn't give her a second glance – how could he? It was like comparing a humble moth with a tropical butterfly. Andrew divided his attention between the two, while with unfailing and natural social grace he talked to his hostess. His easy courtesy made Stewart feel gauche, the expensive tweeds in sharp contrast to his own rough khaki, the well-polished brogues making a clodhopper of him in his army issue boots, the public school voice making him want to hide behind silence.

It was after supper, while they were washing up, that from the kitchen Rhoda and Etty heard the sound of the piano. Pausing in their work, they listened.

Rhoda frowned. 'They should wait until the visitors have gone.' But it was always the same: as soon as Natalie came home, she and Alec would be making music together.

'The chaps won't mind,' Etty said, laughing. 'The soldier could hardly keep his eyes off her – and if Andrew had been less socially trained you bet he would have been the same. Nice that she's home, Mum. She must have lots to tell us, so it's a pity we've got visitors. Where did she find the soldier – Stewart?'

Rhoda told her about the chance meeting on the railway platform, the tale continuing on to how it was he'd been invited to come home with them. On that particular evening she felt a rare sense of exhilaration – she'd been lifted out of the monotonous rut of her daily life, not only by Natalie coming home but by having two visitors and the challenge of stretching a meal to make it feed six instead of four, and yet retain the festive atmosphere she'd planned. If her original plans had included Natalie joining them in the kitchen, in her heart she'd known that wouldn't be how the evening would work out. Etty was her rock, her helper, sensitive to her moods and a willing listener when the unchanging monotony of her daily routine made her feel she was taken for granted. It was somehow impossible to be downhearted for long when Etty was around.

'I persuaded Andrew to come to supper because I especially wanted him to get to know Nat,' Rhoda said as she dried the dishes. 'She must have lots to tell us. But she'll be home for nearly a week so we might as well make the most of having a party this evening. Is that it? Have we done?' Clearly they had done, so she hung her tea towel on the rail in front of the Aga. 'Hark, a duet.'

Opening the kitchen door a fraction wider, they listened.

When Natalie entertained the troops she usually sang up-to-the-minute songs, choruses they all knew and could join in. This ballad dated back more than two decades, a love song from the First World War, a duet for a departing soldier and his lover. Rhoda and Etty crossed the hall and quietly went into the drawing room where to their surprise they found it was Stewart and not Alec playing the piano. All eyes were on the two of them: Stewart playing – and singing – Natalie with her hands on his shoulders, leaning forward so that she could read the words. At the final chord the spell was broken, but not before the scene had imprinted itself on them all. It was as if they realised that the moment had been special, in an ongoing way. Yet where was the reason? By morning Stewart would be gone – they were unlikely to see him again. As for Natalie, at every opportunity she would travel to far-flung service bases, and, even now, five months into the invasion of France, who dared guess how long the war would last? Stewart was just a serving soldier, albeit one with an exceptionally pleasant voice.

'That was – oh, it was gorgeous,' Natalie told him as the song ended. 'I've never sung a duet before. Where did you learn to play and sing like that?'

'When I was a kid I was in the church choir. The organist sort of took me under his wing, gave me extra training and when he saw I was keen, he gave me piano lessons. Even when my voice had broken I still went to him a couple of evenings a week. Funny really, looking back. But at the time it seemed natural. He just seemed to enjoy teaching and never charged a bean.'

'I don't play a note. I just sing because I love to,' said Natalie.

'Of course you do.'

Etty and her mother exchanged a quick glance of understanding. Alec watched too as the young couple sorted through the music to choose what to sing next, his fingers busy pushing tobacco into his pipe. The evening was surely

18

everything he could possibly want, everyone together, his precious Natalie home again. This soldier they'd brought home had a pleasant voice, but he certainly wasn't the sort Nat would find attractive and by tomorrow he'd be gone, then they'd have her to themselves. Drawing on the stem of the pipe as he held the match to the tobacco, he was content. If he were honest with himself, Alec would admit that he hated the thought of losing her to any man – one day it would happen, but that day was far away and for tonight he wasn't even going to contemplate it.

Andrew went home, Etty and Rhoda went up to bed, but still Alec stayed by the dying embers of the fire listening to the music.

'We're quite a duo, aren't we?' Natalie turned to Stewart when finally he stood up from the piano stool, her eyes bright with excitement. 'Why are you wasting your time in the Army, Stewart? Just imagine if you were free. We could give Nelson Eddy and Jeanette Macdonald a run for their money.'

'It was great. Do you believe in Fate?' asked Stewart. A simple question and Alec tried to believe he imagined an underlying message. Stewart Carling was just a soldier they'd befriended, an outsider. By tomorrow he'd be gone.

Natalie considered the question before she answered.

'I've never bothered about it. I just think that we have to decide what we want and then go all out to get it.'

Stewart nodded slowly, giving her words time to impress themselves into his mind.

Upstairs in the cold bedroom, Rhoda undressed and carefully hung away her unremarked-on new dress. With her arms stretched high she was holding her nightdress ready to pull over her head when, instead, she stopped and moved towards the mirror on the front of the wardrobe door. She let herself imagine the feeling of youth and hope. Surely for her it had been more than hope – it had been certainty. She had been

19

about Natalie's age when she had fallen in love with Alec. He had filled her every thought. Had *he* changed? Had *she* changed? And what did she mean by 'changed'? No day passes without it leaving its impression. But, in her case, an impression of what? Day after day the same: nothing to challenge her – unless she counted eking out the meagre rations so that they all felt well catered for. If every life started as a blank canvas, what was she adding to the picture? Nothing! Years ago it had been different. Yes, of course she'd changed, she'd been ground down by monotony and routine, by compromising her dreams and teaching herself to expect nothing except second-hand satisfaction from the family's achievements. Was she being fair? Was it just that reality never holds the heady glory of dreams? If she could see into Alec's mind, would she find that his own thoughts were the same as hers, that he saw her as no more than part of the orderly dull routine of their days?

On his tallboy there was a photograph of the two of them taken more than twenty years before. She'd been so slim, so supple and lithe. 'My elf' was what he used to call her. So long ago ... there was nothing elfin about her now ... yet where was the difference? She was still slim, but she wasn't the same. Peering at the mirror she examined her face. When had youth been lost? Her complexion was clear, her eyes bright, yet nothing was as it had been all those years ago. And Alec? She slipped her arms into the sleeves of her nightdress then, not bothering to do up the buttons, leaving it hanging open as she sat on the edge of the bed, memories crowding her mind. He'd been good looking as a twenty-five year old and still was. His hair had now started to go grey, his face was weather-beaten, but in men those things did nothing to detract from their appearance – if he had grown heavier it only gave him the appearance of strength. Funny to sit here thinking about it, she told herself silently, it must have happened without my noticing. So where is the difference between then and now? The answer sprang to mind, memories exciting her and yet

20

adding to her feeling of loss. Then she heard them all coming up to bed.

She moved to her dressing table stool and started to cream any remaining make-up off her face as Alec came into the room.

'I'd thought you'd be in bed ages ago. You must be frozen,' he said.

'I was waiting for you.' Did he hear the echo of memories in her tone – memories that filled her with longing? It seemed not. 'It's been such a special evening,' she said, as if that would set his thoughts on the same road as her own. Surely it was an evening that should find its ultimate conclusion in bringing them close. She longed to find the joy they'd known long ago, something that had been overshadowed by habit, routine, compromise.

Coming to stand in front of him, she raised her face to his and teased his mouth with hers. Lightly, affectionately and in a way that emphasised the change the years had wrought, he kissed her forehead. And gave her bottom a friendly tap.

'Funny girl,' he said softly. 'Hop into bed.'

From downstairs they heard the grandfather clock chime, then strike. Midnight.

Tying the cord of his pyjamas, Alec went through his nightly routine. He turned off the bedroom light, opened the curtains and pulled down the top window about nine inches. Then he climbed into bed.

'G'night dear,' he said, giving her forehead a light kiss. She raised her face, her mouth seeking his, only to be met with 'Sleep time. It's been quite an evening. You did well, feeding so many. Lovely to have her home.' When he turned his back, she put her arms around him. 'Better turn around,' he told her, his tone one of companionable contentment. 'You won't sleep well like that.'

She did as he said. Of course it had been a splendid evening – yet she felt utterly alone.

So the seconds ticked by as Friday became yesterday.

*

21

Next morning Rhoda carried the carpet sweeper into the dining room to get rid of any toast crumbs left on the carpet. With resignation she'd watched the others drive off towards town: Etty and Alec for a morning's work in the yard; Stewart to chop a supply of wood and stack it in the shed in Russell Street; Natalie to wander around the shops until midday, when she was meeting Stewart for lunch at the Tudor before he caught his train to Wales to surprise his grandmother and spend the rest of his leave. Automatically she pushed the carpet sweeper just as she did each morning, the shadow of last night still hanging over her. She'd been lifted out of the rut of their daily life by the advent of two visitors, then the music, the elusion of being included in the aura of anticipation that seemed to her to surround the youngsters. For her, the glory of youth was lost and yet she longed to grasp at it, to feel herself to be *alive* and eager for the start of each new day, to find joy and excitement in living and loving. If only Alec would share the feelings that drove her. For him life was a comfortable affair, running smoothly on the familiar lines she didn't doubt he found completely satisfying. Pushing the carpet sweeper around the table, she could hear the echo of his affectionate laugh, his 'Funny girl, hop into bed.'

Letting her memory drift back she gave up the pretence of crumb-hunting, propped the sweeper against the wall and sat on the window seat. Had Alec the slightest idea of her frustration? Would he understand the fantasies that filled her mind as they went through the routine exertion of making love and she strived to leave behind the boring – yes boring – routine of life and let her spirit fly free?

It was at that point that her attention was taken by a sports car drawing up outside April Cottage, the only other house fronting the green and situated directly opposite Timberley. She watched a young Air Force officer get out of the car then, after a moment's hesitation, walk up the garden path to the house that had been empty since elderly Miss Lacy had died a few months previously. Rhoda recalled the old lady telling her that she had a great-nephew in the Air Force serving in North Africa. Could this be who it was? Perhaps news of the death had gone astray. Had he arrived expecting to find his great-aunt ready to welcome him?

Without so much as stopping to put on a coat Rhoda hurried across the green to come face to face with the caller just as he reappeared from the side path leading to the rear of the cottage.

'I saw you come,' she greeted him quite unnecessarily. 'You've come to visit Miss Lacy?'

'Miss Lacy? I have an appointment to meet the agent here.' He frowned, looking at his watch. 'Nine o'clock was the time we agreed. It's nearly five minutes past.'

'Then I'm so sorry. Not that he's late – after all five minutes isn't enough to make a fuss about – but sorry for what you must see as interfering.' And without pausing for a reply, if indeed he intended to make one, she stumbled on with the explanation about Miss Lacy and her Air Force relative.

'Don't worry about it. It's not important. Here comes a car ... yes it's coming this side of the green. So, if you'll forgive me.' And without further ado he turned his back on her.

Rhoda returned home disappointed. She had hoped that when April Cottage was sold – or let – her new neighbours would become friends. There were few people she didn't get on with, but instinct told her the stiff-necked flyer was one of those few. Then her conscience brought her up sharp. She shouldn't judge him on that brief meeting. So, in an effort to overcome her resentment that her neighbourly action had been received in such a brusque, disinterested manner, as she shut the gate of Timberley she purposely looked back to where the two men were standing talking and forced herself to smile. Whether the young man noticed she had no idea, but the action made her feel more comfortable with herself.

23

Once indoors she put away the carpet sweeper and made herself concentrate on preparing the rabbits for the cooking pot. It was nearly three hours later when she was tidying bedrooms that her natural curiosity took control and she went to the window of Natalie's room to see whether the sports car was still there. Now there was not only the car but a lorry too. To call it a removal van would have been an exaggeration – it was a delivery lorry of some sort but clearly the young man hadn't much in the way of personal effects to add to the furniture left in the cottage. Standing back from the window, she gave full rein to her curiosity as a thin, balding, middle-aged man prepared to climb up into the driver's seat. First his hand was taken briefly in the new owner's, then a girl came running out from the cottage and hurled herself into the new owner's arms. Staggering behind her was a small boy, a child sufficiently young that he could never be sure exactly where his feet and the ground would make contact. Rhoda's hopes took an upward leap at the thought of a young family living on the opposite side of the grassy patch.

After that brief handshake, the young Air Force officer turned his back on the man who must have delivered their few possessions and on the girl who presumably was his wife and the toddler's mother. He swooped the boy into his arms, hoisted him over his head to sit astride his shoulders and started towards Timberley. After her far-from-friendly reception from him earlier, it was with mixed feelings that Rhoda went down to open the front door. She was already at the foot of the stairs when she realised just what it would do to his opinion of her if she opened the door before he knocked! And, even as she thought it, she faced the truth: to look out of the window and see another human was so unusual that it gave colour to her day. Immediately her resentment was directed at Alec – and not for the first time. It wasn't fair that she had to be content with nothing more in her days than making life comfortable for everyone else. Before the war that had been the accepted way, but now

24

things were different. Why couldn't he see that being *his* wife didn't make her different from other women? Everyone should be willing to play a part in the war effort and she was both willing and eager. A silent honest streak reminded her that it wasn't necessarily that she wanted to help the war effort – what she craved was to be more than what she'd been ground into by the years and to rediscover the person she had once been. Why couldn't he understand? Yet whenever she brought up the subject his answer was the same: 'There's no need for you to work ... there's plenty for you to do here in the house ... you are my wife, your place is at home ... Muriel Wheeler manages the offices perfectly and if she couldn't manage alone, then there's plenty who need the mon—'

At that moment there was a sharp knock on the front door. Moving at a leisurely pace and clutching at dignity that didn't come naturally to her, Rhoda walked across the hall to face her visitor.

'You came over to speak to me earlier,' he said. 'I've come to apologise. If you'd been right and I had been Miss whatever-you-called-her's great nephew, I should have been grateful to you and I'm afraid I wasn't even polite.' Then, steadying the little boy with his left hand he held out his right. 'My name is Michael Matherson and above me you see my son Mickey.'

'How nice of you to come across. I'm Rhoda Harding.' Then, dignity giving way to honesty accompanied by the ghost of yesteryear's elfin smile, 'Yes, you managed to make me feel as though I were the sort of person who peeps around net curtains. I promise you I'm not.' Looking up to the little boy on his high perch, she said, 'Hello Mickey. You don't know how pleased I am that a family is coming to the cottage. That's your wife waving the furniture lorry goodbye?'

'Yes.' Michael hesitated but he changed his mind about whatever he'd almost said.

'I'm looking forward to meeting her.' And again that

25

smile that seemed to strip her of the years. 'I can't tell you how much I'm looking forward to it. Miss Lacy was pretty well housebound and since she died there has been no one. As far outside the village as this, we see almost nobody – especially in the winter. I do hope your wife won't find it too quiet.'

'Jenny will learn to adapt. I'm just thankful to find somewhere for the lad away from where she was living before.'

'Oh look, she's seen that you're here,' Rhoda exclaimed. 'Give her a wave, call her over.'

'No, we must go. I only have twenty-four hours free and, although the place is furnished after a fashion, I want to change things around and must get the bulk done before it's time for Mickey to be settled for the night.'

'Say hello to her for me. And tell her I'm always here.'

His wife had started across the green in the direction of Timberley, walking none too easily as the rain-softened ground was spiked at each step by her four-inch heels. As soon as Michael turned to leave, she stopped in her track and they returned to April Cottage together. Rhoda's reaction to the brief, closer view of Jenny Matherson was disappointment. With her hair piled high into the sort of exotic style that might look in place on a cinema screen and must take her half an hour to arrange, her tight-fitting clothes showing every curve and those unsuitable shoes, the newcomer showed little promise of finding contentment in the isolation of Dewsberry Green. But the little boy looked a darling, Rhoda told herself, trying to hang on to hope as she watched the young family return to April Cottage.

Chapter Two

Although Natalie was only at home for a few days, once Monday came and Etty and Alec went off to the yard she was soon bored by the quiet lack of action. It was different for her mother, she told herself, as she had plenty to do in the house – looking after the family had always been her life. But nothing happened on Dewsberry Green, absolutely *nothing*.

'I know, Mum!' she said, early in the afternoon, 'What if I go across to April Cottage and introduce myself to the new people? His car isn't there so he must be at the airfield and I bet she's fed up with the silence all by herself – well, herself and the child. I'll go and welcome her like a good neighbour. It's better for someone young to go than someone she sees as another generation.'

'That's a nice idea,' her mother replied, giving no hint of the hurt her self-esteem had suffered. 'Why don't you bring them back here for a cup of tea or something? There's no festive fare but we'll make up for it by making them extra welcome. I feel so sorry for the poor girl, her husband a flyer and living here where it's so isolated – she'll have nothing to take her mind off the worry. Her son looks like a dear little boy.' Although she meant what she said about being sorry for their neighbour, she didn't imagine Natalie would have much in common with the girl.

But when, a little while later, Rhoda saw them coming

27

across the green together they appeared to be talking companionably. If she put it down to Natalie's natural friendliness, she would have overlooked Jenny's sudden feeling of hope.

Mickey was in his pushchair where he was leaning over the side and letting Benji, his scruffy toy dog, drag on the grass, no doubt seeing it as walking. Smiling in anticipation, Rhoda put cups and saucers on the tray and some milk in a mug for the little boy.

'Come on in,' Natalie said as she led the way into the kitchen, holding the back door open for the pushchair. There was no suggestion that the boy might walk in on his two feet and leave his muddy wheels behind. In any case, even if Rhoda had harboured such thoughts they would have vanished at the sight of the child's smile. There was nothing shy about him and at first glance he appeared to see Rhoda as a friend.

'See 'oo,' he announced as he beamed up at her.

'That's good. And you've brought your dog with you too.'

In reply two small hands lifted the toy dog and held it in Rhoda's direction.

'You're in,' his mother said with a laugh. 'He's taken a shine to you right enough.' And that was Rhoda's introduction to Jenny.

'Children always like Mum,' Natalie told her. 'I'd better introduce you. This is Jenny, Mum, Jenny Matherson. And this is my mother, Mrs Harding.'

'Me, I'm just Jenny, or Jen to my mates,' the girl said, her diction a far cry from the image she meant to present with her glamorous hairstyle and over-painted face. 'And I don't want to sound pushy, but I'd like it much more if I could call you by whatever your name is. Would you think that's a cheek when we don't hardly know each other?'

Rhoda's previously wounded self-esteem was being restored by the second. 'I'm Rhoda and I agree. Christian names are much more friendly. We shall probably see

28

plenty of each other – there's no one else around. And this is Mickey – he and I met yesterday when your husband called.'

'Yes, this is Mickey,' Jenny said. 'Well, to be honest, he's Michael, same as his dad. But I can't be doing with more than one Michael about the place.'

'It suits him, it's a nice, cheerful sort of name. I'll just take the tray through to the sitting room, the kettle won't be a minute.'

'Do we have to go into the good room?' Jenny said, throwing an anxious glance in Mickey's direction. 'Give him so much as a dry biscuit and he gets crumbs everywhere. If he stays in his chair he can't spread himself too far – that's why I brought it indoors. And it's wet and mucky out there – didn't half bucket down in the night. Did you hear it? The wheels of the chair will make a mess on the floor. Bad enough on the kitchen lino, but they wouldn't do a carpet no good.'

'It's much comfier in there,' Natalie said uncertainly. 'We can soon sweep up a few crumbs.'

'Honest, Rhoda, I'd be easier if we could have a cup of tea out here. Can't natter half as well if I've got to keep an eye on His Lordship.'

Rhoda nodded. 'I know the feeling – I've been there. We'll stay out here.'

Instead of just tea and a biscuit they feasted on toast made in front of the Aga, then shown a buttery knife and smothered with home-made raspberry jam. Mickey was given just half a slice and thoroughly enjoyed licking the jam off and leaving the toast as clean as a freshly washed plate. By that time it had lost its appeal and he discarded it onto the floor.

'Oh Mickey, you are rotten,' his mother told him. 'You got no manners at all.'

It wasn't until Rhoda had taken a clean, damp cloth and wiped first his hands and face, then taken the sticky finger marks off the pushchair that she remembered Natalie's

29

reminder of the age gap. Would the young mother see it as interference?

Apparently not. 'Ta. He's a right mucky pup. I'll have to get used to watching out for Michael's uniform. Get sticky hands on that and the balloon'll go up. But with kids, you can't keep them clean all the time, can you?'

Tea eaten, Rhoda suggested taking Mickey out of the pushchair where he was already getting fidgety. She even went upstairs to the old playroom and found a wooden train for him to play with.

Of them all, Natalie was the first to get bored. She'd gone to April Cottage hoping she might find a companion in the newcomer and even though at first sight she had been disappointed, her natural friendliness had managed to overcome her qualms for the first half hour. Under normal circumstances she wouldn't have attempted to build such an unlikely relationship and it took less time than to make the toast to bring her to the point where she made a silent assessment of Jenny and didn't think much of it. On Saturday afternoon, after Stewart had caught the westbound train, she had come back to Dewsberry on the bus, walked from the village and it was then that she had caught a brief glimpse of Michael Matherson. A good-looking man, dashing and debonair had been her opinion. But his wife fell far short of anything she had expected; in fact, Natalie thought in silent criticism, she looked like nothing but a tart and sounded even worse – by the time she had been in the house five minutes, any initial uncertainty banished by Rhoda's easy manner, Jenny's aitches began to fly.

While Rhoda and Jenny crawled on the floor trundling the train with a gleeful Mickey, Natalie let her thoughts drift forward to where her engagements would take her once these few days at home were over. Fancy anyone as young as Jenny Matherson must be having nothing more exciting ahead of her than living in a one-eyed place like Dewsberry, getting her pleasure second hand as Mickey developed, until finally she would end up with a life like

30

Mum's. It was different for Mum, she wasn't young, and of course she enjoyed looking after them all. But that sort of life wasn't for *her* and in contrast came her vision of her own future: the heady sound of applause, the shouts of appreciation from the men in the audience. Roll on Friday, she thought silently.

In Rhoda, Jenny knew she had a friend but that didn't detract from her disappointment about the isolation of Dewsberry Green. So when, a few weeks later, Rhoda suggested she might leave Mickey at Timberley and have a day in Brackleford, she snatched the opportunity with both hands.

By ten o'clock the following morning she was hurrying into the village to catch the bus to town, her high heels clicking on the tarmac of the lane, her hair piled even higher than normal. She was pleased with life. She adored Mickey with every fibre of her being, but over the last few years she'd forgotten the joy of being free. If only Michael could have been with her. No, don't think about Michael. She couldn't imagine him hurrying to catch a bus for a day window-shopping, and anyway, if he were with her she'd feel that he was watching her to find something to criticise. Like Sunday when she'd put on these pretty bright-red shoes – just because they weren't posh leather like he would have chosen, he looked all tight-lipped and upperty.

All right, she argued silently, so he doesn't think I'm good enough for him – and I'm *not* if what matters is being right and proper – but if only he really loved me he would see past all that. What's going to happen to us? What if he finds some smart bit who's more up his street? It's not the money I'm after. When Mickey gets a bit bigger I don't mind finding a job, but if Michael threw me back where he found me I'd . . .

But she didn't get as far as finishing her silent sentence for as she rounded the corner to the village street she saw the bus was already waiting by the war memorial. Heels

31

clicking, she ran. Having left home full of excitement for her day of freedom she settled into her seat and pushed everything else from her mind.

She gave herself over to enjoyment. Today she could only window-shop as clothes coupons were running short, but she went to the Tudor for lunch, as recommended by Rhoda. Euphoria didn't desert her as she returned home intending to go straight to Timberley to collect Mickey, but as the green came into view she saw Michael's car was outside the cottage.

He heard the click, click of her high heels as she ran. Why wasn't Mickey with her?

'Where's the boy?' he greeted her.

'He's OK. Rhoda's had him for the day so that I could go into town. You're nice and early.' And with the glow of her day still on her she wound her arms around his neck and raised her face, teasing his mouth with hers.

'Careful of that lipstick,' he said.

Laughing, she took her handkerchief and rubbed it hard against her lips, then tried again. A fastidious man, what she was doing seemed to annoy him. The lipstick was smeared across her mouth; her handkerchief was probably ruined.

Moving away he told her, 'I came early because we have to talk.'

The joy went out of her day. What was he going to say? She'd lived in dread of this, knowing that one day it would happen – the culmination of her humiliation in telling him about the baby, the brief pause before he'd said, 'I shall need your stepmother's consent, then I'll arrange a quick wedding.' All of it came flooding back to her as she looked down rather than see his expression.

'Go on, then. Say what you got to say.' Her voice was rough and coarse – she needed it to be, even though it conjured up a picture in her mind of her stepmother who was about to be proved right in the hateful things she'd said about the marriage.

32

'I'm being posted from the base and promoted with immediate effect. I'm going to an airfield in Norfolk.'

Whatever Jenny expected to hear, it wasn't that.

'You mean we got to pack it all in just when you found somewhere for us?'

'Of course not,' Michael retorted. 'I've signed a contract for a year. After that we have the option of extending the lease. You and Mickey will have to stay here. But at least I shall know it's decent for him – and Rhoda Harding will keep an eye on things.'

'Keep an eye on things be damned! It's me who looks after us. Just cos I left Mickey with her for a few hours you think I need watching out for. Well, I don't. Shouldn't wonder you'll be glad to be shot of us, off there in Norfolk.'

'If you behave like this, I shouldn't wonder you're right. Christ, Jenny, why do you always have to fight me? How the hell was I to know when I was posted to Oakleigh that this would happen? No one chooses where they get sent – or when, either. I'm being posted as of Monday. You have a perfectly good home here and the rent will be paid straight from my account at the beginning of each month. So for God's sake act like a grown-up and learn some self-discipline.'

Still she didn't look at him. She felt she was drowning in misery. In other homes when men told their wives they were moving away, surely they would cling together, finding strength in each other. She clenched her teeth as if that would hold back the emotion that was shocking her.

'You always treat me like some kid,' she growled.

'Not true.'

'No, not always you don't. In bed it's different, it always has been.' Now the tears gushed and wouldn't be held back. 'It's like that cow of a stepmother always said: for you I was just a bit of easy fun. That's all I ever have been. If you didn't like me better in bed than you do out of it, then we wouldn't be here at all – I wouldn't have got in the

33

club. I *was* a kid then, but now I'm almost nineteen – and I know a bloody sight more about life than some of the prissy birds you look on as my betters.' Once started, it' was beyond her power to stop the hysterical tirade. ''Spect you thought yourself no end of a good type being prepared to marry me. Well, if you hadn't you'd have been in a hell of a lot of trouble, getting me up the spout at my age. And me? Was that supposed to be the end of it for me? Nothing to complain about – you married me and gave me a meal ticket, is that what you thought? All I had to do was be there for you when you felt like favouring me with—' Her near-scream was cut short when he brought his hand sharply across her cheek. 'Never loved me, you didn't. Not even in the beginning,' she sobbed.

Her cheap mascara was smeared down her face, her eyelids were red and swollen. One hand on her shoulder, he raised her chin with the other, willing her to meet his gaze.

'I have never lied to you,' he said softly. 'Jenny, usually you and I get on, but not when you behave like some half-brained fishwife.'

'Not half-brained, not a fishwife.' She rubbed the palms of her hands across her face, making matters even worse.

'I know it's been hard for you. You were too young to have to be forced into marriage and you would have been happier with someone of your own sort.'

'You reckon you're too posh, is that what you think? Well, I'm *damned* if I do. Getting in the club wasn't just my doing. If you think you stooped and picked up nothing when you took me on, then you can bloody think again. Anyway, I've got Mick. He's the best think what happened in all my life.'

'And in mine too,' Michael answered, speaking softly and ignoring her tone and language. For a second they looked at each other, frightened where her outburst had led them and desperately wishing none of it had happened. 'Come here.' He drew her close and with his own hand-

34

kerchief wiped away her tears and with them a good deal of mascara. 'Now, go and wash your face and we'll walk over to collect Mickey.'

By seven o'clock the following Sunday evening, Michael had gone.

With her allowance from Michael, Jenny had more money than she'd been used to and, using clothing coupons intended for Mickey, she bought herself a new and what she considered glamorous winter coat which she hung away to await Michael's Christmas leave.

'The girl looks like a street walker,' Alec said with a frown as he glanced across the green to where Jenny was watching Etty and Mickey playing his version of football on a Sunday morning a week or so later. 'I can't think why Etty wastes time on her.'

'Time with Jenny isn't time wasted.' Rhoda's voice was sharp. If she were honest with herself she would acknowledge that she was more disappointed than annoyed by Alec's words. Had he always been like this: quick to criticise anything or anyone who didn't conform to his own pattern?

He seemed to be considering her answer before he replied. 'It's different for you, I can see that. But Etty has a broader experience ... she does a man's job and does it well. What possible stimulus can there be for her in the idle chatter of an empty-headed creature like that?'

'And whose fault is it that my own experience is so narrow and that all I'm fit for is empty-headed chatter? Certainly not mine. Five years of war and while other women have worked, what have I done? Nothing. If you think it's beneath your dignity for me to apply to a stranger for a job, then let me come in to the market and do the books like I used to when we first had the business.' Purposely she said *we*, intending to take his mind back to those early days when it had seemed to be a shared venture.

He picked up the newspaper and took his pipe from his

35

pocket, looking forward to his Sunday morning routine.
'Get along with you.' Clearly he didn't even take the
idea seriously. But just in case she took his friendly tone as
a sign that he was weakening, he added, 'Muriel Wheeler
has been there since she left school just before Etty was
born. She's as much part of the business as any of us. Are
you saying you want me to tell her to move over and make
room for my wife? And in any case,' he said with a laugh
as he imagined anything so outlandish, 'let's just be thankful things aren't as tight as they used to be in the days when
you used to help out, eh? And how do you imagine it would
do anything for the war effort for you to take her place?
She manages the book-keeping excellently, I trust her
implicitly. And more than that, I really think she cares
about the business as if it were her own.' Then, with a
sudden smile that almost succeeded in banishing her resentment, 'And you more than manage here. The spirit of the
house comes from what you put into it.' So often she'd
longed for the romance of their youth, yet now she was
made to feel vaguely uncomfortable by the way he was
looking at her, not the sort of casual affectionate glance she
was used to but as if he was seeing behind the façade and
into the secrets of her soul. 'You doing the books was a
long time ago, my funny elf.'
    Yet when he held his hand in her direction she pretended
not to notice. Instead she took the loose cushion from the
second fireside chair and shook it, then put it back in place.
    'Besides,' she returned to what they'd been saying about
Jenny, 'Jenny didn't have time to grow up properly before
she found herself married and having a baby.'
    'And not in that order unless I'm much mistaken.'
    'Hardly your affair or mine either. I know the way she
dresses isn't suitable for the country—'
    'Not suitable for town or country either – except for
hanging around on street corners. God knows the way she's
lived, or how she ensnared that young fellow.'
    'That may be your opinion,' Rhoda answered coldly.

36

'Personally I see her more as a child who's not had a chance, trying to look like some glamorous film star. She's a *good* girl and she adores Mickey.'

'Huh!' Apparently she'd done nothing to change his opinion.

Back in the kitchen peeling potatoes, in her mind Rhoda went over the conversation, surprised at her reaction.

Standing poised with a potato in one hand and the peeler in the other she gazed out of the window, hardly aware of what she was seeing. It's too late, she thought. Now if Alec said all the things I believed I longed to hear, if he touched me not as a body as familiar to him as his own, but as if being close to each other was filling him with burning desire for that mad passionate love I dream of, the familiarity would destroy the desire, make us both feel rather uncomfortable.

Sighing, she peeled the last potato and dropped it into the saucepan. Perhaps she should be gratful for those early years, those and the secret fantasies that fuelled her imagination. With all the vegetables ready for the pot, she started up the stairs to see to the bedrooms but on the way she was sidetracked to the window on the landing, from which she could see the three on the green. As Jenny walked on to the grass meaning to join in the game of football, the high heels of her bright-red shoes cut into the soil like spikes. Just for a moment she hesitated then she kicked off her shoes and ran in her stockinged feet. A tart, that's what Alec had called her. No, beneath the war paint was a character far more complex than he was prepared to see. Sometimes Rhoda worried about what sort of a marriage the Mathersons had – they seemed such an unlikely couple. Yet on the day he'd come home with the news that he had an almost immediate posting away from Oakleigh, Jenny had been crying. When they arrived at Timberley to collect Mickcy, even though her face had its usual thick covering of make-up, nothing had disguised her swollen eyelids. Somehow, Rhoda had found the tell-tale sign reassuring.

That same morning, as Andrew trotted his horse towards the green, he saw a very different Etty from the grease-smeared girl in workman's overalls he was familiar with in the yard. Etty found the sight of him different too but perfectly in character, immaculate as he was in well-cut riding jacket and jodhpurs. She forced herself to imagine him riding side by side with the girl he called Celia, his fiancée, both of them beautiful people.

'Where have you sprung from?' she greeted him in her usual friendly manner. 'There isn't a riding stable within miles.'

'I'm weekending with Celia's cousin just the other side of Oakleigh.'

'Isn't she with you? Well, I can see she isn't.' Perhaps the beautiful Celia wasn't a horsewoman.

'Actually she's not there,' Andrew replied. 'Anyway, Celia and horses don't see eye to eye. I borrowed Hector – this is Hector, a proud name don't you think? – from their stable. A much better form of transport than a bicycle.'

'You look most impressive,' Etty said and still he knew she was teasing. Her mind was going on a journey of its own: he must be like one of the family already, to stay with Celia's cousin without her. Somehow the knowledge made it even harder to keep that smile on her face. The Andrew *she* knew, the Andrew of the yard, was just a small part of the whole person. Firmly she reined in her thoughts.

'What about tethering your friend Hector to the gatepost and coming to play football? Boys against girls. You and Mickey can play against Jenny and me.' Then holding out her hand in Jenny's direction she drew the girl forward. 'This is Mickey's mother, Jenny, Mrs Matherson. Jen, this is Andrew, a colleague at work. But today it's playtime.'

Dismounting, Andrew formally shook Jenny's hand and

took the reins to lead Hector off the green. Then he noticed Jenny's stockinged feet.

'Oughtn't you to put some shoes on? I can almost hear my grandmother's dire warning that by the time you're thirty you'll be a martyr to rheumatism.'

'Yes, but my shoes'd be worse for kicking than my bare feet. All of them got heels.'

'Jen is new to football,' Etty explained, adding with a ring of pride, 'her shoes aren't built for it. I don't know how she walks in them. I'd lend you a pair of my sensible flatties, Jen, but you'd fall out of them. I'm like Clementine in the song. Go and get rid of Hector, Andrew, then let's get cracking. Mickey doesn't want to hang about all day, do you, love.'

The meaning of her words went over Mickey's head but he enjoyed knowing he was the subject of conversation.

'Hoss,' he pointed at Hector, 'me wiv hoss.'

'Wait a minute,' Andrew said, his foot already back in the stirrup, then he was once again in the saddle, 'pass him up to me, I'll see he's all right, Jenny. He can sit in front of me and ride across to the gate. I'll hang on to him.'

He didn't ask himself what had directed him to Dewsberry Green – he simply accepted the way the morning was going. And as for Mickey, no matter how many years he lived, if he dug deep into his mind one of the earliest memories indelibly printed there would surely be that short ride, sitting high from the ground and feeling the strange motion as Hector walked forward.

Mickey was even better pleased with the football match when Andrew lifted him to sit on his shoulders, preferring the importance bestowed on him by his new height to the frustration of never being able to kick the ball as far as he meant it to go. But after a few minutes, by which time Jenny's feet were soaking wet and frozen, they decided it was a goalless draw and called it a day.

'Cor, fancy you never telling me about him. He's quite something Ett,' Jenny said as Andrew rode off at a steady trot. She sounded mystified that Etty seemed to consider a work colleague of such distinction unimportant. 'Tell you what though, he fancies you right enough.'

'Me? Don't be a nut.' It wasn't often Etty sounded flustered. Jenny took note of it and let her romantic imagination have its way. 'If you could see me in the yard, up to my eyebrows in filth and grease, you'd think differently.'

'Bet you a dollar to a dime I'm right,' said Jenny. 'Why else do you reckon he rode all that way – he didn't attempt to go on further, so this must have been where he was aiming for. Why would he have come all this way if it wasn't he wanted to have a decko at what you looked like scrubbed up.'

'Chump! Andrew is engaged to be married; his fiancée is serving in the WRNS – and you could tell from what he said that he is already looked on as part of the family. Jen, you go on in and sort your wet feet out. I'll take Mickey to say good morning to Mum. I'll give you ten minutes then I'll bring him home.'

Jenny was disappointed that Etty could brush the suggestion aside so easily. Too practical, that was Etty's trouble. Romance would do her a world of good.

Michael came home for Christmas, a week that seemed to Jenny little short of pure magic. They collected holly, they bought a spruce tree, she left 'you two boys' – as she christened father and son in that idyllic interlude – to play together while she went to the village where rumour had it a delivery of oranges had arrived to be allocated on babies' ration books. On Christmas Eve she and Michael crept into sleeping Mickey's room to hang a sock of Michael's on the end of the cot to be filled with treasures. No young mother could have been happier. Later, while Michael was upstairs, she switched out the kitchen light and opened the back door. Gazing at the clear, starry sky a strange sensation gripped her – it was as if she'd been surrounded by fog, but now it had lifted. The future was clear.

Oh I know me and Michael will have lumpy patches, she pondered, but they won't be able to do any harm. Deep down, him, me and Mickey, we're going to be OK.

A feeling of utter peace filled her. She felt humble; not humble as a girl who had married out of her station, for that was unimportant, but humble that she should have been found worthy of being so blessed. Yet, when even in her thoughts she tried to find the right words, they eluded her.

That same feeling of wordless joy stayed with her all through Christmas. From somewhere Michael had managed to buy fairy lights for the tree, and Etty, who was a favourite with so many of the farmers, had brought them a duck for their festive meal. Jenny had been brought up to think of decorations as paper chains. Real greenery, the pungent smell of the tree and the shimmer of the coloured lights, logs on the fire, and most of all Mickey's look of fascinated wonder – these things would stay with her.

The duck eaten, in the afternoon they'd been invited to Timberley. Before they went they listened to the King's message on the wireless at the cottage – it was too much to hope for Mickey to be co-operatively silent but she knew that, like people throughout the country, hearing the King was an important part of Christmas for the Hardings.

At half past three, just as he had every year for as far back as Etty and Natalie could remember, Alec disappeared to make his entry a few minutes later dressed as Santa Claus. Nothing had changed his opinion of Jenny: she would have looked more in place hanging around on a street corner than sitting in his drawing room. However, Mickey had wheedled a way into his heart and Michael was a fine young fellow, especially so in view of the ribbon of the DFC on his breast pocket, so he tried to treat Jenny with a courtesy he considered she didn't merit.

So the festival passed. That Jenny's confidence had taken a huge leap forward was based on something different in Michael's manner. They had shared the fun of each day as

41

well as the joy of each night. She felt she wasn't clever enough to understand how the difference had come about, but it had to do with Mickey too. Yes, she decided that was what made it all so perfect.

On the morning Michael had to return to his station they had breakfast together, Mickey wrapped in his dressing gown and strapped into his high chair, making a good deal of mess with a bowl of porridge. Jenny didn't dread Michael's going as she had in the past; this time he would come back as soon as he could. They might be separated by space but nothing could take from her the sense of belonging, of being a family unit. In the Hardings she had believed she'd seen a perfect relationship, been aware of an atmosphere that was solid and unchanging. That was how it would be for Michael and her and their children – Mickey and any more they would have.

'Come back,' she said earnestly as he kissed her goodbye. 'As soon as you have a chance, you will come back?'

'You bet. What a Christmas! Mickey knew it was special too. I'll be back at the first chance.'

'We're gonna be all right, you and me. You think so too, don't you?'

'We're going to be fine – you, me and Mickey. Take care of each other till I come back. Soon perhaps I'll be home for good.'

She nodded.

'Me, me up, me 'queeze,' Mickey demanded, having had enough of being imprisoned in his chair.

'Get a cloth and clean him up,' Michael said, 'then come outside to see me off. I must get on the road. I'll go and get the car started and let it run until you come.' Then, from the narrow passage when he opened the front door, 'I'll slam the door behind me or the house will get cold, it's blowing like blazes. You'll need your coats.'

Mickey was given a cursory wipe with a damp flannel

and lifted out of his chair. Carrying him so as to be quick, Jenny ran upstairs to collect their coats.

'Me toat, me out,' he chattered as she wrapped a blanket over his dressing gown.

Then, leaving him looking uncertain about this unusual style of dress, which in his mind didn't match up to the suggestion of 'out', she turned back to the wardrobe. Her old coat would have done, the one she wore when she shopped in the village. But this occasion was special, the last sight Michael would have of her until he came home. Stopping by the dressing table to freshen up her lipstick and re-anchor a strand of hair to the top of her head, she heard the impatient parp-parp of the car horn, but the extra minute making herself look her best was important. She opened the built-in cupboard where she kept what she thought of as her 'smart things' and took out the coat she'd bought just before Michael's leave. She'd used the last of Mickey's clothing coupons on it so that she would look her very best for Christmas. Pulling it on, she turned so that she could admire the side view in the wardrobe mirror and it was then that she realised Mickey wasn't in the room.

'Mick! Don't you go near those stairs, not without—' she didn't finish the sentence.

Mickey had managed the stairs without help for months, but she'd always been with him and he'd not been hampered by a trailing blanket. For safety's sake, she and Etty had fitted gates at the bottom and top of the steep flight. But on that morning, intent on speed and carrying Mickey, she'd left both gates open. She heard the thump, thump as he tumbled. 'You're all right, Mick, I'm here, I'm coming. Don't cry, Mick.' But why did she say it when the only sound was silence as he lay on the floor at the foot of the straight flight? 'It was that horn, that bloody car horn,' she said as she rushed down and scooped the little body into her arms.

Over the week of Michael's leave the father/son relationship had travelled a long way – one of the things that

43

had bound them had been the way he would follow Michael out to the car and together they would sit inside. What went on between the two of them Jenny had no idea and she hadn't attempted to intrude; she knew how much it meant to her to confide in Mickey, even knowing that his understanding couldn't encompass half she told him. That never mattered, it had been enough to share her secrets with him, to know without doubt that the moments of intimacy meant as much to him as they did to her. And so it must be for Michael. She'd felt proud that it should be so. And that's how it had come about that the sound of the car horn was so familiar to the little boy, for one of his very favourite things had been to sit on his father's knee behind the steering wheel of the stationary car and press his small fist against the button that made the special sound. On that late December morning he had heard it as a message that Michael was waiting for him. In those seconds that Jenny rocked Mickey in her arms, all she felt for Michael was anger.

'It's all right, Mickey, you're OK, darling.' But how could he be all right when he didn't seem to hear her? She sat on the second stair from the bottom, cradling him in her arms, rocking him, cooing to him, holding him so close that if he'd been conscious he would have wriggled away, but still he didn't stir. 'Wake up, Mick. Can't you even hear me? Come on, God, don't pay me back by hurting him. It was me left the gate open, so don't be rotten and hurt my poor Mick. Wake up, Mick. Oh God, why won't he wake up and scream? Come on, Mick love, please, *please* make him wake up, make him open his eyes and look at me, make him—' Hardly aware of what she was doing, as she rocked him, she'd been speaking aloud, but now her wild muttering was interrupted.

'For Christ's sake get a move on, I should be on the road before—' Taking in the scene that met him as he opened the front door, Michael broke off mid-sentence. 'What's the matter?'

'Mick fell.'

'Fell? Where? Come on, Mickey. You can't sit there being cuddled all day. Aren't you going to see—' Michael had been talking as he closed the door behind him, then he reached to take the boy from Jenny. This was no ordinary tumble. Like all small children Mickey could and did fall often, but unless there was visible damage he would usually pick himself up, yell briefly and within seconds appear to have forgotten the incident. 'He's knocked himself out. How the devil did he do that? What on earth were you doing not to see what he was up to?'

'I was upstairs getting a coat. Just turned my back for a second—'

'Why the hell didn't you close the gate? Have you no sense at all?'

If he'd struck her she couldn't have been more surprised. In her misery she looked at him, her eyes brimming with tears.

'For pity's sake pull yourself together.'

'You blew that bloody horn, he must have heard it same as I did. You didn't like having to wait half a mo' while I got our things. He tried to get out there after you, same as he always does. He's only a baby, he doesn't know things are different this morning.'

Michael propped the small inert form against his shoulder as if, like a doll, in being turned upright he might open his eyes.

'Out cold he is,' Jenny said, coming to stand behind Michael so that she could see any reaction. 'D'you reckon we ought to get the doctor? Come on, Mick, come on, darling, open your peeps.'

'Stop twittering and go across to the Hardings and use the telephone.'

She told herself it was only because he was worried that he spoke like that.

'I better take Mick along with me. You got to go, Michael. You'll be in trouble if you're not back by midday,

45

that's the time you said.'

'You think I'd go and leave him like this? Christ, Jenny, he means as much to me as he does to you – and I take better care of him too. If this is the way you carry on, I shan't have a moment's peace worrying about him. Don't just stand there, buck up and telephone.'

Like a chastened child she went.

If Michael had doubts about Jenny's sense of responsibility, he was reassured by the presence of the Hardings. Hearing what had happened, Alec decided they should telephone not for the doctor but for the ambulance. So they all waited together at April Cottage for what seemed like eternity before they heard the distant clanging of the bell and knew the ambulance was almost there. In truth it was less than ten minutes; ten minutes that had seen no returning sign of life in Mickey. Now it was all out of their hands.

With Mickey lifted to a stretcher and borne through the back door of the vehicle, Jenny at his side clinging to his baby-plump hand, the stretcher bearer looked at the group waiting.

'Got the little chap and his mum on board. Now what about his dad? Are any of you his father? Got room for you if you are.'

'Get in, son,' Alec said to ashen-faced Michael, 'Jenny will need you.'

Michael looked at him blankly.

Etty sized up the situation. 'You go ahead,' she told the ambulancemen. 'We'll drive his father to the hospital.'

Michael watched the ambulance go yet he made no attempt to get in the car and follow. He seemed to be removed from the rest of them, caught up in the torment of his thoughts.

'They'll need your car there to get home, Michael,' Alec prompted him.

'Give me your keys.' Etty held out her hand. 'Let me drive. We'll follow the ambulance. When we get there I'll walk on to the cattle market.'

At least her suggestion appeared to have broken through the images he'd created in his mind.

'I can drive myself,' he answered, sounding aggressive.

'Come on, let me take you.'

'There's no need.' Then, as if the fight had suddenly gone out of him, 'The keys are in the ignition.' Like an obedient child he followed her.

By that time the clanging of the ambulance bell had almost been lost on the cold, still air, but Etty meant to catch up with it by the time it reached the hospital.

'He'll be OK, Michael. By lunchtime you'll be bringing him home.'

'Shall I? Shall I?' He took a packet of cigarettes from his pocket and thrust one in his mouth, but his hand was shaking so much he couldn't strike the match. Pulling to the side of the lane, Etty stopped the car and took the matchbox from him, then held the flame to the cigarette. She had had very little to do with Jenny's husband, but on the few occasions they'd been together she had noticed a tenseness in his manner and had suspected it may have been impatience with Jenny who, try as she usually did, so often let her behaviour or speech fall short of what he probably demanded. Perhaps that was part of the problem, but she realised now that there was a far deeper reason.

'You don't know, do you? How can you know, how can any of you, stuck here in your safe and peaceful rut,' he said. He turned his face towards her and, for the first time, seemed aware of her. 'An innocent happy child and in a second an accident can happen.' There was a wild note in his voice, bringing to her mind what her father had said after the Mathersons had gone home on Christmas evening, his concerned expression as he'd muttered something about it being 'more than time that poor young devil was grounded for a spell'. Surely there was terror in Michael's voice as he went on, 'And I've done it to hundreds, to thousands.'

47

'Rubbish,' she replied bracingly, 'You've never dropped a bomb in your life. You're a pilot.'

'What? What the hell difference does that make? We're a team. I'm as responsible as the man who releases the bombs. God knows how many people, innocent people, children like Mickey, have had their lives ruined because of what we do? The enemy, that's what they are, all of them: men, women and children, sick, healthy, young, old. Cities are targeted—'

'Cities are targeted here as well as there, Michael. And do you think every German pilot doesn't feel just as you do?'

'God forgive us.'

'Amen to that. Forgive us our trespasses as we forgive those who trespass against us. We say it without a thought and then all carry on as if what we do must be blessed by some divine providence.'

For a while they drove in silence and when he spoke again his voice had lost some of the near-hysteria she'd heard before.

'She'd got nothing to do but watch after the boy,' he said, 'and she couldn't even do that. Another minute and I'd have gone – wouldn't have known. Imagine having him upstairs and not closing that gate. Hasn't she any sense at all?'

'Jenny is wonderful with him,' Etty defended her friend staunchly. 'I've seen how carefully she fastens the gate on the stairs. This morning she must have been thrown off-balance because you were going.'

'Couldn't wake him.' The fear was creeping back again. 'Why the hell couldn't she have watched what he was doing? Probably plastering rubbish on her face.'

'Probably no such thing!' Etty snapped back, quick to defend. 'Michael, don't start dishing out blame. Anyway, by the time the ambulance gets to the hospital I bet he'll have come round. He must have concussion, poor love. They're sure to keep him in for the day though.'

'Once I know that nothing's seriously damaged, no bones broken, I'll have to make double-quick time. The way things are going it'll be after ten before I'm even on the road.'

Surely he didn't intend to leave Jenny still at the hospital! But that thought was overtaken by another, that he had a responsibility to be back at the airfield. Five years of war had taught everyone to accept that personal lives weren't their own.

'Jot down the number where you can be contacted – on the flap of your cigarette packet will do if you haven't anything better,' she told him. And when Etty gave an instruction no one argued.

Half an hour later she was in the workshops and Michael on the road to Norfolk. He drove with his foot hard on the accelerator, reassured that no bones had been broken in Mickey's tumble.

Chapter Three

The day passed, bringing no message about Mickey. Etty was loathe to drive home with her father, leaving Brackleford without knowing what had happened. Perhaps the little boy had woken up by the time the ambulance got him to the hospital, just as she'd tried to reassure Michael. But if so, and if Michael had taken them home before setting out for his aerodrome, surely Rhoda would have known.

Andrew read her thoughts.

'Why don't we drive over to see if they're meaning to keep him in overnight? If so, Jenny'll be glad of a lift home – and if they've already gone, at least you'll know there's nothing to worry about,' Andrew suggested. Then, his face lighting in a smile, 'I managed to acquire – ask no questions – coupons for a gallon or two at the weekend.'

Alec frowned. Such an admission hinted at black marketeering, something he wouldn't tolerate.

'Nothing too dastardly, I promise you,' Andrew laughed, 'just a bit of surplus from home.' Nothing in his manner to remind them that 'home' was his father's large estate. 'The manager gave them to me. Honest, guv.' He pulled his forelock, his eyes twinkling with merriment. 'Not a ha'penny passed hands – they were a gift.' Then, more seriously, 'And what better way to use them than to find out about the lad? How's that?'

'Thanks a million, Drew,' Etty answered.

Twenty minutes later the two of them were waiting on a far from comfortable bench against the whitewashed wall of a long corridor at the hospital.

'Cheer up, Etty.' Andrew tried to sound reassuring. 'He can't be too bad – the nurse didn't say his father was still here so he must have known it was OK for him to go back to the base.' Etty let herself be cheered. But the emotion was short lived for almost immediately Jenny appeared from a side corridor and one look at her told them the news wasn't good.

'He never woke up. Ett, they say Mick's . . .' Her voice trailed into silence. Etty's strong arms were around her. And that was her undoing. Numb shock gave way to misery as her body was shaken with sobs.

'Tell me, Jen.'

'Jus' told you, didn't I,' came the aggressive retort. Then misery swamped her. 'I kept on talking to him but I couldn't make him hear . . . all he did was sleep away there. The doctor kept coming in, listening with his stetho-scope thing. When they weren't there, I gave him a good shake, tried and tried I did to make him open his eyes. If he'd seen me he would have been all right, I know he would. But Ett, he never moved, not a flicker. Then . . . don't know when it was . . . just now sometime, the doctor listened and said he was gone. Mick gone. Just had his porridge like every morning, happy as happy, now . . .'

Etty held her close, her feeling of helplessness even stronger than of grief and shock.

'Michael doesn't know?' she asked, her voice gentle.

'No,' Jenny snorted, 'I told him the ambulance men said nothing was broken. He said I had to telephone you and someone would come and get us when they said he could come home. Just kept talking and talking to Mick, I did, cos I knew if he heard me he would wake up. But he just lay there, still as still. Then they told me . . . said it was all over. "Sorry," the doctor said, "there's nothing more we

51

can do for him. It's all over." Then they said something about me going home – going home and leaving Mick all alone. They took him,' she sobbed, 'don't know where they took him to ... my Mickey ... don't even know where he is.' And again her words were drowned in tears.

'Stay with her,' Andrew whispered to Etty. 'I'm going to phone your mother.' He didn't know Rhoda well, but instinct guided him.

'Wait.' Etty stopped him, still holding Jenny close with one arm while she felt in her pocket. 'This is the number where Michael can be contacted. Read it to Mum – or Dad – ask them to phone him.'

It was Alec who answered Andrew's call and heard the news then put through a call to the aerodrome, while Rhoda stood helplessly at his side.

'Wouldn't they get Michael to the phone?' Rhoda asked as he put down the receiver.

'No. They were a bit cagey, perhaps they don't allow personal calls. Perhaps the poor young devil is on some raid. God, Rhoda, what a bloody awful mess the world has got itself into.' She was touched by the unexpectedness of his outburst.

'We can't imagine what they're going through,' she said. 'Can't even start to imagine. Mickey was her world.'

Ten minutes or so later they heard the rare sound of a car and knew it must be Andrew bringing Jenny and Etty. Would they come to Timberley or would he drive straight to the cottage? Despite the cold evening, Rhoda switched off the hall light and opened the front door. She hoped Jenny would come to them. But what comfort could any of them give her whether in her own home or theirs? Perhaps a message would have been given to Michael by now, perhaps he was on his way. At the thought, her aching sympathy reached out to encompass him as she imagined him driving the long miles home.

Her eyes growing accustomed to the darkness, she could

see the dull beam of the shielded headlights on the far side of the green and heard the car door slam.

'Jenny! Jenny, don't go home until Michael gets here,' she called as she ran across the green. 'Come back and wait with us.' Then, having covered the space between them just as Jenny opened the latch gate of the cottage, 'Oh Jenny, what can I say? What can I do?' Her arms embraced Jenny, her own tears wet on Jenny's cheek.

'Mick's gone,' the girl croaked. 'Gone . . . they've taken him away somewhere . . . all alone . . . just lying there like as if he's asleep. Never moved, Rhoda, he didn't. Kept on talking to him, but he wouldn't wake up. They wouldn't let me hold him. Can't hold him never no more.'

Rhoda didn't answer, she simply held Jenny and let her talk, hoping that in the rush of words some of the misery would find release. Andrew drove away, dropping Etty off at the gate of Timberley without turning off the engine. He didn't need telling how upset she was. Etty was his friend, his dear friend. If there had been moments when some deeper feeling had stirred within him, loyalty to Celia had made him hang on to the belief they were nothing more than that – just brief moments. But that evening, when all their emotions were touched by tragedy, he felt confused and uncertain, even frightened. He had grown accustomed to an easy life and had been able to pick himself up even when the torpedoing of his ship had led to his being discharged as unfit for service. Now he was unprepared for the blinding truth that seemed to rob him of the ability to think coherently. What he felt for Etty was more than friendship, more than the physical desire he might feel for an attractive woman; it was as if she was part of his very being. Just as Rhoda's spontaneous reaction had been to hold Jenny, so he wanted to hold Etty, to share her sadness. His mind leapt to Celia, the childhood friend who had grown to be his adolescent sweetheart and now his fiancée. Thinking of her only made him more certain of what Etty's reaction would be. Etty: loyal, honest, straightforward and

53

high-principled – to fall short of her standards would destroy the relationship that had become the focal point of his life.

'Thanks, Drew,' she cut across his thoughts, 'you've been a trump. See you tomorrow.' Then thoughts of Jenny made everything else shrink into insignificance, 'Oh Drew, what must she feel? However will she bear it? In a few seconds her whole world's changed.'

It wasn't often Andrew was lost for words.

Jenny's night seemed endless. She ached with exhaustion and yet sleep was a million miles away. If only Michael would come. Yet how could there be comfort even in being with Michael? And would he find comfort in being with her? No one, absolutely no one, could share with them the grief that was theirs; perhaps they couldn't even share it with each other. Mickey, little Mickey ... where had they taken him to in that great hospital building? Did he know he was all alone? But he wasn't alone, her spirit was with him and surely even if he didn't wake up like she'd tried to make him, surely his spirit must know that she would always be there for him. But he was only a baby – what could he know about having a spirit? If only Michael would come.

All that night she listened, but neither that night nor the next day did he come. It was two days after Mickey's fall that the telegram arrived. 'Failed to return' – it told her nothing and yet it told her everything. No one had witnessed what happened to his plane. There was ambiguity in the message.

A week or so later, she sat with Rhoda at the kitchen table at Timberley, drinking a watery cup of mid-morning coffee. 'If Michael had gone, gone like my Mick, don't you reckon I'd know? Michael's alive ... I *know* he is. So why do I feel like as if there's a sort of fog in between him and me.'

'Perhaps it's because of Mickey. Michael doesn't even know what's happened. If you're right – and please God you are and you'll hear he's been taken prisoner – his thoughts of home must be that everything's like it was when he was on leave.'

Jenny clenched her teeth. She wouldn't cry, she *wouldn't*. 'Can't never be like that no more,' she said, her lips held in a stiff line, emotion making her lose control of her slim grasp of grammatical correctness. 'Him, Mick and me. We're going to be all right, that's what we said. Don't you never trust it when you think things are going right for you. It's like as if some rotten god is there watching out for how to trip us up and make us see we can't take anything for granted. You know about me and Michael, how I got preggie when I was just a kid. *She* – Agnes, that rotten stepmother of mine – she'd say that all this is my just desserts, that Mick's got taken away to punish me for carrying on like I did with Michael.' By then she'd lost the struggle, her words almost swallowed up in her tears. 'He never loved me, not back then, not like I did him. I kept on telling myself that it was the same for both of us, that that cow was wrong saying all the spiteful things she did about him seeing me as an easy lay. Blind as a bat I was, believing what I wanted to believe. He married me fast enough when he knew about the baby ... well, like she kept saying, he hadn't got no choice, he'd have been in trouble up to the neck if they found out he'd been going to bed with a kid my age. Anyway, we got married and off he went overseas. Sent me a letter once in a while, wanting to know about Mick after he got born. But when he came back he only looked in, never – well you know, never touched me nor nothing.'

Rhoda didn't interrupt her, indeed she suspected Jenny wasn't so much talking to her, telling her much that she knew already, as being carried along on a tide of uncontrollable misery.

'Then he got the cottage and I thought this would be our

55

real beginning. I tried to believe he must have loved me all the time but just didn't want to see me cos I was living with *her* – that cow Agnes in a right slutty hole she'd made of where Dad and me were before she came along then he got killed in the raid. Soon saw I was wrong when I got here though. Ashamed of me he was . . . made sure none of his mates ever met me. But at Christmas it was . . . it was . . . don't know the words . . . going to be all right, him, Mick and me . . . wasn't just me what thought it, it was him too.' For a moment she fell silent. Rhoda waited, feeling inadequate and helpless. It was as if in the silence Jenny became aware of her presence. 'Funny how things work out,' she said, sniffing and trying to wipe away her latest bout of tears. 'Supposing it had been someone else living in this house, not you and Etty. Don't know what I would have done. You must be fed up with me . . . keep on blubbering . . . can't seem to stop.'

'I feel helpless,' Rhoda answered truthfully, taking Jenny's damp hand in her own, 'But fed up? You know that's not true.'

'How long can someone just be *missing?* Honest, Rhoda, I *know* he's still alive. Got to hang on to that.'

So week followed week. February brought news of raids on German cities, and in England a nation longing for peace became accustomed to the voice of the BBC with announcements of successful raids, the number of planes taking part and the number returning safely. Six years earlier even *one* such news bulletin would have shocked and horrified people, but by the early months of 1945 death and destruction had become woven into the pattern of daily life. Allied forces were advancing on Germany from all sides; air raids, like every horror of war, were a means to an end and must surely promise that soon it would all be over. Only later, much later, did they see photographs of the devastation, and of the hundreds and thousands of those who were homeless pushing their few remaining possessions on handcarts, prams, anything they could find, as they fled, seeking somewhere, anywhere, away from the living hell of defeat.

Through those weeks Jenny too was running away, dreading being alone in the cottage filled with memories she was frightened to let into her thoughts. Despite the bitter winter, sometimes she borrowed Rhoda's bicycle, sometimes she walked miles, often she spent days in Brackleford and hours in the cinema – but everywhere she seemed to hear Mickey's laugh, could almost feel the sweet warmth of him in her arms. Still she clung to the belief that Michael was somewhere out there in the chaos of Europe and one day would come home. It was all she had to hang on to.

Towards the end of February, on a day when she'd been out for hours on Rhoda's bicycle, she didn't wait to wheel it to the shed at Timberley but leant it against the side wall of the house.

'Rhoda! Rhoda, are you there?' she yelled as she opened the kitchen door and charged in. 'I've made up my mind. Listen, tell me what you think.' There was a new look about her, an expression that had seemed to die with Mickey.

'You look pleased with yourself. What have you been up to? You must be frozen, come by the fire.'

'Rhoda, I've got a job. Don't say anything, just listen and I'll tell you all about it. I cycled out to Oakleigh … don't know why. Must have been cos I wanted to look at where Michael was when I first came here. Anyway, I never got as far as the aerodrome because just the other side of Farley Wood, there was this farm place. Not a farm with cows and that, just fields of veg. On the gate there was a notice that they wanted someone to help sort the stuff. Don't know much about veg, not like you do. But I do know how to clean it and pack it nicely so the shops can put it out ready. So in I went. And Mr Ridley, the bloke who grows the stuff, took me on. I'm going to get paid two quid a week and work from nine till four. How's that?'

Rhoda's immediate reaction was disappointment. Now even Jenny would have somewhere to go, a responsibility that made her see herself as a person in her own right, not just part of the background to someone else's life. Then, reality pushed that thought out of the way. Just because Jenny hung on to the belief that Michael was somewhere out there, the truth was that no one would ever know what happened to Michael's plane. Jenny had had her whole world snatched from her – surely she deserved the chance to make a new start.

'Well done, Jen,' she said, giving Jenny a hug. 'Independence! A chance to fly free.'

'Fly free? As if *you'd* want to do that from here? Get on with you, Rhoda. You got a smashing place here, and the family and all.'

'Yes – and I'm ashamed that I get this feeling of being left behind. I expect it's because I've been doing the same thing year after year for so long.'

'It's what most women want. Tell you one thing: I'd rather be like I was back a few months than scrubbing spuds or whatever it is I'll be doing. But – well – I'm not going to be beaten by what's happened. Not the sort to sit and weep. Not that you'd notice it, the way I've been carrying on since I lost my Mick. But if that's the hand Him upstairs has dished out, then I'm blowed—' Then, in a note of defiance, whether aimed at Rhoda or God not clear, 'I'm *buggered* if I'm going to be beaten. Tell you what though, when Michael hears the sort of job I've found he'll kick up rough.'

'When Michael comes home you'll want to give up.'

Just for a moment Jenny hesitated, showing a chink in her armour of trust.

'Yes, sure I will. But he'll kick up rough just the same when he knows the sort of job his wife has been doing. Got no training though, Rhoda. Any road, they were real nice people. Mrs Ridley took me in and gave me a cup of tea and a slice of homemade cake like as if I was an ordinary visitor. The kitchen wasn't like this, all light and bright. But it's not the trimmings that make up a place, it's the people. And they were nice – both of them. I said I'd start the day after tomorrow – that gives me a day to take the bus to town and buy myself a bike.'

'If you're lucky,' Rhoda added with a laugh. 'Like everything else bikes are hard to come by unless you can find one second-hand. But if you can't get one, use mine. The walk to the village won't kill me.'

So by Thursday of that week a new routine began, one that found Rhoda's days back to the way things used to be before the Mathersons had come to Dewsberry – except that she was short of a bicycle. That's how it was that she was the only one to see the green sports car round the bend and drive with familiar accuracy through the open gate and park by the side of April Cottage.

He was home! Jenny's trust hadn't been for nothing. Despite the biting March wind, Rhoda ran, coatless, across the winter-hard grass. 'Michael, Michael,' she yelled even before she came within earshot as Michael rapped on the front door of the cottage. Even though he remembered the back door was never locked, all the way from his base in Norfolk he'd been imagining the excitement on Mickey's face when Jenny opened the door to his knock. The fact that nearly three months would have been a long time in a toddler's memory hadn't occurred to him – he and Mickey had formed the sort of bond he felt was too strong to break.

'Michael, she's not in.'

His quick scowl was almost immediately banished as he imagined Mickey playing with the old toy box at Timberley.

'She's left him with you? I'll come across and collect him.'

In a way things can flash through one's memory, she

thought of Alec's phone call to the station. Through the weeks that had brought no news she had realised that he couldn't have known about Mickey, but surely, when he'd got back to the base, someone would have told him before he set out for Dewsberry. For a second she felt at a loss. How could she tell a man that his child was dead? But she had no choice.

'The evening of the day you left, we tried to phone you at the station. They didn't tell you? Haven't you been there?' Words, just words, as she played for time. Of course he'd been there – how else would he have collected his car? 'Oh Michael, I don't know how to—'

'What? Where's she gone? Where's she taken him?' His voice frightened Rhoda, the way he said the word 'she'. Into her mind came Jenny's tearful outburst, the knowledge that Michael had never loved her like she had him. But to speak of her like that, almost with contempt!

'If only that's what happened. Mickey never came out of his coma. He died that same night.' There! She'd said it. And what was more, she had said it with anger aimed at him, anger that he could speak as he had about Jenny.

Michael might have been made of stone. He stood stock still, his face showing no expression while she, ashamed that she could have felt resentment against a man who had to face such hurt, went towards him with both hands outstretched.

'And where is she now?' he said, not waiting for an answer, 'Kicking up her heels in town now that she's free I suppose – or perhaps comforting the lonely Americans at Oakfield? All she had to do was watch him. She couldn't even do that. Christ! Oh Christ.'

'Don't talk like that about her, not to me. She's at work. She's running away from the loneliness of the cottage without Mick and without you. Michael, she never lost faith that you'd come home . . . she said if you weren't alive she'd know. But she had to be occupied. Can't you try and understand what she is suffering to have lost Mickey?'

60

'And who has she to blame but herself?'

'The accident was no one's fault. Share your grief, Michael don't throw blame at each—'

'No? And what sort of divine providence would you suggest took his young life?' He spoke with an ugly sneer. 'She wasn't fit to look after him. Any natural mother with half a brain would have kept her eye on him.'

'And any man with half a brain would have known better than to call him outside by blowing that stupid car horn. Any man with half a brain would have known it was a message Mickey had come to understand.' She was ashamed as soon as she'd said it, but his answer soon cleared her conscience.

'I suppose that's what *she* said.' He looked round, putting her in mind of a trapped animal. 'What's the point of any of it? Mickey was the only thing that held us together.'

'And Mickey can still hold you together. Your son and hers, he loved you both. Michael, she won't be home for a couple of hours. Come over to the house with me and wait.'

'Where is she working?' For a moment Rhoda thought she detected a calmer acceptance but when she told him about the market garden at Oakleigh she could see she'd been mistaken.

'Sorting vegetables! Just about suitable. Christ, what a ruddy mess I've got my life into.'

'That depends how you view people,' Rhoda answered tartly. 'Personally I look on Jenny as one of the family, just like I did Mickey.' And you can put that in your pipe and smoke it, she added silently, immediately feeling wretched that she could have such uncharitable thoughts about a young man who'd been through whatever horrors his last few weeks had brought him, only to return home to such shattering news.

He went home with her and even told her briefly how his plane had been hit returning from the raid. It was losing

61

height and he'd ordered the crew to eject while he'd tried to steer the bomber over open country. When it had hit the ground he'd managed to escape just as it had exploded into flames and he'd found himself alone in a field bordered by woodland. Unsure where he was, he'd hid in the wood until darkness, then found his way to a farmhouse just as he heard voices from German soldiers searching for survivors of the crash. He'd buried himself in the only available place, a stinking heap of manure, while the search had been made. Only when the soldiers had departed, reassured that everyone must have parachuted from the plane before the crash, had he emerged and shown himself at the farmhouse. The Allies had been moving forward fast and the French farmer and his wife were expecting almost daily that the ground war would arrive on their land. With his foul uniform burned, they had found him old clothes and hidden him in the coal cellar where he'd been for more than three weeks. 'A hell-hole' was how he described it to Rhoda. Hell-hole or not, it had spared his life as the battles outside had raged. Only when the Germans had retreated to take up a position a mile or two to the east had he emerged.

'If I'd known then what I do now, I swear to God I'd not have gone back to the squadron. They could have gone on thinking I was dead,' he said wretchedly.

'It's shock, that's what makes you speak like that. Jenny loves you, Michael – you are her whole world now she's lost Mickey.'

He didn't answer, but his expression gave her no hope.

After a while he told her he was going over to the cottage; he'd wait for Jenny there. Imagining how he would feel going into that little house with no small boy waiting, again her sympathy overcame the antagonism he always seemed to arouse in her. Alec saw him as a fine young man, she reminded herself. Perhaps one man understands another better than any woman can – after all, it was she who saw beyond Jenny's brassy image whilst Alec was quick to scorn her.

As dusk deepened, Rhoda heard the familiar ring of her bicycle bell, Jenny's 'Hello, I'm back' message. But this time, Jenny didn't come in to see her. Watching from the window she saw – indeed she almost felt – the girl's look of wonder at the sight of the car parked by the cottage. Timberley forgotten, Jenny cycled straight across the grassy patch, dismounted and, running, pushed the bicycle through the gate and thrust it against the cottage wall as she rushed to the back door.

Later, when Alec and Etty came home, Rhoda told them what had happened. The things in Michael's manner that had made her uneasy were forgotten. Now that he and Jenny were together they would share their unhappiness and be drawn together by their love for Mickey. Just as Alec turned on the wireless for the nine o'clock news bulletin, they heard the car rounding the green and making towards the village. Frowning, he said, 'I dare say they're entitled to celebrate Michael's safe homecoming, but that's no reason to use petrol. It's no distance to the village if they've gone out for a drink.'

'They'd get short shrift there,' Etty laughed. 'Didn't you see the notice on the door saying the pub's closed until the brewer delivers next week. Dewsberry is on the wagon.'

Rhoda felt uneasy. Was it natural for them to go out to celebrate? Twelve hours ago Michael had been on his way home, confident that Mickey would be there waiting for him. Celebrate? Tonight surely Jenny and Michael should be drawn closer by shed tears rather than celebration.

Next morning, just as every morning, Rhoda was the first to come downstairs. The fire in the kitchen range had to be raked and banked up, the kettle had to be drawn forward to bring it to the boil for early morning tea, the morning routine never varied. As she passed the landing window she looked across the green and saw there was no car at April Cottage. Michael hadn't told her how long leave he had, but surely after what he'd been through he couldn't be expected back on duty after just a few hours! Jenny was sure to call and tell her before she set off for Oakleigh. Then Rhoda had another thought: most probably he'd driven early to the farm to explain how it was that she wouldn't be working today.

But she was wrong on both counts, as she found out as soon as Alec and Etty drove off. Clearly Jenny had been waiting for them to go.

'He's gone, Rhoda,' she croaked as she blundered into the kitchen. 'Been waiting all night to come over.' Yesterday's layer of make-up had been washed away by her hysterical tears; tears that she'd shed alone in the cottage through a night that had seemed to have no end. Now they flowed again, she had neither the power nor the will to hold them back. It was as if she had sunk to rock bottom and wallowed in her misery. 'Him and me, he said it was only Mick what stopped him clearing off before. When I reminded him about how things were at Christmas, he said he'd been making the best of how it had to be cos there was no way out. Just for Mick's sake. Said it was my fault what happened to Mick and he's right . . . so it was. If I'd shut the gate – or if I'd not been getting my good coat out of the cupboard so he'd go away remembering me looking smart – then Mick would be here. He said I got to look on it as Fate – God or something – giving him the chance to wipe out the mess he'd made of his life. Said there were plenty of blokes the sort I'd suit. He'd learnt his lesson and I ought to learn mine. All that, he said. Looked at me like I was . . . was . . . sort of a bit of rotten rubbish. Just about what I am. Expect that's why Mick got took away from me, cos I didn't deserve him.'

Whatever had been Michael's intention, he'd certainly brought Jenny to rock bottom. Rhoda had never known such rage. Gripping the girl's shoulders, she shook her, her action firm but gentle.

'You've listened to *him* . . . now listen to *me*. Oh Jen.

64

Don't cry like that, love. Cry for Mickey, but don't cry for *him*. He's not worth a single one of your tears.'

'Can't stop. Cried all night. Didn't go to bed, I just sat in that little chair in Mick's room. It's like as if there's *nothing*. Just a sort of big load of nothing. Don't know which way to go. Don't want any of it, honest I don't. But ...' and with a sniff that showed more determination than elegance, 'but I can't stay here blubbing like a great baby, I got to get to work.'

Her words surprised Rhoda. The market garden was the last thing she expected to be on Jenny's mind.

'Let me cycle over and tell them you can't come in today. I'll say you're not well.'

Another sniff, this time accompanied by a scarcely visible squaring of her slight shoulders as Jenny replied, 'No. I may be as rotten and no good like he tells me, but I'm not going to start lying to the Ridleys. I'm going in just like usual – except that I must look like something the cat dragged in. And when they ask me what's up, Rhoda, I'm going to tell them the honest truth. Go on, tell me it's none of their business, and you'd be right. But I got to do it. If I start off by running away from it, then I'll feel sort of mean and cheaty.'

'Good girl,' Rhoda said, giving her a hug. 'But you're going to hear what I have to say before you go dashing off. If Michael is so blind he can't see what a gem he has in you, then he doesn't deserve you. One thing's for sure, Jen, not Michael and not anyone else can ever take away from you the love you and your little Mick shared. He was only a mite, but I bet you one thing: if he were old enough to understand, he'd be cheering you all the way. You never did let him down and you never will.'

'I told Mick that in the night,' Jenny said with something like a smile, albeit a watery one. 'Sitting there by his cot and blubbering, I was, but it was like as if he was there with me, his warm little arms round me. Thought I must be going bonkers. But I'm not. And I won't let Michael

65

trample all over me. Well, I suppose I can't stop him, but I'm buggered - yes, *buggered*, Rhoda - if I'll let him squash me flat.'

'If you're going to work - and you're right, the only way to fight back up is not to let yourself be beaten - then pop upstairs and wash your face in cold water. There's some face cream and powder on my dressing table - use that unless you'd rather go home and sort yourself out.'

Jenny shook her head.

'You know what? This is the first day of the rest of my life and I want to meet it head on, not trying to look like something I'm not. I'll have a wash, then get on my way. Thanks, Rhoda. Don't know what I'd do without you.'

'You're not without me, love. And, if you want God's honest truth, I reckon you're a damn sight better without Michael.' As she said the words, she realised that deep in her heart she had never trusted him. Perhaps it stemmed from that first encounter when he had dismissed her with such arrogance.

'Got to have a new start. You know what? I was so sure Michael was alive, and I was right. But - and I can say it now, I couldn't have done before or it would have seemed like tempting Fate or God or whoever it is - I could never picture us together; not without Mick. Michael reckons it was to get him off the hook that Mick got taken away - even though he says it was *my* fault Mick fell. But that's not fair, Rhoda. If he only stayed because of Mickey it's not fair that he didn't tell me so. I would have let him go, I would have done anything, just so long as Mick—' An ominous croak silenced her.

'The trouble is, Jen, we none of us can play God. Run up and rinse your face. You'll have to hurry if you're not going to be late. But come in to me when you get home. We'll make plans.'

'You're a real mate - better than a mate.'

The making of plans was little more than reinforcing Jenny's security in the friendship that had become so

66

important to her. Rhoda was more than 'a mate', she was mother, sister, friend and confidante rolled into one.

During those weeks as winter gave way to spring, the hope of peace became more than a distant dream. Throughout the country confidence strengthened as on all fronts the Allies advanced. The very word 'peace' conjured up images in every mind. For many, thankfulness was overshadowed by a truth from which there was no escape – loved ones lost or maimed so that their lives could never return to those halcyon days before the war, days whose contentment was usually enhanced by memory. Jenny had been just a child, a child at the mercy of an uncaring stepmother, so for her the future was a blank page. For the Hardings, the war had brought no personal tragedy, rather it had profited Alec's business; even so, the thoughts of peace painted a sunny future. Not that anyone's hopes for the future were without a backdrop of horror as one concentration camp after another told its story. Newsprint was in short supply, but that had been the way of things for so long that everyone had become used to a daily paper of four pages, just one folded sheet. In those weeks of 1945, into that small space were crammed harrowing stories of homeless and hopeless displaced persons and of Allied armies moving relentlessly onward through the war-torn scenes of devastation. Sometimes, reading and imagining, Rhoda felt overcome by shame; not shame in the Allied cause, never that, but shame for her own security and for mankind that had let the world be overtaken by such evil. Supposing the scales had tipped in the other direction, supposing it had been in England, there in Brackleford, Dewsberry or more distant Reading, that buildings had been flattened whilst enemy forces and their lumbering tanks moved relentlessly on towards London.

Then at last the guns were silent and the drone of overhead bombers became a memory. On 7 May the armistice was signed, and that familiar and loved voice of Winston

Churchill was brought through the ether to every home with the news that at last, in Europe, it was all over. The following day was given to celebration and thanksgiving.

'Let me carry that,' Andrew said, taking a heavily laden tray from Rhoda's hands. 'Where do you want it? Who's doing the serving?'

'At the far end of the table. Etty will dole out this lot while I get another tray,' Rhoda told him, already starting back to the house.

Like towns and villages up and down the land, Dewsberry was feeding its children with sandwiches, jelly, blancmange and ice cream, thanks to Roger Dunkley of Stockwell Farm, a customer of Hardings and quite unable to refuse Andrew's request made with that never-failing friendly charm, putting the finishing touch of perfection to this memorable meal.

When the vicar had called at Timberley asking permission for the Women's Institute and the Mothers' Union to use the kitchen there to assemble the food for the party that was being organised, Rhoda had been delighted. She had even chosen to ignore Alec's view that they could do without strangers intruding on their domestic arrangements. She knew exactly what gave his face that tight-lipped expression: it was the idea that something was going to disturb the ordered routine of their days. Taken individually, he would have shown nothing but kindness to each of the children and courtesy to every villager – but that didn't imply he welcomed the intrusion of two female societies into his home. In fact, many of the members of the Mothers' Union were also part of the Women's Institute so it was two societies in name only. Rhoda belonged to neither, but she was welcomed to work with them.

All that morning, Etty had helped men prepare for the festivities on the green, erecting the long trestle table and putting up a makeshift stage where later the local amateur jazz band would play. Young, strong and nimble, she had

68

climbed the ladder to tie bunting to overhanging tree branches, while old Eddie James from one of the almshouses had stood on the bottom rung to make sure she was safe. Always she kept an unobtrusive but watchful eye on Andrew, trying tactfully to step in when he attempted something more strenuous than was wise. He never talked about his less-than-fit state, but she wasn't blind and neither was she insensitive to his feelings.

While the food was assembled on the table, the children were sitting cross-legged on the grass noisily enjoying a Punch and Judy show with Sydney Hopkins, the grocer, doing the honours. Some of them were too old for such childish entertainment, but on that May day everyone's goal was to squeeze every drop of fun from any situation that presented itself. There had been egg and spoon races, three-legged races, all the traditional fare demanded by the day. Jenny knew the kitchen at Timberly had been taken over, so she didn't come across to the house. Instead she leant on the garden gate of April Cottage watching. Afterwards Etty blamed herself – she ought to have put herself in Jenny's place and seen her solitary figure as a cry for help.

But Etty had something else on her mind and, if her gaze followed one person, that person wasn't Jenny. The toddlers were lined up to run, stagger and lurch their way to the winning post just as that one person came towards her with a middle-aged man in tow.

'I want you two to meet,' Andrew said, holding his hand in her direction. 'Silas – my uncle if I'm accurate – this is Etty.'

A pair of keen, light-blue eyes were on her. She told herself it was stupid to feel the moment to be important but, stupid or no, she had no doubt. Yet where was the sense? Celia was on leave from the WRNS and perhaps any minute she would arrive to join Andrew for the celebrations. And quite right too, she told herself. Making herself face the facts was one thing, but pretending it didn't matter to her wasn't so easy. Until he'd come into her life she had never so much as toyed with the thought of being in love.

'I believe, even without Drew telling me, I would have picked you out. I'm delighted at last to meet you.' His reply threw her off balance: surely it must mean that Drew – and she'd thought herself the only one to shorten his name – must have talked about her. Probably said that she was more like a lad than a girl, workaday hands covered with grease, more at home in trousers than skirts.

'Me too,' she answered holding out a hand with no sign of grease or grime. 'He didn't tell me he had family coming. That's great. Is Celia here? I've not met her yet.'

'No one but me. He said—'

'Etty, why did Jen go? Was it the toddlers' race?' Rhoda's voice called as she hurried across the green towards them.

'Gone? I haven't seen her. I'd not thought—'

'I was unloading the ice cream so I couldn't run after her. She went into the wood with a shopping basket. What could she be taking into the wood?'

Mother and daughter looked at each other, both of them with a premonition of tragedy, though neither could see the logic.

'Leave the teas. We must find her.' Which one had actually said it? It was in both their minds.

The two of them set off for the path by the side of April Cottage, the path that led to the edge of Farley Wood. Neither spoke as they ran, Etty outstripping her mother.

Behind them Andrew and Silas followed.

'What is there about this girl that puts them in a panic?' Silas wanted to know. So Andrew told him about Mickey and finally about Michael's desertion.

'You think—'

'God knows. She's had enough to make anyone unbalanced,' Andrew answered the unformed question. 'Her sod of a husband looked down his nose on her because her background was rough, but she's a good lass. Thank God

70

you're here; I reckon you might be needed.'

They were led to the scene by the sound of her whimpering; whimpering like a whipped dog. She'd taken the rope from her basket and flung one end over a branch of a tree, slipping it through the loop she'd tied in the end of it. With hands that shook uncontrollably and with vision misted by tears she was trying to tie a knot in the other end.

'No, Jen, no!' Etty yelled as she came in sight of her.

'Go 'way. Go on, clear off. Don't stop me, Ett. Let me go. Don't want no more. Did you see them, all those little ones? Did you see him? I did. I saw my Mick – then he was gone. Can't take no more.'

She was such a little thing, hardly taller than Etty's shoulder. All her strength, all her will had gone out of her as Etty took the rope from her and held her in her arms, rocking her like she might a hurt child. Rhoda took the rope from the tree and was pushing it back into the basket when Andrew and Silas arrived.

Back at April Cottage, Rhoda made tea, putting three spoons of sugar in Jenny's.

'Sorry,' Jenny mumbled. 'Made a real fool of myself and spoilt things for you lot.' Then, seeming to be conscious of Silas for the first time, 'Who's that?'

'My name's Silas. I'm Andrew's uncle. As for making a fool of yourself, you've done nothing of the sort. Sometimes we all have to blow our tops, like taking the lid off a pan of boiling water.'

Watching him, Rhoda was aware, just as Etty had been in his moment of introduction, of those light-blue eyes. It was as if, as he looked at Jenny, he saw into her thoughts and held her in his power. But that was nothing but fanciful imagination – he was a stranger, albeit a kindly one who wanted to help.

Andrew was watching too and it was he who mouthed the words 'Leave them' as he nodded towards the door. What were they doing, letting themselves be ushered out and leaving Jenny with someone she didn't even know? That was the silent question both Rhoda and Etty asked themselves, yet neither of them resisted. It was as they came to the gate and saw how far the jollifications had progressed on the green that they turned to Andrew for an explanation.

'Trust Silas,' he told them. 'By profession he's a psychiatrist. He has enormous powers of understanding but it's more than that – he doesn't send folk off into trances or any of that sort of thing, but it's just as complex. I've heard it said by his colleagues that he has mental power enough to feed whatever it is a person with a mind in chaos needs into his patients. Don't expect miracles, but I promise you Jenny will gain more from half an hour alone with him than she would from a dozen bottles of tranquillising medicine.' Then, as if having put the responsibillity for Jenny onto Silas's shoulders, he gave the boyish grin that was so much part of his personality. 'I say, things have been moving on. You ladies have missed the washing up by the look of it. Look, the band is getting ready for some dancing.'

'Alec must be wondering where I am,' Rhoda said. 'Just look at him standing there on his own. I'll go and report. Call me when your uncle leaves. I don't want Jenny left by herself.'

'Come on, Etty,' Andrew took Etty's hand, 'Let's start the dancing and show them how it's done.'

Neither they nor anyone else could give a creditable performance on the uneven grass of the green, but for Etty the wonder of it was to be held in his arms as they fox-trotted.

'I thought Celia would be here before this,' she made herself say.

'Celia isn't coming. I talked to her last night. Etty, our engagement is off. I was frightened I was being a heel – and honestly, I didn't want to hurt her. I'm much too fond of her for that.' Etty was almost too frightened to breathe, frightened she'd not heard him properly. 'But it would have been wrong to marry her when I love someone else.'

Her arms ached, her tummy was turning somersaults. 'You've never hinted there was someone else, you've only ever talked about Celia. Are you sure?'

'I've not mentioned anyone else because I was frightened of spoiling our friendship. Even now am I being a fool? Etty, how could I marry Celia when I love just you?' Silence. When was it they'd stopped dancing and were standing still as the crowd milled around them? She felt she would choke with happiness. 'Say something, please say something, anything,' he implored.

'So happy – can't talk straight.'

'You mean you feel the same? You mean you'll marry me? Darling Etty, yes, yes, yes.'

'Yes, yes, yes,' she repeated. 'Yes I love you, and yes, more than the whole world I want to marry you.'

Wordlessly, and held tightly against him, they finished the none-too-graceful foxtrot.

Then the band broke into a polka – an ice-breaker the bandsmen thought something young and old alike would join in.

'Alec, just look at those two,' Rhoda laughed. 'They're like a pair of children galloping about. Come on, let's join the fun.'

'We're not dancing folk.' His answer squashed her immediately, but he said it quite amiably and seemed content to lean against the gate of Timberley smoking his pipe and watching. 'Who's that coming out of the cottage with Jenny? I expected her to be out here with an eye to the American contingent from the aerodrome.'

'Then you expected wrong,' she answered tartly. 'The man with her is Dr Clutterbuck, Andrew's uncle.'

The polka had been popular, with cries of 'more' when it finished. Then, as the band struck up for a repeat performance, she watched as Silas led Jenny into the dancing throng. What had he said to her there alone in the cottage? Had he drawn her out to talk? Had he imbued her with strength and comfort, given her a new hold on the will to make something of her life? Whatever had gone on, she was sure she would never know but she felt a new hope for Jenny.

'It's not what I expected, but naturally I'm delighted. There's no better basis for marriage than sound friendship,' Alec said after the nightly ritual of opening the curtains and pulling down the top sash window a precise nine inches. 'Quite an evening,' he added contentedly.

'Etty isn't fool enough to agree to marriage if friendship is all they share,' Rhoda answered, trying none too successfully to suppress her irritation. 'They should be madly, wildly in love.'

'Funny girl you are,' he laughed affectionately, pulling her closer. 'That's all well and good for a bit. I've always known they were good friends. They'll be all right, they have a good base to build on.' Tonight he would make love to her, of that Rhoda had no doubt. Mad, wild, passionate love? She knew the answer. Tonight, though, there was no room in her heart for self-pity when across the green Jenny was alone; alone with memories of how near she'd come to escaping the life she couldn't bear to face. There would be nowhere for her to escape memories of her day, but surely into those memories would be a pair of light-blue eyes that must have seemed to pierce her soul and somehow instil in her the strength she'd lacked.

Chapter Four

'I wish I had something really eye-catching to wear. Meeting your future father-in-law is important.' And, not for the first time in recent years, Rhoda said, 'Damn what the war has made of us all. Haven't we had enough of "make do and mend", for goodness sake?'

'Oh, come off it, Mum,' Etty laughed, her words accompanied by a quick and affectionate hug, 'the war brought out the best in folk and well you know it. We've got plenty to wear – and enough to eat. That's more than can be said for half of Europe.' She flicked through the dresses hanging in Rhoda's wardrobe, most of them as familiar as old friends. 'What about this, Mum? It really suits you.' She drew out the cherry red dress that had gone unnoticed on that evening in November.

'I bought it in the winter. I can hardly wear it out to dinner in May. Well, there's nothing for it, I'll have to make do with my old favourite – at least I've always felt comfortable in the lilac print. Andrew was much too taken up with you at the Victory Party to notice that it was what I was wearing then, and his father won't guess that it's been my summer stand-by for at least three years. More important, what are you going to wear? I wonder whether he'll be a sort of older version of Andrew. Are you nervous about meeting him?'

'It's the first time I've been invited to dinner, but I've

75

met him a few times when I've been doing jobs on the estate farm and he's happened to be at home. In fact, I suppose I met him even before Drew came to Dad for a job. No, he's not a bit like Andrew – he's a little man, sort of cherubic. I got on with him from the first time he stumbled over me – almost literally. I was under the tractor and he didn't notice my legs until it was almost too late. Nice bloke, honestly Mum. Not a bit what I'd imagine a wealthy stockbroker to be.'

'You didn't tell us you'd met him.'

'I guess it hadn't seemed important. I mean, I meet lots of farmers and so forth when I'm doing repair jobs. Anyway, me – you say what am I going to wear? Would it be a waste if I got something new? I mean, most of my dresses are old as the hills and I can't go to dinner in an old pair of trousers. Come into town tomorrow, Mum, and in my lunch break you could make sure I don't buy something too ghastly.'

The next day, armed with Alec's clothing coupon book, which he'd surprised them by offering when he heard about the mission, the two of them went to see what Hawkes and Loveridge, Brackleford's leading department store, had to offer. What they found transformed Etty from the strongly built, practical girl, comfortably at home in dungerees, into an attractive young woman – except for the flat-heeled lace-up shoes which were part of her work attire. They were replaced by plain navy blue courts to complete the ensemble. The assistant was keen for her to choose sling-back sandals, but there were limits to how far Etty would go – besides, court shoes were smart and practical at the same time. Added to that was the silent voice of common sense that told her they would last longer and could be worn after summer had gone.

So often Andrew had imagined her 'de-greased' as she called it, displaying the natural curves of her strong young

76

body. And the next evening when he came out to greet them as Alec drew up on the forecourt of Sedgeley Manor, his home, he was moved by excitement, pride and affection which, in that first moment, almost stole from him his natural charm and good manners.

'Hello Drew. We've made it,' then with a sudden feeling of self-consciousness at her new elegance, she added, 'glad rags and all.' Thus spoke the Etty who was his daily companion, unchanged by the large diamond solitaire she wore. Somehow her manner brought his feet back to terra firma as he held out his hand to Rhoda – Etty, his dearest friend, the woman he wanted with every fibre of his being. For a moment, and taking him by surprise, he imagined her beautiful sister, Natalie, full of charm and knowing exactly how to use it. When he'd met her that previous November evening at Timberley he'd been aware that it was natural for her – without a word but simply by a tilt of her head or a fleeting expression on her lovely face – to encourage men to fall at her feet. Certainly she seemed to have knocked that soldier for six, he mused silently. But Etty . . . Etty, so different, so *complete* – and soon it would be *he* who would, please God, bring alive the desire, the fulfilment, the wonder they would find in their lives together.

All these thoughts flashed through Andrew's mind as he ushered them up the steps to where his father was waiting to welcome them. He was a small man and indeed, just as Etty had said, there was something cherubic about his rosy cheeks and round face. Despite being about the same age as Alec, the impression of being older was probably due to the fact that he'd lost most of his hair; what remained no more than a sandy brown fringe to his shiny pate. Then he smiled, a smile that surely hadn't changed since he'd been a mischievous child.

A quick look passed between Rhoda and Etty, both of them understanding the other's relief. Neither had voiced the niggling doubt they'd harboured that this evening might have been suggested simply as a sop to convention, that

77

beneath a veneer of hospitality there might have festered resentment that Etty had been the cause of Andrew breaking his engagement to Celia, the daughter of family friends.

'These two have given us cause to celebrate, eh what? I hope you're as delighted as I am?' Nicholas Clutterbuck beamed on them all.

'Indeed we are,' Alec answered. Rhoda was irritated: why did he sound so stiff and starchy?

'If we'd been able to choose a son we couldn't have found one we'd rather have than Andrew,' Rhoda added quickly.

'And you, young lady, you and I aren't strangers to each other. Although I'm not so sure I would have recognised you this evening looking so sophisticated.'

'It's an illusion, Mr Clutterbuck. I scrubbed up especially. Look in at the yard by tomorrow and you'll find me grimey as usual.'

'Now this Mr Clutterbuck business won't do. Very soon, yes *very* soon I hope, you'll be Mrs Clutterbuck and then it would just be damn silly. Some of my cronies call me Buck. How would that do, eh what?'

'I think it would do rather well. I like it, don't you, Drew?'

The evening started well and got even better. Even Alec forgot his formal politeness and involved himself in the pros and cons of the Lease Lend aid from the United States and the desperate wait by farmers for replacement machinery. Half listening to them as she chatted with Etty and Andrew, Rhoda felt she understood where Andrew's easy grace came from, but she wished Alec – dear Alec, she prompted herself to add – would widen his horizons. Surely in this wide and glorious world, a world emerging from years of tyranny and tragedy, they ought to have their minds set on higher aspirations, on ways to restore hope in the lives of those who had lost so much.

It was just as Tilly – a none-too-bright school leaver who cycled to the manor each morning and was being 'knocked into shape' by Ellen Long, the housekeeper – picked up the tray loaded with their used dessert plates, that they heard footsteps on the marble floor of the hall.

'The front door was open so I let myself in,' the visitor called as he came towards the dining room. Then, seeing visitors, 'I apologise, Nick, I hadn't realised you had friends.'

'Silas, what a delightful surprise. And quite right you should be here. Let me introduce—'

'No need, we've already met. Andrew, my congratulations! I had a note from Nick this morning telling me the glad tidings. That's why I came – cycled here purposely to tell you I think you're a lucky young man and—' just a slight pause that might almost have been in their imagination '—my feeling was more than pleasure, it was relief. I felt you were a matching pair as soon as I saw you together.' Then, leaning over the back of Etty's chair and planting a light kiss on her forehead, 'A niece I shall cherish.'

More greetings, this time no more than formal handshakes, then Silas drew up a chair to the table.

'I hope you've not arrived starving, for I fear we've eaten everything. However, another cup for my brother when you bring the coffee, Tilly, if you will, my dear.' Well pleased, the girl scurried off to do his bidding. 'Not the sharpest knife in the drawer, but a sweet willing child. I hope there won't be changes when I've gone.'

'Don't be maudlin, Pa, it doesn't suit you,' Andrew said, laughing. 'By the time you hang up your saddle, our little Tilly will probably be married with a brood of children.'

'And that, my boy, is where you're wrong.' The brief statement brought the room to silence, for surely it could mean only one thing. He looked a picture of health, but appearances could be deceptive. Surely if he had bad news to break to Andrew he should have been sensitive enough to wait until they were alone, not drop his bombshell in front of relative strangers.

'Pa ...?' Clearly Andrew had read the same message as the others. His normal cheerful expression had given way to one of uncertainty, even fear.

'Eh? What?' Nicholas Clutterbuck must suddenly have followed the path their thoughts had taken and his cherubic face beamed with enjoyment. 'Hang up my saddle, did I say? Beggar me, no. Saddle up ready to live, that's more to the point. Ah—' he held up a finger, his blue eyes shining with merriment '—no matching me up with some dame or other, either. Indeed, no. Hear me out and you'll see why I'm so delighted by the engagement of you two young things.'

But what about Celia? If his ambition had been to see Andrew married, surely the daughter of his friends must have been a perfect choice. No one voiced their thoughts, but his own must have moved in the same direction.

'With young Etty by his side, I shall have no worries about the lad. You know the most important thing in a young man's life is the right partner, well, that's always been my belief. I had it with Andrew's mother. Where I'd have got in this life without her backing I don't like to think. That's her, there above the mantelpiece – yes, indeed, and that's one thing I ask of you, Andrew my boy, don't shift that painting.'

'Pa, stop rambling. You're leaving us behind.'

Looking from Nicholas to Andrew and back again, Silas was laughing, the lines in his thin face made even deeper.

'A pound to a penny I know your plan,' he told his brother.

'Never thought I'd make it, did you? Eh? What? Thought I'd let my roots grow too deep. But it's always been there at the back of my mind, just waiting till the time was right. And now, thanks to young Etty here, I know the boy's in the right hands.'

'Live your dream, brother Nick.' There was no laughter in Silas's voice now.

Watching him, Rhoda lowered her gaze; she felt she was

80

prying on affection that had no room for outsiders.

'Dream?' Andrew prompted.

'It's always been there at the back of my mind, right from the days before I met your mother. Of course, she bowled me right over; I didn't even have time to feel disappointed that all those youthful plans were to be no more than an empty dream. Then, after I lost her—' and turning to Alec '—well, you know how it is. We strive to get on in the world, make a comfortable nest for our young, what?'

'Talk about walking through a maze,' Andrew laughed. 'Come on, Pa, tell us in simple words, the sort even *I* can understand.'

Nick and Silas exchanged a glance and it was Silas who answered.

'Everyone has a dream, some let it take a clear shape and some only know there is something we strive after but can't grasp, something our lives lack. One thing is certain: whether we chase that dream in our youth or wait as Nick has, turning it into reality is the only way of becoming a complete person. And Nick's dream was America.'

'But you've been there enough times, Pa, and you've never come home wild with enthusiasm.'

'America, son, not USA and business trips. The continent of America from the frozen north right down to Cape Horn. Where else in the world will you find so many different cultures? I want to see – and be part of – each shade of culture. I want freedom to criss-cross east to west, west to east, as I move southward. No fixed abode, no responsibilities, nothing but an open mind – one that means to absorb every nuance of the flavour of the places I see. And I shan't waste my time, you may bet on that. Each day I shall write up my experiences, who I've met, what my emotions are.'

'Then come home and turn it into a book,' Rhoda spoke her thoughts aloud, 'make it so that we all gain from your experience, all have a share in your dream.' She felt rather than saw Alec's quick glance in her direction and understood him well enough to know that he considered she had stepped out of line in taking part in a conversation that didn't concern her. Clearly Nick Cluttertbuck didn't share the sentiment.

'Perhaps I'll do that too,' he answered her, smiling and not even trying to hide his excitement at the prospect of what lay ahead. 'Or perhaps I won't. That's part of the joy, don't you know – free as a bird, ah yes, that about sizes it up. And I have these two young people to thank for it. Hurry up and get the wedding over – or do you want to spend months getting a trousseau together, Etty my dear?'

'I'm not really the trousseau kind. A new dress to make myself respectable for this evening was quite an event,' she said, laughing.

'Just the answer I hoped for. So there's nothing to wait for, what?'

'They've only been engaged a few days,' Alec said, looking to Rhoda for support. 'They should have a decent interval before they rush into marriage.'

'It's not for us to make plans for them,' Rhoda answered. 'Wartime has seen plenty of rushed marriages.'

'This is peacetime and Andrew is a civilian. For Etty's sake – well, you know the way people talk.'

'A shotgun wedding, eh what?' Nick laughed. 'God bless my soul, I never gave it a thought.'

'Anyway,' Rhoda spoke with decision, seeming to put an end to the discussion. 'Whether Etty and Andrew want to marry next month or next year, it's their decision and not ours.' She wished she weren't as conscious of Silas. She felt that his pale bluey-grey eyes missed nothing, that he read beneath the surface of the conversation.

Was that how Etty felt too? Was that why she kept her gaze lowered and looked embarrassed by what Alec had suggested.

Reaching to refill Etty's wine glass, Andrew's words were addressed to her.

'Next month, next year ... next week would suit me better! What about you, Ett?'

She sat a little straighter and looked directly at him as if to cut out the rest of them.

'If I don't have to doll myself up and feel thoroughly uncomfortable, then what is there to wait for? I'd plump for the first date Nat can get home. I can't be married without Nat.'

'Naturally—' Alec assumed everyone would share his opinion '—you'll want Natalie as your bridesmaid. And there are invitations, caterers – although what sort of a spread any of them can produce these days, heaven knows.'

'Let's just see how they want to play it,' Rhoda's firm tone seemed to draw a line under the wedding arrangements. 'A showy wedding doesn't necessarily make for a better marriage.'

'That's it,' Nick beamed. 'The days of our organising their lives are far behind us and quite right too. That's the joy of the freedom these young people have given to me.'

Considering that until recently Andrew had been engaged to Celia, Rhoda couldn't understand why this sudden change of plans meant so much to him. 'Now to other things,' their host continued, his benign expression encompassing them all.

'You know, Andrew, that Henry Dean is retiring?'

'Yes, I know he goes at the end of June. But never mind Henry Dean. You can't drop a bombshell like you have and then change the subject.'

'Ah, I see. I've left you behind again! What have I done to deserve a son who can't see beyond the end of his nose, eh Silas, what?'

With his elbows on the table and his chin resting on his clenched fists, Silas looked at his brother with tolerant affection.

'A bombshell Drew called it. And, for him, I suppose it was. After that he's hardly likely to try to keep up with you. Out with it, man, fill in the gaps.'

At that moment Tilly re-emerged bearing a tray with the coffee.

'Thank you, my dear,' Nick said as she stood looking uncertain as to whether she was expected to pour it or where she should place the tray. 'Let's start as we mean to go on, shall we? Etty, I think as soon-to-be mistress here, you might dispense the coffee, what?'

Mistress here? It wasn't what she and Andrew had had in mind as she'd persuaded him that as his wife it would be in order for her to continue working in the yard and they would find a house somewhere conveniently near to Brackleford. But this wasn't the moment to argue, so she leant to one side so that the tray could be put in front of her.

Tilly would like to have stayed to watch and listen, but clearly that wasn't on offer so she scurried back to make her report to the kitchen.

Nick Clutterbuck was enjoying himself, his gaze fixed on Andrew to see the reaction his words would bring.

'I spoke to my solicitor this morning. I can't find the freedom I'm looking for with this place making me look back over my shoulder. In any case, I see no reason to wait until one dies to pass things on? Better to have the satisfaction in your lifetime, what? Solicitors move at their own unhurried pace, but by the time I can make my arrangements to get across the pond – not easy with the shadow of war still hanging over us, but there are ways and means I have no doubt – the legalities will be tied up. And your first duty will be to find a good replacement for Henry Dean.'

The coffee remained unpoured. The announcement made its mark on each one of them. The nearest Alec had ever come to matchmaking had been to wish Andrew and Natalie might have been attracted, but since that wasn't going to happen, what could be better than that Etty's future was secured? There was no doubt that she had found favour with Nicholas Clutterbuck – and quite right too, Alec considered. Only that morning she'd made it plain that she

84

and Andrew meant to find somewhere to live near Brackleford and continue to work in the firm. Naturally this evening's announcement must make a difference – they would have a longer drive each day but it was one that Andrew was used to and for Etty it would soon become routine. Sure that Rhoda's thoughts must be in line with his own, he tried to catch her eye across the table. But her thoughts had outstripped his and her gaze was held by Silas, aware in those silent seconds that both of them had seen and understood the unspoken message that had passed between the young couple. Then talking broke out, excitement for Nicholas. Coffee was poured and drunk before they wandered out to sit on the terrace as the early summer light faded. If any of them noticed Andrew and Etty disappear in the direction of the farm buildings, no one commented.

'But you told me only this morning that you and Andrew had discussed it and agreed to let things stand as they are.' From his voice, they knew that Alec's initial delight was clouding as they drove home.

'And so we should have, Dad. But that was before we knew Buck – what a nice name for him, it suits him doesn't it? – before he told us what he was doing.'

'You ought to be delighted, Alec.' There was a sharp edge to Rhoda's voice. 'How many times have you told me you object to married women wanting a life beyond fussing around after their husbands.' Hadn't they covered this ground a score of times? This evening should belong to Etty, it should be cloudless. She was ashamed that, despite recognising Alec's disappointment at what Etty had just told them – or perhaps *because* of it – she couldn't resist the opportunity to hit out at him.

'Don't talk rubbish! It was quite different for you – there was never any logic in what you suggested. Etty does a useful and skilled job. Anyway, thank God, the men will soon be home and there won't be a need for women to go

85

out to work. Not that you ever had the need.'

'If I didn't, certainly the same can be said for Etty. I think it's a wonderful idea, Ett. A completely new beginning for you and Andrew. Remember what Silas said about everyone having a dream? Do you suppose Andrew's has always been to run the estate? We know so little about people, don't we, deep down knowing them I mean. Do you suppose Nicholas had that in mind – you and Andrew running it together? Do you think that's why he was so pleased about the engagement?'

'You could be right, Mum. But I know he's always been fond of Celia. You'd think he would have resented me like anything.'

'He's no fool,' was Alec's final comment on the subject. 'Very likely he understands his son well enough to know his feelings about the estate, and he's wise enough to see you as a suitable wife. Well, what an evening. I must say, I took very kindly to Nicholas Clutterbuck but that brother of his is a queer egg. I thought so the evening we met him at the shindig here on the green. Out you get, girls. I wouldn't mind betting Nat has been trying to ring us, wanting to know how the evening went.'

Later, lying awake next to a sleeping Alec, Rhoda let her mind drift back over the evening. Everyone has a dream: some give that dream a shape and make it a goal; others go through life knowing the shape of it eludes them. And where in the great order of things was she?

Wriggling to the edge of the bed, she slipped her feet to the ground then crept across to the window. In those first moments of sleep she knew nothing would disturb Alec, so as quietly as she could she pushed up the bottom window and leant out into the night air. How still everything was, not a murmur. She breathed deeply, savouring the scent of early summer.

But her mind couldn't be calmed. Years ago, back in what seemed like another life, she had truly believed that she had

86

found her dream. Was it her own fault that it had faded and died, or was it the same for everyone once one became part of the routine of daily living? Coming home this evening she had known that despite it not being Saturday, after the excitement of the evening Alec would break from his weekly routine. She had known just how her day would end: in bed, curtains opened, the top window lowered nine inches and the light switched off – only then, not before – Alec would perform the rite of 'love making'. No longer did she try to arouse him in any other circumstances, oh no, a darkened bedroom was a necessary background for his exertions Years ago it hadn't been like that. She remembered a glorious late evening in the first summer of their marriage when he'd tied their punt beneath the overhanging branches of a weeping willow. The idea had been to change into their swim suits and bathe. With abandonment they'd pulled off their clothes . . . now, closing her eyes, she recalled each wondrous second, standing in the gently rocking boat, her warm flesh close to his, sinking to the uncompromising wooden floor rejoicing in the near-contortion position imposed on them. Discomfort had been part of the wonder; surely proof that nothing, *nothing*, could halt the passion that drove them. All of it so long ago . . . why couldn't she accept that nothing stays the same? Instead of following his habitual pyjama-clad ritual of winding the bedside clock and setting the alarm for a quarter to seven – quite unnecessarily for they were always awake in time to turn it off before it rang – opening curtains and window then, with a grunt of satisfaction, climbing into bed; if tonight Alec had torn off his clothes as he had that evening on the punt, if he had carried her to lie naked on the bed, if she could have known that he was driven by desire beyond his control, if – but the images her imagination conjoured up made her feel uncomfortable. She pushed such thoughts away and turned her mind back to Etty and the life ahead of her: mistress of Sedgeley Manor, working in partnership with Andrew, her own input of maintaining the machinery as valuable as the knowledge he had acquired from Henry Dean as, since childhood, his interest had been on the farm. Lucky Etty, she would be an equal partner, she would have Andrew's love, his companionship and his respect too. But here at Timberley what would be left once Etty had gone? Just the daily grind, the monotonous routine, cooking, shopping, washing, cleaning, no one even noticing what she did, no one caring that she craved to be *something*, someone seen as more that part of the background of living. Ashamed, she felt the sting of tears and caught the sob that rose in her throat. Stop it! It's nothing but self-pity because your darling Ett is going, because even Jenny has found something useful to do. Jenny ... how can you be jealous of poor little Jenny: Mickey gone, Michael leaving her and not even hiding from her that he had only stayed because of the boy.

'What are you looking at out there?' Alec's voice cut into her thoughts.

'Just the night. Come over here and take a huge breath of it, Alec. Nothing can compete with the scent of night in the country.'

'Close the window and get into bed. It may smell good, but you'll get cold.'

With a sigh, she did as he said. What was the point of arguing?

'I was thinking of Etty,' she said as she settled back under the covers. 'Who would have thought the evening would have turned out like it did? What a glorious adventure for them, a challenge. They'll make a super team.'

'I dare say. But it's a bit selfish of Clutterbuck to suggest clearing off and washing his hands of everything. Suppose I decided to give up the business, hand it on to someone else whether they wanted it or not.'

'Perhaps that's the shapeless dream we've always had,' she said with a chuckle. 'Think of the adventure, Alec. Stowing our bags in the car and just following our noses.'

'You sound about as logical as that uncle of Andrew's. No, we ought to have had notice of what Clutterbuck intends to do. To replace those two won't be easy. Andrew

88

has brought a lot of custom to the business and Etty is as reliable as any mechanic on the staff. I'll have to be out more if the order book is to be kept full. As for filling Etty's slot – thank God the men will soon be demobbed.'

'Don't you envy him though – Buck, I mean?' But she knew the answer even before she asked the question.

'A pointless waste of time. What's the object of travelling if it's not to reach a specific destination? Are you getting warmer?'

'Wasn't cold,' she answered huffily. But apparently he didn't hear the pout in her tone.

'Go to sleep, there's a good girl.' He kissed her lightly, in the dark his lips making their brief contact somewhere near her left ear, then turned his back and pulled the covers high around his neck.

'Listen Alec, let's talk a while. It was such a special evening.'

'I suppose I ought to take you out more. But after a busy day there's nothing better than coming home,' he said. Then, after a pause, 'We're very lucky, when you think of the lives so many have. Out first daughter marrying a good chap like Andrew, our second climbing up the ladder of her choice. We've done well, you and me.' She knew he was right. Dear Alec, dear unemotional, sensible, loyal Alec. She took hold of his hand and carried it to her lips, just for a moment forgetting her longing to find a shape for that dream. 'I thought something along those lines this evening,' he said when she believed he was already drifting back to sleep. 'Muriel Wheeler always drops into the post office with the letters on her way home but this evening I could see she was anxious about something – I noticed how often she checked the time. You know how independent she is, she wouldn't go a second before six o'clock – if she finishes before that she finds something else that needs doing. So I pretended you'd telephoned to say you'd been out when they'd tried to deliver a parcel and you wanted me to collect it from the post office on my way home. That way I could suggest taking the post myself. Thought she was going to cry, her eyes filled and she said how grateful she would be – it would mean she could get the earlier bus home. It seems her mother is going through a bad patch.' He didn't need to elaborate – they both knew that Muriel Wheeler's life was lived on a tight rein controlled by her mother's fits of depression.

'I don't know how she stands it,' Rhoda said sympathetically.

'I suppose her lifeline is coming to work.'

Imagining the home life waiting for the faithful Miss Wheeler, Rhoda felt a nudge of shame for her own self-pity. Somehow, after that, it was easier to settle for sleep, letting her thoughts drift over plans for the wedding, images of what the years would bring for Etty. But her discontent was ready to catch her unawares, giving shape to her dream just as she drifted into sleep.

'If you are short of coupons for your dress,' Muriel Wheeler suggested tentatively to Etty when she was told the news, 'I would love to give you some of mine. And I know Mother would be happy to help too. She hasn't been out of the house for months, you know.'

'That's rotten for her. I didn't know her arthritis was as bad as that. And you're a saint, Miss Wheeler – about the coupons.'

Muriel felt her pale thin face grow warm with embarrassment. She'd known Etty since, as a baby less than a month old, Rhoda had brought her to the cattle market. She remembered it quite clearly, remembered too her own delight in the tiny, helpless scrap, and her own assumption that one day she would have babies of her own. Don't think about it, she told herself now, be grateful that through all these years you've been safe in your job, that you've made a place for yourself. But here she pulled her errant thoughts up short.

'It's not just her arthritis,' she said in answer to the honesty of Etty's interest, 'it's ever since Father died, ten years and more ago. She has just lost her grip, if you can understand what I mean. I don't like to imagine how she gets through her day when I'm out. She won't go outside the door, not even as far as the shop on the corner of the street. She used to do that, she used to go and get the grocery rations even though she didn't seem to have the confidence to do ordinary shopping. Now all that's finished too. It isn't that I mind, I have plenty of time on Saturday afternoons to get what has to be got – or I pop out in my lunch break sometimes.' It was almost as if she sat outside herself, listening to the voice she didn't seem able to control.

'But that's awful! When do you have time for yourself?' Etty had been standing just inside the office door, but now she closed it and sat by Alec's empty desk, swivelling the chair to face Muriel Wheeler. What a poor little woman she was! Etty had never seriously taken stock of her, rather she had accepted her as part of the background. But now she really looked, trying to see beneath the mousey, pale creature she had always taken for granted. There was something timeless about Muriel, dull at twenty, thirty or now at nearing forty, and yet the very unchangingness of her must surely show a strength of character.

'When you get your holiday, do you go away together?' Then, hearing the words as a sign of sympathy for the poor spinsterly mainstay of the office, she added, 'Mum and I have always been great buddies.'

How could Muriel laugh even while her blue eyes – nice eyes, Etty admitted silently – filled with tears which overflowed as she tried to blink them away.

'Buddies? Mother and me? That sounds like people who *do* things together, who find pleasure in being together. I'm sorry. Mustn't talk about it, it's disloyal and hateful of me. She can't help it. I try not to think about it, just get through each day and am grateful for the hours I spend here. No one could be kinder than your father.'

'He's great,' Etty agreed, her voice hearty and good humoured as always, 'but you don't need to be grateful. Crumbs, Miss Wheeler, this office would grind to a halt without you.'

Muriel wiped away the telltale trace of her unhappiness and, seemingly, found strength in what Etty said.

'I used to kick against the pricks,' she spoke in the unemotional tone they'd become so used to that they hardly noticed. 'I used to resent how it was that if ever I wanted to go out – a day in Reading or an evening at the pictures – she would get so het up that I might have a life outside, perhaps friends, that she'd make herself ill. A migrain that made her lie in a dark room, giddiness that made her frightened of being alone. Within an hour she would be in such a state that she would be physically sick. Oh, you've no idea. But, you see, she couldn't help it. Can you imagine what it must be like to be so miserable, so frightened.' Then, with a determined flick of the lace-edged handkerchief she still held after her mopping-up operation, she spoke with new resolution. 'She's got a heart of gold really. And I know when I go home and tell her I've suggested she lets you use some of her coupons to pretty yourself up for the wedding, she'll be over the moon.'

'You're a saint, Miss Wheeler.'

'Muriel, not Miss Wheeler.' This time her new confidence deserted her. 'I've called you Etty since your mother brought you into the office on your first outing. I know you look on me as old, well of course you do. But I couldn't have been more than about sixteen. I wish you'd call me by my christian name. You and Mr Clutterbuck too.'

'What a good idea. Muriel, Etty and Andrew, that's so much better than a lot of silly misters and misses.'

Pushing her ledger to one side, a sure sign that she wanted to hang on to the moment of intimacy, Muriel picked up her handbag and put her handkerchief in it. Then the bag was returned to rest on the foolscap sheet of paper she always put on the floor to prevent it getting soiled.

92

What a quaint creature she is, Etty thought, poor Miss Wheeler – but from now on it must be Muriel – always so prim, not knowing how to unbend. Yet beneath the surface there must surely be a normal woman, one whose youthful hopes and dreams had been crushed by that domineering mother.

'Are you going to Reading for your dress? What flowers will you have for your bouquet? And I expect your sister is looking forward to being bridesmaid. Your father tells me she has no commitments for that Saturday.' It was as if, the ice broken, she was determined to hang on to the joy of this unexpected moment of confidence.

'Right on the last count, Nat will be home. But Drew and I want a quiet wedding. Anyway,' she added with an un-ladylike guffaw, 'can you imagine me in frills and flounces, tripping up the aisle all decked out with wreath and veil. Don't look so dumbfounded, Muriel, I shan't turn up in my overalls. I scrub up quite well. You'll see. I thought I'd get some material and a pattern and take them along to Mrs Loveridge – you know her little shop in Prince's Street. She's made things for us in the past – I'm sure she'll manage to fit it in. I thought some sort of cream colour – sufficiently suitable for a bride and yet useful for special occasions afterwards. I suppose I'll have to get a hat, the vicar might turn me away from the church door if I arrive bare-headed. What barmy customs they do have! If God didn't want to see my head, what's he given me one for?'

'Oh Etty, what a way to talk!' But the prim Miss Wheeler giggled as she might have done before the respon-sibilities of her life had taken away all semblance of any joie de vivre she might once have had. 'I thought every girl's dream was a beautiful wreath and veil wedding.'

'Not this gal,' Etty laughed. 'You will come, won't you? And Mrs Wheeler too if you can persuade her.'

Muriel reached to lay her hand on Etty's as she nodded her head. There was so much she would like to have said, but that afternoon she found it very hard to keep her emotions under control. She mustn't make a fool of herself, not again, not in front of jolly, practical Etty.

So the plans for the wedding were made. Privately, both Jenny and Natalie thought Etty crazy: here she was, marrying a handsome, well-to-do young man – and a landowner too – and she seemed to have no interest in the excitement of buying a trousseau. Everyone had grown used to making things last, darning runs in stockings, taking shoes to the menders when they were more ready for the bin – even the men in the workshop would have spared a few coupons in the cause of decking Etty out for her big day in a manner they thought fit. But the bride was adamant. Dressed 'like a prize animal groomed for a show' would make her feel uncomfortable and not a bit like herself. Natalie thought she was crazy but she knew her well enough not to be surprised. Jenny, more aware of the ways of the world than the bride might be, found her mind going down the track Alec had feared.

'It was different for me,' she said one evening when Etty wandered over to the cottage. 'I'd put the cart before the horse, that's what that rotten bitch of a stepmother called it. No other way Michael would have married me – he said that too. And she was right, but I never let myself think so.'

'More fool him then, Jen. You're worth much more than Michael and one of these days things will work out for you. They *must*. Oh Jen, what have I said? Don't cry.'

'Not because of him,' Jenny snorted, wiping the back of her hand across her nose. 'If he came back to me now, honest Ett, even if he grovelled on his knees and begged me, I'd tell him to bugger off and leave me alone. But he was my Mick's dad and I thought there'd always be the three of us. If Mick was still here, I know we would have got on right as rain. Do you reckon that's why it happened to Mick? Was it to sort of put things straight cos me and Michael shouldn't ever have got together? If up there in what people say is heaven – and I got to believe it, Ett, cos

94

of Mick I just got to – but if up there there is a God sorting out all the mess we make, do you reckon that's why He took Mick away so He could put things back to how they should be?'

'No. No I don't see it like that, Jen. But I *do* believe there's *something* after we die. Don't ask me what I expect, I just don't know. There's so much we do that's wrong – I don't mean just *us* but everyone; things that hurt people's feelings and make them miserable; things that cause awful wars and all the tragedy they bring. If you ask me what I expect in paradise or heaven or whatever you like to call it, it's a sort of feeling that everything is *right* and being sure we've been forgiven for the things we're ashamed of having done.' She gripped her bottom lip between her teeth, suddenly embarrassed by the serious turn of the conversation and yet knowing that for Jenny's sake she had to go on. 'And more than that, Jen. You know that feeling when for a split second, even in our ordinary lives, it's as if we catch a glimpse but then it's gone. Jen, for Mick that's how it must be, not just for a quick second but for always, even now while we're here trying to find a way to understand. When you used to read him a story as he was going to sleep, I bet that's when he had a glimpse of what it must be like for him now, a sort of warmth of being wrapped in love.'

'But it was me who was there to love him, it was me he wanted just like he must be wanting me now – same as I want him,' Jenny gulped.

'But there's a difference, don't you see? He always has you because your spirit is still with him. And that's what counts. We can make all the protestations of love for someone, but if it doesn't sort of unite your *spirits* it can never be the sort of love that can last for ever and ever and stay with us even when we die.'

Jenny had stopped crying and looked at her friend in something like awe.

'Crumbs, Ett. I reckon your Andrew is a lucky bloke.'

Etty forced a laugh, embarrassment winning the battle over earnestness.

The evening before the wedding, Alec waited alone on Brackleford Station – Natalie was coming home. He smiled in anticipation of the next half hour: driving her home, having her to himself. The very thought of it pushed the plans for the next day from his mind. But when the carriage doors opened and, right by where he was standing, he saw Natalie waiting to emerge, his happiness took a dive. Jumping ahead of her onto the platform, then reaching for her case, was Stewart Carling.

'Good evening, Carling. You're visiting your grand-mother?' he said hopefully.

'No. Gran's decided to live with her sister.'

'Hello Dad!' Natalie hurled herself into his embrace. 'Another wedding guest. Isn't it great, he was able to get a seventy-two-hour pass. We've got great plans for the recep-tion and have been practising. I was at his camp on Tuesday and I thought there was no point in hurrying home so I waited. That gave us plenty of time to do our stuff. We're going to take them by storm tomorrow.'

Alec was aware of the involuntary tightening of his lips but his expression was lost on the young couple. Natalie had eyes just for Stewart.

'I see. Well, you'll have to discuss it with Etty. She and Andrew have such damn fool ideas about this wedding.'

'When it's my turn I won't fail you, Dad. I shall want a real meringue of a dress, and lots of fuss with pictures for the papers. The whole lot.' By that time they were beside the car he'd left parked at the kerbside. Still hanging on to the remnants of his hopes for the drive home, he opened the front passenger door for her. 'Are you OK in the back, Stewart?' Natalie asked. 'I'll go there if you like, you're legs are longer than mine.'

'I'm fine. You sit and talk to your dad.' If he'd said 'to Mr Harding', or even 'to your father', Alec might have been more kindly disposed towards him. He was an uncouth lout – that had been Alec's first opinion and nothing had changed it.

Halfway home they saw a slight figure trudging along ahead of them pushing a bicycle. Coming closer they saw it was Jenny, the rear tyre of her recently acquired second-hand bike as flat as a pancake.

'A puncture,' Alec called as he drew up alongside her. 'I can't offer you a lift as I've no room for the bicycle.'

'There was a nail right through the tyre,' she answered. 'Anyway, don't worry. It's been a real dirty day in the sheds and my dungarees are caked.'

But Stewart, uncouth lout or no, had opened the door as the car slowed to a near stop. 'Give it over here,' he told Jenny. 'I'll push it home for you. You jump in the back.'

'I'm mucky as anything.'

There was no welcoming smile to accompany his words as Alec told her, 'There's an old rug in the boot, get it out and sit on that.' Then, as he drove off, 'One thing, we shall get home before him and prepare your mother for an unexpected guest. As if the house isn't in enough uproar.'

'Dear old Dad,' Natalie laughed, rubbing her cheek against his shoulder, the action going a long way towards placating him. 'A good thing I know your bark is worse than your bite.' Then, with her head still resting against him, and somehow speaking in a tone that told him she wanted to be taken seriously, 'For my sake be nice to him, Dad.'

'You ought to have given your mother more notice of an extra person in the house.' Hardly an answer but it got him through a moment he didn't choose to dwell on.

'You underestimate Mum,' Natalie said, laughing.

And she was proved right. After a quarter of a century, he ought to have known Rhoda better. So it was that an hour later when they assembled around the dining table for what Natalie referred to as 'Ett's last supper', there was not just

97

one unexpected guest, but two. Scrubbed up, clad in an almost skin-tight summer dress and with a fresh layer of make-up, Jenny joined them. Her bicycle was in the shed and Stewart had promised he would have it roadworthy in time for her to set out on the Monday morning.

Rhoda half listened to the chatter around the table – Etty's last evening at home. She would visit, she would probably even come into the kitchen and help clear up after a meal, but no more would she *belong* as she did now. She seemed relaxed, unchanged by the occasion. Anyone looking in and listening would think Natalie was tomorrow's bride – Natalie who held centre stage, steered the conversation and, indeed, monopolised it for the most part. There was nothing unusual about that, but every instinct told Rhoda that this display of charm was to impress Stewart.

'I saw some puncture-mending stuff in the shed,' Stewart said when there was a rare lull. 'Be alright for me to help myself, won't it? I want to get Jenny's bike done on Sunday.'

'Thanks, Stewart,' Etty answered. 'I would have done it in the morning as I don't have to spruce myself up till about eleven o'clock. But if you don't mind, it'll save me getting too filthy.'

Rhoda looked at her dear, honest, unchanging daughter with a rush of happy pride. It was as well as they looked forward to the next day that none of them could foresee the bend in the road that weekend would bring.

Chapter Five

'I suppose she knew what she wanted,' Natalie said as they turned back to the house having waved to the bridal couple until their taxi disappeared round the bend at the far end of the green. 'But you wait till I get married, Mum, that'll more than make up for Ett's silly low-key ideas.'

'It was a lovely wedding,' Rhoda said defensively. 'A white dress, flowers, photographers and all that paraphernalia doesn't count when it comes to the crunch. Etty and Andrew will have a *good* marriage. If I weren't sure of that, Nat, I'd feel very different this evening.' Then, turning to the remaining few guests, 'Now folks, I've finished with being mother of the bride so I'm going to disappear to sort out our meal. All of you go back into the drawing room while I do one or two last-minute bits.'

If anyone thought Natalie might have offered to help, they were mistaken.

'Good idea. Let's go and make some music,' she said. 'Come on, Stewart.' Probably no one else noticed his hesitation, but then no one else was as sensitive to his mood as she was. 'You accompany us, Dad.'

Whether or not the few guests were eager to be entertained didn't enter her head, and because Alec never tired of listening to her he assumed everyone else must feel the same. What that loutish soldier wanted to put his oar in for was another matter and the cause of Alec's tight-lipped expression as he struck up the opening chords from the song sheet Natalie put on the stand before him.

The guests were few: Nicholas, Silas, Rhoda's cousin Stella White and her husband Basil – both of whom regaled their friends with Natalie's success – Alec's older brother Steven and his wife Gwen – conveying at a glance to each other their shared view that the girl 'was a show-off, always had been' – and Jenny, who knew that with Etty gone and Rhoda in the kitchen, she didn't fit in with those left behind. As Alec played the introduction to what she imagined was going to be the full repertoire Natalie and Stewart had rehearsed, she crept from the room and joined Rhoda.

'Crumbs, Rhoda, just look at that wapping great ham!' she said as she came into the kitchen.

'It was a gift. One of the farms where Ett often goes. I haven't seen a gammon like it since before the war. When I think of how I panicked about catering for today, but we have been so lucky. Well, why not? Ett deserved all the kindness and generosity – and Andrew too. A lot of today's wedding food was thanks to Nicholas's own farm – the turkey came from there and so did all those gorgeous tiny potatoes, and they were scraped ready for the pot too. I thought local asparagus was over, but they produced that real feast of it – and the butter to go with it. Home-grown peas, all shelled before they were brought over and strawberries complete with cream.'

'Crumbs,' Jenny said again. 'He's nice, isn't he, Andrew's dad. Sort of easy to be with. Not a bit like the other one, Uncle Silas.'

Remembering the dreadful evening of the Victory Party, Rhoda was puzzled.

'I thought you got on really well with him.'

'He wanted to help me – and talking to him I know *did* help, but it was like as if he turned a tap on and the words came pouring out. I can't really remember half of what I said. Nor what he said either, not in so many words, like. But it was like as if it wasn't quite real, any of it, he sort of pulled me back from – oh, I just want to forget it. Him being there like an ordinary person sort of makes me feel uncomfortable. Perhaps it's because even though I'm not sure what I said to him, I bet he still remembers.'

'We don't know him very well, Jen. Andrew thinks the world of him.'

'I can't put him out of my mind, you know. Oh, I haven't got a girlie crush on an older man or any of that bunkum. But it's as if he sort of printed something on my mind, or my heart or whatever it is. When I'm over there at the cottage on my own, sometimes I sit in that chair where I was the night he talked to me like he did and it's like as if he was there saying all those things again. It's not as if I remember what either of us said – not in real words. But he gave me a sort of peaceful feeling, like as if I could accept the way things had turned out and I was still *me*. You know what I mean?'

Rhoda had no idea what he'd said to Jenny on that fateful night, but one thing was certain: whatever it was, it had chased away the devil that had led her into the wood with the coil of rope.

'He's an unusual person,' she said thoughtfully. 'He seems to understand things that have never been told him.'

'Unusual you call it. More queer, I'd say. I don't want to think about that day, Rhoda. Remembering all that sort of gets between me and Mick, like a sort of cloud of misery.'

Rhoda stopped laying up the tray she was preparing to carry to the dining room and gazed at her young friend.

'I think you're wrong, Jen, about Silas seeing you and remembering all the things you said. I believe Silas knew then what you were suffering without your having to put it into words; and I think he knows where you are now without your telling him. But I understand exactly what you mean; I have the same feeling with him. In the medical

101

world he is a psychologist; I think of him as a healer of minds.'

Jenny looked uncertain, biting her thickly painted bottom lip. 'Can't keep up with you and the things you say.'

Rhoda laughed, giving Jenny a quick hug as she said, 'Oh but I think you can, Jenny my love. Now, be a darling and do Ett's job for me, will you. The cloth is on the table in the dining room and you know where the cutlery lives in the sideboard drawer.'

Jenny went off, well pleased. There was nothing she liked better than to feel she was 'doing Etty's job'.

The meal over and fearing they might be given more entertainment, Steven Harding suggested they might sit outside and make the most of the remaining daylight.

'All right for you good folk,' he boomed, as always his voice making Rhoda aware of just how different he was from Alec despite their physical resemblance, 'but remember Gwen and I come from the sooty Black Country; pure air such as you take for granted is a rare treat.'

'Oh lovely,' chimed Gwen, already on her feet.

So whatever Natalie had had in mind had to be put on hold.

'I'll bring the coffee outside,' Rhoda agreed. 'Who's going to give me a hand? Jen? Nat?'

'You go on out with the others, Rhoda. I'll do the coffee and bring it out,' was Jenny's prompt reply, as much to escape trying to look as though she were at ease in the company as wanting to help Rhoda.

'Good, good, well done,' came Steven's hearty rejoinder. 'We'll all trot along outside and have a smoke while we wait.'

So much for the pure country air. Rhoda was sure her expression wasn't a window to her mind, yet as she caught Silas's glance she knew they shared the joke. As Jenny had said, there was something about him that made one uncomfortable. Half an hour or so later, the coffee was drunk, and

102

Steven and Gwen were on their third cigarette. However did they come by them, she thought, to be able to chain smoke like that? She deemed herself lucky if she could ever buy a pack of ten, let alone twenty, from the newsagent in the village. The contented conversation was a gentle hum when Stewart vacated his place next to her on the bench, taking the tray from Jenny and carrying it back to the kitchen, and Silas took the empty place.

'Peace,' he said softly. 'Peace beyond the end of fighting – at least on this side of the globe. It comes from the certainty of the rightness that Etty and Drew will share their lives together.'

She nodded. 'I've never been more certain than I am about those two. And yet only a few weeks ago I had no idea.' A pause that might have drawn a line under what they'd said. Instead, almost as if she were voicing her thoughts aloud, she went on, 'The house will be so empty without her.'

'Her father will miss her enormously. Don't forget how they've shared their interest in the business.'

How was it she was so sure that this was no polite small talk? It was something to do with the quiet, positive way he spoke.

'Yes, he'll miss her, I know he will. He'll miss both of them and it will mean that he will be out more, covering much that Andrew had taken off his shoulders.' Another pause, one in which she knew she ought to have changed the subject. Instead, making no attempt to hide her anger, she continued, 'Work will fill the void for *him*. What makes men so touchy about their wives wanting ... wanting ... oh, I don't even know what it is I'm looking for. I often think about what you said the evening we went to dinner with Nick, about everyone having a dream, yet for some of us the dream has no shape. I suppose I'm one of those.'

'Your home is full of your personality, of the warmth of your hospitality—'

But she cut in as if he hadn't spoken. 'Years ago I used to feel I was part of the business – when Alec was just starting, I mean, I used to do the books, write the letters. We were working partners and, even though we were hard up, we shared the same dream that the business would be a success.'

'And so your dream has been realised.'

Yet, even as he said it, she was sure he knew it wasn't the truth.

'But I'm not part of it.' Her voice was small. She felt she was talking against her own will; this man was practically a stranger; it couldn't be right to discuss with him anything so close to her heart.

Sensing her unease, he took a packet of cigarettes from his pocket and offered one to her, then held his lighter to it. But she wasn't going to fall into the trap of meeting his gaze in the brief glow and purposely kept her eyes lowered.

'If you filled your days with something outside your home it would be bound to alter you. Your husband doesn't want that to happen. My guess is that the shape of his dream is found in more than the business, it's in his marriage, in the home you make together. In that he has everything he wants.'

'But surely if I broadened my horizon it would add a new dimension to our relationship.' He was silent. Mulling over what she had said? Bored with the subject? She didn't know and by now the warm, summer evening had become too dark to read his expression. 'Are you staying with Nicolas?' she asked in an attempt to get onto less personal ground.

'With Buck? Heavens, no! I'm something of a rolling stone, that's the way I've lived for more years than I care to count. Before September 1939 put an end to the way things had been, I was attached to a hospital in France; then I had a spell in Spain.'

'You spoke the languages?'

'Yes. Always a nomad at heart, I'd had a fascination

with languages as long as I can remember. I suppose my kind of calling – if that's what you call it – is the same in any language. Human frailties don't alter with time or place; grief, confusion, resentment, bitterness, misery – one finds them in abundance the world over. Utopia has never been, nor ever will.' He spoke quietly and she felt privileged, certain that what he said was for her understanding alone. Momentarily she was unsettled by a feeling of excitement but immediately she thrust it away before she gave herself time to examine it. Here in the dark it was more likely that he was no more than voicing his thoughts aloud as his memories strayed down the years of his travels. But when he laughed softly, it seemed to bring her into the magic aura of those footloose, halcyon, pre-war days. 'And a lucky thing for me, or I'd not be able to earn a living out of something I so thoroughly enjoy.'

'The shape of your dream.'

'In part. At least I'm not conscious that there is anything lacking in my life. But you asked whether I lived with brother Nicholas. My plans are never set in stone, but for the present, while my clinics are at hospitals not too far away, I'm housed by an old friend, Matthew Wilberforce. He and I were at Oxford together way back soon after that other war. He deals in rare and antiquarian books, his clients are historical researchers, academics, collectors. Deals in them, did I say? He lives for them. And I can understand the appeal. He's often away, always on the quest for literary treasures. It's not as though he can order from a publishing house; these books are rare and valuable, certainly never to be trusted to the post. He's like a bloodhound after its prey, the way he tracks them down. For me it's a convenient arrangement for the moment. I live above what he calls "the shop", although in fact it's no such thing. It's the two front rooms of an Edwardian house – you may know the properties, on Oakleigh Green – book-lined rooms with nothing shoplike about them. One is a comfortable sitting room, the other a study. Occasionally if I happen to be free of commitments when he's away, I might take a call on the telephone. Even though she couldn't see his expression she knew he suddenly smiled as he said, 'I'm a sort of messenger boy, the bottom of the business chain. Until recently there's been a retired military man who held the fort when Matthew's away, but over the last few weeks the poor old boy has been under the weather. Consequently Matthew has been trying to organise his jaunts so that I can be there when he's away.'

'What about your own work?'

'Naturally that has to come first. But my clinics aren't every day. All too easily I could let myself get too comfortable there. But that wouldn't do. I've told Matthew that the wanderlust is nudging at me. With peace will come opportunities.'

Wanderlust. Well, what difference did it make to her where he went, she hardly knew him; and, as Jenny said, he had a way of making one feel uncomfortable. She was grateful for the darkness, telling herself that if he couldn't see her he wouldn't be able to read her thoughts. It seemed she was wrong.

'I said Major Clifford had been under the weather recently. An understatement. He's had pneumonia. I'm worried that he won't be fit to carry on – at least not for some time. So what price my wanderlust? Matthew is back at the moment but not for long. Then the hunt will start again. As I say, he's like a bloodhound tracking down what a client has asked him for, then he collects the precious volume and delivers it personally; he wouldn't trust a courier.' Silence. Why was he telling her all this? She was certain it wasn't idle chatter. Even so, she wasn't prepared for what came next. 'It would give you the wider horizon you yearn, Rhoda. No,' when he sensed she was about to interrupt, 'hear me out.'

'There's no point. It's one thing your looking after the place when he isn't there, quite another to think that *I* could do it. I've no knowledge of antiquarian books, precious

106

little of history even. I'm just a *housewife*. I cook, I clean, I darn, I weed, I polish, I—'

'You underestimate yourself, Rhoda. How many women who fill days as you have, caring for the family, yes, cleaning and cooking too, doing the hundred things that are taken for granted in a home, and yet have kept the power to – to *enchant,* to still be a whole person, not a *housewife* absorbed into the shadow of those you care for?' Surely even in the dark she couldn't disguise her embarrassment.

'I told you, I don't know anything. You were at Oxford with Mr ... Mr whatever you called him. I left school without even taking any exams. I've done nothing except help Alec when he started the business and I suppose he couldn't have thought much of what I did or he would have let me work there again when the girls went away to school and I wanted to.' This time she made no attempt to hide her angry hurt.

'This is different. You don't need knowledge of the books on the shelves, only to familiarise yourself with what he has in the bookcases and where to look if you are faced with an enquiry. If anyone phones or even comes to Oakleigh, it would never be up to you to put a price on anything. All you would do would be to take details and pass the message to Matthew so that he could make contact. Do you think *I* know the trade? Trade? That's hardly the work for anything so specialised. No, of course I don't.'

'Anyway,' she argued, determined not to let him suspect her sudden surge of excited hope at his suggestion, 'you've already said your friend has a suitable ex-army man working for him. He won't have pneumonia for ever and from what you say it's just the sort of job he'll be glad to get back to.'

Ignoring her protest, Silas went on, 'It's not a regular commitment, there are times when Matthew is there for a week or more at a stretch, then he'll be away three or four days, occasionally longer. Naturally when that happens I can't neglect my work to be there all the time, so there are

often hours when the phone is left unmanned. When I
visited the Major a couple of days ago he told me he'd
decided the time had come for him to call it a day. Think
about it, Rhoda. Surely it could be tailor made for you –
you could have a life outside the home without it being so
demanding that it upset things here.' Then, laughing, 'And
I could find my freedom without my conscience telling me
I was letting Matthew down.'

'Anyway,' purposely she repeated the word, the ungra-
cious sound of it giving her some sort of protection from
the runaway excitement that was surging through her,
'anyway, it's not up to you to choose who he wants to work
for him. He can't be stupid – and that's what he'd have to
be if he was prepared to leave an ignoramus in charge while
he's away.'

'Up to him and up to you, of course it is. You might take
an instant dislike to each other. But I talked to him about
you—'

'How could you have told him about me? You hardly
know me. Anyway—' again that word '—I've never told
anyone I wanted a job of work, only Alec, and he doesn't
even take it seriously.'

He didn't enlarge on how he'd been so sure she wanted
something more in her life than she found at Timberley.
Instead he took his cigarette packet out of his pocket and
tore off the end flap.

'Think about it, promise me you'll do that. I've already
scribbled Matthew's number on here. Put it somewhere safe
– and promise me you'll give it serious thought. In the
meantime, I'm holding the fort as best I can until the Major
makes a final decision – of which I have no doubt.'

She fingered the small piece of cigarette packet, her
imagination running riot. Surely it was her ticket to . . . to
. . . to what? Adventure? Hardly that, spending days on her
own surrounded by books that would be far beyond the
scope of her knowledge. Escape? Yes, escape from a future
that would go on without change, with nothing more excit-

ing than a walk to the village shops when she might at best have a friendly chat with someone in the same position as herself. Did other women feel as she did or was she in some sort of mid-life crisis? Was what she feared no more than that while her years went on unchangingly she was growing older until hope would finally fade?

Coming back into the garden from the bright kitchen Jenny peered through the darkness, hesitating. She could hear Natalie talking and laughing. She envied her the sort of confidence that she supposed came from knowing herself to be beautiful and accustomed to being the centre of attention – as if by contrast she was conscious of her own cheap dress bought last year in the sales and altered to fit her like a second skin. She recalled how she'd patiently taken in all the seams wanting to look glamorous for Michael. Her memory baulked. She wouldn't let herself recall her disappointment when all he'd said was, 'If you like it, that's all that matters.' Today there had been nothing else she could have worn to Etty's wedding, so she'd put on her war paint and pushed thoughts of Michael out of her head.

'Seems they're managing OK without us,' Stewart whispered. 'Not even noticed we've finished clearing up. Let's go back inside and have a quiet fag shall we?' He sensed rather than saw her head nod in agreement as they crept back to the house. 'Don't know about you,' he went on when they got back to the kitchen, where she immediately started to busy herself putting the clean coffee cups and saucers away, 'but I'm not up to much at these sort of affairs. Nat asked me along because of the singing. She and I have got plans for when I get out of the army.'

'You're great together. She's gorgeous, isn't she. Not like Ett – she's about the nicest person I know, she's sort of solid, real down-to-earth honest. I'm not saying Natalie isn't, but I was thinking how different they are.'

'Ah, Nat's pretty as a picture. Wherever she goes, heads turn to look at her. But you got nothing to sound so modest about, Jenny. You're a real corker.'

'Don't be daft.' Surely there was anger in the way she answered – or was it fear? The last half hour had come near to clearing Jenny's mind of memories she didn't want to face, but at his words it was as if she could see the expression on Michael's face on the occasions she'd taken extra pains in dressing herself in anything she'd bought for a special occasion, just as she had the dress she'd worn for the wedding. 'We only came in here to have a fag and now we've had it, so we better get back with the others.'

'Have I offended you? What's wrong with telling a pretty girl she's got what it takes? And you've certainly got it, Jen, in spade fulls.'

'Depends what you're digging for. Anyway, shut up about it and let's go outside. I reckon I'm off home. Someone's got to be first to make a move or they'll have their sitting breeches on half the night.'

Whether or not he'd meant her to take seriously what he considered to be compliments, she didn't know. But she wished he hadn't said it – his 'you got what it takes' brought the echo of her stepmother's sneering comments and, worse, the knowledge that even when Michael hadn't voiced his criticism, in the end he'd left her in no doubt. Now she was glad it was dark outside as she wanted just to creep away. If only Etty had been there she would have braved the visiting Hardings, met their condescending gaze defiantly. Bugger the lot of them – the lot of them except for Rhoda. But as she approached the garden seat where she knew Rhoda had been sitting, she found Silas still with her.

''Scuse me butting in,' she said tentatively, 'but I better push off home. And Rhoda, thanks ever so much for letting me be part of it – sit with you in the church and all that. It was smashing, all of it.'

'Do you need to go so soon, Jen? Nat says she was only waiting for Stewart and then we're going in to listen to them. Why don't you stay?'

It was crazy to feel so scared at the prospect, but Jenny

look around her, the darkness only broken by the glow of cigarettes, the hum of voices to her ears all sounding what she thought of as 'posh', just like Michael's had been. Well, she'd had as much as she could take. It was different with Rhoda, the nicest person she'd ever known – she either liked you or didn't like you, she never put people into slots according to where they came from.

'I'll just go on back, Rhoda. Got things to do. But it was a lovely wedding, sort of ... sort of ... crumbs, I don't know – sort of holy. They're going to be all right, Ett and Andrew.'

Rhoda nodded. 'Yes, that's just how I thought of it. Nothing showy, but so *certain*.'

'That's it, that's what I wanted to say. Blimey, though, nothing'll be the same with no Ett here.'

'That about sums it up, Jen. Thank goodness I've still got you.'

If the words were designed to give Jenny's flagging confidence a boost, they couldn't have been better chosen. Taking herself as much by surprise as she did Rhoda, she swooped down and dropped a kiss on the cheek that was just about discernible, then turned and left them.

'I haven't forgotten your puncture,' Stewart called after her. 'I'll do it in the morning and bring it over to you.'

'You sure you got time? I reckon I could do it if I tried.'

'Not worth breaking your nails for,' he laughed. Then, taking pleasure in the sound of his dignified words, 'It will be my pleasure.' Then he went to join Natalie.

'Poor little Jenny,' Silas said softly. 'Why can't people learn to look below the surface. "Lady!" What a misused word it is.'

Around them there was a movement towards the house. It seemed Etty's wedding day was over; the next hour belonged to Natalie.

A tight-lipped Natalie watched out of the landing window the next morning as, with the puncture mended, Stewart rode

111

Jenny's bike across the green. Too tall for it, as he pedalled he kept his knees far apart, the sight putting her in mind of an errand boy. It annoyed her. He'd been kind to offer to see to the puncture, but why couldn't he have pushed it like any reasonable adult would? She supposed he was trying to put Jenny at ease, and that was the thought she clung on to and enlarged, not wanting anything to dent the excitement he had brought into her life. She found herself in an unusual position: used as she was to young men fawning around her, never before had one of them aroused any great interest. But Stewart was different. From that first evening when he had been brought back to Timberley she had known he would be important in her life. Surely it must be clear to everyone. When they sang together it ignited a spark – spark? No, a flame – that must be there for all to see. That's what she reminded herself as she watched Jenny come out of the cottage garden and walk to meet him.

Natalie loved clothes and her make-up was never less than unobtrusively perfect, so it was no wonder she frowned as she gazed at the scene. Even at a distance it was evident that Jenny's face was plastered with its usual thick layer of cheap make-up, her hair piled ridiculously high, her heels making walking on the green well nigh impossible. Natalie found the sight reassuring as she made a mental picture of herself in comparison. Turning from the window she went on her way down the stairs, sure that once the bicycle was handed over Stewart would be back. Had she waited a few seconds longer she would have seen that, instead of passing it to Jenny, Stewart upended it and presumably proceeded to explain to her how to mend a puncture should another occur.

Jenny listened to every word, imagining the process and being grateful for the lesson that would help her towards independence.

'Nice out here, isn't it,' he commented as he lifted the bike to right its position. 'Not in a panic to rush off, are you?'

112

'Got nothing to rush for.'

'Good. Let's sit awhile, eh?' Carefully he laid the bicycle on its side. 'Sundays are the worst when things fall apart like they have for you.' He held out a hand as if to stifle her protest before it was spoken. 'No Jen, don't get me wrong. I wasn't saying let's not rush off because I'm sorry for you, honest that wasn't it. I meant it because I think you and me got off to a good start, we're friends. Come on, let's park ourselves on the grass for ten minutes. It's not often the sun shines and we've got a chance to enjoy it.'

She ought to make an excuse, she knew she ought. But the nearest she got to it was. 'Just two minutes then. You haven't got long at the house – you and Natalie are off this afternoon. Rhoda told me.'

'I know. It would be rude of me to be away too long. Just a few minutes though, sort of build on the start we made. Last night, Jen, when I said that to you about you being a cracker, I didn't mean to offend you. That's the main thing I wanted to tell you this morning. It just came out naturally – because it's the fair truth. Didn't mean that I was making a pass at you and expecting you to roll on your back and purr. Nothing like that.'

'That's OK. I expect I'm a bit touchy. You see ...' But her voice trailed into silence – she couldn't tell him the hurt Michael had caused her. She could neither tell him nor could she clear from her mind the echo of Michael's final words, telling her that he'd only been prepared to try and make the best of a hopeless situation because of Mick. And almost as hard to bear was the memory of how she'd constantly tried to make herself attractive for him. Would he have preferred her to have gone around looking frumpy? Well, if that was what he'd wanted, even if he'd not gone off and left her like he did, he could have whistled for it. Imagine him sitting out here on the grass with her, saying nice things. Not likely, he wouldn't. Well, see if she cared! It took only a second for these thoughts to crowd together in her mind, and somehow as they did, it was natural to smile at Stewart's sudden lack of confidence. 'Thanks a bundle for doing my bike and telling me how to set about it if I get another. Now look, it's time you got off back to the house. Rhoda is going to have the dinner ready a bit early today because of your train.' Then as they stood up and he pulled the bicycle upright, 'You know what? I'm going to miss Ett like anything. She was a real mate.'

'I don't come here that often, but can we keep in touch, Jen? I'd like to feel you looked on me as a mate too.'

She laughed, the sound suddenly making a child of her.

'I'm not much at writing but I tell you what – if you send me a letter, I'll answer it.' Then seriously, as if she was choosing her words with care, 'You know what? Being here living on the green has been special for me, never known the sort of family Rhoda and her lot are. When it all happened – Mick and I suppose Michael too – don't know what I would have done if I'd been somewhere else. So having you for a friend is sort of right and proper. You're part of them.'

'When I get out of this ruddy uniform, Natalie and I are going into a proper partnership. When I joined up, if I could have heard myself saying a thing like that I'd not have thought it possible. But it's fallen into place so easily. I've got nothing to bring to the partnership, nothing except that since I was a kid I've always loved singing. She's already making quite a mark for herself though and she wants to give up the solo singing and take me on board. I bet being half of a duo was never her plan for the future either.'

'I guess that was before she got to know you. When it comes down to brass tacks it's *people* who matter, people and what we think of them. You and Natalie fit together as if you were tailor-made ... only got to hear you singing some love duet. You know what? I used to try and believe that it was like that for Michael and me. But now, now it's all over, I can see that I was kidding myself, probably too

114

frightened to look at the truth. My little Mick was like a sort of gold chain that held us together.'

'Like I said, Jen, we think we know where the road ahead is going to take us but, by the time the chaps all get home from the forces – and let's hope it won't be long before the Japs throw in the towel – by the time they get to be civvies again, there won't be many who pick up where they left off at the beginning. The way we've lived these last years must have made a mark, changed us.'

She laughed, 'Don't know what the way I'm living must be doing for me then. Cleaning and packing veg up at the farm, sure thing wasn't part of my plans for the future. But there's one thing even more important than what we *do*, it's what we *are*. And I don't reckon that changes, no matter what happens. Like when I was a kid – back before I met Michael even and I was only a kid really when I fell head over heels for him with his posh voice and airs and graces – more than anything I wanted to earn so that I could stand on my own feet. And that's the way I mean to go on. The rent on the cottage is paid up until November, but after that I shall pay for it myself. I don't want *anything* from Michael. Right now I bet he's thinking that because he walked out on me he's got to pay for a roof over my head. Well, I'll show him! He can stuff his charity where the monkey stuffs his nuts – I'm blowed if I want it.'

'Good girl. God, what a fool he must be.'

'Give me the bike. You better be off back to the house, Stewart. Thanks a bundle for doing the tyre. I'll think of you when I pedal off tomorrow morning.'

'It was my pleasure,' he replied, just as impressed with his tone as he had been when he'd said much the same thing the previous night.

Then, to protect her heels, rather than walk back across the green, she hopped onto the saddle and rode the short distance to the cottage garden. Turning back to Timberley, Stewart saw Natalie coming out of the gate. The contrast between Jenny and her had never been more apparent –

Jenny in her cheap, clinging summer dress and out-of-place shoes, and Natalie in pleated skirt and polished leather shoes. At other times her clothes would be as glamorous as her vocation demanded but here in the country she might have stepped from the pages of a county magazine.

'Too late,' he called, 'she's just gone in.'

'It was you I was coming to see. There's still half an hour before lunch will be ready. We could go for a stroll into the wood. There's so much we have to talk about and the weekend will soon be gone.'

They set off along the path bordering the side hedge of April Cottage and, as Jenny came away from the shed where she kept her bicycle, she watched them disappear hand in hand.

The midday meal over, Rhoda waved the visiting family members, plus Stewart, on their way. The family saloon had never been so overfull for, despite nearly six years of wartime fare, middle-age spread had had its way with the older members.

'Almost need a shoehorn to pack us in, eh Alec,' Steven Harding boomed. 'Never mind, we're lucky to get a lift, petrol being as tight as it is.'

Probably Natalie was the only one of the three women who relished the seating arrangement, wives all too aware that with each mile their husbands knees became more numb. Stewart would hardly have been human not to appreciate the way she leant against him on their half of the back seat, one arm unnecessarily around his neck. Once at the station they all parted company, 'the oldies' as she thought of her aunts and uncles going to the tearoom to await their respective trains, while Alec crossed the bridge to the other platform to see Stewart and Natalie on their way.

He waited until the train steamed its way out of the station and was lost to view. For him that was the moment when the weekend ended.

*

116

'We didn't see much of Nat, not by herself,' Alec said regretfully as he settled contentedly into his armchair and opened the Sunday paper.

'We'll have to get used to that,' Rhoda answered, 'now that Stewart's on the scene.'

'Rubbish. In my opinion this singing duo idea will be a nine-day wonder. Natalie has too much talent – she should be a solo artiste.'

'He has an extraordinarily pleasant voice. It won't be a case of Stewart needing to ride in on *her* talent. But I wasn't thinking of that. Natalie has had admirers enough ever since she started to grow up—'

'Not to be wondered at. I thought looking around the church yesterday, there can't be a prettier girl in the county. She makes us very proud, doesn't she.'

'They both do, they always have. But, what I was saying about Nat and Stewart, it's the first time I've ever thought she was falling for anyone.' Then, with hardly a pause, instinct warning her to change the subject, 'Are you ready for tea, or do you want to wait and eat up some of last night's leftovers later?'

'What?' His irritable voice and the way he vent his feelings on the newspaper, closing it and throwing it onto the floor, told her exactly what he thought about her theory. 'Blast the food. Falling in love, that's utter nonsense. She's nice to him, she likes his singing voice, she's caring enough – and I don't mean in the stupid way you seem to believe – caring enough to want to give him a leg up the ladder.' Then, with a final glare, 'That and nothing more.'

Sitting on the edge of the chair facing him across the empty hearth – at least empty except for a flower arrangement she'd prepared especially in honour of yesterday's gathering – Rhoda leant forward as if to emphasise the importance of what she was going to say.

'Alec – no, leave the newspaper where it is, I want to talk to you.'

'About yesterday? It went off well, very well considering what a hole in the corner event Etty was determined to make of it. Honestly Rhoda, if I didn't know the pair of them better I would have the same sort of suspicions as I'm sure most of the village who came to watch events did. Why the devil she couldn't have put it off until at least the autumn I can't imagine.'

Rhoda's laugh was affectionate, her thoughts on Etty.

'I'm with Etty, I can see no reason to arrange your life so that it fits in with what's expected of you. Think how *boring* that would be. But, Alec, I'm going to miss Ett more than I can say. That's why I want you to listen and to try, really *try* to understand. I expect you noticed I was talking to Silas in the garden last night.'

'I was glad you were. He's not my cup of tea and someone had to show him some sort of civility, Andrew appears to hold him in high esteem, God knows why. I wouldn't have thought they had a thing in common, Andrew's naturally an outdoor type of fellow. It must be galling for him to be so restricted; I've noticed it in the yard sometimes, a step too far and he's done in.'

'He and Ett have three good lungs between them and you may be sure that's the way they'll work. She won't molly-coddle him, but she'll keep her eyes open. Anyway, going back to what I want us to talk about: Silas is temporarily living at Oakleigh. He has a friend who deals in antiquar-ian books ...' And so, willing him to hold her earnest gaze, she told him the proposition.

'How often do we have to go through this pantomime for heaven's sake?'

'This could be the last time if you'd come down off your high horse and be reasonable. Alec I don't want us to quarrel over it; there's no need for that. For the present some retired army major is going in when the owner is away, but he seems to be coming to the end of the line. Silas wants to move on but doesn't want to let his friend down. It's not an everyday job, it's only to hold the—'

'God spare me,' he whispered through clenched teeth,

'do I have to spell it out to you in single syllables? Even if I were to agree, which I never shall, what makes you think that you have the capability of being employable?'

His words hung between them. For a moment she was frightened that she would lose her control, that the tears welling up inside her would defeat her. She *wouldn't* let that happen. She daren't speak of the emptiness of her days, of her longing to find something, *anything*, that would bring interest and colour. If she went down that track her control would be gone. So she clenched her back teeth, keeping her jaw firm. One croak in her voice and she'd be lost.

In fact it was no more than seconds before she spoke, but as she battled it seemed much longer. Alec watched her, his expression inscrutable.

'Not everyone sees me the same as you do.'

He raised his eyebrows, his irritation giving way to humour.

'And so I should hope. Rhoda, why can't you behave like other women? Oh yes, plenty of them have had to work during the war years, but they're younger. Surely after all the time we've been here you can find enough to amuse yourself locally. You have a comfortable home, I don't keep you short of money. Perhaps wartime catering has got you down but that's a small price to pay for the way we live.' His anger had gone, leaving him genuinely puzzled. 'If you'd ever been trained for a career I could understand you wanting to prove yourself in it. But for nearly twenty five years you've made a good job of running the home, caring for us all. What is it you want that I haven't given you?'

Don't be kind to me, she cried silently, how can I argue with you when you're like this. But I *can't* give way to you, it happens every time and I *won't* let it happen again.

'I want to be *me*. All I've become is someone who keeps the house clean and tidy, who washes the clothes, darns the socks, sews on buttons, shops for things always looking to find something other people like, who cooks,

119

washes up. I'm a wife, I'm a mother – but I'm more than that, I'm *myself, me.*' Her voice was rising ominously. 'I want a chance to see a world beyond these four walls. You say I'm stupid. And so I must be or I would have stood up for myself ages ago. Etty and Andrew will be equal partners in their marriage, they will run that place together.'

Her voice trailed into silence; silence that she was frightened to break for fear of that rising tide of emotion getting out of hand. By this time they were both on their feet as if that gave their words extra impetus. So they stood, neither prepared to be the first to move.

'Anyway,' she said in an attempt to cling on to her aim, 'Silas gave me his friend's telephone number. Tomorrow I shall ring him.'

'You know my views,' Alec reminded her coldly.

'Of course I do – and you know mine. I don't see what extra pleasure it can add to your full life to know that I'm stuck here like a bird in a cage. Anyway,' she repeated the word with emphasis, 'tomorrow I shall ring him. And we'll take it from there. It's only that he wants someone to hold the fort when he's away; he always delivers books in person, just as he'll be away when he's on the trail of something he wants.'

'I see my wishes count for nothing. I'll just say this: I should have expected you might consider there are plenty of women with greater need of earning money than you.'

She was about to make the quick retort that she wouldn't care whether or not she was paid for her time when she realised that wasn't true – however small the salary, to have money that was her own, truly hers because she had earned it and it was evidence of her worth, was a heady thought.

Alec picked up the Sunday paper before continuing, 'Let's have a cup of tea and a slice of cake or something, shall we? You did well yesterday – all the weekend in fact – feeding so many. Rhoda – you're a good lass. Perhaps I ought to tell you so more often. Is that what's the matter?'

'Of course not.' And neither was it. 'I'll get the kettle on.'

Suddenly she was happier than she'd been for ages. Was is because he appreciated how she'd coped or was it because the door of her cage had been unlatched?

Chapter Six

Cycling from Dewsberry Green, Rhoda had imagined herself knocking at the door, having time to compose herself from her ride before facing the unknown Matthew Wilberforce. Even, at the back of her mind had been the hope that her knock would be answered by Silas, his belief in her ability giving her the confidence she lacked. Instead she found the door of the house open, the sight presenting her with a problem: should she walk straight in and if she did, supposing no one was there, how did she make her presence known?

For goodness sake pull yourself together, she told herself, you're acting like some frightened child. You may dislike the man – and that'll be the end of the affair. But I hope I don't, and I hope, yes really *do hope* that he likes me too and it's the start of something.

'Would you be the lady Silas told me about? Mrs Harding?' A man's voice broke into her reverie.

There had been no logic in expecting that because Matthew Wilberforce and Silas were friends there would be some similarity between them. Whereas Silas was of no more than medium height, wirily slim and with light bluey-grey eyes that seemed to see into her mind, and coarse, steely dark hair that wanted to curl, this man was built like a giant, his hair prematurely white in contrast to the grey of his well-trimmed beard.

Rhoda took the large hand he extended.

'Yes, I'm Rhoda Harding. I don't know what Silas told you. Did he explain that I've had no experience, I mean I've never been to work. I may be no good at all. But Mr Wilberforce, if you think I might be able to, then I promise I'd give it a hundred percent. I'd make sure you didn't wish you'd never given me a chance.' The words tumbled out – she didn't seem to have the power to stop them.

Matthew's dark eyes shone with silent laughter.

'Never known such enthusiasm,' he chuckled. 'Damn me, if I'd made up my mind against you I wouldn't have the heart to send you on your way. Come on inside and I'll tell you what's involved. And now I want you to make up your own mind whether you think you'd be bored out of your brain – you could be, you know, for there will be days when you sit here on your own and even the telephone doesn't ring. When Silas is free from sorting out confused minds he delights in it as it gives him a chance to write up notes with no interruptions. This isn't a fast-moving trade like you'd get at a shop in town. But it's a good deal snugger, I promise you that. Perhaps you knit or some-thing, whatever it is ladies get up to.'

So he ushered her inside and the next half hour was spent in introducing her to his two-roomed collection before finally opening a locked cupboard where his most priceless publications were kept.

'Silas told you about the Major, of course. He says he feels he should pack it in but if, when he is fit again, he wants to come back then the job must be his. I believe that once he knows I have a fill-in doing the job – for that's what I shall tell him – once he knows I'm not dependent on him, he will be only too relieved to give up. Is that arrange-ment of any interest to you? Or do you see it as something and nothing?'

She shook her head. 'I see it as ideal. And thank you for giving me the chance.'

From head to toe and toe to head again he sized her up.

'I shall be here until Thursday night. How about your coming in for one of those days and having a trial run. It's a bit much to expect you to be thrown straight in with no one to turn to. Better bring your sewing or something to read. Give yourself six months and you might prefer to get your nose into what you find here. Antiquity has a way of captivating you, you know. Silas says you have no leaning towards things historical but stranger things have happened. Where do your interests lie, Mrs Harding?'

Interests? Never in her life had she felt so inadequate.

'Ask me in six months. Didn't Silas warn you? He should have. I'm a nothing sort of person – all I've done for the last twenty-five years is live through other people, running a home, gardening. You don't have to take me, Mr Wilberforce. Honestly, I'd understand perfectly if you said I'm not the person you want.'

'I believe you would. But if I'm to be honest with you, Mrs Harding, you *are* the person I want. Silas recognised it in you and so, I believe, do I. Now take a seat – the chairs are better in the other room and we might as well be comfortable while we discuss terms etcetera. No, better still, come with me to see where you can make yourself a drink and something to eat at lunchtime. There's a percolater and meths lamp in the back room here. When we've had a coffee I'll take you up and show you my kitchen where you'll be very welcome to cook up whatever you need. Not very up-to-the-minute perhaps but I think you'll find my elderly oven adequate for warming up anything you bring. Now then, I'll put a match to the meths lamp and we'll soon have a cup of coffee while we talk. Just pass my coffee jar from the shelf, will you.'

This wasn't turning out to be a bit as she'd imagined a job interview, but she felt drawn to the giant of a man and his unconventional approach. Five minutes later she followed Matthew and his laden tray into the second room, the one with the easy chairs.

'The Major is most unlikely to return. A grand chap, I

124

hope his health picks up. I dare say Silas explained to you that I've not long been here so his foray into work in retirement was a short one. I hope yours won't be, Mrs Harding.'

She laughed. 'That's what I hope too, but you may change your mind if I turn out to be useless.'

'I believe in trusting my own instinct – mine and Silas's too, in your case.'

She supposed Silas was purposely keeping out of the way, not wanting his presence to make it difficult for his friend to turn her away. Yet even though she found herself constantly listening for sounds from upstairs, there was no hint that anyone was there. It was half an hour or so later, her terms of employment discussed and agreed, when the telephone rang.

Matthew started to ease his bulk out of the chair, then with a mischievous challenge in this eyes he said, 'Up you get, you answer it, Mrs Harding. I've explained what's expected of you, so let's see how you get on.'

It happened so suddenly that she didn't even have time to be nervous. She answered the call in the same easy, friendly manner that she would have had she been in Alec's office or even at home, taking details of the request and promising that Mr Wilberforce would call back as soon as he returned a little later in the morning. What was said the other end Matthew couldn't hear, but he could tell from her smiling reply that his client had been well pleased.

'See, there's nothing to fear in that? Let me read what you've written. Ah yes, excellent. Now I'll give you a spare door key so that you can let yourself in and once you've seen where you'll find the kitchen, I think we're ready for business. I plan to be away all next week. You just make yourself at home, bring something to do – do you paint? Or perhaps you write. Silas uses whatever hours he's able to spend here very profitably in my absence. But of course he has a pretty full schedule and it's seldom that he can get here.'

'He says he covers a large area.'

'Personally I've had no call for the services of a head shrink, but I understand he's very highly thought of. Top of the tree you might say. So, yes, his experience is called on from all over the place. He left on Sunday but I don't doubt he'll be back when he's this way again.'

He accompanied Rhoda to where her bicycle waited propped against the house, then, holding out his huge hand to her, said, 'I shall call you on Friday afternoon – then and each weekday afternoon until I get back.'

'I'll do my best not to disappoint you, Mr Wilberforce.'

At that he threw back his head and laughed.

'Hey, hey, hey, Mr Wilberforce be damned. We have Silas as a mutual friend, or in your case I suppose almost a relation now Andrew and your daughter are married. I think that means we can manage Matthew and . . .?'

'Rhoda. That's much nicer. And don't tell me you didn't know my name.'

'True. But courtesy demanded.'

On that laughing note she climbed onto her bicycle and left him. It hadn't been her idea of an interview nor did it sound like her idea of a job that would broaden her horizon and add excitement to her days, yet her confidence had been given the boost it needed and she found herself looking forward to working for Matthew Wilberforce. It presented her with a challenge and she was determined to get to know something of the books that lined his shelves. She was also honest enough to recognise that she wasn't suddenly going to become a historian – the best she was likely to do was familiarise herself with what stock he held. That must surely be the first step towards speaking intelligently to callers.

Such was her mood of optimism that as she rode towards Dewsberry Green she even looked forward to describing the interview to Alec, imagining that now it was a fait accompli he would share her pleasure and take pride in knowing Matthew was putting his trust in her. By the time

126

evening came and she heard his car draw up outside the house, her feet were firmly on the ground again. Just as well, perhaps, but he listened in silence to the description of her morning.

'Alec, the way I spend my days makes no difference to you. From eight in the morning until almost seven in the evening you've a life outside while I—'

'Yes, I work long hours. But Rhoda, do I do it for my own entertainment? Whatever I've done has always been for you and the girls, for *us* as a family.'

Back to her came the echo of Silas's voice, telling her that the shape of Alec's dream was found in their marriage.

'I know,' she said softly, filled with sudden emotion that made her afraid to trust her voice any more. Coming close to him she wound her arms around his neck, holding her face up so that her mouth was within inches of his.

'Funny girl,' he laughed, dropping a light kiss on her forehead. The action spoke for itself: he believed she was reconciled to his way of thinking. In that moment her battle for freedom lost its grip, but not for long. Somehow she must make him understand that for her, too, their marriage mattered above all else, but that didn't mean that she was nothing more than part of the home he provided, taken for granted as much as his fireside chair or their well-plumped feather bed at the end of his day. They were equal partners. She even managed to make herself believe that they shared each other's interests and by widening her horizon she would have more to bring to their relationship. Whether she was prompted by guile, wisdom or her longing to hold on to the emotion that temporarily gripped her, she decided to say no more about her plans. Instead she played her part.

'I wonder how Ett's getting on,' Rhoda said later, the ham risotto she'd cooked for their supper turning her thoughts back two days to the wedding.

'I missed her at the yard today, missed them both. I'm very fond of Andrew, but I hope she hasn't taken on too much. He may have the know-how to run that place, but has he the physical stamina?'

'She has enough for both of them.'

'I dare say you're right. And they have the most important ingredient for any marriage,' he said. 'They have a very real friendship. I hope when Natalie falls for someone, it will be something deeper than the froth of romance that attaches itself to a career like hers.'

Rhoda bit back her words. Was he trying to puncture her bubble of contentment?

'Natalie isn't stupid,' she said, then laughing, 'Just hark at us, Alec, the chicks flown the nest and we can't let go. Just us now. When have we ever had the house to ourselves? Not for years. Quite exciting.'

It was hard to read his expression, but her resolve didn't weaken. She *had* to make him realise that the two of them were enough, that just because she looked outside their home it didn't mean that she was wanting more than their life together could give her. And so the evening went on, Monday evening. She knew that for Alec, Monday belonged to the start of the working week. Saturday night – in time gone by often Sunday night too – and occasionally once during the week he would perform the lovemaking ritual. But Monday night belonged to the working week, an evening when he would spend an hour in his study planning the work for the days ahead.

'Let's go in the garden,' she suggested as she piled the tray with their dirty plates. 'These can keep until the morning. Let's take our coffee outside and watch the sun go down.'

'The sun won't be down for another hour or more. Get the washing up done while I have a few minutes – you know I like to look ahead on a Monday. With no Andrew I'm going to be extra busy. Thank heaven Muriel Wheeler is efficient – I don't have to worry about that side of things.'

Already she could feel herself getting irritated, but she

128

made herself nod her agreement.

'I'll hold coffee back for half an hour. Don't be long though, Alec. It's a special sort of evening ... can't you feel it? A sort of new beginning for us too – everyone gone.'

'Don't know about that,' he said, laughing. 'But give me twenty minutes.'

The evening turned out well. She weeded the rosebed in the front garden and then trimmed the edges of the lawn prior to getting out the mower the following day; he tidied the hedge. Just once, glancing across the green, she saw Jenny leaning over the cottage gate. She waved knowing that had she been on her own the lonely young girl would have come over, but she wasn't on her own so an answering wave was the only recognition.

'Poor Jenny, always going home to an empty house.'

'Umph, her and thousands like her. Perhaps when she sees us busy she'll realise there's plenty to do in that garden too. It's turning into a wilderness. If she lets it get too bad I should think the landlord would want her moved. What's the house like? I suppose you don't go in now that she works all day.'

'Jenny is never scruffy,' she said defensively.

'Humph! Not my idea of tidy. I bet she'll let things go now that Etty isn't there to keep an eye on her.'

Don't spoil the evening, let it be good, thought Rhoda, now we only have each other, let it be like it used to be. Then her thoughts shot off at a tangent and she wondered where Silas had gone to, how his depth of undersanding could make him able to guide lost, confused souls.

'Wake up, dreamer, standing there gazing into space. Come and help me sweep up the clippings then we'll have an early night.'

Hope stirred anew. Was he, too, remembering those days so long ago when despite having so little they lacked nothing because they had each other and the certainty of the golden years before them? She fetched the broom and swept up as he piled the wheelbarrow, willingly letting herself rejoice in unfamiliar excitement. Indeed, as she watched the way Alec upended the wheelbarrow to replace it just where it was kept, not an inch to the right and not an inch to the left of its habitual place, she felt a stirring of affection for the never-changing precision he brought to everything he did. If she intentionally encouraged the warmth of her emotion she didn't admit it. Her mind dwelt on all the good things of their world: their two girls, brought up in their own image, given a code of living that would hold them in good stead, but now flown the nest and standing on their own feet. She and Alec had been the foundation they'd built on; she and Alec, the love and security of their home.

Matthew Wilberforce's establishment in Oakleigh belonged to another existence as she encouraged excitement and anticipation to hold her. With the wheelbarrow in place, the shears oiled and the hoe she'd been using hung on its hook, Alec came to join her and she slipped her hand into his as they surveyed their evening's work with satisfaction.

'Don't put those on,' Rhoda reached to take his folded pyjamas from him. 'Don't spoil a lovely warm night.'

'Perhaps you're right. What about you? Do you want your nightdress or are you ready for me to turn off the light?'

'What would I want with a nightdress?' she whispered, coming close and teasing his mouth with hers. 'Leave the light on.' Then, leaning against him, she laughed softly. 'We're free. Listen to the silence. No one here. Just us.'

He said nothing, but she knew his thoughts were following hers and the knowledge thrilled her. Nuzzling her face against his neck, she wasn't sure whose heart was beating so hard, his or hers. This is our new beginning, she told herself, hope, trust and surely deep and abiding love. Tonight I don't want fantasies, I just want us, *us*. 'Carry me to bed, let's make wild passionate love.'

For a moment he hesitated.

'Don't know about carrying you, you're not as light as the girl you were and I'm not in such good shape either. But the rest sounds all right.'

The first suspicion of disappointment nudged her. She ought not to have suggested it, reminding them both of the difference between then and now. Yet it wasn't because he didn't want to play the cave man that she felt let down. What she had wanted was for him to speak with repressed passion in his voice, to let her know his own need was as consuming as hers. Instead he guided her to lie on top of the bed (a slight improvement on the habitual between the sheets performance) then without preamble, thanks to the advances she'd been making, he was ready.

Hardly five minutes later they were in bed with the light switched off and his back turned in his normal sleeping position. As so often, she lay awake long afterwards, but on that night her fall from the heights to the depths was greater even than usual. There was one consolation: on Friday she would turn the key in the lock of the house on Oakleigh Green and thus would begin her new life.

'Can I come in and hear all about it?' Jenny greeted Rhoda through the open back doorway. 'How did you like being part of the working world?'

'Don't know about working,' Rhoda said, laughing, 'I hardly killed myself. But – it sounds daft – but I loved the feeling of having to be there at a certain time, of having to sound as though I knew what I was talking about when I had a phone call. Actually I only had two calls all day, so rather than saying I was busy, I must have had about the laziest day I've known for years. But it was *different*. Does that sound crazy?'

'It ought to, but seeing how sort of safe and cosy you are here, in a way I can see what you're after. A bit of adventure. It sounds jolly different from where I work. No good painting my nails nowadays.' To emphasise her words

131

Jenny held her small childlike hands for inspection. 'I tell you Rhoda, a bit of colour on them and after half an hour there they look worse than if I leave them alone.'

'Why don't you get a pair of gardening gloves?'

The suggestion brought forth an uncharacteristic guffaw. 'I'd feel sort of ashamed, like I thought myself precious. Now who sounds daft? They're a grand pair, the Ridleys, both of them working out there in the fields looking after their veg. Tough as old boots they are but there's something so sort of contented about them, there in their scruffy old gear, hands and faces kind of lined with hard living. And they treat me like one of them. It's nice, that is. So I couldn't wear gloves – it would look like I wanted to be different, posher or something.'

'You're a nice girl, Jenny Matherson, did you know that?'

Too late she wished she hadn't said it. Beneath the piled and sophisticated hair, Jenny's face was pink with embar-rassment.

'Blimey,' she forced a laugh, 'I been called a lot of things, but never that. Anyway, Rhoda, it wasn't me I came to talk about, it was you and this adventure of yours.'

'There's very little to tell, only what I said just now. Yet, Jen, I have a deep-down feeling that today has been an important one in my life, a stepping stone to ... to what? I don't know. I can't see ahead to where it might be leading me, yet I have a feeling, almost a physical excitement, that after standing on the edge for so long I'm in the swim of things.'

'Gosh. And you know what, Rhoda? When I first came here, before everything went wrong – well, all that – I used to look out of my window at this house and think of you and see you as the luckiest, happiest lady alive.'

Rhoda digested her words before she answered.

'Luckiest ... happiest ... Of course I was, and of course I always shall be in the things that really count. You talk about being ashamed to wear gardening gloves, so how ashamed does it make me to stand back and acknowledge how discontented I was when I already had all the things that are worthwhile?' Then, with a sudden smile and a hint of that elfin expression of yesteryear, 'But if *then* I couldn't see the wood for the trees, now all the shadows are gone.'

'Funny things you say. What time's Mr Harding getting home? Got time to come over to the cottage with me and have a cuppa, or do you have to start cooking? I bet he's cocky as anything that you landed yourself a job like that, isn't he, Rhoda?'

'If I'm Rhoda, how is it he's still Mr?' She evaded Jenny's question.

'You told me it was OK for me to call you Rhoda. Remember, that first time I came here, me and Mick.'

'I remember.' She took Jenny's hand sensing more than seeing the dark shadow that had fallen. 'I remember it all, Jen. Dear sunny little Mickey, he held out his dog for me to see. Remember?'

Jenny nodded, her eyes swimming with tears.

'No one talks about him. We ought to talk about him, Rhoda.'

'We'll never lose him, Jen. And he knows it.'

'I'd have gone round the twist if you hadn't been here. Oughtn't to have been like that. Ought to have been Michael I'd talk to. But I couldn't. He couldn't either.'

'Every time you think losing Michael left you heart-broken, remember that,' Rhoda said. 'You both loved Mickey, but you weren't close enough to help each other.'

'Even when we don't want it to, life goes on. We have to pick up the pieces that are left and get on with it, don't we.'

If Rhoda had felt ashamed a few moments ago, that was as nothing compared with how she felt at that moment.

'Come on, Jen, let's see about that cup of tea you were offering me.' Not a hint that she suspected one reason for the invitation was that Jenny dreaded returning alone to the empty cottage.

'Did Silas Clutterbuck show up?' The question cut into her thoughts as they started out across the green.

'No, and from what Matthew said, once he starts treating patients in a different district there's usually no word until his next visit in this area. Matthew's place seems to be where he returns to roost.'

'I expect you're glad he's not there looking over your shoulder. Like I said, he's an uncomfortable sort of person. Ever so kind, I know he is, but just sort of unsettling. He knows too much for folk to be comfortable with.'

Through the following two or three months, Rhoda went to Oakleigh perhaps a couple of days a week, sometimes more, sometimes for no more than the odd few hours while Matthew was making a personal delivery of some rare and precious publication. Only on one occasion did she work for five days at a stretch.

It was during the first week of September, the third and last day she'd be at Oakleigh during that week. Matthew was due back late in the afternoon from a visit to the north, to an ancestral home that had fallen on hard times, like so many others. When at about midway through the morning she heard the key in the lock, she expected he must have travelled south overnight and waited for his customary booming greeting, 'Hello there, good to be back,' his voice in keeping with his oversized appearance.

Instead, what she heard from the 'behind-the-shop' kitchen where she was making a salad for her lunch, was a lighter, unfamiliar tread.

'Matthew, is that you?' She mustn't let whoever it was suspect the way her heart was pounding. What if someone had stolen a key and broken in knowing that Matthew was away? A tomato in one hand, a knife in the other, she stood stock still as the footsteps came closer, down the passage toward the kitchen.

'So he's away? Didn't he tell you I was coming?'

'Silas! I thought someone had broken in—'

'Hence the knife,' he laughed as he spoke, taking both knife and tomato from her and kissing her lightly on either cheek in Continental fashion, the unfamiliar action leaving her speechless. 'That looks good, all straight from your garden?'

'Not the nuts or orange,' she too laughed, suddenly uplifted by the turn of events. 'They're there simply to add colour to a rather dreary assembly.'

'To a hungry man it looks just about perfect. What's with it?'

'Crusty bread, no butter.'

'Nothing better. Now, here's the deal: I'll walk across the green to get us a couple of old Mr Hodge's pork pies. If you've never eaten one before, you're in for a treat. Where he gets his constant supply of pork from I've no idea – one asks no questions about such perfection. In exchange you can give me half of your salad – and a hunk of your crusty bread. You're on?'

She nodded and without her knowing it her dark eyes shone with excitement. The expression wasn't lost on him.

'Wait,' she called after him as he opened the front door, 'my bike's propped against the side wall. You'll be quicker on that.'

Ten minutes later, they sat by the empty fireplace in the sitting room that had never got used to its commercial use, their easy chairs pulled close to the coffee table that stood between them.

'Now tell me how you're getting on here. Did I do right in steering you towards it? Matthew is delighted, but what about you?'

'It's not a bit like I imagined having a job would be. In a way I feel like a cheat to take my money at the end of the week. But, did you do right you say? Yes, oh yes Silas, it's so good to know I have to be at a certain place at a certain time. Funny, isn't it. I bet most people who have worked for years would think I'm crazy. Perhaps you do.'

It was said lightly, not expecting an answer. No wonder

135

she was disconcerted when, with his knife and fork at rest on his plate, he gazed at her long and hard, making her recall the things Jenny had said about him.

Then he shook his head. 'No Rhoda, you are extremely sane. Tell me, are you finding yourself? Are you finding what you were looking for?'

A flippant reply would have been easy, but he deserved better.

'I think I am . . . I'm sure I am. Now that both the girls have gone, now it's just Alec and me, I had to dig deep and rekindle the girl I used to be, I just *had* to.'

'And is she still there or have the years laid her to rest? That's what happens, you know.'

Another question that deserved an honest answer, this time one that made her dig deeper into her mind.

'Yes, she's still there. If I'd been able to lay her to rest none of this would have happened.'

'Shall I get in your way if I'm around the place here? Not all the time, of course. I have a clinic about to open at Brackleford Hospital. War does the devil's work, you know. My patients aren't all from those who've been on the fighting front . . . there are so many whose lives have been torn apart – the loss of husbands, sons, daughters, lives shattered.'

'And you help them find a way to walk on the road peace has brought?'

'I try, yes I honestly try with all that's in me. To understand things that we haven't suffered ourselves is hard. It makes one dig deeper into one's own soul than is comfortable. There but for the grace of God . . . and for all the training, for all the knowledge, how would I cope?' For a moment they sat in silence, then he asked, 'How is our little friend Jenny? A brave heart, but with the cards stacked against her. I'm glad she has you for a friend, Rhoda.'

'She'll get over being deserted by Michael. She's strong and was too good for him in my opinion – although that certainly wasn't the way he looked at it.'

'Humph. So I gathered.'

'But losing Mickey will stay with her always.'

He nodded. 'Of course it will. One doesn't get over that sort of love. Her comfort will come from remembering. That sort of pure love is stronger than the misery and sadness of loss. In the beginning she can't see it like that, but in time that's what she will find over the years.'

'I know you're right. I just wish I could help her more *now.*'

'She knows she isn't alone, she knows you're there for her. I've only ever talked to her on that one occasion, but through all the anguish I knew then that your being there for her was one golden thread.'

Rhoda's mind leapt back to what Jenny had said about being uncomfortable in Silas's presence. Yes, he was different from anyone she'd known; yes, he made one feel that he saw right into your mind. And yet as they shared their makeshift lunch she felt utterly at ease.

'If you're going to be staying here, Matthew won't need me for a while.'

'Indeed he will. I shan't be here that much during the daytime as I have clinics most days either in Brackleford or one or other of the cottage hospitals. He's always happy for me to muck in with him when I'm in the region, but unfortunately I shan't be able to persuade you to make a habit of our lunching together. Shame.'

She forced her face to smile. 'I've enjoyed it too,' she told him.

Only as the days went by and she saw no more of him did she acknowledge to herself just how much she had enjoyed it. The memory would come back to her at unexpected moments, perhaps when she was hurrying to prepare a meal before Alec got home, perhaps when she was working her way through a pile of ironing, even – and increasingly often – while she conjured up those Saturday night fantasies as she reached towards the elusive satisfaction of lovemaking.

*

Muriel Wheeler always sat at the table she chose to call her 'desk' in the comer of Alec's office so that he had become as used to her presence as he had to the sight of the unshaded light bulb or the steel filing cabinet. The room was functional and comfortable and Muriel fitted seamlessly into the background. In the early days there had been no separate space to fit an office worker, but even after he acquired extra buildings and could have given her somewhere away from him, it was something that didn't enter his head. The arrangement was convenient; they worked closely together – all he had to do with the morning mail was read it and write brief messages, and he knew the replies would be on his desk for signature with no further effort. Often he watched her working, sitting as she did with her back to him, and recognised how blessed he was.

However, on a morning in December, Alec's daily routine was being knocked off course. For a quarter of an hour or so he had been delayed in conversation with one of his wealthier clients, making sure he gave no hint that he was anxious to get back to the office and the end-of-month accounts for which Muriel had prepared the cheques so that they only required his signature. The task wouldn't take long but, man of habit that he was, he liked to get them in the post ready for the midday collection.

'Sorry,' he said as he came through the door from the workshop, 'I got held up. Are we still in time for the post?' He spoke without glancing at Muriel, turning his swivel chair to sit at his desk. It was only then that some sixth sense told him all wasn't well with her. His pen already in his hand, he pushed the pile of papers to one side. 'Are you all right?' Surely that sound, somewhere between a sniff and a snort, told its own story.

'So ashamed ... behaving badly ...' came the watery reply.

'Nonsense. Can I help? Do you want to tell me what the trouble is? Is it your mother? Ought you to be at home?'

'In a way it's Mother,' and this time Muriel turned to

138

face him, the sight of her contorted face and reddened eyelids coming as a shock to him. 'Got no business to bring my troubles to work with me. I'm sorry, Mr Harding, I don't usually let things come between me and what I do here. But – oh dear, there I go again ...' And indeed there she went again, tears streaming down her normally pale face, even her reddened nose adding an independent drip to the picture of misery.

Alec crossed the room to the door that divided the office from the workshop and closed it, then went to where the poor dejected creature was trying to mop up with no sign of success.

'Muriel, my dear, if your mother is ill then you should be at home. I'll manage, honestly. If there's typing to be done, Rhoda will do it this evening. Nothing is so vital that it's worth upsetting yourself like this.'

'She's not ill, not like you mean. Sometimes I think she has more energy than I have, the way she cleans and polishes the house. But there's more than one kind of illness. It was soon after Dad died that it started ...' And out poured the story of how her mother had become more and more housebound, giving all her abundant energy to her battle against the slightest speck of dust. She would cook, she would polish until every surface shone like a mirror, no curtain would hang out of line by so much as half an inch, each cushion would be set at exactly the right angle. None of this was a surprise to Alec – piecing two and two together, he had formed his own opinion over the years and surely Muriel was just as meticulously exact in all she did. Yet Mrs Wheeler had not only contributed clothing coupons towards a new outfit for Etty to take on her honeymoon, she had attended the wedding and appeared to be, if anything, abnormally excited by the occasion. So what could have happened to trigger Muriel's uncharacteristic show of emotion?

'It must be very hard for you, my dear,' he said kindly. 'I'm not surprised if sometimes you need to let off steam.

139

I'll put the kettle on the ring, shall I? What about a cup of something, and I have a flask in my drawer – a drop of whisky will buck you up.'

Muriel was about to say that she didn't drink, that she'd been brought up to believe that drink was a temptation of the Devil. But, surprising herself, she gave Alec a watery smile and nodded her agreement. It was after she'd taken the first gulp and felt it's tingling warmth in her throat that she took up her tale of woe.

'It was yesterday morning the letter came. It was from Malcolm Hawkes – you know, the letting agent in Broad Street. We've lived in that house in Western Avenue as long as I can remember. Mother is in a dreadful state. You see, Mr Hawkes says the owner wants us to find somewhere else, but you know how impossible it is to find a place to rent, or even to buy for that matter. We've got notice to be out by the end of next month. It's not for myself I'm so worried, just a bedsit would do me, but Mother isn't in a state to cope with an upset like this. She says it'll kill her. And Mr Harding, from the way she is, I'm frightened that that's the truth.' Tipping back the glass she drained the final dregs of neat whisky.

'I'm sorry, Miss Wheeler. As you say, housing is a dreadful problem and, from the way of things, won't be better for years.'

'I went to the council office during my dinner break yesterday, hoping to take some good news home. But all they could do was put our name on the waiting list for a house. We're number two thousand and three on the list.'

'Then, my dear, we must discount help coming from that direction.'

His kindly tone, the use of the endearment and most of all of the word 'we' gave Muriel more comfort than the tot of whisky she'd swallowed too quickly for comfort.

'I've put a card in the newsagent's window. But no good will come of that – I'm not stupid enough to expect that it might. Mother suggested it, though, and I was simply

140

relieved to think she was taking on board that we have to do *something*.'

'I wonder if any of our farmers might have a vacant cottage,' Alec mused. 'The trouble with being in the country is there might not be public transport.'

He'd been doing little more than thinking aloud and was surprised by her response. With a quick movement she turned towards him, caring nothing now for swollen eyelids or reddened nose.

'No! I want to be in town, I want to be near here. Compared with not being able to come here each day, losing my home is nothing. I'll find somewhere. Don't mention it to any of the customers. Please, Mr Harding, promise me you won't.'

Alec found himself surprisingly moved by her uncharacteristic outburst. Quiet, placid, reliable Miss Wheeler, as much part of his life in the office as his desk or his telephone, yet coming here each day was the most important thing in her poor, narrow life.

'I promise. We've worked together for more than twenty years, so I'm not likely to try to find you somewhere that would mean my losing you. Now mop your face, my dear, and we'll go through the post. This afternoon, instead of coming straight back here after you've been home to dinner, I suggest you take a walk around town, call at all the estate agents, see if they have anything, ask them to keep an eye open for you.'

Just as she was recovering, his kindness was almost her undoing.

'I ought not to bring you my troubles. All the extra work you've had to take on now that Andrew isn't here – he told me I could call him by his Christian name – and I come—'

'And after all the years we've known each other, surely we could manage Muriel and Alec couldn't we?'

She felt her face grow warm – surely he must see the flush, although even she wasn't sure whether it came from excitement or embarrassment. In fact, he didn't so much as notice, for at that second the situation was saved by the shrill ring of the telephone and while Alec was talking to a client she made a start on sorting the mail. That afternoon she did as he said and made a tour of the local house agents, a tour that proved as fruitless as she had feared.

To Rhoda, Muriel Wheeler had always seemed a pitiable creature, colourless in appearance and personality. The impression was bolstered by the fact that for so many years she had resented Alec's dogmatic refusal to have her, his wife, working in the business, her suggestions always being met with the same response: Miss Wheeler managed beautifully, she was efficient and reliable. However, on hearing the news of the Wheelers' threatened eviction any resentment was forgotten.

'But that's dreadful! We can't let that happen, Alec. I'll ask around in the village. That Metal Box firm has been moving back to London. You know where I mean? Beyond the laundry in those warehouses on the Oakleigh road. When I cycled past, I saw the notice saying it was coming up for auction. The workers from there couldn't all have been local, and if they're going back to London they must have lived somewhere down here.'

'Find out all you can. Looking after the home seems to be almost an obsession with Mrs Wheeler – to be stuck in a room in someone else's house would unhinge her. She's in a dreadful state of stress – and of course that all rebounds on Muriel.' Then taking up the newspaper he settled himself while he waited for her to call him to the table. 'Here's you with the sort of situation most women crave and throwing it aside so that you can find some sort of unnecessary independence in that tomfool job, while a woman like Mrs Wheeler's one joy in life is to make a home comfortable and it gets taken from her.'

Rhoda had cycled home from her day at Oakleigh feeling content with life. The working day had given her a feeling of satisfaction that she had coped with no less

142

than four callers, all satisfactorily, added to which she had had Silas for company during the afternoon. Listening to the new angle of Alec's all-too-often-repeated opinion of her taking a job, just for a moment some of that contentment was stripped from her. On that day, though, even Alec hadn't the power to burst her bubble of self-esteem. Silently she voiced the opinion that if Mrs Wheeler thought life shouldn't be more than the chores of housekeeping, then more fool her.

Humming under her breath, Rhoda went to the kitchen to dish up their meal. Alec watched her retreating, his brow furrowed with annoyance. Yet he knew he wasn't being fair. There was more self-pity than sadness in his sigh as he took out his pen to start on the crossword puzzle; why did things have to change? Both the girls gone, Rhoda discontented with their home . . . it seemed to him that only *he* remained constant.

Next day, on her way to Oakleigh, Rhoda went to the manager's office of the Metal Box Company. As she told her story of the mother and daughter shortly to be evicted after being exemplary tenants for some forty years, it didn't occur to her that the reason she was listened to with sympathy and her enquiries met with a willingness to help were in a large part because of her natural charm of which she was quite unaware. In truth, if timid and colourless Muriel had knocked on the manager's door, it was unlikely she would have been given the opportunity to take over the remaining years on the ten-year lease of the cottage he had moved into at the end of 1939. Muriel's letter of gratitude to Rhoda was touchingly pathetic, somehow fitting the image of the one-time girl who had developed into such a doggedly faithful part of the business. And it was because of her move to the cottage on the Oakleigh road that Alec took the country detour to Brackleford each day, collecting her on the way.

Silently resigned to Rhoda's new routine, although his

opinion remained unchanged and he had high principles concerning unnecessary use of petrol, he did suggest on wet mornings that he could go a mile or two out of his way and put her down in Oakleigh. But she preferred her bicycle, an inner voice warning her that if she had to wait in Oakleigh for him each evening so that they returned together to Timberley, it would add fuel to his resentment of her determination to find something for herself outside their home. She walked a tightrope, juggling home life and work, always careful not to give Alec cause to imagine that Timberley no longer counted. Then, too, there was Jenny. That early evening hour with Jenny was important to both of them.

So the year ended, the unchanging routine carrying them into another spring and the first anniversary of the celebrations of victory in Europe. It was in August, exactly a year since peace had come in the Far East, that Etty came to see her mother in the house in Oakleigh and brought the news Rhoda had hoped for: Etty and Andrew were expecting their first child. In November of that same year, Stewart Carling was demobbed and he and Natalie were offered their first engagement together.

'So I suppose that's the pattern of things to come,' Rhoda said to Alec as she read the cutting Natalie had sent them from the provincial newspaper. 'Like it or not, Alec, they are a team and, from the opinion of the local reporter, they are expected to become household names.'

Alec remained tight-lipped and silent. There wasn't a man born good enough for Natalie and most certainly not that uncouth clodhopper Stewart Carling. As for Rhoda, she believed she could see a clear path to the future: Etty in a happy marriage and bringing up her family at the manor; Natalie teamed with Stewart and rising in fame and fortune. And Alec and her? He had been made to realise that just because she looked outside her home to widen her horizons, it didn't mean that he and the girls meant less to her.

Her new-found confidence blinkered her, blinded her to the truth that the wider the horizons the greater the opportunity for trouble.

Chapter Seven

Kind, honest, loving Etty had always found life a pleasurable affair. Until she knew Andrew, falling in love had played no part. She had supposed that one of these days she might be married and have a family but 'one of these days' had had no bearing on the satisfaction she'd found in the work she did and the contacts she made on the farms she and her tool bag visited when she worked in the family business. Then had come Andrew, friendly in a way that had seemed brotherly – or so she had made herself believe as increasingly he had filled her thoughts.

With marriage had come joy beyond anything she had imagined possible. Alec had assumed she and Andrew would build a lasting relationship based on firm friendship, but Rhoda understood Etty better. She had no doubt that she and Andrew would have a good marriage, but surely friendship alone could never reach to the heights that must be the firm foundation on which they'd build. In the intimacy of married life they were more than friends, more than lovers, more even than soul-mates. Together they were complete. Even knowing Etty and loving her all her life, neither Rhoda nor Alec suspected the passion that had lain dormant. Certainly Natalie had loved and admired her elder sister, but never seen her as sexually aware. Only Andrew had been certain of the spark that waited to be ignited and that was perhaps because he alone had the power to stir it to life.

There was nothing shy about Etty, nothing coy or coquetish. From that evening of the victory celebration when he'd told her he loved her, she had rejoiced in the thought that soon their love would be complete. She had held nothing back, she loved him with every fibre of her being – her healthy, strong body was her joy and his too. The family still clung to their original impressions for there was nothing demonstrative about the young couple: they were friends, they were happy; that their ultimate joy in each other was kept behind the closed bedroom door had no bearing on prudishness – for them such a thing didn't exist. They worked together on the farm at Sedgeley, Etty secretly trying to watch that Andrew didn't overstretch himself; they listened to the news and discussed affairs in a world that had been torn apart by war; they found plea-sure in sharing the crossword puzzle in the daily paper, sorting the staff wages, ordering fodder for the animals, all the everyday things that were part of their lives; then at the end of the day they came together in a union they knew was perfect. They wanted children, but had to wait until nature decided the time was right. They had been married almost a year before Etty was confident that she was pregnant.

'Hello Mum. I rang the house but when there was no reply I guessed I'd find you here. Gosh, you've got a cushy number,' Etty said with a laugh as Rhoda opened the door of the house on Oakleigh Green about mid-morning on a day in November. 'Not a customer in sight. I wouldn't mind betting you've got a good fire going.'

'Right on both counts. Lovely surprise, Ett. Where's the car? Did Andrew drop you off?'

'I came on my bike. Now don't look like that, Mum. I may be beginning to look like a young elephant but I'm fit as a flea. The exercise is good for me – and for junior too. Although a fireside seat won't come amiss. Gosh, it's bitterly cold in that fog. Did you cycle over or did Dad drop you off?'

'Yes, I braved it. Alec would have brought me but if I come with him I have to wait until he goes home and that means I can't have a meal ready when he gets back. Cycling is best. But at the risk of sounding like a fussy old hen, I can't pretend to like seeing you riding – what is it? – quite five miles each way. Didn't Andrew try and stop you.'

'He wasn't there so he didn't know. He had an appointment with the accountant so he took the car to Brackleford and left it at the station. He won't be back for ages – he mentioned about the four something out of Waterloo. I hope it's not foggy like this when he gets to London. Can we make some coffee, Mum?'

This was like old times, Rhoda thought, as she poured cold water into the lower globe of the coffee-making machine and Etty put the filter followed by the ground coffee in the upper funnel. Then, the methylated spirit lamp sending its flame to lap around the glass globe, they went back to the fireside, prepared to wait and enjoy the tempting aroma of things to come.

'Mum ...' One hesitant word, but enough to destroy Rhoda's perfect moment.

'Well? Go on. Is something bothering you? Things do, the first time.'

'You mean the baby? Crumbs no, I'm fit as I ever was – if anything I seem to have more get up and go than normal. But Mum, Drew worries me. Don't tell anyone, not even Dad. I ought not to say anything, it's sort of like breaking a trust to talk about him like this. But I can't talk to Drew himself about it. If I did he'd just put up on an extra show. I know he tries to hide it from me so I pretend I don't notice. You know how cheery he always is ... always was ... and nothing has changed. But being with him all the time I've come to realise that an awful lot of it is a sort of façade. Catch him off guard, or see him when he comes in from the farm, and sometimes he looks ghastly. He'll sit down and open the newspaper, hold it

148

open in front of him so that he's hidden, but even then it's frightening to hear the effort he has in breathing.'

'Was he like that when he worked for Alec?'

'I just don't know. If he needed to rest while he was out I wouldn't mind betting he found somewhere to pull off the road until he got over it. When he got back to the market he was always full of beans. So is he not as fit as he was? Ought he to be doing so much on the farm? I could take a lot of it off his shoulders – I'm tough as old boots, you know I am. But it's that silly male pride thing. It would be bad for him if I made an issue of it.'

'Does he have regular medical checks?'

'When I asked him he said yes he did, he wasn't due for one and they were nothing, just routine.' Then, turning to her mother and speaking with none of her normal happy confidence, she said, 'If I told him how worried I am it would be like losing faith. I feel that's what it is even telling you.' Rhoda felt the cold hand of fear when she saw the expression on Etty's face. 'But ... Mum, suppose he's worse than he wants me to know. Mum, suppose – no I can't even say it.'

For Rhoda, fear gave way to something akin to relief. This wasn't a young wife whose marriage was based on friendship alone.

'Then don't say it, Ett love. And don't even think it. Andrew is a sensible young man. He knows he has physical limitations. And perhaps we should all be thankful he has, for if he'd stayed in the Merchant Navy he wouldn't have come to Alec for a job and you wouldn't be sitting here worrying today.'

'Didn't know I could ever feel like this. Didn't know there could be the sort of feeling that another person is a sort of part of you.'

Rhoda took her hand and held it tightly. 'Then thank God that you found out.'

'I do, Mum. Every day I say it. And Mum, I'm glad I talked to you. It's helped me to get things in perspective.

149

Of course he's sensible and of course he knows just what he should do and what he shouldn't. I've got to trust him. That's what you're saying, isn't it?' Then, with a change of expression and that ready smile back in place, 'Coffee's hissing, it sounds as if it's done. Shall I pour or is that your prerogative as hostess here?'

'No, I'll go and unearth a packet of biscuits I've squirrelled away in the kitchen.' That she'd squirrelled them away in case Silas arrived unexpectedly was forgotten. In fact, he hadn't been to the local hospitals for two or three months. Should that mean he was due to come again soon? And, if it did, where was the logic in it mattering to her? Yet, the biscuits put out on a plate, she made sure her question was said casually as she asked if Andrew had heard from him lately.

'There was a letter last week. He says he'd been hoping to get over this way again, but demobilisation seems to produce more rather than less patients. Don't people make a mess of things! People? Politicians? How's Jen, Mum? Talking of making a mess of things, the war certainly did that for her.'

'I don't think that's true. If she hadn't fallen for Michael she wouldn't have got pregnant with Mickey and her life was made so much richer for having him.'

'Blow that, Mum. All she's left with is the agony of losing the poor little darling.'

'She'll never lose the memory of him or the knowledge that he loved her above all else. She must be richer for that, Ett. We can't be afraid to love in case we can't hang on to the moment.'

'You and Silas should get together. It's all too deep and introspective for me! Hark, there's the door, you must have a customer. I'll take the tray and hide in the kitchen.'

Rhoda laughed, getting up to answer the knock. 'You needn't. There's plenty of coffee left – perhaps our enquirer might be glad of a cup. That's the joy of this place, it's more like a home than a shop.' By that time she was almost at the front door, automatically making sure her bearing gave the impression of charm and confidence. But as she opened it, rather than some learned client, she came face to face with someone barely more than a child, someone she knew she'd seen before but couldn't remember where, a young girl with her face red from exertion.

'Mrs Long sent me on my bike,' the caller panted. 'Said to ride as quick as I could.' And then Rhoda realised who she was.

'Tilly, it's Tilly, isn't it? Do you want my daughter? Come inside.' The charm she had believed she had assumed in readiness for an official caller remained unchanged. 'Etty,' she called. But already Etty had heard the voices and was standing in the doorway of the sitting room. In her eyes was the same fear Rhoda had seen earlier.

'Oh Mrs Clutterbuck, m'am, Mrs Long sent me. She said you'd told her you were coming here but we didn't know how to find the place in the phone book, see.'

'What's happened, Tilly? Is something wrong?' A stupid question, for why else would the child have been sent poste haste on a five-mile bicycle ride?

'There was this telephone call you see, m'am. I got the number here on a bit of paper. Mrs Long wrote it out – got them to say it twice, she did, to make sure it was right. It's some place in London, Mrs Long said.'

'It was from Drew? From my husband?'

'No, m'am. Seems it was from the place where he'd gone to up there in London. The man said we got to get word to you so that you could telephone him as soon as you could.'

Etty took the paper.

'The phone's on the desk in the other room.' Rhoda tried to sound calm, but her head was filled with the clamour of those alarm bells. Not Andrew himself, someone phoning with a message, an urgent message. If *her* heart was pounding, what must Etty's be doing?

'Go and have a warm in that room, Tilly. I'll fetch

151

another cup and saucer. There are biscuits on the plate; help yourself.'

Tilly's morning was turning into something special.

On her way to fetch the cup and saucer, Rhoda hovered by the open doorway to the second downstairs room, the one with the desk Silas used to write up his notes when he was holding the fort for Matthew.

'This is Etty Clutterbuck. You rang me earlier. I'm sorry I couldn't get back to you sooner. Is my husband still with you?'

'It was Dr Prentice who called you, Mrs Clutterbuck.'

'Doctor? Who are you? Is that Clarence and Domby's office?' Etty quoted the name of the firm of accountants.

'No, Mrs Clutterbuck. Your husband had an appointment to see Dr Prentice this morning. He arrived but was very unwell. Dr Prentice is still with him. I'm so sorry I can't give you any more details.'

'Can't you put my call through to the surgery?'

'Dr Prentice accompanied your husband to his private clinic. As soon as he gets back I'll ask him to call you again. Are you at home now?'

'No.' How unlike Etty it was to sound so out of control of a situation. 'I'll give you this number. I'll wait here for the call. Tell them I'm waiting. Please, please see someone rings me soon. It must have been the fog got into him. He'll be all right. He will, won't he?'

'I'll see Dr Prentice calls you on that number as soon as he returns from the clinic.'

Replacing the receiver, Etty still stood there, both hands on the instrument, her eyes closed.

'Ett?'

'Mum, Drew must have known something was wrong. Got to wait here – that's OK, is it? Must have been the fog. He told me he was going to the accountant, but really he must have been seeing the consultant. Mustn't he? Or did something happen to him and he got taken there? No, she said he had an appointment. I should have gone with him.

152

It's the fog, it gets right into him, he can't breathe. I'll drive up and bring him home – damn the petrol. He's not to attempt to come home by train.'

'We'll ring Alec. He'll drive you up.'

'What? No. No, I'll go by myself. I'd rather. I expect it's silly, but I want Drew to know that whatever happens we can always manage on our own. Him and me, together, we'll be fine.' Then, forcing her face into a smile, she added, 'You just watch us. Is Tilly having a coffee?'

'I'm supposed to be getting her a cup and saucer. We'll have another cup with her. Perhaps the call won't take long.'

In fact it was more than an hour before the shrill sound shattered the silence. By that time Tilly had set off back to the Manor, keen to be the one to impart such a story. Alec had been alerted and had driven over to Oakleigh so that he could get Etty to the station where Andrew had left the car. He and Rhoda both hoped that they would bend her will to theirs and she would agree to be driven to London. But Etty's mind was made up: she, and she alone, would bring Andrew home.

When the call finally came – and bearing in mind that Rhoda was employed to care for a business, it was she who lifted the receiver – it was after two o'clock. Even knowing that a motor journey to London would be in ever thickening fog and darkness, Etty was already on her feet anxious to be off. But the call threw her plans into jeopardy: Andrew had been taken to the clinic's private hospital and for the present that was where he must remain. He was being given oxygen and every care was being taken for his well-being. A reassuring call and yet one that left Etty feeling utterly helpless and alone.

Always quick to make decisions, Etty's mind was made up. She would take the train to Waterloo, then a taxi to the hospital.

'But you have nowhere to stay,' Alec said, seeing disaster at every turn.

'Don't fuss, Dad. There are plenty of hotels in London and I'm sure I'll be able to pick up a toothbrush and night-dress somewhere. If I can't, then I'll go without. But I promise I'll phone you tonight as soon as I know what's happening with Drew.'

Alec wasn't satisfied. One look at his face told them her self-assurance was only making him more certain she was walking into trouble.

'Let your mother drive us to the station and I'll come with you. You can't be alone there in London without so much as a bed for the night.'

'Dad, I shan't be alone. Drew will be there – and anyway, at this hospital place they won't see me out on the street with nowhere to sleep. By the morning we shall have a much better idea of how he is. Perhaps if I hire a taxi to bring us, they'll let him come home. But as long as I can talk to him, make sure that he is . . . is sort of content in himself about what's happened, then we can start to look ahead. I just have to see him, talk with him.'

Alec knew when it was no use arguing and by teatime Etty was on the train and well on the way to Waterloo.

At the hospital she found Andrew half sitting in bed and half lying, heavily sedated and wearing an oxygen mask.

'By morning we hope he will be stabilised,' the sister told her. 'Tonight he won't be aware that you've come.'

Etty was used to knowing herself to be in charge of the situation. But that night she felt numb, gripped by fear she wouldn't let take shape. She told herself that it was a good omen that she found a hotel close to the hospital. She was ravenously hungry not having eaten since that biscuit during the morning, yet when she asked for something to be sent up to her room, the thought of eating made her feel sick. Sitting by the hissing gas fire, she unconsciously found some sort of comfort in cradling the hump that was their baby.

This is the future, she told herself as she felt the pressure against her hand. Junior, our child. And Drew will be

154

well, please, please make Drew well. I knew something was wrong so why couldn't he have talked about it to me? Was he too frightened? No, we must never be frightened. Whatever we have to face, just so long as we face it together, we'll be fine. Us and the baby. He'll soon be home again . . . things will be like they were.

Taking up her knife and fork she cut into her 'too late for dinner' meal of mushrooms on toast. Perhaps the food helped her find her courage. For it was an hour or so later when, lying awake in bed, she made herself look to the future and see a way forward. Tomorrow she would talk to Drew, she vowed, making herself believe that by the next day he, too, would be ready to look ahead.

Maybe her trust had something to do with it but, whatever the reason, when she arrived at the hospital the next morning she found him awake, propped to sit up in bed, the oxygen cylinder still at the bedside but no longer in use. That she was there didn't seem to surprise him – he would have been more surprised if she hadn't come when she heard what had happened.

Holding out his hand to her, he felt it taken in her strong grasp.

'I should have told you,' he said with a sheepish smile, 'but I knew you'd worry. I thought if I came up to see Dr Prentice he'd reassure me. Did I think that? Or did I just hope? Things aren't too good, Ett. Now, with the baby coming . . . now, of all times, they tell me I've got to live at half cock. I can't make them understand that we have a farm to run, that it's what we do, what we want to do. They've no idea—'

'Darling Drew, never mind all that. Yesterday when I saw you I was so frightened, now today here you are carping about something that you and I together can sort out.'

'Ett, I want to work. We are a team, I'm just not going to give you more than your share to do.'

155

Bending over him she kissed his forehead then rumpled his usually tidy hair.

'Yes, we're a team, Drew. And if one of us has a problem, then it's the other one's problem too. Last night I got it all worked out. I prayed like mad that this morning I would find you on the road back. And this morning we both have to say a huge 'thank you'. If this is the situation we've been faced with, then we'll sort it out together. I'm not daft, you know. I realise that Junior makes me more cumbersome each day and even after he puts in an appearance I'm not going to have as much time on my hands as I had before. So what do we do? I'll tell you. Men are coming out of the forces all the time, men who'll jump at the chance of work with a cottage thrown in. We don't need a manager; you and me like things to be done the way we want. And we're quite capable of training any men we hire. I'm not shirking. I'd willingly take on some of the things you've been doing if I weren't going to be tied up over the next few months. And then, thinking ahead, once this baby is born, perhaps by next year or soon after, there'll be another, and so on. We want a proper family. That's our future Drew. We've always said "children" not "a child".'

His expression frightened her. 'Drew ... Drew what is it?'

'Ett, why should loving you so much make me feel – oh God, I don't know.' Where was the habitually cheery smile? 'Been so bloody frightened.'

'And you hid it from me just as if I wasn't as involved as you were yourself. What sort of a team does that make us?'

'I know. And I'm sorry. Everything was so perfect. It's only these last few weeks that I've felt so rough.'

'Has Dr Prentice given you a reason?'

'He came in first thing this morning.' Then, with an almost normal grin, 'Even before the cock crowed. These chaps work hard for their living. He told me I'd been over-doing things and asking for trouble. It seems that I have an infection in the lung that's left, nothing life threatening as long as it's nipped in the bud – if I'd had two lungs I'd probably have shaken it off with nothing more than temporarily feeling a bit under the weather. However, he wants to keep me here for a while. I would guess a week or so. Then I'll be home, darling, and we'll start to sort out the future.' His expression had gradually changed, the smile being replaced by something she hated to see: not quite fear, not quite depression, yet an expression that was a stranger to his normally bright counternance. 'It's not the way we planned.'

'So what?' Etty carried his hand to her hump, her cheerful smile giving no hint of her sadness for him. 'Feel the kick? Bet you can. Being a dad is as important as being a mum. As for the farm, we're the ones who will be at the helm. We don't need to load bales or get up at crack of dawn to milk cows – our job will be to see that things are done the way we know they should be.' Then, as if she'd turned a page and put all that behind her, she said briskly, 'Listen Drew, if you have to rest up here for another week or so, I'll get on back and go to the Labour Exchange and see if there is anyone suitable waiting for work. You do trust me?'

'You know I do.'

She laughed. 'Thought I'd better just check. Then, when you get home, as soon as you are fit – and I mean honestly fit, not covering up and hiding the truth from me – then we'll settle into a new pattern. There's nothing going to get us beaten, we're a team – you, me and the brood of young Clutterbucks we shall take huge pleasure in producing.'

'A farm won't stand still waiting our convenience,' he said. It wasn't his words so much as his laboured breathing that warned her she couldn't move his thoughts as fast as she could her own. Fear still lurked not far beneath the surface.

'For the moment everything is under control. We have staff enough to cope at this time of year – and if the machinery lets us down I can just about get into my over-

157

alls.' With a laugh that told him how pleased she was with her condition, she told him, 'Providing I don't do up the buttons. Drew, I wish I could stay in London, so I could come and chivvy you along each day. But now I've seen for myself that you are on the mend, I shall go home today and get cracking on finding either a keen and trainable young ex-serviceman or someone with the sort of experience we need.'

'Ett . . .' Just her name, as if he were lost for words.

'Drew . . .' she mimicked. 'Darling Drew. And promise me, scouts' honour, you won't play silly devils with me again, pretending nothing was wrong like that. Don't you see, if we'd shared it we would have been all the stronger.'

'You make me feel a heel. Ett, oh damn it, I can't think of the words without sounding like something in some sloppy film.'

'I know, Drew. Me too. Hurry up and get home, then everything will be right again. I'll phone the hospital every day and as soon as they say you can come, I'll drive up and get you.'

'I don't like to think of you driv—'

'Just think about the return journey, you, me and little 'un here. Honestly, I reckon he/she/whichever is going to be an acrobat.' Then, thoughtfully, as if she was struggling to find the right words, 'You know, over these last months, feeling the baby getting stronger and each day somehow becoming more of a person, I find myself thinking so often about Jenny. How could she bear it, losing Mickey?'

'She lost more than Mickey, she lost Michael too.'

'And good riddance, that's my opinion. How that pompous prick sired Mickey I shall never know.'

Andrew's laugh was spontaneous and reassuring. He was on the road back.

It was two days later, a day when the fog had hung like a blanket over the countryside and the light had faded even earlier than usual for November. Rhoda pushed her bicycle out of the shed and wheeled it backwards along the path at the side of the house on Oakleigh Green, the rear light guiding her. The prospect of the ride home wasn't inviting and she had been tempted to phone Alec and tell him she would wait for him to fetch her. She'd been prevented partly by an independent streak in her nature and partly because it was important to her to be home first, to see that a meal was prepared and the house warm and inviting by the time he returned. What she shunned from letting herself acknowledge was that it wasn't out of consideration for his well-being that she was so insistent that no home comfort should suffer because she worked – on the contrary, especially on nights such as this, she felt resentment towards him.

Once on the roadside she turned the knob of her front light. Nothing happened, not a glimmer. But it had worked the night before and the battery had shown no sign of giving out. Taking it from where it was fixed to the handlebars she shook it vigorously but to no avail. She'd have to unlock the house and go inside to see if she could do anything in the light. But before she turned the key in the lock, a car approached, slowed down and then stopped. Surely it couldn't be a client at gone half past five.

'Good, I hoped I'd be in time to find you here.'

At the sound of the familiar voice her lamp was forgotten. Silas!

'I should have gone, but for the fact my lamp has died on me. I didn't know you were back in the area.' There was nothing in her friendly greeting to suggest that each day unacknowledged had been the hope that he might arrive unexpectedly.

'You don't want to cycle on a night like this. Let's see if we can find something to tie the bike onto the luggage rack with.'

She ought to refuse, she ought to say she would phone and ask Alec to collect her. She ought to – but she didn't. Silas Clutterbuck was showing no more than natural friendship, he was Andrew's uncle and therefore almost family. So why was her heart racing like some love-struck adolescent's? If she heard of any other woman of her age, happily married – yes, *happily* married – for more than twenty-five years being filled with this rush of excitement, she would look on her with scorn. And yet she revelled in the knowledge that ahead of her was the drive home. Alec wouldn't be back until half past six at the earliest, so perhaps Silas would come into the kitchen and they would talk together while she prepared a meal. Would the shepherd's pie be enough for three? She would find something to help stretch it. None of that mattered – for the present there was nothing except the unexpected wonder that he was here. Later she would take herself in hand, make sure that she behaved as was fitting for his nephew's mother-in-law. But for these glorious moments she didn't feel like anyone's mother-in-law. Joy surged through her veins. Willingly she gave herself over to the pure, unadulterated thrill brought by being with Silas. Later she would ask herself what Alec would have thought could he have known that his loyal and affectionate wife was chasing romantic adventure. In those moments she cared nothing for future thoughts; the moment filled her whole mind. Even the wild beating of her heart excited her.

Together they went back into the house where Silas apparently knew just where to find a piece of rope and ten minutes later they were side by side in the car.

'You asked if I was to be working back here,' he said as he closed the door with a decisive slam, the action cutting them off from dark and fog alike. 'No, unfortunately. But I had no appointments today, so I went to see Drew. Then I decided Etty would like a first-hand report.'

'You'd heard about what happened?'

'Jack Prentice is an old friend of mine and he let me know. The lad's doing well, but thank God he had the sense to seek help. Apparently he was in a bad way when he

160

arrived. He was out of bed when I called this morning and straining at the leash to be home. I imagine he's learnt his lesson. Then, as I said, I went to the Manor and talked to Etty. What a great girl she is – no wonder Buck was so delighted about the marriage.'

He couldn't have said anything to please Rhoda more.

'Ett's a gem,' she agreed, 'but gem or no, she'll have a hard time persuading Andrew to do less if it means she has to take on more. As she says, she's as strong as a horse, but no man wants to see his wife doing the heavy stuff.'

Silas had made no attempt to start the car. Instead he took out his cigarettes and flicked his lighter as he passed her the packet so that she could see to take one. Then, in companionable silence, they lit up.

'A gem indeed, a sane and realistic one too. She knows very well that the answer isn't for him to do less while she does more. Apparently she has been to the Labour Exchange and has three men coming to see her tomorrow, one of whom has agricultural experience, one who before the army was a gardener and one with no experience but has said he wants to work on the land.'

'Imagine, probably four or five years in the services and coming home to be out of work. We've been so lucky, sometimes I feel frightened. It's as if life goes on for other people and yet we've been untouched.'

She knew he was looking closely at her, even though it was too dark to see more than the outline of a face.

'Lucky, you say? Lucky to be untouched?'

She didn't answer. Perhaps he didn't expect her to. His words seemed to hang between them, seeming to tell her something she already knew. Life should be *lived,* lived with a capital L. And what had she ever done? She had lived through others, others whom she loved, others who *did* things, worthwhile things. Yet she had been spared tragedy and wasn't that something for which she should be eternally grateful?

She changed the subject.

161

'Are you coming back here for the night? If you drive me home, won't you stay and take pot luck supper with us?'

'No to the first question; I must get back tonight. If this fog hangs on I'd rather drive at night with time on my side than have to travel in the morning in time for my first appointment. But yes please to the second question. I would love to eat with you. I hoped you might invite me.'

With that he switched on the engine and started the car forward. He drove slowly, on such a night he had no choice and she felt they were isolated together, surrounded by thick mist. Perhaps he felt it too; she let herself believe that he did even though logic told her she was being fanciful. Reality caught up when they drew up outside Timberley.

'I'll leave the car in the lane so it won't be in the way when Alec gets home,' Silas said. They were home; Rhoda the housewife was emerging from Rhoda the dreamer.

Two minutes later and they were indoors, the lights on, the morning post – nothing more exciting than the gas bill – picked up from the hall floor, the kitchen range needing stoaking and there was the daily rush to have a meal ready for when Alec returned.

'I'll coax the fire, shall I?' he offered, already moving the safety guard out of the way.

Perhaps the pattern of the evening was different after all. As she hung up their coats and collected vegetables from the rack in the larder, he was raking ashes in a way that told her the job wasn't new to him. It surprised her. The kitchen range had always been her responsibility. Occasionally Etty had been first up in the morning – special treat days like Mothering Sunday or her birthday – but Alec had never interfered in what he looked on as her part of the household.

There was something companionable about scraping carrots while he fed the range with small nuggets of coal before adding a final layer of coke and opening the damper.

'You and ranges are on familiar terms?' she asked unnecessarily.

'We're old friends,' he said and without looking at him she knew he was smiling. 'Buck and I used to spend school holidays with our grandparents at a smallholding in Dorset. Our parents were busy; they ran what we called a hotel but it was really a seaside guesthouse in Hastings. Every inch was given over to letting rooms. They were glad to be shot of us and the plan suited us all. Anyway, Gran had a range that was an ancestor of this and I got thoroughly acquainted with it. That should burn through in no time. Now then, jobs?'

The thrill of excitement was back again. This was like no ordinary evening and it surely wasn't just his easy way of doing what in her experience had never been seen as 'men's jobs'.

'You could put a match to the gas in the dining-room fire if you like – it'll take ages to warm the room.'

'Do you always eat in there?'

'When there are more than just the two of us we do.' She wished she hadn't worded it like that – 'just the two of us' made an outsider of him. 'But, considering you're almost family and it's a wretched cold night, let's lay the table out here in the kitchen instead. Do you mind?'

'Laying the table? Tell me where you hide the cloth and of course I will.'

They laughed, not because there was anything funny in his misunderstanding of her meaning but because in that moment they were both aware of a feeling of elation. Such moments are rare and precious, times when just for an instant there are no clouds, nothing to mar the rightness of where life has brought you. At almost the same second the silence was broken by the shrill bell of the telephone in the hall. For Rhoda it was an excuse to escape, to hide the strange emotion she was frightened to let herself admit.

The call was short, but it gave her time to compose herself so that when she returned to the kitchen there was no sign of the unspoken and half understood joy that had both excited and alarmed her.

163

'That was Alec. He always takes Miss Wheeler – she's the firm's treasure who took over from me when I had Etty so you can see how long she's been with him – anyway he always takes her home now that she lives in a farm cottage on the Oakleigh road away from bus routes. Apparently when he got there the farmer was waiting for him. The milking machine has packed in. So Alec is rolling up his sleeves and getting down to what he likes doing best – righting the fault in some machine or other. He said it looks like being a long job and, rather than his coming home first to get his overalls, the farmer has rigged him out and Mrs Wheeler has invited him to eat with them before he starts work. So there will be just you and me for the shepherd's pie.'

'Let's pull the table over towards the range,' he suggested. They weren't cold, yet supper next to the fire, where already the coals were lapped by bright flames, conjured up pictures far removed from a workaday kitchen. Like children planning a midnight feast they moved the table then, when he added a pair of candlesticks he noticed on the dresser (albeit the kind of old fashioned candlesticks more familiar to Wee Willie Winkie than a dining table; candlesticks that were kept handy in readiness for the power cuts which recently had happened so often) the mood was set. Soon they were eating shepherd's pie, carrots and Brussels sprouts, the fireside area of the kitchen illuminated by the warm glow of the flickering flames.

'Magic,' he told her, and whether he was serious or joking she couldn't be sure. 'Pure magic.'

Rhoda had always been aware of the deep lines on his thin face, but looking at him across the table they appeared etched with greater intensity, their appearance surely all part of what he described as magic in the surreal atmosphere. She nodded her agreement: magic indeed.

Whatever it was that had cast its spell, it was broken by Jenny, calling out as she let herself in through the back

164

door just as she did most evenings. Usually Rhoda looked forward to the few minutes they had together before Alec arrived home; today she hadn't given a thought to the fact that normally she would have been there earlier than this; indeed she hadn't given a thought to Jenny at all.

'Oh blow! Is there another power cut, Rhoda?' Jenny said as she came into the kitchen. Then, pulling up short at the sight of the two sitting in what she considered romantic candlelight, 'Oh, oh sorry. I thought – didn't mean to . . . if there's no electricity I better be off home to see to the fire.'

'Hello Jenny,' Silas stood up as he spoke, holding out his hand in greeting.

''Evening, doctor,' came the reply like a well-mannered child. 'Sorry, come butting in on you when you're eating. I got a bit delayed coming home – that's why I'm later than usual. Well, I'll get on home.' Then, taking in the scene that Rhoda suspected she had misconstrued, 'I just wondered if you knew whether Etty has heard when she can fetch Andrew?'

It was Silas who answered, telling her about his visit that morning to Andrew and in the afternoon to Etty. Whatever magic spell the candlelight had been weaving, her interruption had dispelled it. Rhoda had wanted those moments to last, but she knew there was no way of recapturing them. So she invited Jenny to stay and eat with them.

'Alec phoned that he won't be eating at home so there's more food here than we can manage. Draw up another chair and have some supper by the fire – you must be frozen after your ride.'

'Honest, Rhoda, I better be getting back. The fire will be out in the stove if I don't chivvy it to life pretty soon. But thanks for the offer. I'll look in same as usual on my way home tomorrow. That'll be all right?'

Did she imagine a fireside tête-a-tête was to become a habit?

After she'd gone they were left in the candlelight, but

their special moment was over. Rhoda wondered whether Silas felt as she did herself, rather self-conscious in the make-believe atmosphere. Perhaps he did, for when he spoke it was a reference to Alec and what a rotten night to be unexpectedly faced with working in a milking shed. So he set the scene for the sort of conversation that might develop between any man and his nephew's mother-in-law. When Rhoda carried the plates to the bench by the sink, she muttered something about needing to see what she was doing while she made the coffee before she flooded the room with harsh electric light.

So soon it was all over and she listened as the sound of his car grew more distant. The evening had been the stuff of which dreams are made, every word, every nuance stored in her memory to be relived again and again.

'I found Mrs Wheeler quite welcoming, very welcoming in fact,' Alec said as, with the nightly ritual of light out and window opened, he climbed into bed. 'I dare say what she needs as much as anything is company. If only you weren't so tied to that book place, you might ride over and have a chat with her sometimes.'

'Aren't there other people in the cottages on the farm? I know we were lucky that Jimmy Winbrook had a place vacant, but there must be other workers, other men with wives.'

'I dare say. But I can't see her having anything in common with them. She's not of country stock. Well, you know Muriel, you can see she comes from quite a cultured background.'

Rhoda turned her back with what could only be called a flounce, angry with him for – for what? For being kind about Mrs Wheeler? For speaking with admiration about Muriel? Or simply for destroying the euphoria of her own evening? She needed to argue with him, or at least verbally to hit out at him.

'Depends how you look on things. Andrew is country

166

through and through. Perhaps you consider the Wheelers of too high an intellect to enjoy his company.'

'Don't talk rubbish, you know perfectly well what I meant.' Then, the Wheelers apparently forgotten, 'How did you get on with Clutterbuck? Whatever made you invite him here for the evening?'

'If he hadn't driven me home I should have had a long walk. My lamp packed up on me,' she answered, feeling more aggrieved by the second.

'I could have collected you. Have you seen to the light for tomorrow.'

'I pinched one off that old bike of yours. In the morning I'll stop off at Hopkin's Ironmongery on my way and buy a new battery.' Then, her normal good humour fighting its way back, 'I'll leave you to sort out the trouble with mine. What's the use of having an engineer for a husband?' she said with a laugh. 'If you can sort out milking machines you won't have any trouble with a bicycle lamp – 'night 'night dear.'

'Umph,' he grunted, a sound that told her he wasn't ready for sleep. Honesty made her admit that many a night hope would have stirred in her; now, though, she wanted time to relive the evening, even though that same honesty took her one step further and brought her face to face with reality: she was behaving stupidly, suffering a middle-age crisis and chasing half-remembered emotions of youth. And with Silas Clutterbuck of all people, a man at the top of his professional tree, a man who Jenny had said made her uncomfortable because he seemed to see right into your mind and understand things you didn't tell him. Yet, lying there in the dark, feeling Alec's tentative and out-of-routine fumbling movements, she pushed to the back of her mind the things she didn't want to acknowledge.

'Imagine,' he was saying as his hands explored her, 'I worked till nearly ten o'clock. But I'm not a bit tired. The evening was so different from normal – the Wheelers, then the challenge of what must have been one of the first

167

milking machines we'd ever sold. It was good – made me feel alive. You're not too tired, Rhoda?'

She moved closer to him. Tonight would be different; tonight wasn't just part of the habitual weekly ritual; tonight he sounded excited. Forget the evening, think just of themselves, think of the love they had shared all these years and built their lives on, think of the familiarity of his touch, the precious intimacy that time brings. Turning towards him, she wound her legs around him, her warm hands caressing him. In the confusion of her mind, the romantic atmosphere of the candlelit kitchen reached out to this moment – she could almost believe it had been a prelude to the ultimate joy they would find together.

Minutes later, holding him closer, ever closer, those were the thoughts she clung to. Tonight every nerve in her body was alive, a thousand lights seemed to be flashing behind her closed lids. She heard herself cry out in the final seconds, control of her body lost in the miracle that so often eluded her. Control of her mind was lost too as in those same seconds she seemed to see a thin face etched with deep lines and she felt those far-seeing eyes looking into her soul. The fall from the heights to the depths stripped her of her momentary euphoria and left her alone and ashamed.

Next day Etty telephoned the house on Oakleigh Green; a very different Etty from the worried and frightened girl who had confided in Rhoda less than a week before.

'Mum, Dr Prentice says I can collect Drew tomorrow. And Mum, I've engaged two men.'

'I thought you were looking for one. Does Andrew know you are taking on two? Have you accommodation for them?'

'Yes, I've got that sorted. One is a bachelor – Ben Dickson's wife is going to give him lodging. The third applicant didn't turn up, so he was out of the picture. Mum, do you ever feel that a sort of providence is guiding you?

Or am I turning into a nut case?'

'I know what you mean. Not about being a nut case, you're anything but. So, what made you engage two instead of one?'

'Ernie Waters must be about fifty; he's the bachelor. He's worked on the land all his life and on the same farm for nearly thirty years. His boss has died and the farm is being taken over by some industrial concern for the production of veg for freezing. Not his line; he's always worked a mixed farm and he will be a real treasure, I'm sure.'

'If you talk about providence, I should think that's what brought him to you. So why a second?'

'I'll tell you in a jiff. But about Ernie Waters, he's really nice and I could tell he'd be completely capable, but he's never been used to making his own decisions. That'll suit us fine. If he'd been a big-headed know-it-all I wouldn't have taken him on, experience or no. The other – well, I guess my heart ruled my head. But that's not a bad thing, is it? Drew said he trusted me and I believe he'll understand how it was I came to give Jim Byford a job. They were both here at the same time and seemed to get on well.'

'Is this other one – Jim Byford – I take it he has a wife? You'll give them the cottage?'

'Let me tell you about him and you'll understand why I took him.'

And so she explained and, listening, Rhoda knew she would have done exactly the same thing herself. When Jim Byford had been posted overseas, his young bride had already been pregnant and living in London. He had persuaded her to accept his parents' offer and live at their bakery in Kent, all of them so sure that would be safer and healthier. But Fate had taken a hand and when on a summer afternoon a stray raider had released the last of its bombs as it made for home, the bakery had taken a direct hit. Fate hadn't done with them even then, for what else could account for the fact that all the adults were brought dead from the rubble, while the baby had been protected by the kitchen dresser which had fallen across his pram and allowed a pocket of air sufficient to keep him alive. The authorities had handed him over first to one foster home and then another. Jim was determined to bring up his own son and Etty was equally determined to see nothing stood in his way. No one could have foreseen how many lives would be changed by her warm-hearted decision.

Chapter Eight

Propped against his pram pillows, Christopher Silas Clutterbuck laughed until he hiccupped. In front of him four-year-old Denis Byford crouched out of sight, then sprang like a Jack-in-the-box with a shriek of 'Boo!' From the drawing-room window of the manor house Etty watched them, taking in the sound of their fun, the sight of the fields below Maybury Copse where haymaking was in progress, the smell of early summer. She shut her eyes and breathed deeply. The air was intoxicating – or was that simply the imagination of a young woman who was utterly happy with where life had brought her?

'Young Byford is doing well,' Andrew's voice surprised her, so engrossed had she been that she hadn't heard him come into the room. 'Haymaking ... don't you love it, Ett? The final line drawn under winter.'

'Umph,' she agreed, nodding but not taking her eyes off the outside scene, 'Yes, I love it, but winter was pretty good too. Drew, are you ever so happy that you're frightened? I remember thinking that before Christo was born; I had a sort of gut feeling that because everything was so perfect something would go wrong with the baby. It was there in my mind but I couldn't tell anyone, not even you: that would have been like tempting fate. I was wrong about the reason for it, but right that something was going to change things for us. Now we've got through all that – and we have, haven't we? – now there's *nothing* that can go wrong. There isn't, is there?' It was unlike Etty to sound less than certain.

'No one can ever know what's around the corner,' he replied. Then, as she turned to him and he saw how he had destroyed her moment of perfection, 'We shouldn't expect to be different from other people. We have to take what comes. But honestly, cross my heart, Ett, I can see no clouds. Anyway, I learnt my lesson and I'd always tell you if I thought trouble was going to pounce.'

'You promise me?'

'Honestly, I promise you. Living at half cock the way I'm training myself, I certainly can't be accused of over-doing things.' He smiled at her, the smile that was a hanger-on from the cheeky grin of his childhood. 'I believe we've got a pretty good arrangement going here.' Then, his expression changing as his thoughts took a nose dive, 'Yet . . .' His voice trailed into silence.

'Yet? There *is* something. What is it?'

'It's nothing to do with us, not you, not me, not Christo. If anything ever goes wrong for us – and we'll be remark-ably unusual if nothing ever does – you and I have the strength to stand up to it. Maybe not always physical strength, but that's less important in the end than having the guts to deal with the hand that's dealt to you. No, Ett, it has to do with this great place, with how we live – comfort, space, staff to run it all while we just lord it.'

'Poor Drew.' She took his hand and carried it to her face, rubbing her cheek against it. 'You seem fit, you look fit, I know how hard it must be for you to live by the rules and you're so good and uncomplaining.'

He didn't argue with her. Instead he said, 'It's not really to do with that.' For a moment that teasing smile was back, 'Not that I don't appreciate m'lady's admiration.' Then with a return to whatever it was that was troubling him, he went on, 'I think what's made me think is young Denis Byford. He's a grand kid, isn't he? You know, when it

172

comes down to it, I don't even know what it is I'm getting at. The war mucked Denis's life up, took away his mother and his grandparents. What if Jim hadn't come home?'

'Jim did come home and Denis is a very happy lad.'

'Umph,' Andrew conceded. But none of that had erased from his mind the feeling that somewhere, just beyond his vision, was a signal guiding him towards ... towards ...? Towards what? He didn't know.

Late that same afternoon Rhoda paid an unexpected visit on her way home from Oakleigh – or that's what she said when she arrived.

'Hardly on your way, Mum – you made quite a detour. Shall we phone Dad and ask him to come here after he's dropped Muriel Wheeler off?'

'No, don't do that. I don't know what he's doing about Miss Wheeler these days. I imagine she must have got herself a bicycle like the rest of us. For days he's not been getting home until it's pretty well dark – you know what haymaking time is like.'

'He's taken on two new mechanics recently. Surely they aren't as busy as all that?'

'He certainly seems to be. He's never replaced Andrew so he's out during the day much more than he was. And to be honest I believe he enjoys doing some of the repair work himself.'

Etty chuckled. 'I can't picture Dad coming home all grimey like I used to.'

Rhoda laughed as she, too, conjured up the picture.

'Those days were long ago. No, there's nothing grimey about him. He always goes back to the yard and gets out of his boiler suit or whatever it is he wears. By the time he shows up at home he's scrubbed up and respectable. Anyway, never mind about all that. I came to see my grandson. Can I give him his bath?'

They could all see how the coming of Christo had brought new colour into Rhoda's life. Watching his progress, delighting in the way his baby face would beam its pleasure when he saw her, even using some of her clothing coupons for some small garment that caught her eye, all these things contributed to giving a shape to her future and to banishing that feeling of mid-life discontent that had become so familiar. She who had resented the passing of the years and the loss of youth now didn't give it a thought. She told herself the feeling of excitement that had lain dormant for so long was because of Christo; if some inner voice whispered that she wasn't being honest, most of the time she refused to listen to it. But there were times when the truth couldn't be denied. No matter where she was, no matter what she was doing, somewhere at the back of her mind was the thought of Silas. Shouldn't falling in love belong to the young? She'd always made herself believe that was so, how else could she have lived year after year never stirring out of a rut that had lost all sense of adventure? In the early years there had been the excitement of each small success at the business, then her days (and often her nights too with Natalie, who'd never been a baby to take kindly to an orderly routine) had been taken up with the children. As Alec's business became more established so their home had become more comfortable, the rut smoother - and deeper too, so that she'd had to fight against the temptation to let herself see above the rim to the big brave world beyond. And then had come Silas.

When was it that Alec had ceased to see her, really *see* her for herself and not simply as part of the well run household? If she had the courage, or yet the interest, to ask him, she knew he would deny the suggestion. But of course it was true. If it weren't he would surely be aware that in her mind she carried the image of Silas, that even if he were a hundred miles away she could hear the echo of his voice? At Timberley the routine went on unchanged, only she knew the excitement that bubbled inside her, the hope as she started each day that he would suddenly appear. No

174

word had ever passed between them that couldn't have been spoken in front of Alec and yet she *knew* that what was developing between the two of them was important, as soul consuming to him as it was to her. No wonder her smile was never far beneath the surface, no wonder life these days was spelt with a capital L, and no wonder when Alec performed his weekend ritual (even occasionally once during the week too), she rushed headlong into her world of fantasy. She knew it was pure fancy on her part to imagine that Silas must know where her thoughts were carrying her and that his were united with hers, his heart with hers.

Rhoda wasn't the only one to make the regular journey to Sedgeley Manor on her bicycle. If, back on that autumn day in 1944 when Jenny had moved into April Cottage, anyone had told her that she would become a welcome visitor at one of the largest houses in the district, she would have replied with a mocking, 'Go on! Now pull the other one!' But that had been before she had known Rhoda and Etty. Mr Harding, as she still thought of Alec, was a different kettle of fish, always polite but distant and he made her uncomfortable. But Andrew, he was easy. And as for little Christo, being with him kindled memories that were part joy and part utter misery – holding him and seeing his eyes light up as he recognised her and his face break into a toothless beam carried her right back to those first months with Mickey. Sometimes, as she pedalled homeward after sharing his bathtime fun and watching him settle into Ett's arms for his evening feed, her vision would be blurred by hot tears. She would stop going to the manor – where was the sense in opening old wounds? But it was those very wounds that made it impossible for her to stay away.

On that particular June day, while Rhoda was wrapping Christo in a new hooded bathwrap – a present from his globe-trotting grandfather – Jenny cycled up the long drive to the house, head down as if that way she'd gain speed.

'Too late for bathtime,' Etty greeted her with her never-changing smile of welcome. 'Mum's doing the honours. Tonight she's even going to give him his supper. He's getting weaned quite nicely and she's got some disgusting-looking milk sop to spoon into him. How old was Mickey when you finished breastfeeding?' Joy and agony shot through Jenny like physical pain. She ached to talk about him, to hold on to every smallest memory. Right from the beginning Etty had talked of him openly, somehow managing to bring his happy presence close.

'Younger than the welfare woman said he ought to be. But I never had much to give him, poor little man. So, soon as I could, I used to make him some milky slop with a bit of the ground-up cereal stuff in it and get it down him instead. He put on weight right enough and seemed fit as anything – better than he would have been with what he got from me. Night time I made him a bottle, but he never liked it much . . . used to spit it at me and yell blue murder. I reckon he must have been just a few weeks older than Christo by the time he took everything from a spoon. That "She Devil" used to make cracks like "Another few weeks and you'll be down the chippy buying his grub, never ought to be a mother" – rotten cow she was.'

'Your best day was when you came to April Cottage – best day for all of us, Jen.' At Etty's words, Jenny turned her head away, frightened to show the struggle she was having to keep her face from contorting and letting the threatening tears win the battle. 'If it was right for Mickey, I reckon it's going to be OK for Christo. I'll start sieving vegetables into gravy for him for his dinner. I was just going to find Drew and tell him the news Nat has just telephoned through to us. He's somewhere in the milking shed. Come on, come with me.'

Jenny loved coming to the manor. Grand house though it was, with its stables, its coach houses, its atmosphere of timelessness, she felt utterly comfortable there. Clad in the workman's overalls she found most convenient for a job that was dirty, her made-up face and high-piled hair looked out of place; other than the overalls and 'sensible' shoes, the only concession she made these days was that her nails were unvarnished and sometimes broken too. She called her workmanlike hands the price she paid for the independence she found in paying her own rent for April Cottage. If Michael hoped to be able to divorce her for infidelity, she was bugg – she was blessed if she was going to give him the pleasure. He could wait three years and then he could blame her if he wanted, and say she had deserted him. It should be the other way round, for it was he who had walked out on her, but a stubborn streak in her refused to co-operate. All the consuming infatuation she had felt for the handsome young flyer had been turned on its head. It wasn't in her nature to analyse her reasoning; all she knew was that she wanted to hurt him just as she had been hurt. Somewhere deep in her subconscious was the illogical belief that he had been thankful when they lost Mickey, for without him to hold them together Michael could have the freedom he craved.

'Hello there, Jen,' Andrew greeted her with casual affection. 'I suppose Ett has told you that you've lost your job to mother-in-law this evening. It's time young Byford knocked off and went to get Den's supper. I'll take over cutting for a couple of hours – we don't want to waste the daylight.'

Etty sat on a bale of straw and watched the scene, knowing exactly what was going on in Jenny's mind. A few seconds later she was proved right.

'Tell you what, Andrew. Me and Denis get on like a house on fire. What if you suggest to his dad that I do his supper for him. I don't want to be the one to suggest it, not to go and say it to him, I mean. If he thinks I'm shoving my oar in, then he won't mind saying to you that he'd rather do it himself. Anyway, Ett has something to tell us first. Out with it Etty – what was it Natalie told you?'

So Etty made her announcement. Natalie and Stewart

177

had been engaged for a twenty-minute slot on the wireless on Friday evenings for six weeks beginning the first Friday in August.

'And that's not all,' she added as if there was still the icing on the cake to come. 'They've agreed to sing at a fund-raising function in Brackleford on the last Saturday in July in aid of the repair to the church clock, *and* – and here's the exciting bit – they are coming to Timberley when they finish in Bournemouth this Saturday night and can stay a whole week.'

Of course the contract for the broadcasts was important, but the excitement created by the phone call centred around the following week's visit. Jenny pushed it firmly to the back of her mind while she played a game of snap with Denis, watched him eat two slices of toast with home-made plum jam from the 'big house', gave him a head-to-toe wash in a zinc bowl in the kitchen, and sent him off in his pyjamas to say goodnight to his father with the promise of a story if he came straight back and didn't get 'all messed up again'.

More than an hour later, side by side, she and Rhoda pedalled home, and Jenny was no longer able to escape the confusion of her thoughts. Every few weeks Natalie and Stewart managed a weekend at Timberley and he always came to see her at April Cottage. She told herself she wished he wouldn't make a point of coming, frightened to admit to herself how much his visits meant to her while, at the same time, fearing he befriended her out of sympathy. What other reason could there be? He and Natalie were a team, growing closer all the time. Jenny would imagine the two of them together and then, by contrast, conjure up a picture of herself, dirty from work, with no natural social graces. Oh, she tried, she watched the way they did things at Timberley and tried hard not to show herself up, but to compare her to Natalie was like comparing the workman's overall that was her daily garb with a silk gown. A few years ago she would have battled to hold on to her self-confidence, but that had been before Michael had stripped it from her.

She wasn't the only one to look toward the week's visit with clouded vision. Alec's world was never complete if Natalie was away from home despite his pride in her success, but why did she always have to have Stewart Carling in tow? No one was good enough for her and *he* least of all. In Alec's opinion, his singing success was doing nothing to fine down his rough edges; the fellow remained as uncouth as he had been on first acquaintance. Last time they had come he had been wearing a well tailored suit, the sort of thing he could never have dreamed of buying had Natalie not given him his opportunity, yet he managed to make it appear very little different on him from the one that had been issued when he'd been demobbed. Some people carried their clothes well but whatever Carling wore, nothing could make him anything other than the lout he was. Add to that the fact that Alec wanted Natalie to himself or, at best, to share her with the family, it was small wonder that he made Stewart feel like an unwelcome intruder.

'It's nice to get out of the house and come across here,' Stewart told Jenny on his second evening. 'Honest, Jenny, Natalie's old man makes me uncomfortable. Not that he ever says he doesn't want me there, but I'm not daft, I can tell. I'd make an excuse sometimes and not come home with her, but then I wouldn't see you. You and me, we're pals, aren't we?'

''Course we're pals,' she agreed. 'But Stew, I've learnt not to take any notice of the way Mr Harding sort of manages to knock you down with a look. You know what I reckon? I reckon he puts Natalie above anyone else, sometimes even above Rhoda. And that's rotten of him. Etty must have known she came off second best with him, but she's sort of complete in herself. I don't think she

179

would have got hurt. Even before Andrew came along and fell for her there was something strong and honest about Ett. She's smashing, always has been. When I came here, well I was sort of – how can I say it? – sort of ignorant about things. At the time I probably didn't look at it like that, but when I come to think about it now, I know that's about what I was. But right from the start Etty made me feel that I was OK. Might have been because of Mick ... she was a great one for playing with Mick. Anyway she and Rhoda, they were smashing to Mick and me. Natalie – well I hardly had anything to do with her, of course, cos she wasn't here very often. And as for *him,* Mr Harding, wish I had a pound for each time he gave me that look like as if I was something the cat brought in. So don't you get upset by the way he carries on. Tell you what I think: I think he's a miserable old bu— well, a misery anyway.'

Stewart hadn't taken his eyes off her as she'd talked. Perhaps being pals made it right for them to be so honest with each other.

'Natalie knew I was coming over to see you. She didn't mind.'

'Why should she mind? You and Natalie belong together, we all know that. You better be getting back soon though – it'll be time for some singing.'

'Yep.' He stood up ready to go. 'She said to be sure I was back. She's not daft, you know, and not blind either. She knows jolly well that if I'm not there, her dad will get on the piano stool and try and elbow me out of playing – and more than that, of singing too. Nat wants to make sure we do duets. If we were anywhere else it wouldn't matter, but because of *him* and the way he tries to possess her, I've got to be there to back her up.'

After he'd gone Jenny gazed out of the window at the green where in the long summer evening light a few lads were playing football. Her life was getting her nowhere. She ought to have the courage to give up the cottage, leave Dewsberry and make a new start. But even as she acknowledged what she ought to have the courage to do, her mind baulked at the images it brought to her mind: a lonely bed-sitting room somewhere, perhaps a job behind a bar or serving in a shop, no friends, nothing. There would be young men happy to ask her out, of that she was sure. But after Michael, after the lesson she had learnt of what he had really wanted from her, while in her youthful ignorance she had believed him to be in love with her, she was frightened even to imagine what might be waiting for her if she turned away from the security and friendship she had there on the green.

Turning from the window she caught sight of her reflection in the mirror that hung on the back of the kitchen door. She'd put it there when she'd first moved into the cottage so that she could take a last-minute peek at herself before she opened the door to welcome Michael home each day. More fool her, she told herself. Even so, youth and hope went hand in hand and she was still only twenty years old. So ten minutes after she'd watched Stewart going back to Timberley, she was lying on the bed while the face pack she had bought for fourpence last time she went into Brackleford hardened. A girl had to look after herself. She closed her eyes and let her thoughts drift. It was nice having Stew for a special friend although when he'd said that Natalie didn't mind him coming over to the cottage, somehow it had cast a cloud.

The weeks of summer passed while, at least on the surface, their lives continued in the familiar routine. They could all see and delight in Christo's progress but what went on in their own lives, or in their own minds, gave every appearance of following a changeless pattern.

If haymaking had been the reason for Alec responding to emergency calls that kept him working during the evening, harvest was even busier. One early evening in September when Jenny cycled to Sedgeley Manor, she found Rhoda already there.

181

'They're both busy in the fields. I'm not needed at Oakleigh until next Monday so I've been looking after the boys. I'm glad you've come, we can share them. Christo is going to be lost after tomorrow when Denis starts school.' Her words were drowned by the excitement of Jenny's welcome from both the children. For a few minutes she joined in their game of ball, marvelling at Denis's patience as he sent it gently towards Christo. But Christo had no idea of how to return it when it came his way; instead he clung on to it chuckling as if he was consciously teasing, but with Jenny there the game took on some sort of purpose.

'I brought them some chocolate drops,' she whispered to Rhoda as Denis set off to retrieve her long-distance throw. 'Is it all right to hand them over?'

'Greater love hath no man,' Rhoda said with a laugh, 'than to give his sweet ration. I'd pop one in Christo's mouth when he goes off for his bath, but Den's old enough to really appreciate them.'

'Starting off to school tomorrow,' Jenny mused. 'That would have been my Mick too. Watching Den and seeing how he's getting on – seeing how gentle and sort of grown up he makes himself with Christo – I can see just how Mick would have been. Daft isn't it, but I sort of pretend to myself that Mick knows it's really *him* I'm playing with.'

'It's not daft at all Jenny. And I bet Mickey does know and is glad. If you learn to love Denis – or any other child – it could never mean that you love Mickey less. You must see him as a baby when you look at Christo. And one day, Jen, you'll fall in love and marry . . . have other children. Each one is different, each one has the whole of its mother's heart. Nothing will ever replace your Mick, no love you feel for any other child will detract from what you will always, *always* feel for him.'

Sitting on a deckchair in the shade of a tall elm tree, Rhoda put out her hand to Jenny and was rewarded by the young woman dropping to the grass by her side and sitting cross-legged with all the agility of youth.

'Tell you one thing for certain,' came the determined reply, 'you'll never find me being fool enough to fall in love again. It sort of blinds you to the real truth, that's the rotten thing about love. Loving Mick – that was different, it wasn't all wrapped up with wanting to be better than my best – he liked me just as I was. But you'll not catch me poncing myself up to please some fella. Was it just that you were lucky, Rhoda? I always wanted Michael and me to have a home like you make, one where you can tell everything is hunky-dory. I bet you don't feel you've got to get tarted up when it's time for Mr Harding to come home.'

With a spontaneous guffaw Rhoda answered, 'If I did he wouldn't notice. That's the sad thing about jogging along in a comfortable rut. I bet you if I went to the smartest hairdresser in town instead of washing my hair myself, Alec wouldn't see the difference.'

'Lucky old you. Probably when you get older and your hair starts to go grey he'll still see you as the young girl he must have fallen for. Funny isn't it,' she mused, 'you can't really imagine people who've been married for years and years being young and all starry eyed and romantic.' Then, all thoughts of age behind her, 'Anyway, I'm done with all that romance stuff, you won't catch me falling for it again. So that's that.' Her thoughts were pulled up short by the sight of Etty coming from the direction of the farm buildings, 'Hey Etty, me and Rhoda are going to draw lots to see which one we get to bath. Or have you done working out there? Are you coming to give Christo his bath yourself?'

'No such luck. The tractor packed up in High Meadow, hence my putrid state. I fixed it and off it went when, would you believe, the next thing was the threshing machine konked out. A bit sheared right off. I'm going to ring Dad and ask him if he'll fetch you, Mum, and bring the bit we want at the same time. I haven't seen him for ages – at least a fortnight – so it'll nice to get him over.'

'You may not find him there,' Rhoda warned her. 'Lately he's been working like he used to ages ago and he told me not to expect him home this evening. It's sometimes ten o'clock by the time he gets in, but he seems so pleased to be doing what he loves best. For anyone as good at his work as he always was, it must be galling to be left behind with the ledgers.'

'The ledgers and Miss Wheeler,' Etty laughed. 'I'll make sure he has an evening off this evening.' And with that Etty disappeared into the house to phone him. A few minutes later she told them that he was already out. She'd spoken to one of the men who had promised to have ready the part she wanted so she was going to drive straight over to Brackleford and pick it up.

The evening progressed, Rhoda dealing with Christo and Jenny going off to the Byfords' cottage where she helped Denis into his new grey suit, white shirt, red-and-blue-striped necktie and school cap so that he could show her how smart he was going to be in the morning. She looked at him but she saw Mickey; her heart ached with love for the child she had lost, but it was Denis she hugged.

'You look – oh my goodness – you look smashing. Bet you'll be the smartest boy there.'

'I 'spect I will. Mr Clutterbuck took me into the big shop in town and bought me all my things. See, he got me two ties, four pairs of socks that pull right up to my knees, two shirts, my posh suit and a pair of new shoes. Money doesn't grow on trees, that's what Dad said, and Mr Clutterbuck said neither did coupons. So Dad gave him his clothes ration book and Mr Clutterbuck paid a whole load of money. And all for me.' Denis had learnt young not to take good fortune for granted.

Jenny spent a long time with him that evening, knowing he was too excited to go straight to sleep. By the time she came away from the farm cottage, Etty was back from Brackleford and busy repairing the threshing machine.

Bumping along in the second tractor, Andrew was towing a load of straw bales to where the rick was being built. It was at moments like these that Jenny's mind would leap backwards and she would seem to smell the summer dust of the city, hear the rattle of tramcars, see the overflowing bins in the alley by the side of the 'She Devil's' house. Breathing in the summer scented air, she shouted to Etty, 'I'm off Etty. Be all right if I come in after work tomorrow? I want to see how Den gets on.'

'Of course it's all right, silly. See you tomorrow.'

Jenny smiled, even starting to hum softly as she went back towards the house and her bicycle. Rhoda had settled Christo in his cot and was back in the deckchair by the elm tree. But she wasn't alone, for sitting at her feet was Silas. Jenny's immediate reaction was annoyance; annoyance rooted in the fact she was never comfortable in his presence. That was swiftly followed by disappointment, for she had an uneasy premonition that now he had come Rhoda wouldn't be in a hurry to cycle home. And she was right.

'Then I'd better push off on my own,' she said. 'There are things I got to get done. I just told Ett I'd look in after work tomorrow. Will you be here or will I see you back on the green?'

'I think it's a help to Etty if we both come while they're so busy with the harvest. I'm not needed at all at Oakleigh this week and I can't resist the temptation of looking after Christo while they're working. There's nothing to keep me at home with Alec out pretty well every evening.'

From the shade of the elm tree they watched Jenny pedal away. Rhoda felt like a child playing truant – she ought to have gone too. You can't tamper with fire and not expect to get burnt. But the thought hardly had time to form before Silas shot it to pieces.

'We have an evening before us and I have that same length of rope on the back seat of the car. Your bike travels quite safely on the luggage grid and you, Rhoda, my very dear Rhoda, will harm no one by letting me take you out to dinner. I found a delightful pub in Tagworth, the Stag and Hounds – you may know it. Their food is excellent – steaks like I haven't seen for years. What do you say?'

'I should say "no".' She didn't enlarge on why it was she should say 'no' and neither did he ask. They held each other's gaze and didn't flinch. 'But I – I . . .' For a moment she hesitated – what she meant was 'I *can't say no*', and they both knew it even as she finished the sentence. 'I have nothing to hurry home for this evening. During this busy period, if Alec knows he'll be late he has something to eat at the Red Lion before he goes off on a job.'

For more than two months, Silas had been based at Brackleford Hospital, travelling to clinics in other parts but always coming back and, just as he had in the past when he'd been in the area, he had been living in Oakleigh with Matthew Wilberforce, who enjoyed his company. Surely two men could hardly have been less alike in personality or interests, yet their adolescent friendship had never wavered. Matthew made no comment and asked no questions, and even though he was out of Oakleigh a good deal of the time Rhoda manned the establishment, he wasn't blind to what he saw as an easy friendship between two middle-aged people who could be called relatives-in-law. Silas and Rhoda had shared lunch many times during these two months, and often in the evening when she locked 'the shop' he had tied the bicycle on his car and had driven her home. At the back of her mind was always the memory of that first time, the magic of the candlelight, the strange wild excitement that told her something extraordinary was happening in her unchanging life. Since that day, though, excitement had developed into a nameless joy; joy that was tinged with shame and with fear too.

On that September evening, Rhoda refused to admit to the fear of where she was heading. Instead she indulged in the joy and excitement of knowing she wasn't just something that merged into the background – she was *noticed*. She knew she walked with a lighter step, that she held herself taller, that her smile came more readily. Deep in her heart, too, she knew that it couldn't last for ever.

Tagworth was some eight or nine miles away, companionable miles. Silas's interest in Andrew and Etty was as great as her own and, because of his medical training, he had a better understanding of Andrew's problems. Talking of the young family created the bond between them – or that's what Rhoda told herself. Once inside the Stag and Hounds, they found a table by the window where they looked out across the open countryside to where the sinking sun was casting long shadows. The proprietor's wife was Swiss and it was she who had introduced fondue meals to the dining room that led off from the bar.

'I only discovered this place the other day,' Silas told her. 'You've been here before, I expect.'

She, been here before? She shook her head.

'We usually eat at home,' she said. 'No, not *usually*, we *always* eat at home.'

'Alec knows that what you prepare can't be bettered.'

She wished he hadn't said it as somehow it cast a shadow between them. She shrugged her shoulders and didn't attempt to keep the annoyance out of her voice as she answered, 'How would he know that if he never tests it against anything else? Anyway, tonight I don't want to think about home cooking.' Then, with a smile that put her right back on course to enjoy everything the evening offered, 'I've never had a fondue. We cook it ourselves don't we?'

He laughed. 'And here you are wanting to have a meal prepared for you.'

'This'll be fun. I've read about fondues. Lots of exciting sauces – now that's a change from the sort of thing I put on the table.'

And so it proved. Steak cut into small cubes, an array of dipping sauces, lots of laughter as time and again they lost their steak from the long skewers and dug around in the boiling oil. It was at one of those moments, when the sizzling meat refused to be re-spiked and she was laughing with all the innocent glee of a child, that his mood suddenly changed. Looking up from the bubbling cauldron, his gaze drew hers and she had no power to look away.

'You know, don't you?' His voice was quiet, each word making an indelible print on her memory. 'We both know.'

She nodded slowly then, needing all her will-power, the nod changed to a decisive shake of her head.

'I know it's no use. Please, Silas, please, don't let's spoil everything. Don't let's say things that change what we have.'

'Is what we have enough?'

'Yes. *No.* I don't know.' She was frightened and confused. But she couldn't tell him less than the truth. 'Yes, I do know. It puts all the colour into my days. But even hearing myself say that makes me ashamed.' She seemed to hear the echo of Jenny's voice telling her how she dreamed of making a marriage as happy and secure as they had at Timberley. *And so we have* she told herself What am I but a middle-aged housewife fighting to squeeze the last drop of romance before the memory of youth is gone for ever.

Silas was watching her closely; she could almost believe he was following her thoughts.

'You should feel no shame, my darling Rhoda. We are friends, are we not? And is it wrong for friends to have affection for each other?'

'You make it sound so decent and normal.'

'What I feel for you is perfectly decent and normal.' He shrugged his shoulders helplessly. 'So I have to be content with less than that which every fibre in my body tells me is right for us. But nothing will spoil what we have.' Then, his thin face creasing into a broad and boyish smile, 'Now, whose piece of steak is that getting charred in the pot? That fiendish-looking yellow sauce is good. God knows what's in it but you'll like it.'

188

It was a clumsy effort at putting the evening back onto the rails where it had been running so smoothly. So she made an effort, fishing the overdone steak from the cauldron and dipping it to give it a lavish coating of sauce. For all their determination, what really lifted them from their moment of truth was her expression as she carried the yellow-coated morsel to her mouth. Too late, he warned her – the yellow fieriness put paid to all that had gone before, making her eyes water, tickling the back of her nose and making her sneeze. The atmosphere was restored; laughter returned. Only later, and often over the weeks that followed, would memory carry her back to what had gone before.

When Silas drove her home, Alec's car was already in the drive.

'Are you coming in to say hello to Alec?' she asked just as if the two men were bosom friends.

'No, I'll untie your bike then go straight on. Thank you for this evening. If I'm away from the hospital in time I dare say, like Jenny, I shall look in on the youngsters tomorrow to see how Denis enjoyed his first day at school.' They both knew it was tantamount to saying that he would see her again the next day. Later, the day over and alone with her thoughts, she would remember every nuance of the evening, then there would be no fear in facing the truth – it would bring her joy that nothing could take from her.

From indoors, Alec saw her hurrying up the drive, his expression giving no hint of his thoughts as he watched Silas drive away.

'Poor you,' Rhoda greeted him. 'I thought you were sure to be late, especially when Etty heard that you weren't at the yard when she tried to phone you. Then she drove in to get some spare part or other.'

'I left in reasonable time, quite early in fact. I took Muriel home. Rhoda, never mind about food, I've already eaten. Sit down, I want us to talk about something.'

189

Something must be wrong! Her first thought was Natalie. 'Is it Nat? What's happened?' She could feel her heart pounding.

'Nothing to do with Natalie. Thank God for that at least. Listen, Rhoda, and tell me honestly what you think we can do – if we can do anything. I told you I took Muriel home. We went early as she was in no state to work. Poor girl, she has no life at all, you know. And when you see the unsuitability of where they are having to live you can understand why Mrs Wheeler is so depressed.'

'From what I've heard, she always was a pain in the backside even when they had their own home.'

The expression was so out of character that he looked at her in surprise, bringing from her a spontaneous chuckle.

'Etty's description, but I'm sure pretty near the truth. I'm sorry for Muriel Wheeler but what she should have done was move away years ago while she had two parents and an escape route. If you ask me, she hadn't the guts. Anyway, never mind all that. What is it we need to talk about?' The serious, sit-down-and-concentrate discussion could hardly be about the Wheelers' domestic arrangements. Her thoughts took a leap in another direction: by now Silas would be almost back at Oakleigh. Did Matthew realise what was happening to them? She *wasn't* a middle-aged woman, frightened that youth had gone, she was *herself* and never more so than when she and Silas were together; never more so than this evening when for that brief moment there had been nowhere for either of them to hide from the truth.

'. . . enough room to swing a cat,' Alec was saying. Surely he couldn't still be worried about the Wheelers. It seemed he could. 'Their furniture is in store. They have no hope of finding anywhere to rent and even if anything suitable came up for sale – and small hope of that these days with housing being so scarce – they haven't a hope of being able to get a mortgage on what Muriel earns.'

'It's rotten for her. And an awful worry for her, without the added misery of going home to a mother like hers. If you think she's worth more, then why don't you give her a rise? In her, you've got a secretary for life . . . she'll never move on.'

'If I were to suggest paying her a higher wage she would see it as charity and would be offended, hurt even.'

Rhoda's sympathy span wasn't as all-enveloping as his.

'It's thanks to us that they found the place they're in – and you go out of your way to collect her. At least it's a place on their own – they aren't like so many people coming home from the services to live with family or in-laws. Anyway, a home is what you make of it. Look at Jenny, see how hard she works doing that wretched job so that she can keep her independence.'

'You can hardly compare Jenny Matherson's talents with Muriel's. She's been an essential part of the business almost as long as I've had that place. But she can't go on as she is. I tell you, Rhoda, it's draining her. Her mother is constantly on her mind. Today the poor girl was at rock bottom, so that's why I took her home early. When I suggested to her that we should go and collect her mother and I'd take them both out somewhere to eat, she was – damn it, Rhoda, she actually cried. Can you believe it? Cried because someone was showing her consideration.'

Rhoda tried to put herself in Muriel's place and felt a tug of sympathy. So often in her heart she had resented the 'treasure' who did the job she'd felt should have been her own. Muriel was five years or so younger than she was herself, but she had no spirit of youth. What kept that spirit alive? Love, the thrill of desire, the hope that came with each new day? In those seconds, Muriel was pushed aside as her thoughts carried her on a journey of their own.

'We weren't even sure her mother would agree,' Alec went on. 'You know she's turning into a hermit, frightened to go outside her own door.' He assumed he had kept her undivided attention.

'She came to Etty's wedding and seemed as normal as

191

everyone else. I think Muriel Wheeler sees her as worse than she is. And who can blame her? She's not much younger than I am and what has she got to show for her years? Nothing but a table in the corner of that office and an over-possessive mother. I bet when you turned up with an invitation to go out to dins, the old battleaxe jumped at it.'

Alec laughed, remembering. 'That's right. She was all smiles and, to be fair, while we were out she was most sociable. She has an incredible grasp on what's going on in the world – she must read the paper from cover to cover each day.'

'I thought she was just a cleaner and polisher.' Rhoda tried to sound interested.

'She's that too. The living room is no bigger than our outside lobby, but it gleams with cleanliness. For some women a home is the centre of their world.'

Did she detect criticism in his tone?

'Life isn't always fair is it?' she mused. 'Before I started going to Matthew's, I used to wander around this house like a lost soul. Four bedrooms plus the attic playroom. I used to go up there quite a lot, you know, remembering the girls when they were little. We ought to bring the lorry across from the yard one day and take some of the things to Etty – the old rocking horse, that train she used to ride on. I can't imagine Christo would want Nat's doll's pram but there are lots—'

'So many rooms,' he interrupted, 'and how many do we use?'

'Most of the time these days only one bedroom and the kitchen. But you can't shrink or stretch a house according to your needs. Awful though to think how many people have nowhere to call their own. Imagine what it must be like for young couples starting their married lives in parents' houses.'

He reached forward and took both her hands in his in a most un-Alec-like movement.

'Suppose we suggested they come here until they can find somewhere more permanent? Mrs Wheeler would look after the place. I'm not suggesting she'd interfere, of course she wouldn't, this is *your* home. But I know she would delight in seeing everything was kept immaculate, she's almost antiseptically clean.'

Rhoda laughed. 'Sounds terrifying. Are you serious, Alec? You really want to bring them into the home. What about when Natalie and Stewart come home? Where would we put them?'

'You don't imagine I'd suggest touching Natalie's room? As for Stewart, perhaps he might get the message that sometimes it would be a treat to have Nat to ourselves. But if he still hangs on, then we could get a camp bed put up in the old playroom. And you're right about the children's things in it, they ought to go to young Christo.'

When Rhoda had been warned they were to have an important discussion, this was the last thing she had imagined. The idea of having this paragon of home-making loose in Timberley didn't appeal to her but before she could think of a valid reason for opposing the scheme, Alec had taken advantage of her hesitation and moved the idea forward.

'It would be easier from my point of view,' he told her. 'It would save me doing that detour in the mornings and evenings. And I should have thought you would have jumped at the idea. All very well to say how you used to wander around the empty house, but now the home has to take second place to this mad attempt to find a career, if you can call it that. If you're completely opposed to the idea, then the Wheelers must put up with things as they are, but to my mind that simply shows the imbalance of society. Muriel works every bit as hard for the business as I do myself. I would lose nothing by offering them use of the empty rooms in this house. Perhaps you might be able to bring Mrs Wheeler out of her shell, introduce her to a few people from around here

193

so that she isn't always inward looking. You would have less to do here in the house and, Rhoda, if you're completely honest I'd have expected you to jump at the suggestion. You can't deny you find no pleasure in the demands the house makes on you.'

'That's not true.'

He held her gaze, his eyebrows raised enquiringly.

'Yes,' she was the first to speak, 'before I started to go to Matthew's, I felt left behind. You, Etty, Natalie, even Jenny, poor sad Jenny, all of you *did* things with your lives. You resent what I do, you don't even try to understand; it suits you better to pretend it's because I'm fed up with Timberley. And that's not fair. Anyway now, what with going to Oakleigh quite often and then there's Christo . . .' Her voice petered out. She didn't want to quarrel with Alec; to quarrel would be to cast a cloud on her private world.

He was suggesting bringing strangers into their home. For even though Miss Wheeler had been part of the background of the little office in the cattle market for more than twenty years, she had remained just that - Miss Wheeler. Rhoda was sure that if she set herself against the idea, he wouldn't press her - it was only a sudden burst of kindness on his part that had put the idea in his mind.

For a moment their gaze met and held. She was the first to look away.

'You'd better speak to Mrs Wheeler,' she said. 'She won't like it if the suggestion comes to her second hand through her daughter.'

'I'd rather you called to see her. Asked her to come as a favour to you, perhaps explained to her how now that you insist on working, the house is becoming a burden.'

She opened her mouth to argue, then changed her mind. Freedom beckoned and she was ashamed of the eager excitement she felt at the prospect of being able to follow where it called her.

*

194

The next morning the shrill bell of the telephone alerted her just as she slammed the front door, setting out on her errand of mercy to see Elizabeth Wheeler; another few seconds and she wouldn't have heard it. It was Matthew. Even as she listened to what he was suggesting, she had no idea that his small request could have such a life-changing outcome.

Chapter Nine

Rhoda observed the highly polished furniture, the sparkling windows and the shining silverware which looked so out of place on the dresser in the one-time labourer's cottage. It was all very much what she had expected, except for the appearance of Elizabeth Wheeler herself. Certainly at Etty's wedding she had been well turned out, but having heard what a paragon of domesticity she was, Rhoda hadn't anticipated the door to be opened to her by someone with the dignity of a duchess.

'Mrs Harding! Is there something wrong? Do step inside, and pray don't look around you.'

'But why not?' Rhoda answered with a smile in her voice as she followed the older woman into the room which, as Alec had told her, was little larger than a good-sized cupboard. 'How cosy you have it in here.'

'Don't be kind, please don't be kind. The place is an abomination; sometimes I look around at what I have come to and I – I – well, I don't know how I find the courage to carry on at all. But there's Muriel. I have to think of her and how alone she'd be if she hadn't me to care for her.'

'These are hard times for so many people, Mrs Wheeler,' Rhoda spoke purposely in what Etty called her 'no nonsense voice', 'Families having to share accommodation, houses bursting at the seams.' Then, realising she was sounding insensitive, she relented as she rushed on,

'We've been so lucky, Alec and me.'

'I remember thinking what a lovely home you have when you were kind enough to invite Muriel and me to Miss Harding's wedding. I do my best and keep this little hovel as nice as I can. But, oh dear, I'm sorry.' She tried to hang on to control but once the tears found their way to escape they kept coming. 'Don't know what's the matter with me,' she snorted and gulped, nothing of the duchess about her any longer, 'behaving so badly when you're kind enough to spare time to call on me.' She was an elderly woman with no hope on the horizon, a woman whose confidence was shattered. Rhoda remembered what Etty had told her of how difficult Muriel Wheeler's life was, ruled always by her domineering mother. But surely it wasn't as simple as that.

'May we sit down?' Rhoda suggested, guiding her tear-blinded hostess to a well-worn sofa. 'I came here because there's something I want us to talk about. It's just an idea and you may think nothing of it, but Alec and I discussed it last night and to us it seemed a good arrangement all round. Did you know I have found myself a job?' Despite what Alec had said, Rhoda hadn't intended to bring that into the equation.

'Yes, Mr Harding mentioned it to Muriel, I believe.' The way Mrs Wheeler looked at Rhoda spoke for itself.

'You think I'm crazy, working when I have no need?'

'If you want the truth, yes, that's what I do think. Young women these days all seem to think they have to be out there earning, and perhaps some of them do. When I was young, we learnt to cut our coat according to our cloth, and lived on the wage our husbands brought home. After all the years you and Mr Harding have been married I'm surprised you don't see things along those lines too.'

The outspoken opinion certainly surprised Rhoda and made her look at Muriel Wheeler's mother with renewed respect. Too frightened to leave the house, too wrapped up in her own miserable outlook to fight for a way out of their present predicament, that was the impression she had been given and, no doubt, that was as Muriel saw it.

'Never mind about *me,*' she said, 'it's you I want to talk about, you and Miss – you and Muriel. Now that the girls have left home, Alec and I rattle around in Timberley. Living here you are so cut off, there isn't even a local shop or a post office within walking distance. Dewsberry may only be a village, but it has most things one wants and we have two spare bedrooms. You are more than welcome to use them until you are able to find somewhere really suitable. You and your daughter could share what used to be Etty's and use the second as a sitting room of your own, or perhaps she would rather turn the second into a sort of bed-sit. It really would be up to you and it would give you the chance to get some of your own things out of store to have around you. We'd have to share the kitchen, but it would be up to us – you and me – to see it worked.'

'Can't believe what I'm hearing. You would really do that for us? Mr Harding has always been kindness itself to Muriel. She's a good girl, better than I sometimes deserve. That office means the world to her – if he asked her to work through the night she'd do it and willingly too. Nothing else in her life, you see. She's never had a young man, never filled her head with romantic nonsense. The way some of the girls chased after anything in uniform filled me with shame for them. I've always known that it had to be up to me to care for her. Even at school she never wanted to bring friends home. There were just the three of us, Muriel, her father and me. We'd given up all hope of having a family when I found myself expecting her. She was born on my fortieth birthday.' Her tears were forgotten as the words tumbled out. 'In the mornings before Mr Harding calls for her, I have her coat on the back of the chair ready for her to slip on, make sure her handkerchief matches her cardigan – all the little extra touches a mother thinks of. Well, I don't need to tell you, you have girls of your own.'

Rhoda thought of timid Muriel Wheeler and imagined the scene.

'If my lot had waited for me to see they had a clean handkerchief they'd have been left sniffing,' she laughed. 'What do you think she will make of the proposition?'

'What do I think? I don't *think*, I *know*. She will feel heaven has dropped into her lap. And if there is anything Mr Harding would like done in the evening I know she will be only too pleased. I tell you, Mrs Harding, that place is the be all and end all for her.'

'Her evenings are her own, Mrs Wheeler. And lately even I haven't seen much of him in the evenings.'

'It's a busy time of year for all of them. Now, may I offer you something? A cup of tea or perhaps you prefer coffee?'

'Neither, thanks all the same. I'm on my way to Oakleigh. At the weekend, Alec and I will clear those two rooms and you can have your stuff brought any time you like after that. I'm sure it'll be a very happy arrangement.'

'It will make it easier for Mr Harding, too, not having to make a special journey for Muriel as he has been. So kind of him. To tell you the truth I was worried she might have to get to work on her bicycle and I know how nervous that would make her. She'd rather do anything than go on her bike. When she first started to work for Mr Harding, we bought it for her, thinking it would be a nice easy ride. But it was no use. She'd walk two miles rather than ride one. And that's what she used to do when she first started work - if she hadn't enough money in her purse for her bus fare she'd set off early so that she had time to walk. So frightened of falling off those two wheels, poor little soul. Always such a timid little mouse she was. So you see, that's why I've been so thankful that she worked for someone as kind and sensitive as dear Mr Harding. Your girls have grown up so well, both of them standing on their own feet and seeming to be part of today's world.' Rhoda felt lost for words. The long monologue was so unexpected, but Elizabeth Wheeler appeared not to notice it was a one-sided conversation. 'I see to it that she does the shopping and feels she's playing her part, but one of these days she won't have me to depend on. That's my constant nightmare.'

'I think perhaps you underestimate her, Mrs Wheeler. Alec wouldn't be without her.' Rhoda wanted to be gone – there was something unnatural in the relationship between mother and daughter. Did they understand each other at all? They each saw the situation from such opposing viewpoints. 'I must dash. Like it or not, I have to make my journey on a bicycle.'

'Perhaps when we get settled at that lovely home of yours, Muriel will find the courage to have another go.'

It wasn't until Rhoda was at Oakleigh propping her bike against the side of the house that the words came back to her. She wasn't interested enough to give it much thought, assuming that one of the men would be delegated to take Muriel home on the evenings that Alec went off on some mission of mercy.

'Here I am,' she called as she let herself into the house on Oakleigh Green. 'Oh, you poor soul!' One look at Matthew Wilberforce's swollen face and she forgot her own excitement at the task he was entrusting to her.

'Not a pretty sight,' he mumbled, his whole face feeling too stiff to let him form the words. 'Silas got the dental chap to see me first thing this morning, but he won't touch it until the swelling goes. Got tablets to take. Bloody painful it is too.' Then, pulling himself up before he drowned in self-pity, he asked, 'You don't mind doing this for me?'

'If you want the truth, I'm excited. And flattered, too, that you ask me to go in your place. Have you told Professor Hitchens what to expect?'

'I telephoned him. Here are my car keys. You'll find enough petrol in the tank.'

*

200

And so Rhoda set out on her first errand. For that's all it was: simply an errand. Professor Hitchens, as he was still known even though he had been retired for some years, was finding life a financial struggle and bit by bit was parting with his book collection. In his experience there were those you could trust and those who were out to make a 'quick buck' – an expression he deplored just as he did so much more about post-war Britain – and Matthew Wilberforce was one of the former, indeed what the elderly professor called the 'old school'. Rhoda's mission was to collect from him the books he had set aside for sale and transport them carefully back to Oakleigh. That in itself gave her a feeling of importance. Anyone who could drive a car could have carried out the errand, but for Rhoda the whole afternoon took on an aura of significance. As she drove through Brackleford and saw the women out carrying their shopping baskets, she smiled a secret smile of satisfaction at where life had brought her. She found the elderly professor talkative and hospitable, and after sharing a cup of tea with him and eating a stale Petit Beurre as if it were just the way she liked it, she carefully wrapped each valuable publication in tissue paper, packed them all safely in the box Matthew had given her for the purpose and drove back to Oakleigh. There was nothing to suggest, as a little later she cycled towards Sedgeley Manor, that the afternoon was to be the first of many such occasions. She assumed that within days Matthew would have had his wisdom tooth removed and would be doing his own journeying just as he had previously. Listening to Denis's excited description of his day at school, she almost managed to put her own adventure out of her mind.

But no day passes without leaving its footprint, and the outcome of that first trip was that although Matthew travelled to buy, when it came to delivering he was more than pleased to stay behind in Oakleigh. As he said to Silas, 'There are times when a pretty woman is more use than years of experience. Wherever she goes I get glowing reports of what a

201

charmer she is.' He let the observation settle without probing for Silas's reaction, but he was neither blind nor stupid and what he suspected was happening worried him. A woman with a quarter of a century or more of a good marriage behind her and a man whom Matthew believed had a void in his life, despite the success of his career, produced a situation that could only spell disaster.

At the weekend, two of the men from the yard came to Timberley to help shift furniture from the two rooms Muriel and her mother were to use, dismantling beds and carrying each item down to the cellar. The following Tuesday the furniture van arrived and the Wheelers took up residence, Muriel keeping the larger of the two rooms where there was space enough for her single bed and some sitting-room furniture, while her mother had her own bedroom suite in the smaller. Somewhere to sleep, somewhere to relax, it had sounded so straightforward, but it was the sharing of the kitchen and the bathroom that inevitably made for a changed atmosphere in the house.

'I reckon you must get fed up with having them about the place,' Jenny put into words what Rhoda very soon felt. 'And with you being out quite a lot, I bet the old bag feels real cock of the walk.'

'It may not be for long,' Rhoda answered with more hope than expectation. 'We are all keeping our ears and eyes open.'

'You may be, but I bet she isn't. Got it made, she has. And that prissy daughter of hers too! Honest Rhoda, when I think of her queening it there in Etty's old bedroom, it narks me. Go on, tell me it's none of my business.'

Rhoda laughed, looking with affection at Jenny.

'Of course it's your business, silly, we are your friends.'

Jenny looked at her with a warm smile. 'You and me are friends, that's for sure. Don't think Mr H is so keen. And why should he be; I'm not really up his street, I know that. But Rhoda, from what I've seen of prissy Miss Wheeler, I wonder how he puts up with her. She makes me think of when I was just a nipper, when my mum was still alive. Now that I'm older I can see that Dad wanted to take her off to bed for an hour after she'd cleared up the Sunday dinner. That's why they used to send me off to Sunday School – it wasn't as if they ever went to church themselves. Bet that's why most kids get packed off ... give a man a good dinner and an hour on his hands. Anyway, like I was saying, that Muriel Wheeler takes me right back to those days. The teacher was just like her – even wore a silly shiny hair slide like she does. Came from Woolies but tried to make it look like a diamond.'

'That doesn't sound like you, Jen. If we can't afford diamonds, sometimes what we buy at Woolies makes us feel good.' Rhoda had a feeling that they were talking their way around what was really on Jenny's mind.

'I should know, I got myself up often enough with bits and bobs from Woolies. Can just see the way Michael used to look. And here am I behaving just like he did. Of course it's fine to deck yourself out in the best you can afford, whether it's Woolies or the poshest shop in town.' Then a pause while Rhoda waited. Knowing Jenny as well as she did, she was sure there was something churning in her mind. 'Rhoda, I got a bit of a problem. Well, you may not think it's a problem, you may see it clearer than I do and see what's right for me to do.'

'Something at work?'

'Crumbs, no. It's a rotten dirty job, but I don't really mind that. They're nice people, the Ridleys. No, it's not work. It's Jim Byford. Rhoda, he's always given me the feeling that he – well, he fancies me.'

Rhoda's laugh was spontaneous. 'Not surprising. Jen, you honestly don't seem to realise how pretty you are – smashing figure too. No wonder he fancies you, as you put it.'

'Don't say that. Makes me feel I look tarty, like Michael said.'

'Tarty be damned. You know that's not what I meant. But

203

why are you suddenly bothered by Jim Byford? He hasn't tried anything funny has he?' Rhoda believed that any man who made an unwanted pass at Jenny would soon have been knocked off his perch, but she couldn't account for the girl's worried expression.

'Not the way you mean. I don't know what to do. You see, he's asked me to marry him.'

Whatever Rhoda had imagined, it certainly hadn't been marriage.

'Are you in love with him?'

Jenny shook her head. 'He's a nice bloke; him and me get on fine. And I really do love little Den. Sounds daft, but it's almost as if God, or whoever it is, has sent Den into my life because Mick got taken away. Just the same age ... you know I've told you sometimes that when I watch Den I feel I'm seeing my Mick. Perhaps all little boys are Mick. Don't know what to do, Rhoda. If I said yes to Jim I could go and live at the cottage and be a mum to Den. He'd like that. I would too. So why don't I jump at it? I mean, going to bed with Jim, all that sort of thing, well that wouldn't be so awful because I think he's as much in love with me as he could be with anyone after Betty – Den's mum. What do you reckon?'

Rhoda gazed at her, considering the situation: if she wasn't in love with him, what was to say that she wouldn't fall in love with someone else? Or, once she lived with Jim, would love follow?

'What do I reckon? Perhaps you ought to tell him you'll think about it. You're not free to get married yet. Give yourself time, don't rush into it. You have your independence – and that is very precious. What if you meet someone you really do fall in love with?'

There was something she didn't understand in the girl's sudden change of expression. Or did she imagine it? Almost immediately Jenny had control again and answered as she had so often, 'Shan't do that. Been caught out once; like I told you lots of times, you won't catch me being that sort of a muggins again. But, what I was saying about Jim: he's a nice guy, he's been through a rough time with losing Betty and his people like he did. But now he's got a home for Den and him, and he's getting back on track, sort of. We could get on well enough. He likes me the way I am.'

'He'd be very stupid if he didn't. Jen, love, no one can tell you what's right for you to do. Don't do it on the rebound from Michael though.'

'Rebound? Not bl— not likely! I don't expect I was the only kid to fancy herself in love with some handsome chap all kitted out smart as paint in uniform. If it hadn't been for the war, for the unnatural sort of way we were all living, then he wouldn't have looked at me – or me at him. But now it's all done and over, I'm glad it happened. Most of all, I'm grateful for having Mick. And even the other, the good times I thought we were sharing – well, I guess I learnt a lesson from them. But Jim, with Jim it would be different, sort of solid if you know what I mean. We'd never have much money, but money isn't everything. I reckon, being good friends like we are and sharing Den, we would make it a good home.'

Seeing the expectation in her blue eyes as she waited for confirmation of her hopes, Rhoda thought as she had so often just what a complex person Jenny was. With her hair piled unnaturally high and her face with its thick layer of cheap make-up, it was likely that most people's first impression of her was much the same as Alec's. But they'd be wrong, just as he was. Scratch the surface and she was pure gold.

'Marriage needs more than friendship,' Rhoda warned.

'Course it does. But however you start off, you've got to work at it, haven't you? I mean, there can't be a sort of magic that keeps everything like when you first clap eyes on someone and think you've fallen in love.'

'You're a wise girl, Jen. Stardust can get in your eyes. You both have to work at it. Time brings routine and habit.'

Jenny nodded and from her expression Rhoda believed her

205

to be imagining the safety of the rut habit would bring, something so different from her chequered background, imagining the comfort of routine and apparently liking what she saw.

'If I say yes to him, Rhoda, I'd get on with it. Like you said, I'm not free to be married, but if I decide that's what I'm going to do I'd move in with him and Den, start making it a proper family home. And there's another thing,' and this time Jenny laughed as she spoke, the serious moment over, 'if I moved out of April Cottage, you'd be able to give prissy Miss Wheeler and her ma the push. She could still cadge a lift to work with Mr H but you'd have the house to yourselves again. You can't pretend that your nice cosy routine hasn't been upset by them hearing every movement.'

Loyalty to Alec, who seemed to have taken remarkably kindly to the Wheeler invasion, stopped Rhoda from agreeing.

'It can't be easy for any of us,' was all she said. But Jenny knew her well enough to read behind the spoken words. That was towards the end of November, some two months after the Wheelers had moved in. To start with, on the days when Rhoda was at home, Elizabeth busied herself in her own rooms; she even organised their food so that when she knew Rhoda would be cooking, she and Muriel managed with the gas ring in the bed-sitting room. Gradually, though, at first tentatively and then with growing confidence, on the days Rhoda was to be out until it was time to prepare something quickly for Alec, Elizabeth relished having the place to herself. At first Rhoda would find the vegetables prepared, but by that day at the end of November the situation had moved on. Wanting to encourage hermit-like Mrs Wheeler to gain confidence, it had been Rhoda's idea that they should walk to the village together so that she could introduce her to the local grocer and butcher where she would draw their weekly rations. Muriel maintained that she had to do all the shopping because her mother had become a recluse; Elizabeth had explained that it was to draw Muriel out of

206

her shell she was encouraged to take charge of the shopping. Either way, from the time they moved in to Timberley, Muriel's responsibilities in that direction ceased. From being introduced to the shopkeepers, it was only one small step for Elizabeth to enjoy her daily walk into the village; first tapping meekly on the door of the room where she expected Rhoda to be, she would offer to collect anything that was wanted. From that it was only one more step for her to buy sufficient for all of them so that when Rhoda came home from Oakleigh she would find the meal well on its way, the fire burning brightly in the kitchen range and Elizabeth with a frilly pinafore over her 'afternoon dress'. A meal for four – what more natural than that they should all four eat together. Alec appeared to have no objection, indeed he was attentive and charming to the elderly woman whose confidence grew day by day.

So it was that when Jenny made her caustic comment about being able to 'give them the push', Rhoda gave it her silent agreement.

Less than a fortnight later on a Saturday afternoon when she'd braved the cold to cycle to Sedgeley Manor, it was Etty who told her the news.

'Have you seen Jen today, Mum?'

'No. She works on Saturday mornings, remember.'

'She won't mind if I tell you, will she? Well, I'm going to anyway. Jim Byford is over the moon. He and Jen are getting engaged. Isn't it great? And Mum,' she added a little tentatively, 'until she's free to be married she's going to live with him and Den in the cottage. You don't seem surprised.'

'I've lived longer than you have, my love. I saw it coming. And it's wonderful for little Denis too.' For all her smiling reply, she wasn't entirely happy. Was it right that a person needed time to think about it before giving a reply? If you need to hesitate, then surely the right thing to do is to refuse.

'There they go now.' She pointed to where Jim was disappearing down the drive on his bicycle with Den strapped into the child seat on the back. 'He's going to collect Jen from work and they're all going into Brackleford to buy her a ring.' What she didn't tell her mother was that Andrew had given Jim four crisp, white five-pound notes when he congratulated him, notes that were safely in the young farmhand's wallet with the other few pounds he'd managed to save from his wages. Had his engagement been to anyone else Andrew probably wouldn't have been so generous but like Etty and Rhoda, he had grown very fond of Jenny.

There must have been enough people on the estate agent's waiting list to fill April Cottage over and over, but Jenny knew just what she was doing when she timed her visit to Timberley the next morning. From her front room window she could see the activity in the garden, Muriel raking leaves and Alec coaxing flames into a smouldering bonfire. That meant that Rhoda must be preparing Sunday dinner and it would be Jenny's guess Mrs Wheeler would be trying to look as though she was helping while, all the time, she would be giving unwanted advice. Quite time that she and that dreary daughter of hers found somewhere else, and Jenny was going to see to it that they had no choice.

'Can I come in?' she called as she opened the back door without knocking.

'May you?' A question or a correction from frilly-pinafored Mrs Wheeler? Either way Jenny ignored it.

'Rhoda, Ett said she told you. I've come to show you my ring. See how it shines when the light catches it.' Proudly she held her hand near to the kitchen window, moving it in the hope that a glint might appear in the tiny cluster of diamond chips set on the gold band. There followed the customary congratulations, hugs from Rhoda who called to Alec and Muriel to come in and hear the news. It was all working just as Jenny had planned – except that she hadn't

208

envisaged Alec would produce a bottle of sherry and five glasses (she suspected playing bountiful host to impress the Wheelers rather than because he was interested in drinking to the forthcoming union).

'Well,' she said, putting her glass down having taken the first large sip, 'well now, that's only half what I came to say, so it's good having all of you here. Tomorrow I'm going to cycle in to Brackleford to tell the estate agent that I'm moving out.' Rhoda could feel a laugh trying to escape as she watched the triumph in her young friend's smile as she turned to the Wheeler's. 'I know what a job you're having finding a place – well, of course you are, places to live are like gold dust. I wouldn't wonder you've got your name down with the agent in case he hears. But if I tell him about you, ask him to let you have it, then I bet you anything he'll agree. Names on lists are one thing, but a mention from a friend is what counts. That's what makes it so tough when you're a stranger in a place, like Michael was when he persuaded them to let him have the cottage for Mick and me.' Was recalling her happiness here on the green with Mickey rubbing salt in the wound? Rhoda wondered. The truth was that Jenny had recognised what she called the 'toffee-nosed look' on mother and daughter's faces at the inference of friendship; she needed the mention of Mickey; belonging to him – and he to her. It was her strength. 'Wouldn't that fit the bill just right? You'd still get your lift to work, Miss Wheeler.' Her temporary loss of confidence restored, Jenny beamed at them all, only Rhoda noticing the hint of a wink in her direction.

'Isn't it strange the way things work out,' Rhoda said as if the arrangement was already finalised. 'If you hadn't come to Timberley to stay, Mrs Wheeler, you might never have heard about the chance of getting the cottage. You won't know yourselves with a place of your own after being so cramped in those two rooms.'

'It's a pleasure to have you here,' Alec told them, hearing Rhoda's comments as their dismissal. 'But at least

April Cottage is conveniently close. As Jenny says, Muriel, we shall still drive in together each day.' Then, his remark meant as a jibe at the neighbour he had always viewed with contempt. 'And I'll be able to give you a hand knocking that jungle of a garden into some sort of shape. But Jenny, I fail to see what your hurry is to vacate the cottage at all. Surely your divorce can't be finalised for some time.'

'That's right, it can't. But what's the point of hanging about? Me and Jim can't tie the knot until I'm free, but there's enough room for us all at his cottage.'

Alec was genuinely appalled. 'Unmarried? And you're contemplating giving up your home and going to live with him?' Then, with a scathing look that took in Rhoda as well as Jenny, 'I'm not surprised. Clearly we haven't all the same standards of morality.'

Jenny was starting to enjoy herself. Mentally she pulled herself up short as she made her laughing reply.

'Lucky for me and Jim we don't all think the same. Andrew and Ett are all in favour. What's the difference whether we sign along the dotted line now or a bit later? The best thing we can do is get cracking making a proper family together with Den.'

'And quite right too,' Rhoda agreed. From their expressions, it was clear that the Wheelers saw things differently.

At that period, divorce was a slow process. Michael had deserted her but when she'd received the first letter from his solicitor it had referred only to the fact they were no longer living as man and wife. When Rhoda had suggested that if she replied that she was willing for them to live together there would be no case, her answer had been a firm 'Not Pygmalion likely! Even if I was pining away wanting him I'm— I'm bothered if I'd live with him now. I know what he always thought about me. And I'm not pining, that's the God's honest truth. I'll bide my time, I'm in no hurry to be free. Like I said, I'm not letting some other chap make a monkey out of me.' So at the time she

210

planned to vacate the cottage, she still had two years or so before the case would be heard.

On the last day of 1947, Jenny and her few belongings were taken from April Cottage and transported by Jim Byford in a well-scrubbed horsebox from the stables of Sedgeley Manor. The scene was watched by Elizabeth from the window of her bedroom, her expression saying it all as she took in the scene: fancy Rhoda Harding being out there in her old gardening clothes helping to carry that 'common-as-muck' girl's bits and pieces of furniture. As if it wasn't bad enough for her to be moving in to live with a man who wasn't her husband, but from the fuss and excitement you'd think the immoral situation was cause for celebration. The more Mrs Wheeler saw of some of the day's younger generation, the more grateful she was for dear Muriel. And of one thing she was certain: Mr Harding's opinion was in line with her own, her own and Muriel's. The surprise was Etty Harding, or Etty Clutterbuck as she was since she'd done so well for herself with her husband inheriting Sedgeley Manor. You would expect in her position she would have set a better example than to encourage such a liaison. Ah, now, they were shutting the door of the horse-box – and what a way to move house!. Hugs and kisses, then, all tarted up in those silly high heels, her hair piled up like a guardsman's busby and, no doubt, her face plastered with its usual coating of rubbish, Jenny Matherson climbed into the seat next to the driver. Hardly like a bride and groom, Elizabeth scoffed silently, but about as near as they'd get. By the time the wretched girl is free to marry they will have been together so long the shine will have worn off – if, indeed, he ever married her at all.

'Don't be late will you, Rhoda. Ett said six o'clock so that Den can be there too. I wish you could have come with us now.'
    'Looking like this?' Rhoda laughed, her words almost

drowned by the throb of the engine as Jim waited to pull away. 'This evening is a celebration; I'm not going to turn up in my old gardening togs. Etty said she would phone Alec and make sure he picks me up in good time. And Jen —' Just for a second she hesitated, there were a thousand things she wanted to say but instead, her smile encompassing them both, she made do with, 'Jim and Jen, bless you both – and Den too.'

Jenny nodded, frightened to relax the tight hold she held on her jaw. Memories crowded in on her. She was leaving the green, leaving the first real home she and Mick had ever had – the first and the last. For a second her eyes met Rhoda's and each read the other's thoughts.

Then the horsebox started forward. Rhoda watched it until it had rounded the bend and the green was lost to it. One last glance at April Cottage where the ghost of little Mickey seemed to be everywhere, playing peep-o around the apple tree, trundling his toy dog along the path, jumping with excitement as he saw the green sports car draw up. And if that was how she felt, how much harder it must be for poor Jenny, who had to pick up the pieces chance sent her way and make a new life for herself. Desperately Rhoda tried to believe that for Jenny the future was bright, yet in her head there was the memory of the day she'd watched as the young family opposite moved in. Make things work out well for her, she pleaded silently. How much misery is any one person supposed to stand? She deserves to be loved and Jim certainly does love her.

Perhaps it was evidence of their own contentment with life that when Andrew had suggested a reception party in the house on the evening Jim brought Jenny to make his family complete, Etty had embraced the idea. Neither Jim nor Jenny had family to invite so those who expected to be there to mark the occasion were workers from the farm, staff from the manor house itself, Rhoda, Alec, Silas and, of course, young Denis Byford.

'There will be raised eyebrows – folk will delight in the gossip and could well make life difficult for Jenny,' Andrew had said. 'We know her pretty well, Ett, so it has to be up to us to make our approval evident.'

Etty had agreed.

'You're a nice chap, Drew,' she had told him, leaning over his chair and dropping a light kiss on his forehead.

'More truthfully, I'm a lucky one. And I know it.'

'I'm off to phone Dad to make sure he's getting away from the yard early.'

Dressed for the evening, Rhoda waited for Alec. It was already a quarter to six when the telephone rang.

'I've called Etty and explained,' Alec told her. 'We can't possibly get there until later. I still have a lot to do before I can think of getting away. Muriel's just gone to the post but she'll come back here and wait for me.'

'What in the world can be so important it can't wait? This evening is *really* important – even more than if today they'd actually been able to get married. I want us to be seen to be backing Jenny.'

'Be reasonable. I have a business to run.'

'So you will have tomorrow; one evening isn't going to ruin the business.' Her voice took on a tone as icy as his own.

'If you're so keen, then you go ahead on your bike. I'll get there when I can to bring you home. I'm afraid in my book the sort of liaison they're setting out on is no cause for celebration.'

No reply from Rhoda. He got his answer from the click as she replaced the receiver. She wanted him to feel her rage. He *knew* the evening was important to her, *knew* all Jenny had been through before this second chance had come her way. Glancing by chance into the hall mirror Rhoda was shocked at the expression on her face – it was more than anger or disappointment, it was ugly and ageing. Without so much as calling goodbye to Elizabeth Wheeler,

213

she tied a headscarf around her head, pulled on her overcoat and went out, venting her feelings by slamming the front door. The evening was dark and cold, and she had some five miles of country roads ahead of her on her bicycle. It wasn't so much the certainty that she'd arrive with her hands blue from cold, her nose red and her hair a mess, as the impression it would give that Jenny's new start wasn't of sufficient importance for her to be punctual. All her venom was directed at Alec: it wasn't work that was keeping him away, it was a mean and petty way of showing Jenny what he thought of the step she was taking.

So angry was she that she wasn't even aware of the sound of a car approaching until it pulled up outside the house and the voice that haunted her called to her.

'Never mind your bike. Hop in. I was there when Alec called to say you'd be late.' Then, with an affectionate laugh, Silas added, 'Etty told him exactly what she thought – and I bet you did too.' Then as Rhoda got in and took off her headscarf, 'The evening starts well, my darling Rhoda.' Taking her hand he carried it to his face, rubbing it against his cheek. 'And what could be better than it's you and me who are there to see little Jenny step into her new role. I know you care deeply about her and from that first evening when she and I talked, I believe I can understand and appreciate her. This is a good move for her, it will help lay her ghosts, or at least those whose memory brings her no happiness.'

As he spoke he started the car forward. These moments were their own, shut off from the world, too dark now to see each other and yet aware of each movement, almost of each thought.

'The ghost she would never want to lose is Mick. He was her whole world.'

'I know that. In Denis Byford she will still hold on to Mick – not as a baby who died but as a little boy growing up. Loving Denis won't detract from her love for Mick, nothing could ever do that. There's room in her heart for both.'

214

In the dark she peered at him. Was there a hidden message in his words?

'I know,' she said quietly, both of them aware of the importance of her words. 'I used to resent the routine, habit, concessions, all the things that go to make up marriage, all of them taking their first root in love.'

'Used to? And now?'

For a moment she didn't answer, the atmosphere between them was charged with emotion.

'Now you've set me free. My marriage is still there, the daily grind is still there, but – my life is more than that. Let's not analyse our emotions. Let's accept what we have as a God-given gift.'

'Rhoda, don't run away from what is between us.' He took her hand in his, still looking straight ahead as he drove.

She shook her head. 'I couldn't run away from it if I wanted to. And I don't want to. It's because I love you that I can accept all the rest.'

He steered the car off the narrow lane to stop by an entrance to a ploughed field. Then she was in his arms, her fingers caressing the back of his neck as his mouth covered hers. A thousand memories crowded her mind, memories of the first time Alec had kissed her, their early years of struggle with the business, all of it like looking back at two different people from the ones the years had made of them. In those same seconds she seemed to see the girls when they'd been small, remembered the pride she and Alec had felt when they'd managed to scrape and save so that they could send their children to her old school. So how had the change crept in without her being aware? How had it become no more than soulless monotony with passion diminished into routine lovemaking? None of the images stayed with her, rather they crowded to fill her head while her heart raced with excitement and she wanted the moment to last for ever.

'So many years gone. Rhoda, is this all we can ever be

215

to each other, just two people who have nothing more than furtive kisses, stolen moments? Why couldn't we have met when we were young?' he whispered.

'Perhaps we wouldn't have looked at each other,' she laughed softly. 'The time wasn't right. This is *now* . . . and the time is right.'

'Youngsters like Jenny and young Byford, Andrew and Etty, they'd see it as ridiculous. They think love is for the young.'

'And so it is – it's for young and old too. And we are neither one nor the other. Old enough not to be deceived by moonshine, young enough to want – want—'

'Want to find everything that has been missing in our lives. We ought to thank God for bringing us to each other. Darling, we can't go on like this. You are dearer to me than life itself – and I swear to you that is the truth. Are Jenny and young Byford braver than you and me? Let's make a new beginning. I've been approached to move to mid-France to a clinic about to open. Heaven knows there are enough people on that side of the Channel whose lives have been broken. Come with me. Look into your heart, my blessed Rhoda. Does it take you back to the life you've lived for these last years, or does it guide you to a new beginning with me?'

'You mean leave Alec?' In the darkness of the car, she peered hard at Silas. Follow her heart, he said. She was torn with guilt, frightened to think of all she and Alec had shared; frightened too to look ahead. Later she would have to face where the years she'd known Silas had brought them. Time doesn't stand still, it brings changes. Would she have fallen in love with him a quarter of a century ago? Probably not, or he with her. If she were to meet Alec today, would she fall in love with him? She pulled her mind up short, not letting herself face the answer: he was the same man, he had done nothing, *nothing,* to deserve her unfaithfulness. For wasn't it the same to be unfaithful in thought as it was in deed?

216

'Better drive on,' she whispered. 'There's only *us*, us and Andrew and Ett who really celebrate what Jen and Jim are doing. The others hardly know Jenny and, people being what they are, I'm sure behind their backs they'll take the same stiff-necked attitude as Alec and the Wheelers.'

At the manor a buffet supper was set out, farm produce making it possible. Home-cured ham, off-ration oatmeal biscuits, cheese, butter and cream from their own dairy, potatoes baked in their jackets to add bulk, all were made to look more festive by a huge bouquet in the centre of the refectory table. Dennis was wide eyed with excitement and pride as, holding tight to Jenny's hand, he listened to his father.

'It's real good of you all to come along to see me and Jenny start out, me and Jenny and young Den here. I know it's not the usual way round for things to be but, tell you what, let's make a date: all of you promise to come along and have a bit of a party with us when Jen and me can tie the knot all neat and legal.' All the time he spoke he fiddled with a piece of paper, although once he started he didn't glance down at it. Listening to him, Rhoda silently told herself that Jim Byford was a good young man, rough at the edges perhaps, but a *good* man, one who was worthy of Jenny, and that was more than could be said for that self-opinionated pipsqueak she'd fallen for before. Catching Etty's glance, she half-smiled, sure their thoughts were on the same line. Around her, those gathered were applauding Jim's efforts and she joined in while her mind was on a journey of its own.

Love ... it came in many guises: look at Etty and Andrew, on the surface even now, after two and a half years of marriage, they appeared as casual as brother and sister. Yet she knew their love was complete – she had seen the fear in Etty's eyes when he'd been ill, and in his when Christo was born. Friendship was the best basis for marriage, Alec had said, but she had been so sure he was wrong. Yet look at Etty and Andrew now and doesn't it show that perhaps he was right? Could that sort of relationship develop between Jenny and Jim? She sent up a silent prayer that it might be so. Poor Jenny, she thought as she saw the young couple and little boy off, how must she feel setting out to share the rest of her life with a man she respects, likes, perhaps feels some sort of affection for, but isn't in love with?

Still Alec hadn't arrived. Hurt on Jenny's account and angry on her own, she accepted Silas's offer to drive her home. In truth, had Alec arrived at the last minute, added to her other emotions would have been disappointment and resentment too. She wanted to be alone with Silas, sure there wasn't one single thought that had forced itself willy-nilly into her head during the evening which she couldn't have told him knowing he would understand. And yet as soon as they were together in the car, the rest of the world shut out, neither of them talked for fear that what they'd said earlier would be waiting to trap them.

'Alec must have had a sudden emergency,' Silas eventually suggested.

'I expect he got someone else to bring Muriel back. She isn't working tomorrow as it's the day their furniture comes out of store and they start to get sorted out in April Cottage.'

Just for a moment he dropped his mask.

'April Cottage ... poor little Jenny ... she's great strength of character, and Denis will be her salvation,' he said, briefly taking Rhoda's hand in his.

'Yes. And Ett will be there for her. But married or not, the promise she's making in her heart is a lifelong commitment.' Dangerous ground. She changed the subject before he had time to move onto the track on which she had stumbled. 'Den is on top of the world. He adores her. And who would have thought to see her that she'd spent the best part of the day humping furniture and cleaning up?'

'The height of glamour,' he laughed, as relieved as she

218

was that they'd avoided the pitfall. 'Well, here you are, home sweet home.'

'Will you come in?'

With the engine still running, he turned to look at her very directly, answering in a voice that had suddenly lost all its assumed light-heartedness. 'You think I can stand by and watch? Husband and wife, tied by years you call routine and habit? Goodnight my blessed friend, my dearest friend.'

She felt the hot sting of tears but, in the dark, he knew nothing of that, simply the light touch of her mouth on his cheek and the sound of her whispering just the one word, 'Silas' as she opened the car door and left him.

Going into the house through the back door she found the kitchen in darkness. Alec must have had a call-out after the men had gone home. For years he had done no more than promise a mechanic would be sent first thing the following morning; only through these last months had he donned overalls and gone himself, leaving poor Muriel to wait for her lift home. This evening someone else must have brought her, for from the sound coming from the rooms she and her mother occupied, they were busy getting ready for moving the following day.

Rhoda pulled the kettle forward to the centre of the range to bring it back to the boil, then spooned coffee into a jug. This time tomorrow the Wheelers would be gone, the house would be their own again. Stirring the boiling water onto the ground coffee, she imagined she and Alec on their own again, trying to make herself believe they would be glad to find each other again. But would they welcome being alone? Would they find each other? They *must*. She must stop filling her heart and mind with memories of Silas or with dreams of him either. Poor Alec, what had he ever done to deserve the way her thoughts were turning? He never changed, he was loyal, caring – she knew he was, even though he never put his feelings into words and, in truth, neither did she want him to. Hadn't that always been his way? Oh, there had been times, times galore when they'd been young and first married, when life had been full of joy simply because they were together. Surely after so many years, all that was incidental to the dependence they had grown to accept. What was the matter with her that Silas was constantly on her mind and that, knowing he was falling on love with her, she did all she could to encourage him? She wanted to laugh with him, (when did she and Alec last laugh in the light hearted way of youth?), she wanted to discuss world affairs with him, affairs of the England they loved and of the future of those whose lives had been shattered by war (and what would Alec's view be? He never put himself in the position of those whose thoughts were different from his own); she wanted to tell Silas her opinions, as she so often did when he had a chance to join her in the book-lined rooms at Oakleigh, knowing that even when his views differed from hers he was prepared to listen so that both of them enlarged their own views by listening to the other (Alec brushed her aside, there was his way of thinking and the wrong way); she wanted to share all that she was with Silas so that they belonged to each other's body and soul. So often Matthew was away and for hours the telephone didn't ring while she and Silas sat together by the fire talking. Both of them knew that at the front of both their minds was the tantalising image of the room upstairs where he slept, the isolation from the world, and above all of the complete love they longed for.

Her reverie was broken by the sound of footsteps on the stairs, footsteps she recognised as Alec's.

'I thought you must be on a call-out,' she greeted him. 'Were you too late to come to Etty's for the celebration?'

'Celebration? Is that what you call it? I find nothing to celebrate in that relationship. Rhoda, you and Etty both amaze me. Thank God for Natalie, at least she has morals. She telephoned before the show this evening and when I told her where you were she agreed with me – agreed in every respect. The girl is a tart, she always was and if you needed proof surely you have it with the way she's behaving now.'

Rhoda chose to ignore his jibes.

'Natalie phoned you at the yard? That's unusual. Nothing wrong, was there?'

'I was at home. Mrs Wheeler said your friend had taken you.'

'So why—'

'Why didn't I follow you over? Damn it all, Rhoda, after all the years Muriel Wheeler has been with the firm, let alone the fact that they've been living in our house, I might have expected you too would have been prepared to stay to give them a hand.'

She glared at him. 'Then you can just go on expecting. Are they packed up ready to be off?'

'Mrs Wheeler looks quite done in. She's been cleaning up after that girl ever since she left.'

'She'll have got a kick out of that, something to complain about. Here's your coffee. And thanks for your enquiries, the party went off very well. Alec, don't be such a miserable grouch about Jenny and Jim. Can't you see how much better it will be for little Den?'

'If they'd done the decent thing and waited until Michael Matherson was free of her, then I would have agreed with you. But what sort of standards are they setting the child?' Then, tiring of the subject, 'You'll have eaten, of course, and I had something with the Wheelers. The evening is nearly gone. I'll read my paper out here in the kitchen – it's not worth putting a match to the fire in the other room at this time of day.'

'There's no amazing news. Why can't we just talk for a change?'

'What did you want to talk about? Nothing wrong, is there?'

Turning her back on him she made a play of putting more coal on the range. Nothing wrong? What if she told him that she had fallen in love with another man, a man who filled her every thought, who never bored her, who made her laugh, who listened to what she had to say, who was a companion and who she longed to be a lover too?

When she didn't answer, Alec opened the newspaper at the crossword and took up his pen.

It was the following Tuesday when she had an excited call from Matthew. A first edition he'd been trying to track down had come to light in the private collection of an elderly member of the gentry who was finding that the income that had kept him in pre-war comfort was no longer enough to maintain his customary standards. Armed with his cheque book, a heart full of understanding for the old man's predicament and fair intentions, he wanted to leave by the late morning train and would be away until Thursday. This was the way Rhoda liked it – a sudden call and a rush to get her bicycle, throwing her ordered existence into disarray. It wasn't the first time he had sent for her suddenly; the uncertainty was partly what she liked about working for him. That day, knowing Silas was in the area, there was added excitement about the sudden call.

She telephoned to tell Alec she might be late home then, as he wasn't in the room, left a message with the faithful Muriel, and she was on her way. Pedalling as hard as she could, little did she suspect that she was living through the day that would have such repercussions.

Chapter Ten

Sometimes Rhoda wondered why Matthew employed her at all, or indeed why he saw the need to employ anyone. On that particular day she hadn't answered a single telephone call; instead she had spent her time forcing herself to concentrate on life in the sixteenth century. Handling the ancient book with such care that it might have been made of gossamer, she deciphered the lettering and tried to conjure up a picture of English life four centuries earlier. She had no illusions about herself: she didn't hide from the fact that she didn't possess a solid rock of historical knowledge on which to build, but she was determined to learn all she could and not disgrace Matthew when she was the initial introduction to his empire. Today, though, her mind insisted on wandering. Had people of long ago been different from those of the present time? She believed not, not in the things that mattered. The book forgotten, her thoughts went back to the previous evening. Love, honesty, kindness, humour and something more, something she couldn't put a name to, a sort of invisible cord that bound your spirit to someone else's. She was afraid to try and look ahead: to go with Silas would be to destroy the foundations of Alec's world just as it would the girls'. Even Jenny had looked on theirs as a perfect marriage and Timberley a perfect home. Perfect? Perfect because they never quarrelled, perfect because the meals were always on time and the house clean

223

and welcoming? But where was the perfection that came from twin spirits? Without Silas, what joy would there be? And here her imagination dragged her down into a world of grey hopelessness. Each day would be the same, even the words she and Alec said to one another were part of the routine in the monotony of their never-changing days. Up and down the country there must be millions of homes just the same – wasn't unchanging routine a sign of a good marriage?

With no conscious effort on her part the whole picture changed. Somehow it was Silas who was there in her mind. She leant back in her chair, her eyes closed; willingly she let herself remember the times she had spent with him, hours there in the very room where she now sat dreaming, hours spent in his car, or by the range at Timberley, or making a snack lunch in the little kitchen at Oakleigh, moments when their gaze had met and had told them so much they'd tried to avoid putting into words. But truth and honesty must prevail, they both knew now there was no way of hiding from the truth. Somewhere in the world, was there the perfect partner for each person? And, if so, how often did Fate bring them together? She ought to be thankful for—

The shrill bell of the telephone cut into her reverie.

'Oakleigh three nine four.' In a voice of eager charm she spoke into the mouthpiece, anxious to build the foundation for some satisfactory transaction.

'Rhoda, it's me, Alec.' Alec? Nothing unusual in his calling her, but when had she last heard him speak like that, in a voice full of anticipation? 'Shut the door on that place and be ready for me to pick you up. I've just had a call from Natalie. There's been a fire at the theatre where they were booked for this evening so the programme is cancelled. They go on to Sheffield tomorrow. So she decided to come home just for the one night.'

'That's marvellous. Both of them, I take it?'

'Just Nat. She said she'd expected him to come too but

he had other plans. I've always told you there was nothing between them. He's probably picked up with a girl of his own sort. Well, thank God for that. Anyway, he's not important. The thing is, to get home she has to change trains and get across to the Great Western on one of these country lines – you know the sort, about one a day in either direction. Apparently there's emergency work on the track and her train has been cancelled.'

'Will it make her very late? I'm glad you've given me warning. I'll make sure there's something she likes waiting when she gets in.'

'Don't keep interrupting, just listen. I've told her that we'll drive out to join her and stay overnight. She's booking us in where she's staying. The yard can manage without me tomorrow. We'll see her on her way to Sheffield in the morning before we start home.'

'The yard might be able to do without you, but then you're your own boss. Matthew is relying on me being here until he gets home.'

In the pause that followed before Alec spoke, she could feel his anger.

'So you propose to put sitting by a silent telephone before seeing Natalie!'

'I propose to keep my side of the bargain, if that's what you mean. Of course I would love to spend the evening with Nat, but I can't just cut and run like that. She'll understand. She wouldn't walk away from an engagement because something at home cropped up.'

'God spare me! Surely you don't liken the hours you waste there with a career such as hers!'

'I suppose I do really. In my book, to break your word is just as important in any circumstance.' If he had pleaded with her, even though she wouldn't have let herself be persuaded, at least her voice wouldn't have been as icy toned. Then, thinking of Nat and imagining her being disappointed when he arrived alone, 'Give Nat my love - and, Alec, *please*, even if you can't see things from my

225

point of view, at least make her understand why I'm not coming. I truly am sorry to disappoint her.'

'I'll see to it that she isn't disappointed.' He might have been agreeing to her request, but picturing the excitement when the two of them met she took his words as conveying the message that, with him there, her added presence would have gone almost unnoticed. And wasn't he telling her what she already knew? 'I'll go home and pack an overnight bag, then get on the road.'

'Alec, don't be beastly about my not coming. Whether you're a private or a general you have the same obligation to duty.'

'Very well. I'll see you late in the day tomorrow.' Then a sharp click and the hum of the dialling tone.

Rhoda walked to the window and looked out at the deserted winter afternoon, her disappointment overtaken by a new sense of freedom. Tonight Alec wasn't coming home – the hours were her own. So many thoughts and images crowded her brain, all adding to an unfamiliar and only half-understood excitement. Would Silas be free in time to get to Oakleigh while she was still there? If he was late it would make no difference; in her new freedom, she could wait for him. This evening they could go out to dinner together, or they could rustle up something to eat by the fire in the book-lined room where she spent so many hours, or she could take him back to Timberley and they could eat by candlelight as they had that other time. Even as she thought it, she pushed the last suggestion away – Timberley belonged to her life with Alec, a life that mustn't intrude on the gift of these precious hours. Hours or a lifetime? In those moments nothing else mattered to her except being with him. Hours or a lifetime? Staring out of the window she willed him to appear, feeling light headed, frightened to imagine the moment when he would hear what she had to tell him.

In her new-found confidence, she was brave enough to let herself imagine what her life would be if he accepted the

226

post he'd told her about and moved away. She couldn't let that happen – she would go to the ends of the earth with him, but she couldn't face the emptiness of life without him Don't be late, she begged silently, please don't be late. Come *now*. And surely a good omen for the evening, right on cue his car emerged from the road through Farley Wood.

Reality is so often at variance with expectation. As Rhoda had watched for Silas to come she hadn't doubted that they would clutch at these heaven-sent hours. She could see the scene almost as if it were happening: eagerly she was telling him of her freedom, not giving a thought to Alec, who by that time would be travelling to meet Natalie, never doubting that his faithful wife would lock the door of the house on Oakleigh Green at the appropriate time and cycle home to face a lonely evening.

In reality, he found time to call at April Cottage to make sure the day had gone well for Muriel and her mother's move. Knowing his faithful secretary as well as he did he was confident she would find time to go across the green to Timberley during the evening and make sure Rhoda was all right on her own. And with that reassuring thought, he put everything from his mind except the evening he and Natalie were to spend together.

For Rhoda, reality followed the pattern she had anticipated as Silas listened to her excited words.
　'So what shall we do?' she ended. 'We can go out for a meal and then come back here. Is that what you want? If you prefer, we'll go to Timberley, but ... well ... but—'
　'Rhoda, we have more than one evening to talk about.' Taking hold of her shoulders he held her at arm's length.
　Hadn't she made her decision moments before? A life without Silas was unimaginable. So winding her arms around his neck, she drew his head towards her.

'I know,' she whispered, her mouth close to his. 'We have the rest of our lives. It's all I can think of . . . just us, a new beginning, just us and all the years ahead.'

So that was her answer. With the curtains drawn against the deepening winter darkness, they shared the large and comfortable armchair in what at one time had been the drawing room of the house. With her cradled on his knee, they might have been a pair of teenagers rejoicing in first love rather than a couple more than twice the age. They both knew where the evening was heading – there could be no other way. So with the front door locked and the telephone earpiece dangling on its cord, like people about to sample stolen fruit, side by side on the narrow stairway they went up to his room.

This evening was like no other. In spirit she and Silas had been close for so long, they knew the depths of each other's minds; in the early hours of that winter evening their knowledge of each other was complete. Between them there was no false modesty, between them there was nothing except the longing to share all that they were. Mother of two adult daughters, grandmother . . . for a moment she longed for her lost youth.

'I wish I was different. I wish I was young for you.'

'No. I want you as you *are*. Youth belongs to yesterday for you and for me. You are perfect, you are beautiful – the only woman I could ever love. And I *do* love you – heart, spirit, with all that I am.'

And so, that evening, fantasy played no part. Afterwards, still lying close in each other's arms, she was the first to break the spell of silence.

'I wish we never had to move and these moments could last for ever.'

'This is only the beginning.' Then a long silence. Where were his thoughts taking him? she wondered. The last hour was like a beacon beckoning her to their future but reality, like a cloud of misery, swamped her.

'I'll phone Etty and Andrew and tell them we want them

228

to give you a bed for the night.' His voice cut across her thoughts. Reaching the pull-switch above the bed, he turned off the light, leaving the room in the glow of the hissing gas fire with its none-too-realistic appearance of burning coke. Then he pulled the eiderdown over them and once more drew her close.

'Why should I stay at the manor?'

'Perhaps to please me,' he answered. 'Tomorrow I shall talk to Alec; until after I've seen him, stay with them at the manor. I don't want you to have to explain to him what's happened.'

She buried her face against his shoulder as she mumbled, 'Don't let's talk about it. Not now, not yet. Let's have a bit longer here like this. I don't want to think. I wish we could switch ourselves off like you did that light. Just now – five minutes ago, half an hour ago, I don't know, time doesn't matter – I never knew there could be such . . . such glory. I don't know what else to call it . . . like having a glimpse of what paradise must be. I'll never forget it Silas. I know it will stay with me as long as I live.'

'And with me. The first time and every time.' His hands were warm. She wanted just to push to the back of her mind those thoughts that had been enveloping her. Eagerly, guided by instinct, experience and the need to hide from what she was frightened to face, she reawoke his passion and her own too. There could be room for no unwelcome thoughts; there was room for nothing except here and now.

But escape was only temporary and an hour or so later, both of them dressed and she with her face and hair attended to, they knew time had caught up with them.

'I'll ring the youngsters,' he said, reaching for the telephone on the wall in the narrow passage between the two front rooms.

'No!' The sound of her voice surprised them both as she barked the one word.

'We can't hide it from them. Etty and Drew have to be

229

told – do you believe it will come as a shock to them? They must have seen how we felt.'

'Don't ring them, just take me back home.'

'If you won't go to Etty, then stay here with me.'

Where now was the glory? With her hand clenched she gripped the knuckle of her thumb between her teeth.

'We'll work it all out, darling,' he told her gently. 'Stay here with me, forget about going to Etty or to Timberley. By morning we'll be ready for what has to come next.'

'I've got to go home,' she rasped, biting on her hand so that her words were indistinct. But her expression told its own message.

Holding her by the shoulders he willed her to meet his eyes.

'What are you telling me? That you've changed your mind, that you want me to go without you?'

'No! Yes! I don't know. I can't think of being without you.'

'But . . .' he prompted. It hurt him to see the way her teeth clenched her knuckle in an effort to keep her control. Gently he drew her close. 'But . . .?' he repeated, his only answer being a muffled snort.

'Don't know,' she wept, all hope of stemming her tears lost. 'I don't know what to do. I know what I ought to do . . . but . . . Silas, I can't bear it.'

'You can't bear it and neither can I. Don't you believe that sometimes – not often, perhaps, but sometimes – two people know they are meant for each other. I knew it that evening at the manor when Buck told us he was going to America, going to live his dream. Remember? We looked at each other and the die was cast.' He felt her head nodding against his shoulder.

'I remember. And I know Alec didn't understand about having a dream,' she croaked. 'We talked about it on Etty's wedding evening—' another gulp '—that's when you said he had no dream because his life was all he wanted.'

'I'm not going to take you home.' He changed the subject without loosening his hold on her. 'Tonight we'll

230

stay here together. We'll wake up together. By morning we will think more clearly.'

And so it wasn't all over just yet. Through the night they lay close in each other's arms, not making love but simply absorbing the nearness one to the other, drifting in and out of sleep, hardly speaking a word, wanting the night to last. Time hustled them on, though, and all too soon the long hours of a new day dragged them forward.

'Just once more,' he said as she passed him a cup of steaming coffee. 'I beg you, Rhoda. Together we can make the way ahead smooth.'

She wouldn't, or couldn't, look at him as she answered.

'Smooth for us, but what about the others? Not just Alec. The girls have always taken their parents for granted; every child has a right to do that. If I were to leave Alec and go with you, it wouldn't only be us, us and Alec, who'd be affected. What would it do to Etty and Andrew's marriage? Her mother and his uncle – it could rebound on them.' At the start she had been answering what he said, but as she talked she had closed her eyes, shutting herself off from her surroundings. 'And Nat, away from home, picturing Alec there on his own. If Nat really loves anyone then it's him. They would blame me – of course they would. Alec has never changed; none of this is his fault. His days go on unendingly the same – there are no highs and no lows, no light and no dark, everything's the way he likes it. It's all been my fault. Why couldn't I have been content the same as every other woman? He's worked hard, given me a good home.' She might have been talking to herself, her tone held anger, resentment and even self-loathing. 'He's never angry, never excited, he's fair, he never does anything on the spur of the moment without thinking it out first.' She seemed to feel the chains tightening their hold on her. 'Order, order, order, everything in its place, not a thought out of line.' Her eyes shot open and she

231

was back with Silas. 'You've brought me to life. When you're gone I don't know how I'll bear it.'

He knew that was his answer. And perhaps she was right, he admitted silently. Today he would write his letter of acceptance and for the remainder of the time he was working at hospitals in the area he would stay at a hotel. There must be no looking back. Instead he should be thankful for the career change and the challenges it would bring. That's what he told himself in that moment when he knew he had to accept the answer he'd dreaded. And yet, wasn't she right? For them to be together was natural and right, they both knew it; yet, if she had agreed to turn her back on her past she would have been ashamed of putting her own happiness before that of a husband she saw as loyal and unchanging. Loyal? Of course he was loyal to her; to have looked outside his marriage would have upset the comfortable, even tenor of his life.

'I must go,' he said, putting down his coffee cup and getting up from the table. 'Today I shall write a letter of acceptance. Rhoda . . .' His words had started so firmly, but as he said her name and she moved towards him, his will-power gave up on him. She was in his arms. 'Don't be unhappy, my precious love. When you feel trapped back in that comfortable cage, don't be unhappy. You will never be alone. Remind yourself that always, every day and every night of my life, I shall be loving you.'

'Don't,' she murmured, her head moving against his neck. 'You make it harder for me to do what I know I must. But nothing alters, not for you and me – nothing, except we shall be miles apart, the Channel between us, you helping so many poor, damaged spirits to find their way again and *me*, *me* whining and moaning and doing nothing, absolutely nothing except live life through the family.'

'You will be doing more than that: the thought of you will be keeping me sane in a world that is trying to find a purpose again.'

'When will you go? Shan't I see you?' It was actually

232

happening, the moment had come and the abyss before her had never been so frightening.

'As soon as I can be released. I shall stay in a hotel until then.' His words brought down the final curtain. Biting hard on her bottom lip, she was frightened to speak. 'But, yes, of course we shall meet in the future, many times I'm sure. Your daughter and my nephew will see to that. There will be family parties, births and baptisms, all the occasions that bring families together. None of them will know how much those times will be meaning to us, no one except ourselves.'

She nodded, grasping at the one straw of hope for the future.

'And when we see each other, all the time between will ... will ... I don't know how to say it, but all the times we've been together in spirit will take shape. I don't know how to make you understand what I'm trying to say.'

'I think you're saying what we know to be true: no matter how far apart we are, in spirit we shall be close. When we meet, it will be confirmation of that closeness.'

She nodded, even managing a watery smile.

'Nothing can take that away from us,' she said softly.

'Nothing.' Cupping her chin between his hands, he gently kissed her then turned and went out of the side door. She stood rooted to the spot as he started the engine and reversed down the narrow side path to the road, then she ran to the front window, willing him to turn just one more time. But staring straight ahead, he drove away.

Somehow those winter months went by. There were the usual highlights, the local pantomime in Dewsberry Village Hall where, by tradition, Alec looked after the stage lighting and Rhoda took the money for mince pies and coffee during the interval, a job that also entailed washing up the cups and missing the second half of the show. How they'd ever got into the job she could never be sure – it had to do with them coming across the writer and producer of the pantomime with his car broken down on the road from

Brackleford some eighteen years before. Alec had stopped and performed the miracle of getting him mobile again, then in conversation had heard they needed someone able to organise the stage lighting for *Mother Goose*. It was Alec who had offered Rhoda's services. How young and hopeful she must have been to imagine it might have been the beginning of – what? She hadn't looked for a social whirl of activity in the district; simply, she had needed to feel that she was *herself*, something more than wife, mother, laundress, cook, child carer. By the next year, Natalie had been given a role in *Babes in the Wood*, Etty helped with the washing up and the Hardings' participation had become established. Now the girls had both gone their own way, Rhoda and Alec were no longer 'that nice young couple' but part of the background.

Of course that Christmas of 1947 did have a new magic to it, for Christopher was old enough to delight in the fairy lights and to believe, as is the way with the very young, that other people's jollity makes life uproariously funny. With Etty and Andrew for parents it wasn't surprising that he was a good-humoured child, but that Christmas his gleeful whoops were enough to drive away the darkest gloom. Watching Alec with him, Rhoda, found herself imagining how different life might have been had he had a son of his own. As it so often did, her conscience smote her as she remembered the days just after Natalie's complicated birth. She made herself rekindle the scene when the surgeon had asked Alec to attend the hospital, told them both that further childbearing would be dangerous and recommended he should perform a hysterectomy. At the time her reaction was one of relief: her pregnancy had been wretched and thank goodness she wouldn't go through another. It was only later, her own health restored, that she acknowledged what having a barren wife must mean to a man like Alec, who must have hoped for a son. Yet he had never hinted at his disappointment. There had been times when she'd longed for him to say, 'As long as I have you, that's all that matters.' But Alec had never been a man to show his emotions.

So 1947 gave way to 1948, winter melted into spring and any news of Silas came second-hand from Etty. On one occasion he sent some snaps he'd taken of where he was living: a stone house set in the middle of a village.

'He sounds OK there,' Etty said. 'You can read the letter if you like. These other two snaps are one of the hospital and the other a view from his back window – miles of open country. Drew says he's always had the soul of a nomad, having worked all over the place, but France has been his second home. I do wish he was nearer, don't you, Mum? You and he got on so well'

'He was – is – my dearest friend.' Rhoda had to hear herself say it.

'*Is*? You mean you still keep in touch with him? You've never said.'

'Of course not.' She knew she ought to have changed the subject, but a wild impulse forced her on. 'Why do you think he went away?'

Etty's honest face was always a reflection of her thoughts. Now she looked at her mother in concerned disbelief.

'You mean he fell for you? You sent him packing yet you say he is still your dearest friend? I don't understand, Mum.'

'I shouldn't have told you. I suppose you think we're too old for romantic affairs. And I dare say you're right. For Silas and me it wasn't like that, it was like a meeting of twin spirits. That sounds like something out of some "penny dreadful", but Ett, it can happen.'

'Did Dad know?'

Rhoda shook her head. 'How could he know? Nothing changed at home. He objected to my going to Matthew's,

235

he objects still, but as far as he could tell nothing else had changed.'

'And that's why Silas ran off? I wonder he didn't want you to go with him.'

Rhoda was beginning to wish she'd not fallen to the temptation of talking about it. She was angry with herself that the snapshots giving her a glimpse of his new life could have made her so desperate to hang on to what they had had.

'He did, if you must know.'

'And you chose to stay with Dad. So no harm was done and you still look on him as a good friend.' How simple it all sounded. It was a relief when Andrew came into sight with Christopher on his shoulders. 'Is Dad not so busy this haymaking? You never mention him working late and getting his hands dirty like you did last year. Just a flash in the pan while he chased his youth, was it?'

'I think it must have been. He brings Miss Wheeler home as regularly as clockwork just before six and now the evenings are getting longer he likes to get out in the garden, either ours or at the cottage giving them a hand. They seem to have settled quite contentedly. I don't see much of them; Muriel is seldom there and, to be honest, Mrs Wheeler and I don't have much in common. My fault perhaps.'

'Rubbish!' This from Andrew who joined them in time to hear what she said. 'When I took the trailer into the yard the other day to collect our new harrow I had a chat with Muriel and I'd say that the move to Dewsberry Green was the best thing that had happened as far as giving her some freedom. She's positively blossomed. And she was telling me that her mother has joined one of the church groups – St Luke's Ladies Circle or something – that she goes to a sewing party at the Rectory one afternoon a week and has been invited onto the committee organising the annual functions, Summer Garden Party, Harvest Supper, Christmas Bazaar, all that jazz.'

'She could have done all that sort of thing years ago

instead of sitting at home and moaning,' was Etty's opinion.

'Indeed she could,' Drew answered with his usual good-natured laugh, 'but it's never too late. And it's freed up poor downtrodden Muriel no end. Apparently the Rector or his wife brings her mother home at the end of the meetings or whatever they get up to, and the new system appears to have worked a miraculous cure on her health. Remember how we always heard how poorly she was if ever Muriel wanted to escape for a few hours?'

'It's easier to be happy with a busy life than an empty one, no doubt about that,' Rhoda said. 'And talking of that, I must get my iron steed and pedal homeward. I haven't seen Jenny today – perhaps she's out in the fields with Jim.'

'It's parents' sports afternoon. She and Jim have both gone. They all seem fine and Den went off as cocky as anything with a dad and a mum coming to make fools of themselves. No, wait Mum! I can see them coming. She and Den must have taken the short cut along the side of the fields. Jim was late getting ready, so he went on his bike.'

If it crossed anyone's mind to wonder that he hadn't got home before the walkers, it was only a fleeting thought and in the excitement of Jenny's arrival, Jim was soon forgotten. After a few more moments, Rhoda started towards home leaving an appreciative Christopher shouting with excitement as Denis demonstrated the expertise that had won him first prize in the hopping race.

'You hadn't given Jim an errand to run after we finished?' Jenny enquired of Andrew.

'Certainly not. He's taking his time for sure. But you know what he is. He's everybody's friend and I expect there are folk to talk to.'

But an hour later, there was still no sign of him at the manor and it was stretching even Jim's garrulous nature to the limit to imagine he might still be at the school. It was then that the local policeman, PC Arkwright, pedalled up

237

the drive. A tall, thin man on a bicycle that stood inches higher than any other in the neighbourhood, he had only to walk down the village street to have the effect of making the children stand a little taller and lower the volume of their voices; yet there probably wasn't a kinder man to be found.

'Afternoon sir,' he said, pulling off his tall helmet, 'and ma'am and er ... er ... yes, well.' Clearly word of Jenny's marital situation had spread. 'Perhaps, sir, I could have a quiet word.'

'What's the trouble, Constable?' came Andrew's friendly answer, clearly not anticipating any such thing as he led the way towards the farm office.

'There's been an accident. I'm told the young man worked for you, something to do with the girl out there with your Mrs Clutterbuck. Byford, that's what the school-marm said his name was.'

'Jim Byford is his name. Yes, he lives here on the farm with his son. His fiancée is with my wife.'

'Ah, I thought that's who the young lady was. But Byford, a bad business. Worst bit of news it's ever been my job to carry. Gone, killed outright.'

'What the devil do you mean? What's happened. When? He only had to cycle from the school for God's sake.'

'One of those nippers from the school had been let down and his Mum hadn't turned up. He lives up on the ridge, a good mile from the school, and the poor wee chap had had a tumble and had his knee bound up. So Byford gave him a lift home on his kiddie's seat on the back of his bike. It was after he'd dropped him off that he came belting out of the track from the kid's house making up for lost time, head down so the driver said – the driver of a steam roller. Not a chance of stopping. Shaken to pieces the poor chap is, crying like a baby and couldn't stop shaking. Well, I mean, what a thing to happen. Not a hope in hell of pulling up. Straight out onto the lane Byford came. Nothing can stand up against one of the road-making machines. Ah, it's a

238

shaker. I can see it's knocked you, sir. Just you sit down a minute.' The kindly constable pulled a wooden chair towards them and gently pushed Andrew into it.

'We must tell Jenny.' But Andrew made no attempt to get up. He looked helplessly at the standing policeman. 'He went through the war only to come home to find his wife and his family killed by a doodlebug; only the boy escaped. He and Jenny and the lad, they seemed the perfect family.' His thoughts went in another direction and he was back in the car taking her home after Mickey had died. 'Jenny, I must tell Jenny.'

'I ought to do it. That's what I came for. And the poor little lad, what sort of a world must he think this is? If you think it might come more kindly from you, you knowing her, then I can't pretend to be sorry not to have the job. All the years I've been in the force, until today nothing like this has come my way, thank God.'

Andrew nodded. 'Yes, I'll talk to Jenny. Some of us go through life so lightly, some get hit time and again.'

'I've thought that sometimes. But I reckon the tough nuts get sent to those with the guts – faith, hope, trust, whatever it is that makes a person strong – I reckon those are the ones that get the real back-breakers. I just hope the young lady out there is one of the strong ones.'

'Please God she is.' Where now was Andrew's habitual cheerful expression?

The next morning, opening the front door of the house on Oakleigh Green to the uncertain knock, Rhoda found herself face to face with Jenny.

'Come in, Jen. Put your bike round the side. Is Den at school as usual?'

Jenny nodded. 'I took him on my way. Best to let him feel things are normal.'

Rhoda was aware of a difference in Jenny's manner; her tone was level and unemotional, yet she sounded lost and unsure of herself.

'Jen, I'm so desperately sorry.'

Jenny nodded. 'It's not fair. He was a good bloke, a really *good* bloke. What did a thing like that have to happen to *him* for?' Biting her bottom lip she looked around as if the book-lined walls would give her inspiration then, seeming to have made a sudden decision, she plunged on. 'I've been awake nearly all night—'

'I'm sure you have.'

'Been going round and round in my head, it has. Got to talk to someone, Rhoda, really talk – like people are supposed to do when they go and confess to a priest. I've seen it when I've been to the pictures and I've always thought it daft that by telling someone the secrets you keep locked up inside you, you suddenly feel sort of free. But I just got to talk. Ett's my mate, honest I love Ett like as if we were equals, even though she's richer and cleverer and all that. But I can't talk to Ett about this. I mean, she and Andrew, they done everything the right way round; they got married then they had Christo, they got all they want in just the three of them – more babies later I expect. But Rhoda, you know life isn't all smooth and cosy, and we have to make what we can of things.' Could this be the girl who used to long for a marriage like Rhoda and Alec's?

'Everyone's life takes courage at some time or other,' Rhoda said to fill the sudden silence and to encourage Jenny to share whatever it was that was troubling her, for clearly it was something less simple than grief for the young man who was her husband in all but name.

'Like I said, Jim was a real gem, good through and through. I suppose it must be sad that anyone's life is lost at his age, but I tell you one thing, I bet if there is a heaven and Betty – that was her name, Den's mother – if she was waiting for him there, I bet he was happier to be with her again than ever he could have been married to me. That's why I don't feel sort of broken hearted on his account. But I do for Den. He can't remember his mum, of course, but his dad was the apple of his eye.'

'I'm just so thankful he still has you.'

'Yes, but Rhoda, that's what's scaring me; that's what's going round and round in my head. I don't have any legal claim to be his mum like I would have if Jim and I had been married. What will some judge or whoever makes the rules think about me? He'll see me as someone ready to shack up with Jim for the sake of somewhere to live. That's what makes me so frightened, that's why I was awake all night worrying. I was there like a housekeeper—'

'Rubbish! You and Jim were as good as married.'

'That's what I expected when I said I'd go and live with him, and that's what everyone else thought was going on – all those who came to the party Etty and Andrew gave for us. But the truth was, I never went to bed with him, not once in all that time. I suppose that's why I'm so sure he'd rather be up there with Alice.' Rhoda's spontaneous thought was of Alec and the opinion he'd always had of their young neighbour. And how wrong he'd been. 'He'd shown me where to put my things in his room. There was an empty cupboard all ready so I thought – well, naturally I thought – it would be like you said. But the night Ett gave the party for us, when we were back at the cottage and Den was tucked up in bed, that's when Jim told me he'd taken his clobber out of the cupboard to make room for me and he'd made up a bed in the little room. I felt rotten, like as if I wasn't keeping my side of the bargain. So I tried to get him to change his mind, but it was no use. Wasn't that I wanted to go to bed with him but it seemed to me that that was my side of the bargain. So, you see, Rhoda, what I was doing wasn't a bit like it seemed. I'd said yes to him knowing I didn't love him. Well, I told you that ages ago. I was ever so fond of him, honest I was, but I used him to run away from being in love with someone else.'

'Somebody else?' Perhaps the son of the people she worked for, Rhoda thought. But why run away from that, for what could have been better for her? If she hoped to be given more details, she was disappointed.

'As soon as we were married, then we could sleep together, that's what he said, even though he knew I wouldn't be free for ages,' Jenny went on. 'Up 'til then he would be in the little room. So you see why I felt rotten. If he'd really wanted me, *me* for myself and for all that, and if he'd got what he wanted, then I would have felt the bargain was fair and square. But when he said that, almost like as if he was running away from me, that's when I suddenly knew, clear as day, that for him there would always be just Betty.'

'But you told me he said he was in love with you.'

'That's what he said right enough. And I reckon he tried, all the time I've been there, he tried to believe it was true. He was a real good bloke, Rhoda, and once or twice I came real close to telling him about loving someone who belonged with someone else. Then I stopped myself. It was best I played the same game as he did and we both pretended. That way it might have ended up all right, both of us pretending, then suddenly we might have found it had turned into the real thing. I did love him, truly I did – well you couldn't help loving him, he was so nice.'

'Den is the problem, and we must see how we can get it sorted out,' Rhoda said, seeming to take the weight of Jenny's worries onto her own shoulders. 'Will you let me talk to Andrew? You know he's been made a magistrate. I'm sure his opinions will be listened to. If he goes out of his way to speak up for you, I bet you anything they'll let Den stay on in the cottage with you looking after him. Poor little man, losing his father is bad enough without being sent off to strangers.'

Jenny agreed to enlist Andrew's support, but they both knew that would be no more than half the battle.

That evening, to Rhoda's surprise, Alec brought up the subject of Den's future and, like a conjurer pulling a rabbit from a hat, she told him how wrong he'd been in his opinion of Jenny.

242

'If she'd been living as his wife she might have had a stronger case for keeping him,' she ended with a worried frown.

'If he hadn't touched her you may be sure it wouldn't have been for want of opportunity. He was just an idealistic boy; a man with more experience would have seen her for what she is. If you want my opinion, the child would be better being put into a good God-fearing home with other parentless children, or farmed out to a foster family. Of course, she won't want that. I suppose she thinks that if she's given custody of him she'll be housed and paid whatever it is foster parents get for looking after a child.'

'Sometimes you appal me,' she said in disbelief.

'By speaking my mind? Anyway, it's no concern of ours. I hope Andrew is able to shift them from the cottage though. With the boy's father gone, someone else will have to be taken on and the accommodation will be needed.'

Without answering, Rhoda ladled soup from the tureen and passed it to him. As they ate in silence, she let her thoughts go back over the afternoon. A telephone call to Andrew had brought him to her book-lined sanctuary where he'd listened in silence as she'd made a case for Jenny keeping the boy.

'Leave it to me,' he'd promised with his never-failing smile. 'I already had every intention of pulling every string within reach, but I'm glad we've talked. To be honest, I wondered whether, with Byford gone, Jenny would want to be tied down. Thank goodness she does. Ett and I have seen how much she means to Denis and now, of course, more than ever. Don't worry about it, Mother-in-law, I will guarantee they can keep their home and, if she needs character references etcetera, then we've known her a long time. What a pig life can be sometimes, though. Just when it seemed everything was starting to go right for her, the chocks get kicked from under her again. A good thing she's a gutsy lady.'

Rhoda listened to him with affection, but said nothing.

Jenny's half-told secret was safe with her. In love with a man who belonged to someone else? Andrew? In appearance, manner and character, he was enough to turn any girl's head, and how many young men did Jenny know? And was that the real reason why she didn't want to talk to Etty? And could that be why she didn't want to leave the cottage?

'It's strange timing that this should come up now. Ett and I have been mulling over a plan. Maybe it's a far-fetched dream, but if we don't explore the possibilities it'll never be anything more. How's this for an idea? What was it my favourite uncle said about everyone having a dream? You probably don't remember – it was that evening when Ett had just promised to marry me. He was talking about Dad of course but it's the same for everyone, and certainly for Ett and me. The more we've thought about it and talked about it to each other, the clearer it has become.'

Chapter Eleven

The idea had first come to Andrew when he'd been in London for his half-yearly medical visit to his consultant. By that time they had all become adjusted to his restricted lifestyle. With tact that Etty hadn't realised she possessed she had seen to it that he worked within the limitations imposed by the list of 'Thou shalt nots' handed out to him after the scare they had had the winter before last and, despite his show of bravado, he knew better than to fall into the same trap as previously when enthusiasm for what at that time had been his new life on the estate had taken him that step too far. He had learnt that there was more to running the concern than physically working the land, so he had taken over the role of manager and fortunately had found it pleasant and rewarding. Sometimes he might drive the tractor or give a helping hand at milking time, but never would he lift heavy loads or work until the fatigue that was always waiting in the wings caught up with him.

On the day his dream was born, a minor road accident was all it had taken to cause a hold-up in the busy London street, but with the skill and knowledge necessary to all black-cab drivers, the taxi was taken on a detour. They drove through streets still recovering from the city's wartime battering, where buildings wrecked beyond all hope had been cleared and had become areas of derelict land, places where local children played.

To country-loving Andrew, the bustle of London held no appeal and, in contrast to the noise and rush, he visualised Sedgeley and its wide open spaces and tranquillity. And that's where his thoughts were as he noticed a group of children playing cricket where once must have stood a terrace of houses similar to those boarded up on the opposite side of the street. One side of the street still standing, the other side gone. Small boys with a piece of wood for a bat and a rubber ball, and this the only place for them to play. As if by contrast, into his mind came the image of Christopher, the clean air he could breathe, the space where he could play.

Wherever the thought might have been leading him it was broken by the driver telling him, 'Won't be long now, Guv. A longer way round but we made up for it by getting away from the traffic.'

So it wasn't until he was on his way home, the city smoke giving way to the fields of grazing cattle, that the image came back to him and, at first no more than half formed, the idea was born. That night, lying in bed, both he and Etty gratefully aware that his reward for obedience to the rules had been a good report, he told her about the boys.

'It seems so unjust, Ett. Poor little devils, honestly, it would have torn your heart out to see them playing there on a bit of space cleared from where perhaps the houses had belonged to people in their own families, people who'd been killed. So bloody unfair. We've got all this; we're so lucky. Not a bit of green, just boarded up houses and rough ground.'

'I love you, Andrew Clutterbuck,' she said, taking his hand firmly in hers. 'You're a thoroughly nice guy – has anyone ever told you?'

'I seem to remember your mentioning it,' he said, laughing. 'But seriously, Ett, there ought to be something, *something* we could do for kids like that.'

And so it was that their plan was born. Before it could

246

come to fruition there would have to be alterations in the domestic management of Sedgeley Manor and, that afternoon when he mapped out to Rhoda what they planned, the project had got no further than the drawing board.

'You're the first person to be told. This is what we have in mind,' he said, the only-just-beneath-the-surface cheery expression giving way to a beaming smile as his imagination took wing in the telling. 'The house is much bigger than we need – who wants eight bedrooms plus the servants' top floor? I ask you! Through the war the place was packed with evacuees, or at least it was until their parents decided London was safe again. Most of the time I was away so I didn't see much of them, but I know Dad enjoyed having them about the place. Anyway, what Ett and I want to do is this: the manager's house has been empty since Dad handed the reins over to me so we'll move in there. It's a good house, four bedrooms, two living rooms, not cramped but a comfortable size to run. Our idea is to live there and engage someone to be in charge of the big house.'

'Engage someone? But where's the logic? Are you intending to turn it into a hotel or something?'

So he told her about what he'd seen on the bomb sites.

'It's all a question of chance, don't you see? Some poor little devils have nowhere else to play except the streets – they don't know the smell of new-mown hay or see the sun going down over the hills far away. I'm not turning into some sort of a nutter, but don't you see, those are the sort of things that give one ... give one ... don't know what it is I'm trying to say—'

'Give one faith. Is that it?'

'I suppose it is. Not just faith in a religious way, but faith in nature, faith in something beyond ourselves, faith in tomorrow and ever after.' For a moment neither of them said anything. Where his thoughts were she didn't know, but hers were much the same as Etty's had been when he'd first told her about the street urchins who had so moved

247

him: what a thoroughly nice young man he was. 'Do you think we're masters of our own lives, or is some sort of Fate steering our ship for us? I mean, just think, Mother-in-law, five minutes ago we were talking about Jenny. I'd promised she could keep the cottage but if I'm honest I know it'll be much easier to get a good replacement for poor Byford if I can offer somewhere for a chap to bring his family.'

'You mean you'll have to tell her to find somewhere else?'

'No, no, not that. Everything is so up in the air. Ett and I will need someone living in with us. Ett spends a lot of time on the farm and there's Christo to be considered.' What he was suggesting seemed to bring a cloud down, darkening Rhoda's image of Sedgeley's future. Not for the first time she wondered whether it could be handsome, kind Andrew whom Jenny imagined herself in love with. 'But that's no outlook for Jenny,' Andrew cut across her thoughts. 'Listen! I've a better idea – we'll set her up to run the manor. Can't imagine why I didn't see it before. I bet you a pound to a bob that when I get home I'll find Ett has had the same idea.'

Whether he won his bet Rhoda didn't know, but once their scheme became more than just their shared castle in the air, things started to move. Of course there were hurdles: hurdles in getting dockets to allow them to buy the necessary furniture to turn previously elegant bedrooms into dormitories – bureaucracy hadn't loosened its grip with the end of the war; in fact it was ready to thwart them at every turn. Inspectors arrived to examine the accommodation; in the kitchen where for years Ellen Long had reigned supreme a man in a pinstripe suit and making no effort to remove his Anthony Eden hat opened cupboards, wiped his finger around the jets on the gas cooker, wrote his findings on paper attached to a clip-board and generally antagonised the housekeeper and her underlings.

248

Then came the next stage. To imagine deprived city children thriving in the freedom of the countryside was one thing; to bring the dream to life quite another. By the time each individual hurdle had been approached and overcome, many months had gone by and Christopher had been promoted from a pushchair to being pushed on his new tricycle on the back of which a long handle was attached so that, even while he imagined he was propelling himself, he was being pushed. During that time Andrew, Etty, Christopher and Tilly, the young housemaid from the manor, had established themselves in the former manager's house and the necessary alterations had been carried out. During that time, too, Rhoda had moved steadily along, the daily routine never changed by highlights, or lowlights either. She asked herself why it was she was able to accept it all without the bitterness and resentment that had sometimes seemed to poison her soul, for where now was the difference? She still escaped to Oakleigh, but sitting alone waiting for infrequent telephone calls, or trying to educate herself with the learned books that lined the shelves, could hardly be said to add spice to life. The difference was that deep in her heart she knew nothing could ever be as it had; between herself and Silas was something that neither time nor separation could touch. So she rose at seven each morning, raked the fire and drew the kettle forward so that it would boil; she cooked Alec's breakfast and accepted his perfunctory farewell kiss; on the days Matthew didn't need her she cleaned a house that never had the chance to get that lived-in look she'd once taken for granted; she washed, she ironed, she shopped and finally had a meal ready for half past six, by which time Alec would have delivered Muriel to April Cottage and returned home.

It seemed a long time since she'd sent Silas away, months during which he'd made no personal contact with her. Was he imagining her making a fresh beginning with Alec, rediscovering the love they'd known so long ago? If the thought entered her head it was only to be abandoned almost before it was formed. Somewhere, some day, they would meet; nothing could take from them what they had found in each other. So she lived through her days, the highlight of her life being the changes at Sedgeley where on the third Saturday of July the first contingent of children would be arriving, brought from their orphanage in Sedgeley Manor's new bus.

'Rhoda, come and look at this,' Alec called from where he was looking at the evening paper while she dished up their meal. 'Never mind what you're doing. Come here. See what's on tonight's radio page.'

'Tonight? Nat and Stewart's night. We must hurry up and eat so that we can go in the other room and listen to the wireless.'

'Buck up with it then. But first, come and see,' he said. 'Nat's picture in the national paper – how about that then!'

Putting the casserole on the table she came to lean over his shoulder.

'That's fantastic. Of all the programmes for the evening they choose theirs. Nice photo too. Don't they make a handsome couple.'

'Thank God that seemed to have died a death. When did he last come home with her? That ought to tell you there was nothing in your stupid fancies.'

'Maybe there isn't,' she admitted. 'Perhaps he just gave that impression, wanting to use her as a way to a career,' she conceded, 'but I was certainly fooled. The same as I was pretty sure Nat was ready and willing.'

'Humph! Utter nonsense.'

Rhoda had learnt when there was no point in arguing, so, taking the peaceful way out, she changed the subject.

'Shall I serve your vegetables?' For from his faraway expression he seemed to be gazing into the recesses of his mind while his meal cooled on his plate.

'Not too many, we haven't long. Your trouble is you read too much romantic nonsense – and you don't give

250

Natalie the credit she deserves. As for that clodhopping fellow, I've seen him as bad news since the day we brought him home. As if Nat, with the world at her feet, would look twice at him.' And with that he took up his knife and fork and attacked the meal with not a second to waste.

By seven o'clock the dishes were stacked ready for her to wash up after the programme and the two of them were seated expectantly, one on either side of the wireless. This was the last of Natalie and Stewart's weekly series of songs, a series that had put them firmly on the map. The path was surely leading them to where Natalie had laughingly suggested so long ago, an English version of Jeanette Macdonald and Nelson Eddy, so loved by the film-going public.

Rhoda smiled at Alec with pride and satisfaction as they listened. No matter what else had changed for them through the years, the one enduring constant was, and always would be, their family.

'Well done,' Alec murmured as Natalie's pure soprano held the final note. Rhoda nodded, smiling as she held his glance of pride. So neither of them was prepared for what came next.

'And so we say a final goodbye to a partnership we have come to love,' came the voice of the announcer. 'Natalie and Stewart have decided the time has come for them to go their separate ways. No doubt each of them will be back, but not together. Natalie Harding is commencing a new programme on this station each Sunday evening at seven o'clock and Stewart Carling starts on a concert tour next week. Be sure, we shall hear plenty from them in the future but in the meantime, sadly, we close this series.'

'There!' It was rare to see Alec beam with such delight. 'She's got rid of him now once and for all.'

'And we shall hear her again on Sunday,' Rhoda's pride matched his. 'I'm glad, though, that Stewart has got engagements. You may have resented him – you'd resent anyone you thought staked a claim on Nat – but he's a nice chap and he's so easy to listen to.'

'A concert tour can mean anything! I dare say he'll get taken up by some dance band or other. Easy, sing-along sort of stuff is nearer his mark. Nat is worth much more, and thank God she's had the sense to see it for herself.'

The broadcast over, Natalie and Stewart took a taxi to their favourite restaurant in Soho.

Always lovely, on that evening she had taken even greater pains than usual to enhance the good fortune nature had bestowed on her.

'Once you get out there on the road, it may be ages before you have a chance to see the family,' she said, turning her attention to Stewart as the waiter moved off with their order. 'They've missed you. There's nothing Mum likes more than visitors in the house. With me gone, Etty gone and always so tied up with Christo as well, she can't have much chance to get over to Dewsberry.'

In his mind's eye he could see it all, almost feel the warmth of Rhoda's hospitality. Certainly he'd been less sure of Alec but had readily believed Natalie when she'd said that he'd always been over-possessive of her and resented any friends she brought home.

'A lot has changed since that night they befriended me on the railway station. Etty married, strangers in April Cottage—'

'Hardly strangers,' Natalie cut in, laughing. 'Miss Wheeler went to work for Dad when she left school. She's been there simply for ever. What sad lives some women do have. You've never been to the cattle market and seen Dad's office, but I promise you it's not smart. It's not much more than a shed, with a desk and proper swivel chair for him, and Miss Wheeler's sort of kitchen table with a typist's chair. A steel cabinet of filing drawers, a two-bar electric fire and an electric light without so much as a shade

252

– that has been her life. Can you imagine anything more pathetic?'

'Posh offices don't necessarily make for a happier working life.'

Natalie chuckled, holding his glance and knowing full well just how irresistible she looked. 'You could have fooled me,' she said, teasingly. 'Anyway, never mind poor Miss Wheeler, just think about Mum and how pleased she would be if you visited like you used to.' Then, thinking of his insistence that they split up as singing partners and frightened that clinging on to him might only make him more adamant that he wanted his own space, she added, 'I'm tied up, but you're free until the end of the week. Honestly, she'd be so pleased if you visited on your own.'

Just for a moment he seemed undecided.

'Hark, there's the phone,' Rhoda said. 'I'll go. I'll call you if it's anything important.' By 'if it's anything important' they both knew that what she meant was 'if it's trouble'. Then, pulling on her dressing gown, she ran barefoot down the stairs to the telephone in the hall. It was twenty to eleven and, as always, they had turned off the radio, put out the milk bottle and climbed the stairs. Quicker than Alec, who hadn't yet wound the alarm clock or opened the window its customary nine inches, she had been just about to get into bed when the shrill bell had shattered the silence.

'It's Natalie,' she shouted up to him as soon as she recognised the voice and, just as she knew he would, he came barefooted down the stairs, the clock still in his hand. 'Of course,' Rhoda was saying into the mouthpiece. 'Tomorrow I shall be at Oakleigh, but I'll leave the key under the usual stone ... what a pity it can't be both of you ... of course I understand. Don't ring off, your father wants a word.'

He had his word and from the way his expression changed from pleasure to disappointment Rhoda knew his

253

feelings towards Stewart remained the same. It seemed that a career split didn't mean the end of a relationship he had so resented.

Stewart intended catching a mid-morning train from Paddington to Reading where he would make the connection for the half past one to Brackleford arriving just before two o'clock. Feeling she wanted some sort of family support to counteract Alec's attitude, Rhoda telephoned Sedgeley during the morning to tell Etty of his visit. At least he would be sure of a friendly welcome from Andrew, Etty and the ever-cheery Christopher. In fact, they went even further: when he climbed down from the train, there on the platform was the Clutterbuck family waiting for him.

'Mum told us what train you were coming on, so we thought we'd cart you home with us, then drive you over to Dewsberry this evening. Is that OK?' That was Etty's greeting while Andrew shook his hand warmly and Christopher tugged at his trouser leg.

Was it OK? Indeed it was more than that. These two always put him at his ease, something he found remarkable when he remembered his first visit to Timberley and how gauche he had felt in comparison to the elegant Andrew. So what had changed? Andrew was no less elegant despite managing the estate instead of spending his days driving from farm to farm, charming Harding's clients into spending their money. As Stewart analysed where the intervening years had brought them, he realised that the change must be in himself, for where now was that clumsy soldier? Gone, buried deep by the success of his name being linked with Natalie's. But without her, how far up the ladder would he have climbed?

'You're looking very fit Andrew. You're keeping well?'

'I'm fine and Ett sees to it that I keep that way. A change of direction can sometimes be a very good thing. I hope it will be for you too – for you and for Natalie. You've certainly created quite a stir as a duo.'

'Natalie will always do well – probably even better without me. I owe a great deal to her. As for me, well, having got a start, if I can't keep going, that will be telling me "I ain't that good",' he laughed. 'We all have to work to our limitations.'

So the chatter went on, but as Stewart talked, his mind wanted to go off on a tangent of its own. He wasn't blind to what Natalie wanted for them. So why did he hesitate? Most men would snatch at the opportunity she was offering – if not offering in so many words, leaving him in no doubt. Married to her, their partnership not only secured but also strengthened by the sure fact that the public liked nothing better than a romance, their future would be golden. She was lovely, she was good fun, she was generous and affectionate, and so what made him hold back?

'How's Jenny?' he asked casually as they drew near to journey's end. 'As if that poor kid hadn't had troubles enough.'

'She's been splendid,' Etty said. 'She's throwing herself heart and soul into the plans we have for the manor. We'll let her show you for herself. She cycled into town this morning to order the bedding we shall need, so she was out when Mum phoned to tell us you were coming. She was going to stay out to get something to eat, and then pick Den up from school on the way home. Licences, dockets, permits, it's all designed to make life more complicated than it need be. After all, in the end we get permission to buy the things that are needed, so why they have to make it all so difficult, I can't think. Here we are, home. This is our new home. What do you think? Nice isn't it?'

'I reckon it's great. Small compared with the big house, but – well, it looks a proper home.'

Etty laughed, getting out of the car with remarkable agility while still holding Christopher, who had travelled on her knee on the front passenger seat.

'Home is what you make of it, cottage or palace. We were always fine in the big house, but this is snug as

255

anything. And Stewart, it's all so exciting, watching the alterations taking shape. The bureaucracy has been enough to drive us bonkers, but it's all fixed now and our first contingent of children arrive the last week in July.'

'The trouble is,' Andrew took up the tale, 'summer is so short. 'About seven weeks, that's seven batches of children brought for a week of freedom in the fresh air, then unless we can get any more in the Christmas holidays or at Easter, we're at a standstill until another summer. It's not really what we had in mind.'

But Stewart wasn't listening.

'Look who's here,' he pointed to the figure approaching them on a bicycle. 'I thought you said Jen wasn't coming back 'til she fetched the kid from school.'

As soon as the greetings were over, Andrew suggested that Jenny should take the visitor to the manor and show him how it had been altered to meet the needs of the children.

'Bit of a surprise finding you here,' Jenny said in her most sisterly voice. 'Why didn't Natalie come with you? I suppose she wanted to stay home and talk to Rhoda.'

'Nat's in London. It was her idea I should come for a few days, and you know Rhoda – there's no one more welcoming than she is.' If Jenny spoke with sisterly friend-liness, his reply seemed stilted, guarded.

'Rhoda's lovely. Don't know where I'd have been without her.'

Silence, broken only by Stewart clearing his throat as if preparing for a speech. Then, 'I wanted to write to you when it happened – when the kid's father was killed. Jen, honest to God, I've been thinking about you. You've been at the front of my mind and I just felt so bloody helpless.'

She turned to look at him, the uncertainty and perplexity on her over-made-up face telling him more than her words.

'Wanted to write? So why didn't you?'

'I suppose it sounds daft, but I felt you'd think I was butting in. I was an outsider; I didn't even know him. But

256

Etty wrote to Nat about it all and from the things she said I knew he was a right good chap. Seemed a cheek for me to put my oar in.'

'I wish you had, Stewart. We were always friends. And, yes, Jim was just what you called him: a right good chap. We were waiting until I got my divorce through, then he was going to get the licence so we could be married.'

'Ah, I know.' And he knew too that she'd been living at the cottage with him. 'They say marriage is only a bit of paper, but what happened about the lad? I asked Nat but she didn't know.'

'That's probably because up to now nothing much has happened. Andrew's been a star. IIe's gone all out to try to make them say I can adopt him, but so far the bigwigs who seem to think they rule our lives won't give the go ahead. One thing for sure though, if they say he has to go to a home – oh Stew, they couldn't do that to him could they? – if they do then I'm sure Andrew will get to work again to make them see he'd be better left at the manor. Ett says that if they say he must be in the care of a married couple then she and Andrew will be responsible, so that for him and me it will be like it is now. That's what I keep on telling myself, telling myself not to panic and think he'll be taken away. But I've not got any real rights. I'm not even his stepmother. So you see I haven't got a leg to stand on – and not much of a history if they dig into my past.'

'They couldn't dig up anything bad about you, Jen. OK, you got in the club when you were a kid, but you fancied you were in love with him. And Mickey, well no one had a better mother than you were to him. Hey, Jen, Jeh what have I said? Don't cry, Jen.' He took her hand in his as he saw her eyes well up with tears.

'No ... mustn't ... got to go and get Den from school soon ... my eye-black will be all smudged.' She gave her nose an almighty and inelegant blow, and then managed a watery smile. 'It was just your saying that about Mick when I wasn't expecting it, sort of caught me off guard.

Come on, we must get cracking if we're going to see what's been going on indoors before I go off to get Den.'

Rhoda welcomed visitors, but that evening she found herself doubting the wisdom of offering hospitality to Stewart Carling. Yet why should she let Alec's prejudices rule who she could invite to the house. If he didn't like the company he could always go across the green and talk to the Wheeler women. The reason her thoughts followed that path was the conversation she'd stumbled onto when she came into the drawing room with the coffee.

'Andrew is a thoroughly good fellow,' Alec was saying, 'and this is a most worthy idea on his part. But sentiment and success don't always go hand in hand. Some of these children – perhaps all of them – will come from deprived backgrounds; for them it could be an insight into a better way of life. The great shame is that Etty and Andrew haven't the time to run the place themselves.'

'Etty and Andrew have a hundred per cent faith in Jenny.'

Was it simply the natural antagonism between the two men or was there some other reason for Stewart's sharp response? Rhoda wasn't sure, but she sensed an atmosphere that didn't portend well for the evening.

'As far as looking after the farmhand's orphaned son, no doubt they have. But it's more than being looked after that these poor youngsters deserve. This could have been a golden opportunity for them to see a more cultured way of living, to mix with people who know how to speak the King's English and who will see that they learn how to behave at the meal table. Probably some of them have never even been used to sitting down and eating as a family, let alone being familiar with civilised behaviour.'

'Oh Alec, for goodness sake!' Rhoda chimed in. 'They are coming to the country to learn to run free in God's clean air, not to be instructed in how to hold their knives and forks.'

'Did I say anything about instruction? Of course not. But

258

the young are receptive. What they find at Sedgeley will be different from anything they've been used to; they will absorb it like a sponge absorbs water. That's the way children learn. If they were to sit to a table with Etty and Andrew they would find themselves learning instinctively. Did we ever instruct our own children? Of course not, it wasn't necessary.'

Stewart was looking from one to the other. 'It's Jenny you're knocking even if you don't come straight out with it. I'm not daft. I know how you always looked down your nose at her.'

If Alec was taken aback by the angry outburst, Rhoda was no less so. Of course he was right in his accusation, but the gauche young soldier they'd first brought to Timberley would never have had the courage or confidence to oppose Alec so bluntly. She felt a bubble of laughter trying to escape even while she shied away from what might come next.

'Jenny or anyone else, my opinion would be the same. And you imagine things – Jenny has always been made welcome in this house.' With that Alec opened the newspaper and retreated behind it.

'I guess I was rude,' Stewart said, 'and if that's how it sounded then I'm sorry. But she's had knocks enough without people who ought to appreciate what a trump she is getting at her too.'

'Jenny is a darling,' Rhoda backed him, 'and I tell you what I think. I think that any child who comes into her care is lucky. There are more important things in life than whether you spoon your soup towards you or away from you. Now Stewart, tell us about you and Nat. Are you both getting bookings on your own?'

So the moment was saved, the conversation moved on and even though Alec took no part in it he listened intently enough, thankful for the unspoken confirmation that he'd been correct in believing there had been no romance involved in the partnership. Rhoda's thoughts were her own

259

as she heard Stewart's itinerary. She acknowledged that he wasn't in love with Natalie, but that didn't prove her wrong about Natalie's feelings for him. So was Jenny his reason for visiting the area? And, if so, did he too suspect that her heart belonged to Andrew; Andrew who was her friend but whose affection belonged entirely to Etty?

'Give us some music, Stewart,' she invited. 'The piano was tuned the other day and unless Nat comes home no one will touch it.'

'Good idea,' Alec agreed, folding his paper. 'If you two are all right without me I shall slip across to the cottage. When I dropped Muriel off this evening her mother had a quiet word out of her hearing. The sitting-room curtains are back from the cleaners and have to be rehung. She didn't want Muriel to go up the ladder as if she reaches up she gets giddy – that's what her mother said. Naturally I made them promise to wait until I got there. All the years I've known Muriel and it's only since Mrs Wheeler has talked to me that I've realised what a nervous girl she always was.'

'Off you go then, Sir Galahad,' Rhoda laughed. Then she settled more comfortably into her armchair and prepared to listen to Stewart. And of course she did listen, but the music didn't keep her thoughts from winging where they would. France, surroundings unknown to her, different customs, a different language, a full life too, so how was it she knew, positively *knew* that his thoughts turned to her as often as hers did to him? The demands of everyday living, responsibilities, duties, none of these things touched what was surely the very essence of their being. But what would happen to them as the years went by? Would they feel differently as they grew older, elderly? Would it have been different if the day-to-day routine had been shared with Silas? She closed her eyes letting the gentle tone of Stewart's voice wash over her as she imagined how it might have been.

'Are you OK, Rhoda?' She was brought out of her

260

reverie by Stewart.

'I think you must have almost lulled me to sleep,' she said, laughing, and then was saved any further enquiries by the telephone ringing.

'Mum? It's me, Ett. Guess what! We've just had a telephone call from France. Uncle Silas is coming over especially for our party.'

'That's splendid.' Almost frightened to believe she'd heard right, Rhoda's hand tightened its grip on the receiver. He was coming. In less than a fortnight he'd be here.

'Mum? Are you listening?'

'Sorry Ett, you caught me off guard. Stewart was playing the piano and I think I dropped off! Yes, I heard. Silas is coming to the opening party. That's splendid.' Somehow Rhoda answered, just as if the news were no more momentous than that of a visit from some maiden aunt. 'Just for the weekend?'

'He didn't say. It was only a three-minute call so he just told us what time his ferry was due to arrive at Dover in the morning and that, all being well, he would be in Oakleigh by afternoon. He's staying at your bookshop place.'

'I bet Andrew is pleased. Have you found a driver yet to fetch the children?'

'No. Drew's licence covers driving the bus, but mine doesn't. He's upstairs so I can say it: Mum, I don't want him to drive to London on his own. It's not like going up in a car – a vehicle like that must be heavy to drive. Jen would go too of course to look after the children coming back, but she can't drive. Supposing – hush! Drew's coming.' Then as Andrew came within earshot, the anxiety vanished from her tone, 'So we're over the moon, not just because it'll be lovely to see him but that he is taking the trouble to come. Mum, find out from Stewart whether he's free that Friday. I don't know if once he starts touring on his own he stays a week in each place or whether he's just giving concerts. Find out for me. It would be nice if he could be here.'

'Yes, I'll pass on your message. I'm sure he'd like to be there if he's free.'

'It's important, Mum, so don't forget.'

Some of Rhoda's joy vanished, pushed aside by the nagging worry of misplaced affections. From the way Etty spoke it seemed all too clear to Rhoda's overactive imagination that she, too, suspected Jenny's feeling for Andrew; the only consolation was that she must be sure that Andrew either was unaware or looking for a comfortable way of steering her in another direction. And that other direction was towards Stewart, so they must have formed the same opinion as she had herself: his interest was Jenny, who was probably the real reason he'd come on this visit at all. So after Etty had rung off she went back into the drawing room to give him Etty's message. Without hesitation he accepted the invitation.

'I have to be in Slough by Saturday afternoon to run through a few things ready for the evening. It's jolly good of them to invite me. If I can borrow a bike in the morning, Rhoda, I'll ride over and thank them. Jen took me round the house, showed me the bedrooms – dormitories I suppose they are. And that's good. Pack a group of kids in together and even the shy ones won't be able to be frightened and lonely. It got my back up, the way Mr Harding was talking, hitting out at Jen. It seems to me that it's because she's never had it soft, that she's just the girl for the job. And isn't it about time something went right for her? All she gets is one knock after another.'

'I think she'll be splendid. And no one will ever walk over her. She may have had a tough time, but she's never let herself be crushed. I'm extraordinarily fond of her. You are too, Stewart.'

At her statement he looked uncomfortable, blushing like the heroine in some Victorian novelette.

'Does it show? I've never told her how I feel about her.

262

And now, of course, just when she's picking herself up and trying to make a fresh start after losing young Den's dad, well – well, if I stuck my oar in now it might frighten her off altogether. After that sod of a husband of hers walked out on her she told me she'd done with romance and all that. So I never pushed her; I thought it best to let her know I'd always be her friend. Perhaps I was daft, perhaps I ought to have come out with it right back then. Don't know much about girls, Rhoda, that's the trouble. Until I chummed up with Nat I'd never really known one, not properly I mean. Nat's been a real pal to me. I know jolly well that if she hadn't been there to give me a leg up and throw her hand in with mine I'd never have had the chance to sing for my supper.'

A shy, unconfident young man – or so he used to be – but once he started talking he let the words tumble out.

'Why did you decide to break up?' Rhoda asked him.

'I guess it was my doing. And it wasn't that I'm not grateful. But I saw the red light. Not just for me, but for Natalie too. Wherever we went, it was the two of us. And that's no good, not at our time of life. If we'd been older, both of us hitched up to other people, then it wouldn't have mattered. It was for her sake as much as my own – more really. She's the best-looking girl I've ever clapped eyes on, and a real nice one at that. But I don't have to tell you *that*.'

Rhoda laughed, agreeing.

'She's a good lass and a pretty one. I honestly thought you two were destined for each other. But there you are – doesn't it show how wrong outsiders can be.'

'Me and Nat?' He laughed at the thought. 'We're different as chalk and cheese. But with me always in tow she was never going to meet anyone – if one was invited anywhere it was always "both of you, of course", as if we were joined at the hip or the like.'

'She'll miss you. These have been good years.'

'Oh aye,' he agreed, 'and I'll miss her too. I bet one

thing, that her dad is glad about the break-up. He's not daft and he always knew she's too good to have her career tied down to being half a duo. As for me, well, to tell you the truth, Rhoda, I reckon I've had enough of it, always travelling around, living out of a suitcase. I love singing, I have since I was in the church choir. But you don't have to deck yourself up in evening dress and stand in front of an audience to sing.'

'What about making records?'

'Fair enough,' he conceded. 'But – oh hang it, what's the point of talking about it? What I really want is some nice little job that would bring me in enough to keep a wife and kid or two, a bungalow or a cottage or something with a garden. Jen, and me—' he looked helplessly at Rhoda as he said it '—she's the only girl for me. We used to be good enough mates, but lately she's stopped writing, never told me what she was up to, not even sent me the address where she's moved to. Last time I wrote, the letter got sent back by the post office with "Gone away" on it. It was Nat who told me about her falling for this chap on the farm and going off to live with him. After that, even though I knew where to write, I got the message that she wanted to be done with me. She deserved a fresh start if anyone ever did and I wasn't going to get in the way of it.'

Rhoda knew him well enough to be sure that it didn't come easily for him to open his heart like this. She passed him the cigarette box then took one herself, both of them needing something to do with their hands.

'Tomorrow morning you take a bike out of the shed and off you go to Sedgeley. If you and Jenny used to be good friends, then be sure nothing has happened that will have changed that for her. And she needs all the friends she can get. If the powers that be don't let her keep Den – oh but they must.'

'They jolly well ought to – and if the people who decide knew her, then they would. But she's single and likely as not they'll say the kid has to go up for adoption to a

264

married couple. She said Andrew is speaking up for her.'
He sighed, frightened to look ahead on his own account and
on Jenny's too. 'I remember Nat once saying to me something about Fate sorting things out for us. It must have been
Fate that made you take pity on me when Gran wasn't
home that night, and see what came out of that.'

'Fate or some inner voice,' Rhoda replied.

He looked at her questioningly, not understanding. She
didn't elaborate. An inner voice, call it that or call it
conscience, but surely if you listened and obeyed, oughtn't
it to bring you some sort of peace? For a second she drew
deeply on her cigarette, letting her mind carry her to that
unknown corner of France. He was coming, but would they
have any longer than that single evening surrounded by
family. Tomorrow she was going to Oakleigh and would
ask Matthew if Silas had told him how long he was staying.

Next morning, arriving at Oakleigh just as Mathew was
preparing to set out for Cambridge, that's exactly what she
did.

'Etty and Andrew are delighted that he's making the
effort to come so far. Is he coming especially or is it the
beginning of a vacation?' she asked in the tone of nothing
more than a casually friendly in-law.

'A short break, that's what he called it. How short I have
no idea. He knows there's always a welcome here and his
room is there for him. I'm expecting a call from Professor
Duckworth. If he rings while I'm away I think you can give
him all the details he requires – I've written a note for you
here. I should be back before six o'clock so if he wants to
talk to me personally perhaps he'd give you his number.
Off we go then, hat, car keys, briefcase, wallet, that's me
set. Have a good day. You'll find a remarkably good fruit
cake in the tin. Help yourself with your coffee.' And he
was gone.

Stewart cycled to Sedgeley where he accepted an invitation

to stay for the rest of the day. In the evening there was nothing in his manner to hint at whether or not he'd made any progress with Jenny, and with Alec sitting there doing the crossword Rhoda could hardly ask him. Of course, visiting the manor at Etty and Andrew's invitation, Jenny would have shown him friendship, but that wasn't the same thing as wanting him there on her own account. So she assumed the love-starved girl continued to weave her dreams elsewhere.

Stewart broke into her thoughts.

'Etty and I had a chat this afternoon while Andrew was out in the barn with the men. She tells me they want to engage a driver for the bus they've bought to transport the children.'

'I know,' Rhoda answered. 'Andrew has had a test and his licence allows him to drive it, but she's not a bit happy.'

'Not happy?' It seemed the crossword had only held half Alec's attention. 'Andrew's an excellent driver, I'd trust him anywhere,' he said. 'Although once they find someone I doubt if he'll ever have any call to drive that bus thing.'

'It's the first trip, the day the place opens,' Stewart said. 'She doesn't want Andrew to know how worried she is so she won't say anything in front of him. But, as she says, this won't be like an ordinary straightforward journey. They're picking the kids up somewhere in east London, a district he doesn't know. Jen will be there, she can map read for him—'

'Perhaps she knows the area – probably even came from it,' was Alec's opinion.

'Actually she doesn't. I know it vaguely – it's a labyrinth of one-ways. If only I hadn't got an engagement in Slough I'd suggest to him I might come along and navigate. Tell the truth, I could share the driving as I got my licence driving in the Army. He gets overtired very suddenly – and, if it turns out to be a bit of a panic, that isn't going to help.'

'Did you know about this?' Alec asked Rhoda, 'Did you know Ett was worried.'

266

'Ett worries a lot about him. I wondered if she might go with him as well as Jen, and I'd volunteer to have Christo.'

'Rubbish! What could she do? Leave it with me. Driving a vehicle like that is much harder work than driving a car. I have a licence for heavy vehicles. I'll go with him.' Then, with a laugh that almost turned him back into the Alec of old, 'Don't look so doubtful, I shan't tell him I'm doing it on account of his health. I'll simply say that I fancy being there when he collects the first batch and would like to come along. Then I'll play it from there.' He folded the newspaper with his usual precision, then stood up. 'I'll give them a ring. Don't panic,' he said with something akin to a smile. 'I can be the height of tact when the need arises.'

Rhoda watched him go out to the hall and close the drawing-room door behind him.

'Poor Jen,' Stewart murmured, 'that's going to put the kibosh on her day. She's up in the clouds with excitement, coming into her own she is, going up to get the first lot for her to look after.'

But Rhoda had more to think about than Jenny's disappointment. Saturday week ... the whole day would belong just to Silas and her.

Chapter Twelve

Around them was the hum of conversation and the party was going well, something that had been by no means guaranteed by the mix of guests. Across the room, Etty and Andrew exchanged glances that carried a silent message of satisfaction and humour. Who would have expected the Chairman of the Rural District Council capable of displaying such charm? He was usually spoken of as a pompous man who reigned supreme at the council offices a mile or so outside the boundary of Brackleford borough, yet here he was smiling pleasantly as he listened to Jenny expounding on their plans for the children who would be brought to stay at the manor. Then there was the plumber who had been responsible for turning one half of a large one-time bedroom into cubicled showers, and the other half into three WCs and a row of washbasins; from the way he was talking to Alec it was clear they'd found a common topic. Stewart Carling was handing round plates of finger food which had been prepared under the hawk-eyed Ellen Long, who was now engaged in conversation with Mrs Wheeler. A fleeting second of unease crossed Etty's mind as she looked at mother and daughter – it had never crossed her mind to invite them until Alec had suggested it.

'But surely you don't mean to leave them out?' he had said, looking puzzled at how such a thing could have come about.

'I never gave them a thought, Dad. Neither did Drew. But if you think they'd enjoy it, then of course they're welcome. I'll drop a note for you to take back with you, shall I?'

'I'll see they get it. You've known Muriel all your life, Etty, so I'm surprised you weren't going to include them naturally, without prompting by me – especially as they stayed for a while at Timberley and moved into the cottage where Jenny had lived. You should see the changes they've made there: the place is immaculate now, just as you'd expect, and Muriel has worked on that jungle of a garden so that the place is unrecognisable. I hope you know what you're doing entrusting Jenny with the responsibility of this place.'

'Don't worry, Dad. You've always had a warped vision of Jen just because you don't like the way she dresses.' Then with a sudden laugh, 'Can you just imagine her if she decked herself out like poor frumpy Muriel Wheeler!' Had it been then that her first feeling of unease touched her, or had she spoken like it subconsciously to see his reaction? She'd always talked freely to him, said the first thing that came into her head; sometimes their opinions were in agreement, sometimes not. When they came at their decisions from differing viewpoints they could always argue amicably. But on this occasion it was as if a shutter had come down between them. 'I'm not mocking her, Dad, I really am quite fond of her. I suppose her life has made her what she is. Can you imagine Mum being such a pain as Mrs Wheeler is, though, and making sure Nat and I never had the chance to make our own lives?'

'The trouble with youth,' he'd answered critically, 'is that you think you know it all. Muriel has been a rock to her mother – just as she has to the firm. I don't care to hear her spoken of as if she's someone to be pitied because she knows what loyalty is.'

That had been the previous week. Now as Etty caught sight of Muriel standing a few feet from where her mother was talking to the housekeeper, her first reaction was that she ought to go over and speak to her. Then she noticed something else, something that made her shy away. If a sixteen-year-old let her gaze rest on her idol in the way his loyal secretary was looking at Alec, it might be forgivable. But Muriel Wheeler was no sixteen-year-old. Instinctively Etty moved across to Andrew.

The double doors that divided the dining and drawing rooms had been opened but, although that gave plenty of space for moving about, most people stayed in the vicinity of the dining-room table, which had been moved to stand against the wall and was laden with food. For this special evening, caterers had been called in to prepare the food, working in the kitchen of the manor and no doubt made aware of the housekeeper's eagle eye. Most of the ingredients had been provided either directly from the farm or from Andrew's personal contacts. None of it was 'black-market' but all of it, and especially its decorative presentation, made up a buffet table the like of which none of the visitors had seen since before the war. Still held in the grip of rationing, it was a rare treat to indulge in the festive fare which Andrew had insisted should be shared by family, friends and most especially by all those associated with the running of Sedgeley Manor and its renovation.

Rhoda had longed for Silas to arrive, each day imagining how it would be. Never had she felt uncertain, frightened that something would have changed for them. The dress she had seen in the window of the most exclusive shop in Brackleford had been wildly extravagant and she tried not to think of how willingly Alec had told her she could take his coupons when he heard she had none left of her own. Her conscience was mollified when she made her entrance into the sitting room where he was ready and waiting, for he made no comment on her appearance; in fact he barely glanced at her. She knew if she'd asked him his opinion he would have said as he always did, 'What do you look like? You look very nice, you always do.' So she

270

hadn't bothered to draw his attention to the expensive creation that secretly gave her confidence a huge lift.

'Ready at last? Aren't you taking a wrap or coat or something? The others are in the car waiting. I put the old lady in front with me – it's easier for you and Muriel to get in and out of the back.'

None of that mattered; Silas would be at the manor.

Yet when he came across the room to greet them, for one instant she knew panic. It was but a brief instant and was gone even as Etty came to welcome the Wheelers and Alec moved in the direction of a neighbouring farmer whom he'd known for years.

'I'm glad you came.' Even as she heard herself say it, she realised how silly it sounded. Glad? So glad she wanted to shout for joy just to be standing here with him again.

He looked at her, his eyebrows raised, his eyes shining with silent laughter.

'I'm glad you're glad,' he teased. 'Otherwise it would have been a long journey wasted.' Then, more seriously, 'You look very lovely. Lilac suits you.'

'My old stand-by best frock was lilac.' And, again, what an inane thing to say.

'I remember it well. Let me get us some food. Is there anyone amongst these esteemed guests you ought to talk to or may I carry you off to the window seat in the drawing room. Folk seem to prefer to hover near the food.'

'How long are you staying? Matthew is going to London tomorrow so I have to be there.' She said it quietly, urgently, frightened that if it wasn't said straight away they might not have another opportunity on their own.

'I know,' he answered, his tone matching her own. 'I'll forage for some food. Are you hungry?'

She shook her head. In the last few moments she hadn't been aware of anything except that he was here and nothing had changed for them.

'Nor me,' he told her, 'but when in Rome ...'

As they made their way to the vacant window seat, she

271

knew Alec was watching, but she didn't care. Trying to hang on to some sort of sanity, she let her thoughts dwell on the fact that hers was the most attractive dress there, that it was a joy to stand tall in high heels, that there was a feeling of luxury about the celebratory gathering. From the large entrance hall with its marble floor came the sound of music and she remembered Etty telling her that Jim's replacement, Sidney Payne, had promised to ply the gramophone with records.

A few more people carried their food to the drawing room and Rhoda did have a fleeting moment of guilt as she saw Alec pulling an occasional table towards an armchair for Mrs Wheeler, fetching a chair for Muriel and then fighting his way through the folk who swarmed around the buffet to fill plates with tempting morsels for them. Oh well, she told herself, let him get on with it, they're his friends not mine. But having the group in such close proximity cast an uncomfortable cloud and ensured that the conversation between Silas and her was fit for public hearing. It was only later, throwing caution to the wind, she felt herself taken in his arms as they were the first to dance. Soon others followed. Men who had brought their wives automatically partnered them; those who had no wife or sweetheart either looked to the kitchen staff or stood idly watching. Guilt nudged again at Rhoda: she was failing Alec, who would surely like to be rescued from the Wheelers. But as one record finished and the next started, Silas kept his arm firmly around her and her hand didn't move from his shoulder. It was with something like relief that she saw Alec circling the floor with Muriel.

The party was breaking up, the first couples saying their farewells to Etty and Andrew, and the indoor staff having all disappeared, when Alec approached across the almost empty dance floor.

'The youngsters suggest that I stay the night with them,' he told her after a brief nod of acknowledgement to Silas. 'Andrew wants to be on the road soon after seven in the

272

morning so that he can get the children back here with half the day still ahead of them. So will you take the car and drive Muriel and her mother home, Rhoda? I think they've probably had enough and are ready to leave.'

'Of course I'll drive them. But I can't come here to collect you in the middle of the day tomorrow – remember I'm working. Will Andrew or Ett want to leave just as the first batch of children arrive?'

'Damn, I'd forgotten you won't be at home. I'll have to take you all home then come back again. Better to do the journey tonight that have him worrying that I won't get here by the time he wants to be on the road. Say goodnight to Etty and Andrew and we'll get on our way.'

It was Silas who answered, he and Rhoda poised ready for the music to start again. She felt the increased pressure of his hand as he suggested, 'Keep your car here, why don't you? I'm going back to Oakleigh for the night and can easily make a detour and drop them all off first.'

'I'm obliged,' Alec thanked him. 'I'll go and have a word so that they know what's going on. Muriel can see her mother is tired; she's getting their coats now.' Who but the Wheelers would have worn coats on such a glorious summer evening?

Alec moved away just as the crackly tone of a waltz prompted the start of the next dance.

'Some of the records have outlived their time,' Silas said, his comment no more than an excuse for the silent happiness they shared as they moved round the floor together.

Watching Alec helping the Wheelers into their light-weight overcoats, Rhoda saw them all as being removed from everything that mattered. She stood apart from her past and from her future too – all that mattered was that she and Silas moved together to the rhythm of the scratchy record.

That evening, Mrs Wheeler returned to April Cottage

sharing the none-too-comfortable back seat of Silas's coupé with her daughter, while Rhoda sat at his side. When, before he started the car, he offered cigarettes to those in the back as well as the front, the offer was refused with an expression that made no secret of their disapproval. For a lady to smoke in the privacy of her own home was bad enough, but to indulge in such an unwholesome habit outside was little short of disgraceful. Mrs Wheeler was surprised Rhoda Harding didn't know better. The two in the front shared another moment of silent laughter as their glances met in the light from his match.

For Rhoda there was still a feeling of unreality, unreality mixed with excitement, guilt, joy, uncertainty and indecision that could so easily be overcome by the vision of the future she longed for. Knowing how close she was to following her dream, guilt took over. Alec was a truly good man, she loved him, yes she *did* love him and she always would. What a moment to remember her old lilac dress, the one that had stood her in good stead almost since the beginning of clothes rationing, and then in her mind to compare it with what she had been wearing on this special evening. Was Alec like that faithful, well-loved dress? Was Silas no more than a wildly expensive and fashionable replacement? A stupid comparison, she told herself. She almost wished none of it had ever happened, that her life had known nothing beyond the daily routine, which for Alec had always been enough. Now she must stand by and watch Silas go back to his life in France. She must be strong. For although no word about the future had been spoken, she knew without doubt that the evening had shown him as clearly as it had her the emptiness of their lives without each other.

First he drove to the far side of the green, stopped the car and helped Mrs Wheeler and Muriel out, taking their key and opening the front door, before switching on the hall light for them. Then he got back in the car and turned to Rhoda.

274

'Don't ask me in, my darling Rhoda. If you do, I might weaken and that's not what I want for you. You can be sure there will be prying eyes watching to see how long the car is outside. Tomorrow—'

'. . . and all our tomorrows; that's how it ought to be,' she whispered 'It's what I've dreamed of and this evening it seemed all to fall into place. Yet I know I can't let myself turn my back on everything just to snatch at what I want. If Alec were different . . . but he's – oh I don't know – so content with where life has brought us – I suppose he's *innocent*. You can't hurt an innocent person. Say something . . . tell me you understand. Tell me we still *have* each other even if we're apart.'

'We can neither of us be all that we are if we can't be together, always there is something missing. That's the truth.' His mouth found hers as with something like reverence he kissed her. 'Goodbye, my darling.' Yet neither of them moved. Did she expect him to try to persuade her to act against her conscience? She knew she didn't and yet it hurt her to hear the acceptance in his firm tone when he said, 'When you get to Oakfield in the morning I shall have left,' he told her, 'I shall get the midday ferry.'

She nodded. 'I wish—'

'It's no use wishing,' he said with a hint of bitterness. 'We only live once, there are no second chances.' Then, tilting her face to his and peering at her through the darkness, 'Whatever path you take, my dearest Rhoda, what I want for you is happiness; not recriminations, not guilt, nor yet regret that you put faithfulness before love.'

'It's not just Alec,' she said miserably. 'The girls . . . the girls would be so hurt. I'd be destroying their trust.'

He leant across her and opened the car door. 'The girls, Andrew, even poor little Jenny who has faced so many knocks, all of them would feel the ground had given way under them. But it would pass; they would learn to accept and gradually to understand.'

She shook her head and in silence stepped out into the

summer night. As he eased the car slowly forward, did she imagine his expression of misery? They would meet again: for Andrew's uncle and Etty's mother it would be inevitable – christenings, special anniversaries, perhaps school prize-giving days if Christopher developed into a winner, and through the years surely each parting couldn't be as heart wrenching as this.

Familiarity guided her key into the lock of the front door and without turning on the light she went up to her bedroom. Her bedroom . . . hers and Alec's – and she had never been more thankful to have it to herself than she was as, still in the dark, she undressed. Then, naked, she flung the bottom window wide open, her expression not pretty as she imagined Alec and the precise gap he allowed at the top. Damn him, damn him and all of it, she thought. What am I in this house but some sort of an automaton, someone to turn muddle into order, dirty linen into clean, money into meals, someone to be there when his mind isn't taken with other things and he feels like ending his oh so interesting day rolling me on my back? What am I? I'm *me*. Her thoughts became words as tears of misery and self-pity filled her eyes, '*me*, and I'm so lonely. Sent him away, tomorrow he'll be gone, haven't even got tomorrow, nothing . . .' There was some sort of comfort in the sound of her weeping.

Leaning out of the window she felt the warm night air on her nakedness. And that was when she heard the sound of a car coming towards the green. He must be coming back! He couldn't bear for them to part! And in that moment she was deaf to conscience. In the morning they would cross the Channel together. She would leave a note for Alec. It took no time for her decision to be made, no more time than it did for the headlights of the car to cast their long beam. But it wasn't coming to Timberley; instead it went round the green and drew up outside April Cottage.

Had she put the lights on in the house her eyes wouldn't still have been accustomed to the darkness, she wouldn't have recognised that it was Alec's car that stopped and it was he who was getting out. He didn't slam the door but shut it carefully. It seemed she wasn't the only one to have heard the engine for, pulling the cottage door to behind her, then glancing up at her mother's window where already the light had been turned out, Muriel hurried down the short path. Rhoda shrank back into the room but she didn't move away from the window. Had he forgotten something he wanted her to do in the morning? It was Saturday tomorrow and Muriel only worked until one o'clock. But how would she get to the cattle market with no Alec to take her? As if it mattered; how she got there was *her* concern. Rhoda found delight in the uncharitable thought. She wondered why it was she felt such antagonism towards the Wheelers, an elderly widow and a woman who had had no interest or excitement in her life. She considered the question and decided it was because she saw them as an endorsement of Alec's view on life. She shivered, tears and night air combining to chill her. What were they saying? Why was Alec holding her by the shoulders like that? A minute earlier Rhoda had been crying, now a giggle bubbled to the surface as aloud she told herself, 'Pity it's not light, he won't be able to see the sheep-eyed look she's giving him. Poor mutt you are, Miss Wheeler. Have you fancied yourself in love with the boss all these years?' It was a nice safe dream anyway – nothing there to upset Mummy and her demands. No, all the time you've been casting your furtive glances at him you must have imagined him home here with me. What a bloody mess we all make of things. Look, Alec's getting back to the car. He must have changed his mind about staying with Ett. I'll be asleep. Couldn't bear ... couldn't bear ... and she wouldn't even let herself imagine what it was she couldn't bear.

In bed, she listened. But the engine didn't start so, curiosity getting the better of her, she knelt up and peered across the green. They were both inside the car, the passenger door open. He must be explaining to her what it was he wanted her to attend to for him in the morning. Rhoda was honest enough to acknowledge that Muriel was the epitome of conscientiousness and she would never fail him.

So she got back into bed putting both of them out of her mind and yet frightened of the empty loneliness that engulfed her. Emotion must have tired her for in no time she was asleep. She woke to the sound of the bottom window being closed and the top opened its customary nine inches.

'I thought you were staying with Etty,' she said, then wished she had let him think he hadn't woken her.

'I was worried about the Wheelers. Surely you must have seen how Clutterbuck offered to take them home and then kept them waiting. I wonder *you* didn't have more consideration even if he didn't – you could have reminded him that Muriel had said her mother was tired. She walks a tightrope over her mother's health.'

'Rubbish. Mrs Wheeler is a selfish woman who expects to have everything her own way. I can't think why Muriel doesn't put her foot down. She must be as weak as her mother seems to imply.'

When he didn't answer she supposed that to be the end of the topic and that he must be settling for sleep. A minute of so later he surprised her by saying, 'There's a difference between weakness and kindness. Muriel is sensitive to other people's feelings.'

'That's nice then,' she said in a voice that showed neither kindness nor sensitivity. 'We ought to go to sleep if you want to be at Sedgeley early.' What was she doing, lying here talking to him as if this night were no different from any other, as if she really cared what time he needed to be away in the morning, as if there wasn't a grey fog over the future? When he answered her she felt too removed from him and from everything that made up her daily life even to be angry.

'Andrew's making a detour so that he can pick us up here. Muriel suggested coming too.' Then with something that sounded like a contented chuckle, 'It had been on the tip of my tongue to tell her what a relief it would be if only she were there for the children, when she suggested it herself. If she could be any help, that's how she put it. She'll be a godsend.'

'What did Jenny say?'

'I've no idea. I telephoned Andrew and told him when I got indoors just now and said that I'd told Muriel how grateful we were.' Putting out his hand, whether intentionally or by accident, he touched her. 'You're not wearing a nightdress,' he told her as if she didn't know.

'Goodnight,' came her reply.

'It's not terribly late.' His hand moved across her as he showed signs of breaking the habit of years and treating Friday night as though it were Saturday. 'It was a good party, wasn't it. Rhoda, you're not tired are you?'

'Yes, I am tired. Tired, tired, *tired.*' Just as it had half an hour or so before, misery enveloped her as she heard her voice croak and felt the hot tears. 'Tired of everything.'

'Oh God, what's wrong now? Is it Muriel, is it because she's coming to London tomorrow? If you weren't always tied up in that bookshop you might have had the thought to offer yourself.'

'Shut up,' and this time she held her voice in control. Sounding disagreeable was her salvation. 'Course it's not Muriel Wheeler. If she's so kind and sensitive you'd think she would have offered her services to Jenny not to you.'

'Don't let's talk about it. I didn't think it would upset you.'

'What, Muriel having a day out with you?' She blew her nose, then turned her back on him with a movement that couldn't be misunderstood. 'Good luck to her, if that's the way she enjoys spending her day off.'

Alec sighed. He was out of his depth. Sometimes he despaired of understanding women – Rhoda in particular.

279

Most of the time she was easy enough and they rubbed along very comfortably. And it had struck him this evening that she really looked quite pretty still. Funny how living together you really never saw each other. It must be the same with her, she must just take it for granted he was always there.

He moved restlessly. Damn it, he was wide awake. Rhoda was his wife. If he moved a few inches her way he would feel the warmth of her. Got to be up early in the morning – ought to be asleep. Was Muriel asleep already, making sure she was ready to be collected by seven o'clock? He tried not to think of Muriel and wondered whether Rhoda had really dropped off.

She breathed deeply and evenly, wanting just to be left alone in her misery. But when Alec wordlessly eased himself onto her she submitted to the inevitable without protest and without passion. Somehow it fitted the pattern of her misery; submission, blind obedience to duty that made a prisoner of her. Less than an hour ago she had known that she had told herself that she truly loved Alec, yet as she lay as still as the effigy in the village church waiting for the ritual to be over, she neither loved nor hated, she felt numb and drained of emotion. Alec didn't analyse why it was that he behaved in a way so out of character but as, satisfied, he turned away and settled for sleep he was content in the thought that she must have been pleased with his unexpected demands. That should have got rid of whatever it was that was upsetting her. Funny girl, she was.

'Jen, I wish I could have stopped it, but it was all arranged that she should drive up with you before I knew,' Rhoda told Jenny on the Sunday afternoon.

'I was wild when I heard she was coming. But to be fair, she wasn't a bit pushy. She said she thought if the kids were little and needed a bit of looking after, I might be glad to think there were two of us there. She meant it kindly.

But the journey was a piece of cake, the kids and I sang choruses we all knew and I'd got some bags of popcorn for them. No, it was great and most of the time Muriel just sat up front with Andrew and Mr Harding. Funny woman, isn't she. But I tell you what, Rhoda – she's head over heels for Mr H – can't take her eyes off him. You must have noticed. Doesn't it nark you?'

Rhoda laughed. If anything could banish the aching misery she felt, it was the idea of Alec being swept off his feet by any woman – least of all anyone as unlikely as Muriel Wheeler.

'She's been around so long we just take what she's like for granted. She hero-worshipped him from when she was sixteen so I'm not going to get into a state about it after all these years. Now tell me about everything.' Did she speak a little too brightly? If anyone guessed at the dull misery she felt, she couldn't bear it.

'They're having a whale of a time Stewart and the kids out there on the grass playing some sort of game of rounders.'

'Stewart? I thought his tour of engagements started yesterday?'

'That's right. But he's only got occasional bookings. I think his next is up north a week next Friday.' For a moment she hesitated, but she was much too excited to hold back. 'Rhoda, what I told you about me wanting a chap who wasn't free, well don't you see? I thought Nat and him were all set for each other, but – oh don't you see?'

'You meant Stewart?' Rhoda started to laugh, 'Why didn't you say? I even wondered if you'd fallen for Andrew and that was why you liked coming here.'

'Come off it, Rhoda. He's a smasher to look at and a real nice bloke, but can you really see him and me pairing off? You know what I think? I think the most important thing is that you mate up with someone you sort of fit together with, like a couple of bits in a jig-saw. Me and Stewart, that's how it's always been with us. Mates, that's what he used to say we were. I was real sort of empty when he stopped writing to me. But, you see, he stopped because he thought I'd fallen for Jim. Well, you know that wasn't true; I told you all along there was someone else. But Jim was such a good bloke. Honest, Rhoda, if things had gone like we expected and we'd been married, I wouldn't have let him down. It was just that there at the back of my mind was always knowing that the person who was right for me was Stewart.'

'And you thought Stewart was in love with Nat? To be truthful, so did I.'

'There, you see!' Jenny chuckled excitedly, 'Funny, but now I can look back at being with Michael as just part of growing up – him being so grand and handsome. And he was my Mick's dad, which was what made me go on believing I loved him. You know what? When Stewart told me about how he'd always felt, it was just as if I'd sort of been lost and I'd found my way home. Remember what I said to you about my dream being I'd have a marriage like yours with Mr Harding, sort of safe and solid. Well, when Stewart turned up all unexpectedly this morning – he came in a taxi all the way from Brackleford station, just walked in to find me and told me that all the time it had been *me* – I felt, well, sort of like I said, as if I was home and *safe*. I'm not clever with how to say things, but you know how it is at Timberley, well that's how it's going to be for Stewart and me.'

Rhoda gave Jenny a bear-like hug, moved with affection for her.

'Your life will never be as routine as mine, Jen my love. Marriage to a celebrity – for that's what he will be if his career so far is anything to go on – that's very different from marriage to a man who goes off and comes home at the same time each day.' She mustn't let her own depression creep into her tone.

'That's where you're wrong,' came Jenny's excited laugh. 'You know what? Stewart says he loves to sing, he says he even thought in the beginning that he would want to chase after being a celebrity as you call it. But he says he's had enough. Standing up there on the platform, all decked up like a dog's dinner and singing to entertain people who pay to come in and look on it as part of having an evening out, he says that's not for him. He wouldn't half have liked our ride back from picking up the kids,' she chortled, 'there on Andrew's bus, all of us singing at the tops of our voices. Even Andrew joined in when Mr Harding was doing the driving. Not her though, not Miss Wheeler. Must be rotten to be so sort of shy that you can't let rip without being embarrassed. She still sat up front on her own, with just Mr H driving. Singing is part of being happy, that's what Stewart says. I reckon that's how it was for him when he first took up with Natalie. And if they had been really keen on each other I expect he would have kept on feeling that way. Anyway, like I was telling you, he's not going to take any more bookings – he's telling his agent tomorrow. I think he has about four he's got to do and then him and me are going to get married just the moment I'm free – be a proper mister and missus looking after the kids together. He gets on a treat with Den, so there will be the three of us.' As she said it a cloud seemed to come down on her. 'Silly to sort of tie Den and Mick together, I know it is, but—' She broke off, undecided how to find the right words and not even sure whether she could expect to be understood.

'I bet you one thing,' Rhoda said, purposely phrasing it just as Jenny might herself, 'I bet Mick would be pleased.'

Jenny nodded. 'It's sort of like being given a second chance.' Then, seeming to give herself a mental shake and speaking positively, 'We had a talk with Andrew and Etty this morning – well, I say "we", most of the time it was just Stewart cos I was sorting the kids out for a treasure hunt. This is what they've come up with: what do you think of it for a plan? Smashing isn't it?'

So she gave Rhoda details of the outcome of the

morning's discussion. The children who were at Sedgeley were orphans in local government care. Andrew's plan was to try to keep them at the manor, enrol them into the local school, become responsible for their well-being.

'I said to him, could he afford the money to keep all that lot?' Jenny explained, 'And he said he thought there would be some help from the government. I don't know about things like what money they got, him and Etty, but his dad seems to have made sure they aren't short. And here on the farm, well there's usually stuff like milk and butter and that. I think the idea is that they turn more ground over to growing their own veg and that, and the lads would all help. What a cracking way to grow up. The people in the local authority can't possible think it would be better for the kids to go back where we picked them up from – honest, Rhoda, going to pick them up yesterday made me think of where I used to be when I was stuck with *her*, that miserable old cow my dad married. A lovely hot day like it was and everywhere had that funny hot-dust sort of smell – not like here where if you shut your eyes and take a big sniff you can almost *see* the country.' Rhoda had never heard such contentment in a sigh. 'Cor, talk about life giving a person a second chance! I want to keep on pinching myself to make sure I'm awake. But like I was telling you, they had this discussion this morning and I wasn't there for most of it cos of the kids, but what they want is for me and Stewart to be like a proper mum and dad. Poor little scraps, they must have been in that miserable place we fetched them out of since they were quite tiny cos for most of them it was the war put paid to their real families. Den is chuffed to bits to have the place swarming with boys about his own age.'

Later Rhoda heard about the scheme from Andrew and Etty.

'The only thing that bothers me, Mum,' Etty said as they sat in the garden of what used to be the manager's house, is Nat. I thought she'd fallen for Stewart – and for her to fall for anybody would be a first. He's not the sort of chap to lead her on then ditch her; if she did have ideas about their future then I'm sure he didn't realise it. Dad says it was all in my imagination, so let's hope he's right. He and Jen are so *right* for each other.'

'He'll be giving up what was a promising career.' Rhoda answered, seeming to hear the echo of Jenny's voice. Right for each other? Like she and Alec?

'Promising, if that's the way you want to spend your life,' Etty answered. 'Personally I can think of few things I'd hate more. Because it's what Nat always wanted, I suppose we got used to looking on it as a great challenge. I tell you what, though, I reckon making that bunch of poor kids happy is far more worthwhile.' Then, with a complete change of tone, 'Drew was disappointed Uncle Silas vanished so quickly. We hardly saw him on Friday, then on Saturday he telephoned from Dover to say goodbye.' She waited as if she expected something from her mother. Then, 'Mum, you and Uncle Silas, you still get on really well, don't you?'

Rhoda nodded. 'You know we do. He's my dearest friend.'

In true Etty fashion she gave a hearty guffaw. 'That's going it a bit! You hardly see each other.'

Rhoda shrugged her shoulders. 'We'd better go and dig your father out, it's time we went home. He's over in the barns with Andrew, I think.'

Etty didn't refer again to Silas. Rhoda couldn't be sure whether it was just in her imagination that this daughter who had always been so close to her was watching her and probably understanding more than she'd been told about his quick departure.

For once, the wheels of authority turned quickly, perhaps because Sedgeley Manor had so recently been certified as suitable to take in the children or perhaps because the home they'd come from was glad to shed some of its occupants and open its doors to those who were in need.

By the beginning of the Michaelmas term, the boys from the manor started with Denis at the local school, each one turned out as resplendently as he had been on his first day. No wonder they strode off with such pride. On day two there was something additional to add to their morning routine: each one had been given a shoe-cleaning kit and before they sat down to breakfast came the job of polishing off yesterday's dirt. They could no more come to the break- fast table with dirty shoes than Jenny would let them see her without her high coiffure and painted face.

Before the end of October Stewart had made his last public appearance. He would miss the money he earned, but Jenny's divorce was through and they had their future mapped out there at Sedgeley.

'You ought to get away for a honeymoon,' Andrew had told them when the wedding was arranged for the first Saturday after the curtain had come down on the up-and- coming tenor Stewart Carling. 'Ett and I can look after Den and the lads.'

Jenny shook her head. 'I reckon honeymoons aren't for me,' she laughed, remembering her wedding to Michael and his immediate return to the station. 'No, me and Stew want the kids to be involved – especially Den of course. I wouldn't go off holidaying as if they weren't important. Right from the start, we want to be like a family. Crumbs, talk about the old woman in her shoe!'

Andrew, Etty, Rhoda, Stewart's grandmother and her sister who travelled from North Wales and Den went with the bridal couple to the register office. That Alec didn't come surprised no one. For Rhoda, the wedding brought a real sense of delight and it was only as she watched the two of them signing the register that she let herself acknowledge how anxious she had always been for Jenny.

Even when Jenny had appeared to be happy there had always been a feeling of unease at the back of Rhoda's mind. She supposed that in the early days at the back of her mind had lurked the memory of her first introduction to Michael Matherson – pompous young upstart, she thought, remembering, as she listened to the registrar's scratchy pen.

It was as that year of 1949 moved towards its end that Rhoda heard that Silas was leaving France. With Alec and Natalie, she was at Etty and Andrew's house at Sedgeley on New Year's Eve for, as Etty had said, it was important for them to be together for this was no ordinary New Year – it was the start of a new decade and should be celebrated accordingly. In the manor, the boys had all gone to bed, Stewart and Jenny were in their own rooms and below stairs the staff had been given two bottles of sherry to toast the striking of midnight.

'Drew had a letter from Uncle Silas,' Etty said, coming to join Rhoda by the open door. Now why was it she didn't say it to the room at large? 'He's leaving France, Mum. Has he written to tell you?'

'Coming home?' How hard it was to ask it casually, glancing down at her watch as if to see how many seconds of the old year were left.

'No. Not even to say goodbye. I think Drew was hurt . . . well I *know* he was but he'd never say so. No, instead of coming home he's going to the States. California. They're big on analysing each thought and action, aren't they? He says there's been someone visiting his clinic – I don't mean as a patient – someone who must have clout in the States. He must have or he wouldn't have been in a position to make Silas such a tempting offer. Head-hunted him – isn't that the up-and-coming way of saying it? And he hasn't written to tell you about it? I thought you were such friends.'

'You don't have to write to each other or tell each other

everything to be friends. Is he just going for a short time – or for good?' No, she screamed silently, don't let it be forever.

'He didn't say. I'll show you the letter before you go home if you like.' With her face set in a smile, Rhoda nodded. Yes, she must know where he was. Even if she never wrote to him, never heard from him, at least she'd have something. 'He's always moved around a lot apparently. Perhaps he and Buck will meet up,' Etty was saying. 'Chasing rainbows ... do you suppose that's what they're both doing?'

'Lovely thought, Ett. If only there was a sign of a rainbow to chase.' Only to Etty could she have said it.

'Poor old Mum. You enjoy that book place though, don't you?'

'Yes, I truly do. I've learnt a lot since I've been there. I really believe I'm some use to Matthew now. Hark, you can just hear the chime of the church clock.' Andrew was approaching with a tray of champagne. 'Happy New Year,' they all called, each turning to kiss the one nearest at hand. Natalie was held in Alec's bear-like hug, Etty and Andrew mouthed a kiss at each other as he moved around the room making sure everyone had a glass, then Etty gave her mother a loud and loving peck on the cheek.

'Happy New Decade, Alec,' Rhoda made herself say brightly as she moved to him.

'And you, Happy New Decade,' he replied touching her face with his. 'This one ends on a very different note from the last,' he spoke to the room at large. With the striking of midnight the 1940s had slipped into history.

So many who'd seen the start of that fateful decade weren't there to see its end, so many lives shattered beyond recall. Rhoda felt the sting of tears and was ashamed that the emotion that threatened to choke her was so much more personal. Ten years ago had she still clung to the belief that her marriage held all the colours

288

of the rainbow she longed for? Ten years ago, before she met Silas had she been happier in her ignorance of the joy life could hold?

'Don't look so sombre, Mother-in-law,' Andrew's voice broke her reverie. 'A new decade – a better one than the last. We'll make sure of that.'

Her smile held very real affection. 'You're starting it on the right course,' she told him. 'Think how what you've done has improved the lives of those poor children.'

'And think how much better their lives would have been if we hadn't made such a mess of things so that they lost their own parents. Has Etty told you yet?'

'Told me what?'

In answer, he held his hand in Etty's direction and she came to join them. Such was the way with those two that he didn't have to prompt her, she knew exactly why he had called her over to them.

'We're having another baby, Mum. That's our news for this shiny new decade. And don't say "about time too". Christo will be three and a half, but I seem to have been tardy – we'd planned for no more than two years' difference.'

The news spread around the room, a new life soon to be amongst them giving extra cause for excitement, resolve and hope during the first moments of the new year.

But as the winter weeks went by that old routine took hold and now, even though Rhoda exercised her mind at work and became increasingly useful to Matthew, all that was no more than an escape. Just as she always had, she cleaned the house, she washed and ironed, she sewed on buttons and darned Alec's socks, resenting that so long after the end of the war they still had to live within the limits of clothing coupons. One break with the habit of years was Alec's Saturday night routine and the other was her relief that often even then he gave her a cursory peck on the cheek and wished her goodnight, just as he did from Sunday to Friday. No longer did she dab perfume behind her ears as she got ready for bed, or lead him towards what she had always hoped would be that elusive miracle of love. They never argued, they never discussed anything meaningful, they never laughed; instead, they lived side by side moving on parallel lines, one on either side of the deep and unchanging pattern their marriage had become.

And so winter gave way to spring, then summer appeared over the horizon.

'I had a long talk with Nat this afternoon,' Alec said one evening in late May, speaking as Rhoda stacked the dirty dinner dishes onto a tray. 'As she said, it would be no use her telephoning here – you're never here.'

'She knows where to find me. I gave her Matthew's number ages ago and she's only called me once – and that was because your line was always engaged.' Then, forgetting to be resentful, 'Is she OK? Is there any news?'

'News? Nothing special. It's always nice just to listen to the way she chatters on all about nothing in particular. I was out when she called so I rang her back. Muriel took the first call, of course, and she said they talked for ages. I was delighted.'

'Nat's always good with people; no one remembers to be shy with her. With so much to say, surely there must be *something* worth telling me.'

'Not really. I couldn't really keep up with half of what she said, but that didn't matter, it was just nice to hear her. She talked of after-show suppers with friends, all that sort of thing. Always so full of life ... I wish she were still living at home.'

Rhoda's answering laugh held no humour. 'It's not very likely she'd be bubbling over with life if she were living here!'

Alec's mouth tightened into a hard line as he got up from the table.

'I'll have an hour in the garden,' he said. 'You never seem to have time for it lately. Neither time nor interest.' For a moment he stood still, seeming uncertain. Then, sitting down again at the table and indicating for her to do the same, he went on, 'Rhoda, it's time we stopped waltzing around the truth and had a talk about the future.'

Chapter Thirteen

Whatever the future might throw at her, surely Rhoda would never forgot that moment as they faced each other across the half-cleared dinner table.

'I'm sorry that I have to do this to you. Honestly, from the bottom of my heart, Rhoda, I am truly sorry. But we can't – I most certainly can't – go on living like this. I ought to have been honest with you ages ago – years ago.'

Rhoda was at a loss. What was he talking about? Was he still harking back to her insistence on taking a job? But after all this time, that was ridiculous. And what difference had she ever let it make to his life, anyway? None.

'I think it was talking to Nat this afternoon, seeing Muriel's pleasure that Nat looks on her as a friend, somehow it made me realise how we're wasting our precious years. And they are precious. You'll be fifty in a few weeks, I shan't see fifty-three again. Muriel is—'

'Never mind the Wheelers. What are you trying to say?'

'Do you honestly not know? She says that if you don't know, then that must show the failure of our marriage.'

'She? Nat said that?'

'Christ, no. I've never actually talked outright to Nat about how I feel, but I believe – no, I'm certain – she understands without having it spelled out to her. I've tried to fight what I feel, but Rhoda I can't go on like this. We live side by side, we share a bed, yet we never come close.

292

I don't mean physically. God knows, I've tried to give you what you wanted. I feel a heel. If I wasn't as fond of you as I am I wouldn't be prepared to shoulder the blame. I'd bluff it out, I'd try to make you see a lot of it is your own fault. Muriel says the fault isn't all mine, that if you'd been more content and really cared about me, then it wouldn't have been in my nature to look to her for understanding.'

'So what are you saying? That you fancy prissy Miss Wheeler, and that when you occasionally roll me on my back – to do your duty and I suppose imagine it's her you're so-called pleasuring—'

His fist came down on the table with a thud.

'Christ! You sound like a common fishwife with your hateful coarse language. It's no use – the way we live is a charade.'

Even thinking of something intelligent to say seemed beyond her capabilities.

'The girls ... you say Natalie must know. Is she looking on me as a figure of pity, poor old Mum, a liability—'

'Of course not. She's seen enough of the world to understand that we're not alone; when I talked to her, not directly about us but I believe she knew what I was getting at, she said she has come across a good many couples who have realised they are better apart. One of them moves on without the other. Haven't you always moaned about looking after the home, seen it as giving you a blinkered existence. And I suppose there was truth in it. You've not had the strain of building a business, you've had no responsibilities.'

She started to laugh, frightened of the sound that seemed to hold more hysteria than mirth.

'And Etty?' she asked, determined to stay in control. 'Have you had a little heart to heart with her too? Or Andrew, perhaps, one man to another?'

'No. I wanted to say something the other day, but she hasn't seen as much of life as Nat and I was frightened of upsetting her. In her condition ... well, I thought it would be better for you to talk to her. If she can see that you understand, then it will make it easier for her.'

She sat looking at him, saying nothing. This was Alec, kind, dull, routine loving, Alec. In love with dowdy Miss Wheeler, in love with the open adulation she bestowed on him. Jenny's remarks after the London trip came back to Rhoda. If only she'd known the truth then! Her years had been wasted, the loyalty she'd had to fight to hang on to hadn't even been wanted. Had Muriel blossomed overnight into an object of his desire, or over the years had he too become bored with the routine of home and found excitement in that never-changing devotion? And did it matter how or when it had happened? Did anything matter now that Silas had gone?

'. . . you're to go on living in the house. We shall find somewhere in Brackleford, somewhere near the yard. Muriel is very anxious about her mother, but if you're nearby, even if you keep that job you insist on doing, she won't be entirely alone.'

Even though the first part of his remark had been lost on Rhoda, she could hardly believe what she was hearing.

'Me here – Mrs Wheeler across the green—'

'You're thinking what I'm thinking? I hoped you would. It seems the obvious and sensible thing.' Alec said, a sound of relief in his voice. 'I haven't even suggested it to Muriel and her mother, but it's really the obvious thing, isn't it. This place is much too big for you on your own and Mrs Wheeler would be company and would feel safe.'

'Here? Oh, no! *Oh, no*! Alec, you say you've had enough and want to be free of our marriage. Why in heaven's name couldn't you have been honest and told me this when you first realised it? "You're my wife, your place is at home",' she mimicked none too kindly. 'That's what you used to say when I wanted a chance to do something with my life. So what did I do? I'll tell you. I turned my back on the chance to find real happiness, to be a complete person, to be *myself* instead of a tool that makes the wheels of this house turn smoothly.'

Her outburst appeared to have done nothing to destroy his calm. 'You're being hysterical,' he told her tolerantly. 'It's been a shock to you, I do realise that, Rhoda. But you can't think that even if you'd got a proper job it would have given you some wonderful new life. Be practical. Even when you used to harp on that work nonsense we both knew you hadn't the knowledge or experience to do anything better than the sort of job you finally found. You look after this house very well, and that's a skill in its own way.' Rhoda said nothing, but her expression carried its own message. 'I'll see you have enough money to live on and I shall continue to pay the rates and electricity here.'

'Frankly I don't care who pays the expenses. Certainly it won't be me. Whatever I do, I shan't stay here.'

'Rhoda, damn it Rhoda, can't you see I'm trying to make it easy for you. I don't want you to give up your home. Let Mrs Wheeler have a couple of rooms by all means—'

'Let her have the whole damn lot for all I care. I shall move out.' It sounded grand and positive, not a hint that her future was lost in a fog of uncertainty. 'I earn a certain amount of money, not enough to pay rent as well as keep myself, but I'm not destitute. You know exactly how much I have in my account, so you can be sure I shall find somewhere suitable to live.'

'Thank God I never let us touch the money your parents left you. In those early days when we were hard up it would have been so easy to do as you wanted and put it into the general kitty. Now, though, it's there for you and it has earned you good interest through the years. Even so, I shall be responsible for making you an allowance once everything is finalised.' Alec was never known to lose his temper, never known to be overexcited; but even so his calm matter-of-fact voice came as a shock to her. How long had he been thinking along these lines while she had believed his life held everything he desired? 'Do you want a hand with the dishes?'

Her answer was in the contemptuous look she threw at him.

'This must be a night for "firsts",' she said sarcastically.

'That's not fair. Often I used to help.'

'Never mind the dishes. I assume you mean to move out? Have you and the delectable Miss Wheeler found a cosy love nest yet?'

He frowned, irritated.

'There's no immediate rush. She has to break it to her mother – she promised to speak to her this evening but it won't be easy.'

But Rhoda had hardly listened beyond the first sentence, that he saw no immediate rush.

'You mean you want us, you and me, to go on as we are?'

'Of course nothing can be quite the same, not now I've talked to you about the future. But, oh damn it Rhoda, we rub along very well – where is the need to be over-dramatic about all this. While we're sorting things out surely we can go on as we have been.'

'With me washing your clothes, cooking your meals, sharing your bed – is that what you expect?'

'Perhaps I shouldn't have told you how I felt until I'd found somewhere to move into. But Rhoda, we've never fallen out, we've always respected each other. As for sharing a bed, if you want me to move into another room then of course I will. But I can see no reason why we can't sort things out in our own time. Obviously now that you know how things stand we wouldn't have physical contact if that's what's disturbing you.'

Picking up the tray, she turned to leave him.

'I shall wash these dishes. I wouldn't want to leave them for Miss Wheeler.' She took courage from the cold tone of her voice. If this was the way to the freedom she had dreamed of, surely there was no reason to feel like this – as if the ground had been knocked from under her feet. Then, her face wearing a sneer that was far from pretty,

296

'She'll want clean sheets on the bed, I don't doubt. I'll leave them out ready, shall I?'

'Stop it, Rhoda. It's not like you to talk like that.' He looked puzzled, even hurt.

'Do forgive me,' she answered with exaggerated sweetness, 'I suppose I've not had a lot of practice of situations like this. Now, why don't you run along and see how the faithful Miss Wheeler is getting on with Mummy. Tears and tantrums perhaps, or an attack of the vapours.'

If there was any consolation at all to be found in the situation it must have been in his look of bewilderment.

'Put that tray down and listen. Surely it doesn't have to be like this. When have we ever quarrelled? Never. But why can't you be honest and admit that all that was keeping us together was habit?'

'Admit I was bored? Oh yes, bored, bored, bored. And did you care? No, as long as you got your meals on the table and the house was clean and shiny for you, I merged comfortably into the background. If only you knew how I longed to be free—'

'So now's your chance,' he said on a note of hope.

'Yes, now that it's too late. For everyone there is a soulmate, and if yours is the prissy Miss Wheeler then I wish you well. I found my soulmate too, so I know about temptation. But I sent him away because of duty, faith, loyalty to you and the girls.'

Alec felt trapped. He had come home from Brackleford dreading what he had to say to her, expecting tears and being prepared to offer her a shoulder to cry on as she listened with sadness and even with shame that somewhere she must have been found wanting. He had felt genuine sympathy for her. But her reception of the news hadn't gone as he'd imagined and after her last remarks he felt she held the trump card.

'I said just now,' he told her preferring to ignore her references both to loyalty and to the girls, 'the very fact that you could have believed I was content shows how far apart we'd grown. This soulmate you talk about, if he had really wanted you and been as close to you as you believe, then do you think he would have accepted your refusal and left you? Of course he wouldn't. More likely he saw you as a safe liaison for a spell of so-called romance. It happens in middle age, so I believe.' If she needed to hit out, so too did he. He closed his eyes and in that second Rhoda felt she saw beneath his blustering manner. He looked vulnerable. When he spoke again his tone had changed: anger, fear, resentment, guilt, whatever it was that had made him speak as he had, being replaced by honesty that brought close to her the Alec she had always known. 'Loyalty, you say. And yes, my loyalty should be to you. I should put your happiness before Muriel's or my own. But Rhoda, I do truly love her. She isn't as tough as you – she's easily hurt. Above all, and may God forgive me for letting it happen, but above all I want to be with her.'

'Bully for you,' came Rhoda's uncharacteristic reply. 'Better get off over there then and give her a helping hand with that spoilt mother of hers.'

'Can we still be friends, Rhoda?'

'If you mean am I dying of a broken heart because you were as bored as I, then I'm not. I don't think my heart comes into it. And that's terribly sad. I'm sad too for the girls – even for Jen who saw ours as the perfect marriage.' It was as if the fight had gone out of both of them. How could years of building what had been seen as a perfect relationship have come to this? Habit, routine, compromise, the words hammered in Rhoda's brain and yet looking at Alec she felt swamped by sadness. 'Such wasted years,' she said quietly. 'We get one life and we've spent more than half our years building towards *this*.'

'Stay here, Rhoda. If you don't want me here – and I suppose I have no right to expect you to – then I'll get a room for the night in town. Tomorrow we'll talk again. We'll be calmer. You'll have had time to think.'

'Do as you please.' Polite words they both heard as 'I don't care what you do'.

He went upstairs to their bedroom, packed a few things in a suitcase and without coming back to where she stood at the sink washing the dishes he went across the green.

Minutes later, upstairs in that bedroom filled with a million memories, Rhoda too put a few essential things into a holdall, then stripped the bed and put the linen into the laundry basket. It was over. The early years of dreams, the later ones of frustration and loneliness – gone, vanished like the snow in sunshine. Standing with her head pressed against the window pane, even with her eyes closed she seemed to see the garden, each tree, each shrub and flower, all as familiar as the lines on her hand. To be divided by death must leave one with the comfort of memory; for a marriage to end like this left her with nothing. She heard his car drive away. Had he gone alone, or was Muriel Wheeler by his side? By his side just as she had been for years, driving off with him each morning, coming home with him each evening – and no doubt taking the thought of him to bed with her each night.

Picking up her holdall Rhoda walked out of the room without a backward glance, going down the stairs without touching the rails of the banisters as if she'd already severed any connection with the hold the house had on her. A few minutes later she was pedalling towards Sedgeley. She ought to be rejoicing – hadn't Alec just opened the door of her gilded cage? Yet she felt numb. And what if Silas had been here? Would she have been able to shed off the hold of nearly thirty years of marriage and go to him without a backward glance? She dreaded facing Etty and telling her what had happened and yet, if anywhere there was one person she wanted to talk to then Etty was that person. Throughout the years, even as a child, she had always understood things without having them spelt out to her.

Even so, Rhoda wasn't prepared for the way her news was received.

'Stupid sod,' Etty said. 'Muriel has doted on him for years and if you expect me to be surprised, I'm not. It's worried me for ages, Mum. Remember the summer when he was supposed to be helping with repairs because he said the men were all busy? I went to the yard on one of those evenings to get something Drew needed. There was no urgent work and the men weren't rushed off their feet. That was when I first suspected and so – and I'm not proud of this but I had to do it because I didn't want to have to believe what I suspected was going on – so after that I made a point of going in, of talking to the blokes, not asking outright. I know them all so well, just chatting to them seemed natural. It used to come out quite innocently from them that Dad and Muriel had pushed off at the usual time. No one else ever took her home. I suppose she told her mother a tale that she'd had to work late just like he did to you. They make me sick, the pair of them.' Etty heard a note of hysteria in Rhoda's laugh and put her strong arm around her. 'I'll tell you one thing for free, Mum: I don't want either of them visiting here. If he'd really fallen for someone and come clean about it, then perhaps I might have made myself accept it. You know what, though? I'm almost glad it's out in the open and you've come to tell me. Ever since I've suspected that's what was going on I felt . . . well, sort of not able to talk to him. I felt I didn't really know him. All the time I worked there in the yard he and I got on fine, but . . . oh, I don't know. What a bloody fool he must be.'

How strange it was that Rhoda took no comfort from Etty's condemnation of him.

'I never told you either,' she started. 'Alec wasn't the only one to be discontented with life and to find what we wanted outside.'

'Uncle Silas, you mean?' Etty noticed how the hot tears sprang into Rhoda's eyes at the words. 'Don't you think that's why he's taken himself off to America?'

'Was I a fool, Ett? Ought I to have done what Alec has?

But I couldn't do that ... I thought that for him everything was fine ... I thought our marriage was everything he wanted. He says – and Muriel apparently says too – that had it not failed already I would have realised he wasn't content. Anyway, I did the only thing I could: I sent Silas away and resigned myself to years, years, years of the same routine.'

'Poor old Mum. It's frightening, you know, how time can bring such changes. You know what I think? I think if Dad had had a hap'orth of sense he would have got you involved in the business. Even as a kid I remember how you used to want him to let you go in and help. But no, he had to be the Man of the House and you had merge into the background.'

'Don't let it happen, Ett, with you and Andrew.'

'Not likely,' she guffawed. 'Me and Drew are a proper team. If the tractor plays up it's my job; if the accounts have to be sorted out it's his. We're as necessary to each other as a knife and fork. It's never a case of home and Christo being my job and outside things Drew's. We muck in together. And, Mum, I'm so thankful it's like that, because that way I can keep an eye on him, make sure he doesn't overdo things.'

Rhoda nodded. How good it was to be with Etty, sensible, understanding, unchallenging Etty.

'Tell you what though, Mum, Nat's going to be shattered when she hears. For her there has never been a man to compare with Dad.'

'I know. Ett, I don't want to be the one to tell her, and I know he doesn't. Will you do it?'

Afterwards, all Etty told Rhoda was that Nat had made it easier than she'd feared. It seemed she knew lots of people who had split up. What she didn't repeat to her mother was that in Natalie's opinion if a woman couldn't hold her husband then she should look to herself for the reason.

'When can you say Mum ever failed him?' had come

Etty's immediate and defensive retort. But if she'd expected an answer, she'd been disappointed.

'I dare say it's rotten for her. No one likes to know they've lost out. And you've always been the same – Mum could never do any wrong as far as you were concerned. Well, *my* sympathy is with Dad. If Mum had made him feel great sometimes instead of always grizzling that she wanted to do something with her life, then she might have held on to him. He'll be OK with Muriel Wheeler – she adores the ground he walks on. And she understands about the business too.'

'So Mum could have understood if he'd not been so pigheaded. Nat, this hasn't happened in a week or two. Honestly, I've suspected it for ages. And all the while he's taken Mum for granted, the same as he always has. It's so *sad*, Nat – for her, for us and for him too once he comes to his senses and sees what a damn fool he's been.'

For a few seconds Natalie had been silent, weighing up Etty's words. Then she answered, her tone even and unemotional.

'I guess you feel like that because your life looks like being about as narrow as Mum's. Well, that was your choice. Personally I've seen more of the world; these things happen. And why be sad for Dad? He's found a new beginning and it's up to us – yes, *both* of us, you as well as me, to welcome Muriel if that's what he wants. And as for us? Why should we see it as sad? We're not children – we've got our own lives. If Mum was making his life unhappy then they're better apart. I'll give him a ring at the yard and tell him he has my support.'

'Well, he damn well doesn't deserve it and he certainly doesn't get mine,' Etty had answered decisively. Another long silence and then the dialling tone. Natalie had rung off. If in her heart Etty had clung on to the hope that the whole thing would blow over and the family would get back into the old mould, her conversation with Natalie had put an end to hope.

302

Although the sisters were so different, they had seldom quarrelled. But there was no doubt in Etty's mind that nothing would ever be the same between them. It was as if they had put their forces behind opposing armies. Honesty made her recall what had been said and try to see things from Natalie's point of view, but the effect was only to make her more angry. She knew her sister well enough to be sure it hadn't been an emotional outburst of support for her adored father, but simply a statement of facts as she saw them. So all Etty told her mother was that Natalie had taken it very well and, because she had known so many couples who had split up, she had been able to accept it.

The next day, alone in the house by Oakleigh Green, Rhoda put through a call to the theatre before Natalie went on stage.

'Mum, if you're phoning to get me on your side, you're wasting your time.'

'Don't talk like that, Nat. There are no sides to take.'

'I've had a long talk to Dad. You grizzled for ages that you want a life of your own ... well now you've got it. Dad's such a loyal man, so don't be mean, Mum, don't play on his feelings and mess things up for him. Give him his freedom, let him start with a clean slate.'

'You don't imagine I shall try to make him change his mind, surely?'

'I don't pretend to know. I just know he wouldn't have done this without jolly good cause and he deserves to be happy. I told Etty yesterday how I felt.'

'When shall I see you?' Rhoda asked, trying to turn the subject and at the same time give the impression that she, too, was looking to the future.

'I shan't come to Brackleford for a while. Dad's bringing Muriel to the theatre next week. After that I shall wait until they're settled before I come home.'

'I shan't be at home.' Surely Alec would have told her.

'Of course you won't. But once you've gone, there's no

303

reason why Dad won't keep the house on. He says that Mrs Wheeler is happy to be responsible for looking after things and he and Muriel will still work together.' She laughed as she said it, applauding his change of heart over working wives. 'I pulled his leg about his views on working wives, but as he said, these circumstances are very different. He and Muriel have worked as a team for so long. And of course that's true, it would be crazy for her to stay at home fripping about with a duster.'

'I must ring off, Nat, there's someone at the door,' Rhoda lied.

'OK. Keep in touch. And promise me you'll not make things difficult for him.'

'I should hope I have more pride than that! Must go.' And she hung up.

A house divided: the girls who had grown up knowing stability and love were being wrenched apart. Natalie stood behind her father, Etty behind her mother. It wasn't fair – the foundation they'd built on had been torn from under them. It mustn't be like that, not for the girls; none of this was their fault.

Staring unseeingly ahead of her, Rhoda tried to believe that emotions were only running out of hand temporarily. Look ahead, she told herself, wait a while until the dust settles. It had to be up to Alec and her to set an example and make it easy for Natalie and Etty to hang on to the love they'd always felt for both their parents. At any rate mentally she squared her shoulders, and let herself imagine the future that surely, surely, now was hers to take.

From the bureau draw she took writing paper and an envelope. Her pen ran away with her.

When Matthew returned from his visit to a book collector in Newbury, she got ready for her bike ride back to the manor.

'Rhoda, I've been thinking,' he said, 'What you told me this morning about you and your husband has been on my mind. I'm afraid you'll be looking for a fresh beginning, pastures new. Now, my thought is this: you have become very useful to me here—'

'Don't fib. Matthew.' she laughed, 'some days – and this was one of them – I don't so much as answer the telephone.'

'That's the way of it in this line. You told me you'd left Dewsberry Green and are staying temporarily at the manor. Now my suggestion is that you use the room I keep for Silas. He'll not be using it now that he's gone off to America. You'd keep your independence and yet you'd still be close to your family.'

'Matthew, this is a bachelor establishment. You're comfortable as you are. But I do appreciate it, honestly I do, more than I know how to tell you.'

'My advice would be that you don't rush things. When you go back to Sedgeley this evening have a good heart-to-heart with your daughter and her husband. I'm not a family man myself, a loner is the way I've always been. That's why Silas and I get along so well. He's a rolling stone, gets the wanderlust. Me? No, that way isn't for me, I seem pretty self-sufficient. But that doesn't mean you wouldn't be very welcome to settle into the other room upstairs. You can do that while you're adjusting if you like. Then I hope you might decide you're comfortable enough to stay, or at least to stay in the job even if you prefer to find somewhere else to live. You've fitted in here remarkably well and I don't want to lose you.'

Cycling back to Sedgeley, Rhoda stopped by the letter box on Oakley Green. She told herself how blessed she was: Etty and Andrew had made it plain they would be happy for her to make her home with them; Matthew had proved himself a real friend. But hearing her envelope fall onto the pile awaiting the evening collection, her imagination took a wild leap forward.

At the manor, Etty was told of Matthew's suggestion.

'You don't have to give him an answer tomorrow, do

305

you? Promise us you'll give it a few days without thinking too much about any of it – give the dust time to settle. Promise?'

'It's got to be faced. Ett, I love it here, you know I do. But I'd never let myself become "Granny who lives with us and hasn't a place of her own".' Looking at Etty with complete honesty she said, 'For so many years I just longed for a chance to be *me*. Now I have no alternative – it's exciting, yet I'm frightened to let myself believe. Oh, Ett, why couldn't he have been honest with me when my dream was there to be lived?'

'Silas?'

'Silas, always Silas.'

Etty didn't answer except to say again, 'Promise not to rush into anything, give yourself a week or two with us. Look on it as a holiday if you like.'

It was two days after that when she was in the upstairs kitchen at Oakleigh making a ham sandwich for her lunch that she heard a car draw up outside. Automatically she rinsed her hands and went to the window. What a fool she was that after all this time the rare event of a car stopping outside could make her heart hammer like this. It would be days before he even had her letter, and yet in her mind's eye the sound conjured up the image of his Singer. Despite herself, peering through the upstairs kitchen window her immediate reaction was disappointment as she saw the black Renault outside the house. Then the driver's door opened.

If her heart had been hammering at the sound of the engine, now it was beating a tattoo that echoed in her throat and tingled in her arms. But how could it be *him*? He was in California. It couldn't be . . . but it *was*! He was here . . . he'd come back. Or was this another dream? Would she wake and find herself sitting downstairs? She ran down the stairs, her footsteps keeping pace with her racing mind. Then, just as he put his key in the lock, she flung the front

306

door open and a second later was held close to him, so close she could hardly breathe.

'You can't have had my letter already. You've come back,' she gasped, even as she spoke thinking what a stupid thing it was to say.

'Of course I've come back,' Silas said softly. 'As soon as I heard I got on the first plane I could. In we go, let's shut the door.'

And there they were, back in just the same place as they'd parted company the summer before, the months between melted into nothing.

'You said "as soon as you heard",' she said after a minute or two. 'Did Matthew send you a telegram or some thing?'

'Drew telephoned.'

'Did he know you were coming?' For hadn't Etty made her promise to wait a few days before she made a decision?

'No. I didn't speak to him. I was away from the clinic so he left a message with my secretary. He simply said his mother-in-law was staying with them as her marriage had broken down.'

So she told him the whole story, holding nothing back. What joy it was to talk to him. 'You know what Jen said to me when she and Stewart got together?' she said as her tale finished. 'She said she felt as if she'd found her way home. I know now exactly what she meant.'

He nodded.

'Home and we'll go roaming no more. From now on, wherever we are we'll be together, wherever we're together for us will be home. And this evening we'll go together to Sedgeley and tell the family.'

After that they had decisions to make. He still had three months left of his contract in California; then they had to decide whether he should stay on out there, go back to France or work in England. Rhoda started to laugh, a laugh that held an emotion far more complex than humour: she was to return with him to America and after that, where?

The door of her gilded cage had been flung wide, yet where they lived counted for nothing. Wherever they made their home, in the icy north or in the tropics or in Brackleford, the routine of life would weave its web. The cage that had held her had had nothing to do with the demands of Timberley, it had been created by loneliness of the spirit.

Looking at Silas she could see a glint of laughter in his eyes and knew his thoughts had moved with hers.

'I like coffee for breakfast, no sugar,' he teased, 'well done toast ...'

Together they laughed, the sound filled with the hope and confidence of youth. The difference was that their vision wasn't clouded by dreams of romance – they knew exactly what life would demand of them.

'As if one's come home ... I always knew Jen was a wise girl,' Silas said softly. 'We'll come back here from Sedgeley – tonight this will be our home. And tomorrow – the world.'

Also by Connie Monk, available from Piatkus Books

To Light a Candle

Cynny Barlow is just eighteen when she falls helplessly in love with the dashing Ralph Clinton, an ambitious and talented actor visiting her home town for the summer. However, when Ralph is talent-spotted by a film producer, he puts everything behind him and leaves for the big time, with no idea that Cynny is already pregnant.

Whilst her daughter Suzie is a toddler, Cynny can see no way out of her life of drudgery, working at the grocer's during the day and as a barmaid in the evenings to make ends meet. Her one friend in the village, the vicar's wife Kate Bainbridge, is sympathetic, but has her own problems. Although the face she shows the parishioners is one of contentment, Kate yearns for more passion in her life than her husband Richard seems able to give her. Lately, she has been charmed by Richard's old friend, Perry Sylvester, a famous jazz pianist.

But everything is set to change for all concerned, for when Perry makes Cynny's acquaintance, he recognises in her a rare singing talent, one that would perfectly match the jazz he plays in the nightclubs of London ...

The Long Road Home

Sophie and Lydia Westlake have always been close, and think of each other as sisters, despite the fact that they are really cousins. Sophie has always been the prettier, more light-hearted younger sister, whilst Lydia has grown up in her shadow and is more serious and reserved. But until dashing young architect Christian Mellor arrives in town on the day of the annual summer fete, their differences have never mattered. Both girls immediately fall for Christian's charms as he becomes a regular visitor to the family home, having been commissioned to do some building work for their father. Working in the office of her father's building firm, Lydia forms a friendship with Christian, friendship that, for her, deepens into love.

But it is Sophie who marries Christian, blissfully unaware of her sister's secret passion for him. Lydia is devastated and tells no-one how she really feels. But she cannot let go of her feelings for Christian, especially when Sophie confides that she is unhappy in her marriage ...

Fast Flows the Stream

When war breaks out in 1939, Sally Kennedy and Tessa Kilbride have already enjoyed several years of close friendship. Although superficially very different – Tessa is married to glamorous film star Sebastian while Sally's husband Nick is his accountant – they feel as close as sisters. Warm-harted Tessa is content to be a home maker but Sally yearns for more, something Nick dismisses as mere fancy.

But with war comes change – by 1940 both Nick and Sebastian have volunteered for the armed forces and Sally has landed a job translating foreign broadcasts at a nearby listening station. Later her son Jethro becomes a soldier while Tessa's daughter Zena pursues her ambition to become a successful actress. None of them imagines how anything other than war could shape their destiny, but nothing prepares them for the unexpected challenges and heartache peace-time will also bring . . .